Agatha

&

The Scarlet Scarab

Book 1 of The Cairo Chronicles

Chapter 1
The Thunder Machines

The Thunder Machines were coming and with them the smoke and fire.

The Thunder Machines were coming and that is how it all began.

In the darkness of the attic, Great Aunt Florrie sat with her great-niece, Agatha, under the moth-eaten canvas that hung suspended from the rafters and shaped like a tent. Florrie's unmistakable hair bun was silhouetted against the single candle as she spoke, exhaling a cold cloudy breath into the chill of the night air.

'Shall we play the *Thunder-and-Lightning* game?' Florrie whispered; her face lit up ghoulishly from the flickering flame below. 'You know the one,' she continued. 'It starts when you hear that first clap of thunder and then you begin your count.'

Of course, Aggie knew the game. It had been a consistent part of Florrie's repertoire ever since the Luftwaffe and those 'damn doodlebug strikes' had blighted the capital. The twist in this version was that the counting started as, and only when, the Thunder Machines – or doodlebugs as most people called them – fell silent and paused, before erupting with an explosion.

Great Aunt Florrie said that it was scientifically proven that each second counted out equated to a linear mile, 'As the crow flies, of course', and, therefore, you could accurately plot the distance of the bombs by counting in-between strikes and navigate, with reasonable accuracy, where those 'damned' devices would have deployed their destruction.

On this clear autumn's eve, the first strike was distant and barely audible, but wily old Florrie heard it nevertheless.

'One…(one hundred). Two…(two hundred). Three…,' Florrie began to count, beating the numbers onto her chest rhythmically, over-accentuating each number, and contorting her face to dissuade her young charge from fearing what was an unlikely strike on their home. 'Remember, for every number you increase your count by–' Florrie instructed, demonstrating the count on her outstretched fingers, 'the number of miles away the lightning will strike,' Aggie interrupted, finishing the sentence for her.

'SEVEN…EIGHT…NINE…TE–' they continued, nodding together.

Before reaching double figures, the distant sound of explosions ripped across the city.

Aggie ran towards the part-opened window at the gable end of the attic where cobwebs danced through the draft. The most famous of London landmarks was perfectly framed in the window. Aggie peered through its panes, across the rooftops; its circular outer and wooden quadrants reminiscent to that of a sight scope on a fighter pilot's plane. The city, which plunged into darkness during nightly air raids, offered distant views of firelight burning against the unmistakable silhouette of St Paul's Cathedral.

'It's still there.' Aggie said with delight.

Great Aunt Florrie laughed, as she often did during these raids, professing her opinions on the bombing strategy and inefficiencies of the murderous enemy.

'Of all the gigantic, come-blow-me-up *Bull's-eyes* you could have in any city, the Fuhrer still fails to hit our beloved St Paul's. And, therefore, I trust, both Parliament and the Palace?'

The three Ps as Florrie so often referred to them.

The Thunder Machines began to rumble again before extolling their silent anxiety across the London boroughs.

In unison, both great aunt and niece initiated their count again.

'ONE … (one hundred). TWO … (two hundred). THREE … (three hundred). FOUR … (four hundred). FIVE … (fi–)'.

BOOM!!!

An almighty explosion sent a cacophony of noise across the rooftops and through the alleyways. Light and fire lit up bursts of amber-framed

4

yellow, sending shadows of houses into the night sky. The incendiaries were getting closer and were relentlessly indiscriminate in their pursuit of destruction.

Great Aunt Florrie decided that five miles was close enough to warrant immediate evacuation from the precarious attic room, and to descend to the safer confines of their basement bunker.

'Don't forget your mask!' Florrie said abruptly, pointing over Aggie's shoulder.

Aggie looked around and grabbed the wooden box. She opened it, but it was empty. She looked shocked at the vacant container before apologetically looking towards her great aunt.

'How many times must I tell you, Agatha!' Florrie announced, rolling her eyes in disbelief. 'You'd better take mine,' she continued, handing her gas mask over, and immediately, she led Aggie from the attic.

Aggie detested being called Agatha. It was Florrie's preferred method of chiding. Overhead, the Thunder Machines' deathly murmurs were beginning again.

'One, two…' Aggie whispered beneath her breath as they descended the twisting flights of stairs. The basement had several gas masks in it. It was just a matter of minutes before Florrie could safely have a replacement.

In normal circumstances, the descent was an awkward route. The narrow stairways, walls covered in an eclectic mix of mirrors, pictures, maps, and all manner of Florrie's paraphernalia, simply cluttered the way. In blackout and Florrie not as agile as she liked to think she was, it was taking longer than expected.

'Three–'

BOOM!

Although, according to the thunder-and-lightning method, the bomb had dropped three miles away, the tremors were felt throughout the house, shuddering its foundations. Chandeliers rattled, a shattering of glass volleyed its way up from the basement, and just a little more than a sprinkling of dust in the air caused them both to cough and wave their hands in the muted darkness.

'Put that damned thing on!' Florrie barked at Aggie, without even glancing back at her.

The young teenager wilfully did as she was told. This was not a time for questioning anything, as she so often liked to. It was unlike her great aunt to be so forthright. They had been through this scenario dozens of times but this time Florrie was genuinely agitated.

The Thunder Machines were coming closer, and it wasn't long until their dull, deep whirring, sent a shiver through their home. They were hovering over the city and would soon, indiscriminately come to choose their next victims.

Aggie began her count again. 'One…Tw–'

BOOM!!!!

An earth-shattering explosion came from outside, shaking the house to its very foundations. Aggie lurched forward, stumbling down several flights of stairs. Great Aunt Florrie, slightly ahead of her, fell the last few stairs and hit the ground floor landing with force.

'For Christ's sake!' Florrie cried out. It was rare indeed for her to cast such blasphemy. She clasped her head and managed to sit herself up.

Smoke was already beginning to seep through the threshold of the front door. It filled the air with its acrid taste and began to pollute the dimly lit hallway. Florrie was beginning to wheeze and cough. Her eyes began to shut as the dust-filled room took its toll. Then, without warning, as if a marionette having had its strings cut away, she slumped forward, motionless.

Aggie knelt down to her guardian and cradled her head. Removing the borrowed gas mask, Aggie placed it over Florrie, its rightful owner's head, but even then, with little life in her body, the old lady managed to shake her head and refuse it.

'Put it on, girl!' Florrie slurred with as much energy as she could muster.

'But, Auntie, I can easily retrieve another from the bunker.'

'Now! Put it on now!' Florrie ordered, managing to raise her voice before she collapsed onto the floor.

Aggie put the mask back on. The hallway had almost lost full visibility. This wasn't like anything she had imagined. From beneath the front doorway, the smoke billowed in. She clutched Florrie's hand. It had lost all grip.

'Auntie! Auntie…!' came Aggie's muffled shouts as she shook Florrie's shoulders hoping to revive her. There was little response.

BANG! BANG!

Two abrupt shots came from outside the front door. Startled, Aggie looked up, but could only peer into the smoky black pitch the hallway had now become. She heard glass smashing outside and several voices arguing. From the basement, it sounded as if the rear doorway had been blown in and a flapping door was now banging against the bunker walls. She was sure she heard footsteps too. The smoke began casting its cloudy veil, as her visibility was quickly lost. Her senses adjusted themselves, with her vision impaired by the dark, her hearing amplified everything around her.

'Aunty, Aunty…' she repeated, shaking Florrie to wake. 'I think we're being invaded. They're here; the Nazis!'

Florrie lay motionless. There was still no response. Aggie was petrified; she had always hated the dark. Luckily, she no longer heard footsteps from the basement, but the voices from outside the front of the house grew ever louder. They must be close to her home. She listened, intently. They had British accents for sure. Only one thing for it, she thought. She stood up, removed her mask and hollered for all her worth.

'Help! Help us !' Aggie cried.

Although the acrid smoke continued to envelop her, she heard the footsteps approaching. Wheezing and coughing she struggled to breathe without the mask on even though it was the briefest of moments.

'Heeeellppp!' she bellowed one more time.

It worked; the footsteps slowly ascended the stone steps leading to the front door.

'We're in he–' Aggie moved to shout, but before she could finish her sentence a hand came over her right shoulder and clasped a tight grip across her mouth, its forefinger and thumb pinching her nose stopping her breathing.

'Ssshhhhh,' whispered a deep, rasping voice into Aggie's ear. 'Put on your mask!' it came again, wheezing asthmatically.

Muffled from behind its own gas mask, it was calm and direct, definitely belonging to a man. A man whose breathing was heavy and words were slurred. Aggie tried to wriggle herself around, but using his strength to hold her in a vice-like grip, he manipulated her like a puppet master, ushering her hands to place the gas mask back over her own head.

Terrified, she duly complied.

Thud! Thud!

Two ham-fisted knocks came from the front door. The stranger released his left arm and moved it slowly down by his side.

'Is there anyone there?' came a muffled voice from outside.

Sensing an opportunity, her left hand now free, Aggie reacted quickly, whipping off her mask and screaming out loud. The stranger could not react fast enough to stop her and before he knew it, the front door had come thundering in. Tightening his grip across her chest and grasping her mouth once again, he dragged Aggie back further into the darkness of the hallway, unseen from the front threshold. Aggie tried pinching the man but he didn't react. His skin was not normal, not as Aggie knew it, but somewhere between scaly and smooth. His snakelike strength constricting, restricting Aggie's breathing.

The open doorway produced pockets of light, and Aggie could just make out the silhouettes of two men. A violet and blue hue lit them from behind, reflecting off of their rain-sodden clothes and hats. It wasn't the fiery light from the usual incendiaries that felled the city. The two men wore standard home-guard fare; enamel hats, sou'westers, and protective gas masks that covered their faces.

'Is there anybody in here? There's been a gas leak,' one of them said.

That explained the strange light and why, on her count of *two,* the explosion had taken them by surprise because surely, as the crow flies, the Thunder Machines should have been two miles away.

'We must evacuate everyone. We heard your voice, ma'am. Ma'am? Where are you, ma'am?' the men continued.

Aggie was still hidden back within the hallway's darkness, beyond their visibility. Her assailant continued asserting his hold, breathing slowly and deeply, remaining calm.

The two men, unaware they were being watched, spied the limp body of her Great Aunt Florrie laid out upon the floor.

Aggie desperately tried to move, stamp on the stranger's toe, or rake his shin; anything to give an inkling of a sign that she lurked in the shadows, captive. Her captor remained motionless and ever-increasingly tightened his grip to ensure she didn't make a sound. He wouldn't make the same mistake twice.

The two men tentatively stepped across the threshold. Aggie watched from behind her misted mask, as from beneath their cloaks they each drew a pistol. 'What on earth would the home guard do that for if it was a gas leak?' she thought, or perhaps they knew there was an assailant in the vicinity? That was it. They knew her captor was dangerous and taking refuge. They couldn't take any risks.

From over Aggie's left shoulder, the stranger slowly stretched out his arm. From the corner of her eye, Aggie saw a thin metal barrel reflect the light from the doorway. She knew he was taking aim at the two men. Dipping her shoulder she jolted forward, the would-be assassin stumbling as he lost his balance.

The noise drew the two guards' attention towards them. From his left hand, the intruder lit up a torch, not a firearm. It projected a brilliant beam, which temporarily blinded the guards. It was violet-coloured, not the white beam of a standard torch. It was reminiscent of the hue of the gas leak seeping through and around them. Releasing his right arm and systematically shoving Aggie to the ground, the assailant rapidly drew his own pistol, releasing two deft blasts. The sparks of light from the bullets fizzed over Aggie's head and instantly found their mark. With just two shots, the home guards dropped where they had been standing, dead.

'Noooo!' Aggie screamed, stumbling towards the two bodies.

Ripping off her mask, she crawled towards the motionless men splayed out on the floor. The assailant's arm beat her to them as he pulled one of the guard's masks away. Directing the violet torch beam over her, it highlighted symbols and markings across the guard's face. There, in the middle of the forehead, an image of a brilliant blue eye was illuminated by the torch's beam. The bullet hole had neatly penetrated it where the iris should be and it now wept blood down the guard's face.

Aggie dashed to run, but her legs would not work properly. She was too weak. She felt faint, giddy, and was struggling to breathe. Her sight began to move in and out of focus and what little she had been able to see was now just a terrible blur. The stranger extended his hand towards her, clasping a gas mask.

'Put on your mask!' he slurred as he breathed deeply through his own. The blurred outline of his dark presence moved slowly towards her. 'Put on your mask, or you will die!' he concluded.

Chapter 2
Morning at the Museum

The morning after any sustained bombing campaign, the brave citizens of London rallied around as always, utilising any resources available to them. Their resilience could not be broken, unlike their homes, and their determination was second to none. Men, women, and children poured out from their air-raid shelters, underground stations, and any other places of refuge taken from those long, fearful nights. To observe them from the pigeon-eye-view of St Paul's spire or the belfry of Big Ben they appeared insect-like, hurriedly scurrying about their business, working together as best they could to patch up their tumbledown city.

For a dedicated few, those who were charged with protecting our heritage, great art, and scientific endeavours, their days were full of cataloguing works, hauling masterpieces, recording manuscripts, and ensuring that, when the time would come and one stray Thunder Machine met its target of any of the great museums and academies, we would still have most of that knowledge and culture intact, and hopefully stored many miles away from the Luftwaffe's bomb path.

The National Museum of Science and Nature was an impressive and imposing building. Its monumental brick facade framed with yellowed sandstone and marble, it stood strong and proud in the centre of the city. The carved images of gargoyle primates and mammals protected it as much as they could from the fire and brimstone that so often rained down from above. Sabre-toothed tigers and the mystical Gryphons stood alongside modern-day Mammalia, all defiantly protecting the museum in their stony silence.

The Museum had not been immune to air attacks but had survived almost intact apart from a severe explosion that targeted its Eastern Quarter.

The Botanical Library & Entomology Department that had been based in the Eastern Quarter had lost many rare and irreplaceable works. Insects of all shapes and sizes, pinned meticulously in their teak and walnut exhibition cases, numbering in their thousands, were literally crushed and turned to dust the day that specific Thunder Machine came. Where once stood the world's most extraordinary collection of 'Plants and Bugs', there was now a skeletal framework of ceiling joists and plaster that lay decimated and fallen as if a mighty wooden beast had collapsed from the imposing rooftop through the floors to the gallery below. Now, while this was an impressive and world-renowned research facility, insects and seeds stood little chance of much attention when the likes of a Blue Whale or the replicated Woolly Mammoths were in residence. The sheer scope and size of the collection were immense and to preserve the already preserved was a momentous undertaking.

There was so much work to be done, yet so little time, and the man in charge of this huge operation was Sergeant Major Boyd Collingdale.

Collingdale suffered neither fools nor had a terrible liking for creepy crawlies. A stout, bald-headed man who sported a large clamshell moustache, he now carried the burden of this huge operation to package, protect, and dispatch the Museum's most valuable objects. A product of several wars, he was a soldier first and foremost; certainly, no diplomat or scientist. He would never deviate from a direct order and often exclaimed, 'My orders are from Churchill himself!'

So, woe betides anyone trying to change his mind.

Collingdale would march, quick smart, around the Museum with a small army of actuaries and registrars who noted every request, every order, and would wriggle back to him, wormlike, when an action had not taken place, naming and shaming the person responsible. In his right hand, he still carried a bamboo cane, an antiquity of previous and numerous encounters; 'The Peacekeeper', as he called it. No one had seen him break out the 'peace' but the imminent threat was enough to keep people on their toes. Every day, at 8 a.m. sharp, he rounded the likes of Asiatic Elephants, Spectacled Bears and Siberian Tigers, all staring anonymously at him through their glazed cases and labelled for dispatch to various corners of the country. When passing the long avian corridors of stuffed birds, such as the impressive hornbills or colourful toucans, he always felt a sense of nausea as he approached the Eastern Quarter.

In stark contrast to the military man, the curator and Senior Professor of Entomology, 'Meticulous' Meredith Malcolm was a man who liked to dress, whatever the weather, in pure white linens. No one really knew why, particularly in the dust and detritus that followed a bombing. He preferred a straw boater and was commonly seen in the company of a large butterfly net, despite living in such a densely populated city environment. It was more than polite to say that Professor Malcolm was a constant thorn in Collingdale's side.

These two distinct opposites of men, with possibly the only similarity between them being the love of an eccentric moustache, were at loggerheads since the Eastern Quarter had succumbed to the Fuhrer's most recent blitz. People had wagered that the 'peace' could be broken through Meticulous' consistent requests and badgering of the Sergeant Major. He was possibly the only person who was not terrified of the man. It was not because of great bravery, Meredith was of a naturally timid character, but because he was somewhat detached from human interaction, didn't understand the imposing body language or specific threats amongst men, as his sole interest was his beloved bugs. He could spot when a spider might corner the fly, but not if a man was raising a large bamboo cane in his direction. The war that raged outside, so obvious to everyone else and which engulfed them every day, was nothing more than a daily distraction for him, and for the past two weeks, since the bomb had struck, it had been an unbearable inconsideration to continuing his life's work.

It was because he loved his 'creatures' so much, alive or dead, preferably alive, that he spent endless hours under the magnifying glass, creating great glass terrariums and trying as often as he could to breed and understand them. For most people these were nothing but a nuisance; irksome little beasts to be crushed beneath one's boot. For Meticulous, they were the greatest wonders. There was an innumerable volume of species under various genus, and his life's work would never end. Every day lost studying them was an unbearable stagnation of progress and thus his passionate confrontations with Collingdale continued on a daily basis.

At 8:05 a.m., as Collingdale's rounds passed the many exhibition corridors – which now appeared decked with the familiar images of Kitchener and his pointy-fingered recruitment posters – stood the immaculately turned out 'Meticulous' Meredith Malcolm at the archway entrance of the Eastern Quarter. The antithesis of any hand-mounted tiger or large jungle cat, he stood there in purest white, net in hand, decked atop with his red-ribbon boater and eagerly examining his silver pocket watch. As the Sergeant Major rounded the glassed boxes of some of the world's most superior beasts, his party of scribes noticed Meredith first and the ripple of humorous anxiety forced Collingdale to look ahead.

'Oh, for pity's sake,' the military man grumbled under his moustache.

'Sergeant Major, Sergeant Major!' Meticulous shouted out, waving his net hand aloft.

'I can bloody well see you, Meredith. You're dressed in summer linens amidst a backdrop of dirt, rubble and debris,' slammed the stout man impatiently. 'I have told you to come back in a fort–'

' –night?' pounced Meticulous eagerly. Tapping the dial of his pocket watch, he continued, 'Yes, a fortnight, sir!' he exclaimed. 'And according to your records, if your entourage care to check.' He nodded to the host of scribes already eagerly thumbing their ledgers. 'You will see that today is exactly two weeks hence our discussion and at 8 a.m., although according to my timepiece now 8:05 a.m., I can re-access the Eastern Quarter.'

There was a momentary silence from Meredith as Collingdale drew a large breath through his moustache.

'I'm willing to forego the five-minute delay and, rest assured, will not inform your superior,' Meticulous concluded.

The professor was oblivious to the Major's increasing wheezes and was not intentionally goading the man, but with the final remark – a poor attempt of kinship – Meredith had certainly pressed a few buttons. The scribes were taken aback. Literally, they took a step back from the military man, much of them aghast at the foreboding. Collingdale was known to have a temper, known to have flushes of colour that ranged from a light fleshy pink to an anger-induced crimson. At this current moment, all they could see was a purple swelling from his neck upwards and the venting of a deep nasal steam as if a boiler was imminently going to explode.

'You silly little man!' he screamed in an almost inaudible screech.

'Can't you see how much work there is to be done?' he bawled furiously, gesturing with the 'peacekeeper', and coming within a fraction of Meticulous as he did so. 'One stupid movement, or ill-placed footstep and the whole bleeding lot could come crashing down on you,' he began to explain, slightly calming, but crimson red nevertheless. 'Today, I have to move a *Bloody* Blue Whale, Professor!' he swore loudly, beating his bamboo cane against his outer thigh to every syllable. 'It's the largest sodding creature on the planet and, guess what? We're not even in the water! So, unless your little beetles and butterflies can flitter by and help.' He mimicked a ballerina as he spoke. 'Then we are done here!'

Meticulous was looking directly at the increasingly angry Major Collingdale, but every emotion on his face was symbolising that he wasn't listening to a single word.

'So, can I enter the Eastern Quarter or not?' he asked quietly.

'AAAAGGHHHHH!' the Major screamed. He had cracked. He picked up the peacemaker and began swiping it at an unfortunately placed ostrich that stood nearby, just feet away. He hit the bird with such force that the bamboo cane splintered. If it could have, the mighty bird would have buried its head in the concrete floor below, but as it stood there, stuffed, yet proud, an eerie standoff preceded between the military man and the scientist.

It was uncomfortable for the Major's entourage, and no one was brave enough to offer up a solution, so the two men just stared at each other in an indefinite stalemate.

Clip, Clop, Clip, Clop came a distant sound. It was subtle but, nevertheless, it was enough to break the silence. *Clip, Clop, Clip, Clop*. It grew ever louder.

The peculiar *clip clopping* echoed through hallways and around the animal exhibits. The entourage, with the exception of Mr Meredith who was now intently focusing on the rear of Collingdale's head, turned around to see what it was. It sounded like the patter and slow movement of hooves as if one of the taxidermist's creatures had suddenly come to life. The Major, temporarily distracted from his current nemesis, squinted towards the direction of the *clip clopping*, focusing his gaze. Meticulous Malcolm, still focused on the bald man's head, reached inside his inner breast pocket and slowly drew out a tortoiseshell hilt. With the slightest flick of a button, a six-inch blade sprung forward.

Major Collingdale, oblivious to the entomologist's weapon drawn directly behind his head and atop of his spine, then lowered his voice.

'Now, nobody move,' he whispered.

'I couldn't agree more,' Professor Malcolm whispered back.

Collingdale ignored him, far too focused on the intruding sound clip-clopping its way closer.

'This is most peculiar,' the Major continued.

'I should say so,' agreed the Professor, still ignored by everyone else, but intently focusing his gaze and blade towards the Major's spine.

'What is that sound? Can you all hear it?' Collingdale asked.

With the exception of Meredith, again, everyone nodded in unison. The Major slid his hand downwards, reaching for his sidearm. He popped the leather holster catch and drew it slowly to his midriff.

Just as he did so, and as all noise was amplified to within the nearest pin drop, the bug man thrust the knife forward towards the rear of the Major's neck. The glint of the blade flashed enough to cause the Major's reflexes to react. He broke focus from the alien noise making its way towards them, swivelled sharply, and using his un-cocked firearm he knocked Meredith's blade arm away. He was just about to draw his arm back and fire when an additional frenzied movement from the end of his adversary's knife made him glance over. There, impaled on the tip, frantically thrashing its eight legs and snapping pincers while its sting curled and uncurled itself, was a sand-coloured, luminously striped beast. The silence was replaced by screams of panic from the scribes as they backed themselves away from the venomous little monster. The Major withdrew his gun and stepped away from Professor Meredith.

'What abomination of a creature is that?' asked Collingdale, holding the gun barrel directly to it.

'Fascinating!' exclaimed Professor Meredith as he drew it closer for inspection. The creature thrashed with one last attempt to sting him before it curled up and died. '*Leuirus quinquestriatus…*' he pronounced, holding it up like a proud lecturer to a class of unwilling students. 'The Death-stalker scorpion!'

The aggressive arachnid, which had shifted their attention so quickly, had erased the very immediate concern of the *clip-clopping* creature that had consumed the Major and his cohort only moment's prior. The acoustic archways and corridors of the Museum, which had amplified that sound, were now silent. A welcome sigh of relief from the Major broke the tension and everyone took a momentary pause while he holstered his gun and straightened himself. No one had spotted that just twenty feet away, the *clip clopping* had stopped for a reason.

There she stood, standing over six feet tall, a long golden mane draping below her shoulders, covered in the purest amber fur, and staring directly at the Sergeant Major with her piercing blue eyes.

As one scribe raised a finger directed over Collingdale's shoulder, the Major slowly turned around to be confronted by the new presence.

'Good grief!' the Sergeant Major exclaimed.

Chapter 3
Taken

Agatha awoke, shrouded in darkness. Across her chest, a tight grip held her down horizontally, though the sinew and muscle of the assailant's forearm had now been replaced by a broad, leather restraint. Across her midriff, a brass buckle rubbed and etched itself sorely into her stomach. Her head felt as if her brain was swelling to escape her skull, and as the slow rolling motion of her surroundings emphasised her giddiness, she felt she could vomit at any moment.

As her thoughts flooded back to her, Great Aunt Florrie was at the forefront of them. Was Florrie dead? If so, did that mean that she, Agatha, was orphaned again? Of course, you cannot be orphaned twice, and Aggie had never fully understood the circumstances of her parents' deaths but, for as long as she had known, Florrie had looked after her and raised her as her own. Despite the huge age difference, she was a mother to her all the same, and she loved her dearly.

Was Florrie dead?

Aggie felt her emotions overcome her. Her eyes welled up and dispersed their tears down her cheeks, creating mascara lines out of the dirt that had accumulated onto her face. Anger, fear, sadness and hatred all mingled themselves into a desperate cocktail of unhappiness. Then her thoughts shifted again. What if Florrie had survived? Surely, she would be captive too, maybe even in a room next door? Until she was absolutely sure of it, she decided her great aunt was still alive and she would do her utmost to find her and rescue her.

Wherever the answers lay to these thoughts, the more immediate concern was why she was being held captive, and where she was being taken. Aggie, as sore and sickly as her head now felt, could not understand what purpose an everyday fourteen-year-old girl or her elderly aunt would have to them. If this was the Nazi invasion, why was she so special? Why hadn't she been herded up and shot or taken to one of those atrocious POW camps she had seen on the Pathe newsreels? Where were they taking her?

As the to-ing and fro-ing, which she had originally thought was a symptom of her sickness, grew stronger, she sensed a whiff of smoke. Not the acrid, mouth-smothering stench she had recently experienced, but a lighter, passing cloud of coal puff. Although she lay there in the pitch of night, very occasionally, through a tiny crack in the wall, a dash of light splintered the darkness. She wasn't being shipped anywhere, at least not a boat as she had suspected. She was captive and being transported, on a steam locomotive. Did that mean she was still in England?

As Aggie's senses became more acute and familiarised themselves in their new surroundings, the occasional creek of boards from outside was out of kilter with the cabin's motion. She was confident she was being guarded and someone was patrolling up and down the carriage.

As she lay there, trying to figure out how to free her restraints, an overwhelming nausea came over her. Her head began spinning and she struggled for breath as her insides contorted and cramped. She screamed out in uncontrollable pain and just managed to turn her head as she felt herself overcome from the inside and vomit projected itself across the carriage floor.

'Aaaggghhhh!' she cried out.

A prolonged, uncontrollable scream wrenched from within her, drawing the attention of the stranger outside. Several pairs of feet shuffled down the corridor. Muted whispers of multiple people came from outside until the slightest click of a key unlocked the door and the un-greased, high-pitched screech of an old door handle being forced downwards, led to it opening.

Aggie lay back into a false sleep, peering through the slit of an almost closed set of eyes. Though there was little more light, possibly a single paraffin burner that came from the corridor, Aggie could make out three blurred silhouettes. Firstly, a smaller stout figure, possibly a lady; then, a man in what appeared to be a fedora; and, at the back, a step or two behind, was a second gentleman in a gas mask. It was too dark to see obvious features but a combination of their muted voices and distorted shapes suggested that two men and a woman were her captors. She lay back still, her eyes barely ajar.

BANG! Outside a single gunshot rang out and echoed all around. It was deafening.

All of a sudden, the carriage came to an abrupt halt. A screech of breaks sent the bed she was shackled to, rolling across the carriage. The carriage door swung open enough to offer a view. Her sight was far better now and with each moment her eyes regained focus as her sickness subsided. She peered along the corridor at the unveiling commotion. Several figures, in long dark coats and accompanying hats, flung open the carriage doors to the outside world. They carried pistols by their sides, their features covered by gas masks. She listened, intently, their accents were English, not quite the King's English, but definitely an assortment of English accents. Not German.

As the noise and immediate rumpus died down, she heard a voice shout out.

'False alarm!'

Soon after, the men re-boarded. The last man took his time scouring into the darkness outside. He was timely and precise as he moved his head from left to right and then up and down. Once he was satisfied it was a false alarm, he slammed the door shut and pulled twice on the cable above it. He then twisted the brass knob of the paraffin burner down, dimming the light, and ensuring minimal exposure from within.

Slowly, the train began to amble away once more. Once the train had gained momentum Aggie, ensuring there was no one in the corridor beyond, twisted and manoeuvred herself until she was able to make out more of the darkened passageway as occasional moonlight flickered through shrouded trees and woodlands outside. Wherever they were going, it wasn't anywhere familiar to her. All her trips across London, above ground, and even the rare trip to the coast, never seemed to have so much covering of forest. Perhaps this was already another country, she hadn't thought of that. Maybe, even, the great **Black Forest of Bavaria?** And the English accents, of sorts, could belong to double agents or **spies**.

As her thoughts began to race once more, the immediacy of the train pulling to a halt startled her. Two brilliant beams of light from outside blindingly lit up the inside of the train. Rain had begun to fall, and the reflective streams of drizzle now began peppering the outside windows.

Along the corridor, the shuffling of feet now moved towards her carriage. Three silhouettes opened the door wider to reveal her lying there. This time they entered and came closer.

'She's still out,' came the first voice. Aggie had been right; this was a lady's voice, for sure, though the accent was unfamiliar and foreign.

'She's fooling no one!' slurred the second voice.

Aggie recognised it at once, the asthmatic wheeze, the controlled tone. It was the intruder from her house. Her eyes opened in fear and there, staring back at her from behind his gas mask, was the assailant. She could now set eyes on him and stared defiantly beyond the mask's glass exterior. The patch that covered his left eye detracted from the piercing stare from his right. She sensed a broad smile come across his face.

'This may sting a little, sorry!' he exclaimed.

The sharp chill of a needle pierced Aggie's vein at her elbow joint as the masked man held her down. She tried to struggle, but all power from her body had subsided within an instant, and she fell limp. Her visibility began to fade once more. She could see the two men leave the carriage; the masked man and the man in the fedora. The lady remained, holding her wrist in the way that nurses feel for pulses. It was only a matter of moments before her eyes rolled and Aggie retreated back into darkness again.

Chapter 4
Ambledown

Aggie awoke, her eyes squinting at the piercing morning sun. For the first time in what had seemed days, she was not restrained. The room she now found herself in was not shrouded in darkness. Sunlight presented itself through slender arched windows where dust particles danced in the lightest of breezes. As her eyes adjusted, the edges of her sight were blurred with a sepia tint that made her vision like an old photograph. Squinting, mole-like, she sat up from where she lay.

First checking her wrists, which were barely bruised, despite the recent restraints, and then her stomach, which had a small pink rub mark where the brass buckle had been tightened around her waist, she found that for the best part she was unscathed. She pondered what had actually gone on. Nothing really made much sense. Aggie sat herself up and turned herself around so her legs hung over the bedside with her feet dangling just above the floorboards. Tentatively she placed a single big toe onto the cold floor. She did not want to make a sound or suggest to her captors she was awake. Allowing the rest of her foot to ground itself and then slowly adding her second, she raised herself up from the bed, stood and surveyed her surroundings in more detail.

The room, which looked to have been untouched for many years, had several small diamond-leaded windows. They were not large enough to escape through, not even for the smallest of children. At one end of the room, with generous helpings of cobwebs and neglect, the floor ran crooked with dark, twisted oak beams doing their best to hold it together. The walls appeared to be made of flint with a light sand mortar. It reminded Aggie of the Tower of London, which she had visited as a much younger child, and where Florrie had regaled to her stories of beheadings and betrayal. She desperately hoped this was not to be her fate. A very small, dark oak door, much smaller than an adult could fit through, was sunk into the floorboards; it appeared to be the only entry and exit point. An inkling of a light source, perhaps a single candle, wrapped the worn edges. Aggie crouched and squinted through below. A lack of light offered nothing more than the views of a descending passageway.

Next to the bed was a small table. A swan-necked terracotta pitcher placed within a bowl, which was much too large for the table, dominated it. Aggie had seen one just like it many years ago at Florrie's. A single pewter goblet stood accompanying it. The two objects were from very different parts of history. A large chest, covered in dust, sat against the end of the single brass bedstead, and against the far end of the tiny proportioned room was a large mirror that covered almost the entire wall and was as big as any man. The dust and ample scattering of dirt was not the type of filth that enveloped you following a bombing raid, engulfing and choking everything in sight, but the type of dust that lent itself to years of isolation, somewhere that time itself had forgotten. There was a rug in the middle of the room, possibly Persian, or of the Orient, its vibrant colours now shrouded in dust, apart from a small set of darkened footprints that looked as if they had recently led to and from the bed, via the mirror. No doubt her captor's footsteps, Aggie determined, as she scrutinised them further. Definitely two sets, one much larger than the other, but what of the third person she recalled from the train? The woman, the man in the gas mask, and the Fedora man. There had definitely been three.

Her thoughts began to race again. Mostly to that of her great aunt's fate. She couldn't be sure if she was dead; it certainly felt as if the smoke had overcome her, lying there limp-wristed and unable to respond as she had been, but Aggie couldn't be sure. Florrie had always taught her that until the absolute facts were presented to her and beyond any shadow of a doubt then she should keep an open mind. Aggie grasped on to this strand of hope.

'What do you see? What would Poirot see?' she heard her great aunt's voice echo in her head. For her namesake, influential towards her education, had led her to a healthy appetite in reading Christie's books and to develop an art in problem-solving. Florrie and her five tutors had always encouraged her to be inquisitive.

'Remember, a curious mind is an active mind!' she heard Florrie rattle around her head again. Though tearful and painfully scared, Aggie knew that until she was presented with the purest evidence to say otherwise, she still had hope that she would see her aunt again.

Sitting back on the bed, she dragged her legs up into her chest, and curled herself up into a ball, resting her forehead on top of her knees, thinking deeply, and running through scenarios. It was incredibly silent, peaceful. It allowed her to think, to compose herself. Hungry and thirsty – Lord knows how long since she had last supped – she turned to the pitcher on the table and the single goblet next to it. The pitcher was full of a transparent fluid but she couldn't be sure what it was. It could be poison; after all, a quick ncedle prick had ensured she ended up in this place. Then again, if her captors had wanted her dead, they could have easily disposed of her by now. There must be some purpose to why she was where she was. She was so parched but refrained from drinking it.

The chiming of bells broke the silence and shuddered through the dusty, leaded windows. She counted seven chimes in all. Wherever she was, it was seven o'clock in the morning, the dawn light ensured that. 7 pm in the evening would have been much darker by now. She tiptoed to one of the windows at the rear, looked out and saw old ruins and battlements. At least, they looked old, made of similar stone to the room she was in, but many a time in London, the buildings had come crashing down and looked as if they were ramparts from days of yore, so she wasn't quite sure if they were as old as they looked or a product of a brutal blitz on this town. Creeping quietly to the front windows she could now hear a few faint voices. The window, if you could call it that, wasn't diamond-leaded like the rear one. Instead, it was far too slender, a tiny slit in the deep-set stone and mortar. Aggie peered through it. It was only just about wide enough to fit her fist into, but was as deep as her outstretched arm. Glass sealed it in at its end. The sand-coloured masonry edges gradually slanted inwards, forming a natural viewing perspective. There was no escape, no matter if you were as small as a bug.

From her elevated position, she could just make out the steady gathering of people walking up the slight incline of the hilly street below. It was difficult to hear anything due to the thickness of the walls and the distance to the street. Florrie's house was on several stories, and this seemed much higher, considering the diminutive size of the people. Aggie continued to watch eagerly. They looked ordinary, not dissimilar to those in London, almost familiar in many ways. Certainly, they were not in any type of military uniform; no long black leather coats or skull-emblazoned headwear; which is what she feared the most.

As Aggie watched from on high, surely no one knew of her spying, she thought. That was until she saw a boy pointing upwards towards her direction. Both an older girl and a younger girl accompanied him. As they passed, the boy encouraged the smaller girl to look upwards and Aggie immediately took a step backwards. Perhaps they had spotted her? Perhaps they could help her?

Aggie was desperate to understand where she was. Where on earth had she been taken? Who knew she was there? Did anyone, apart from her captors, know she was there?

Outside, the little girl let out a scream that was just about audible to Aggie who in turn took a further step back out of view. The older girl clipped the boy around the ear, then grabbed both of her charges and began marching them up the hill. Aggie glanced one more time and saw the older girl stare back momentarily. She made eye contact with Aggie directly but didn't break stride.

Chapter 5
Kitchener

At 7 a.m., roughly an hour before Collingdale's daily round had begun, a large black removal van pulled into the delivery car park of the National Museum for Science and Nature. Several men, dressed in non-descript brown overalls and flat caps, alighted from the rear of the van carrying multiple rolled-up posters, buckets and brooms. After a brief discussion with the sentry guard, during which they unrolled one of the posters with an all too familiar image on it, they entered the Museum.

Sitting opposite the Museum, a large black car watched on as the men went about their business. The front of the car had a magnificent silver bird, with long beak bowing and feathered plumage arched backwards. It sat atop of the car's immaculate chrome radiator. In the front, sat the chauffeur, impeccably dressed and staring attentively straight ahead. To the rear, the passenger gazed on intently as she monitored the men moving in and out of the building. In her left hand a silver timepiece was running. Its two main black hands that were set on a pearl background were almost motionless, with a third crimson hand speedily revolving clockwise. In her right hand, she carried a palm-sized cigarette case. It was not silver, as was the typical fashion, but a dark jade embellished with gold edging. The clasp was curved like an 'S' and two interlocking pincers wrapped around the case and enclosed it as they intertwined. She thumbed it gently as if stroking the tiniest of pets.

As she looked on, her brilliant blonde hair was somewhat out of place in the deep, dark pitch of the car. Her ankle-length overcoat was as bright and burning as the fiery embers that still simmered in the hearts of the ruined buildings nearby. Her sapphire-blue gaze broke only to blink and, only then, very occasionally.

After forty-five minutes, the men sporting overalls left the building and, with one final daub from their buckets and broom, plastered their final posters directly on the entrance to the Museum.

'BRITONS, HE NEEDS YOU!' pronounced Lord Kitchener's famous pointing finger as it motionlessly addressed the passers-by.

At 7:50 am, a now often unseen method of transport, the Penny Farthing, cycled passed the onlookers' car and rounded the wood-and-wire barricade into the Museum. On drawing to a halt, Professor Meredith Malcolm, immaculately presented in white linen, hopped fluidly off of his vehicle in a single motion carrying his butterfly net. With a swift look at his pocket watch and the tiniest twiddle of his moustache, he headed past the sentry and straight into the Museum. The onlooker glanced at her timepiece and smiled.

At 7:55 am, a military-grade green truck pulled up, passed the barricades, and from the passenger seat out hopped Sergeant Major Boyd Collingdale. His moustache twitched as his voice bellowed, and from the back of the truck came, perversely, not soldiers, but an army of clerks and actuaries. They marched to the cue of the man's beating bamboo.

At 8 am, the chauffeur of the large black saloon arose from the front seat, rounded the impressive automobile and opened the rear passenger side door. The occupier was no longer focused on the time; she simply flicked the catch on her cigarette case and the pincers opened with a fluid motion. Inside, the lining was of violet silk that was in stark contrast to its external jade casing. Within its two halves, it harboured two distinctly separate supplies.

Firstly, there were half-a-dozen slender cigarettes, more often associated with European capitals such as Paris rather than London, and each beautifully filtered with a violet silk ribbon to match the inlay. On the other half of the case lay two ebony lengths of a single cigarette holder. She took the two parts out and meticulously screwed them together. Taking one of the immaculate cigarettes and placing it within the holder, she pursed her lips and passed a single gentle breath through it. A wisp of soft violet hue floated around the car until it evaporated into its surroundings.

The chauffeur opened the rear passenger side door and, holding the cigarette holder in her left hand while she grasped the case in her right, she was escorted by the elbow from the vehicle. Gliding graciously across the tan leather coachwork, she slid effortlessly out of the vehicle in one single movement. Standing an impressive six-and-half foot tall, she was adorned in a full-length tiger-skin coat that set ablaze against the dreary bomb-broken background. Her platinum-blonde hair swayed as her clip-clopping saunter began to cross the road to where passers-by and the occasional car stopped to stare in wonder. A short puff of her cigarette and exchange of pleasantries had persuaded the sentry to allow her access to the Museum, against Collingdale's strict rules.

Clip-clop, her high heels sounded, echoing through the acoustic hallways of stuffed exhibits, her tiger-skin coat swaying against the motionless creatures behind glass. It wasn't long until she came upon the man she sought.

'Good grief!' Collingdale exhaled incredulously, staring at the stunning woman standing just yards away. He lowered his gun. Also transfixed by this newcomer, the scribes were all rendered motionless too. Draped in amber fur with its formidable striped pattern, as if she had just sprung from one of the mahogany exhibitions herself, she inhaled from her extended cigarette holder and emitted a light wisp of smoke through her drawn lips. The puff of foreign tobacco flitted amongst them and then dispersed itself into the ether.

From her coat pocket, she drew out a crisp white business card and presented it to Major Collingdale who in turn glared at it intently observing the brilliant red lettering.

'The Official Society for the Improvement and Rehabilitation of Injured Servicemen.'

'Correct,' came the response from the stranger in an unrecognisable foreign lilt. 'Please,' she said, placing her hand upon the Major's hand and rotating it counter-clockwise. 'Read the back too.'

Collingdale gyrated his wrist and there on the back was a gold embossed crest with the initials RA emboldened beneath them. 'By Royal Appointment eh?' he responded, forehead wrinkled and moustache pouting and twitching with nervousness.

'Correct again, Major,' came the mystery blonde's response. 'But not your King. I represent a regal benefactor from a neutral state.'

'A-ha! I couldn't place the coat of arms. You're Swiss!'

The lady flirted with a little laughter as she withdrew her card and placed it back in her coat pocket.

'My name is Sabine, Sabine Erket and I represent benefactors keen to help and improve those tormented in this terrible war. I require some assistance.'

'Of course, ma'am, ummm…I'm not sure how I may help,' the Major replied humbly.

'Oh, it's not actually you, Major Collingdale. It's your entomology professor I am interested in.'

'What?' exclaimed the serviceman, jealous like a school child. 'I mean, I beg your pardon. What on earth for?'

Ms Erket just smiled, drew on her cigarette again, and puffed the smoke directly towards the increasingly reddening army man.

'I need Professor Malcolm – YES?' she said, staring directly at Collingdale and his band of supporters.

'Yes!' he replied subserviently and his entourage nodded in unison.

'You may go now. YES?' she nodded back.

The Major popped the Peacekeeper under his arm, made an about-turn, and carried on with his business.

Meanwhile, 'Meticulous' Meredith Malcolm had retrieved his knife and transfixed his glare onto the curled-up creature impaled on its blade with little interest for the proceedings going on around him.

'Professor?' Ms Erket said as she knelt down beside him as he studied the scorpion. She once again presented her business card.

Malcolm broke from his intrigue at the now-dead arachnid. His index finger gently pushed his brass spectacles on to the top of the bridge of his nose so he could read what was on it and then gave it back.

'Fascinating little monsters, aren't they?' he said, drawing his knife so the scorpion sat at the blade pinnacle and between his sightline and hers. Sabine Erket once more drew on her cigarette and gently exhaled towards Meredith as they both stood there gazing.

'An apex predator for his size, the wolf of the desert some say, although scorpions don't hunt in packs.' The professor half-smiled looking upwards at her.

'I really wouldn't know, sir.' She smiled back.

'The interesting thing about this little beast is that I am certain I have never bred them or kept live ones in this museum.'

Ms Erket stood up calmly, not quite as composed as she had been, inhaled a large drag of the cigarette and puffed it directly downwards at Meticulous' face.

'You're a very smart man, Professor Meredith Malcolm – YES?' she said, piercing her glare through his spectacles.

'Yes!' he responded in a single monotone.

'And you are going to help me – YES?'

'Yes!' he replied in the same tone.

'Good,' Ms Erket responded. 'Shall we?' She ushered the Professor towards the entrance of the East Quarter where a temporary red-and-white-bannered cordon separated exhibits from the debris. A half-fallen column was propped up fretfully at forty-five degrees and allowed a small but dangerous opening to crawl through, which they duly did. As they passed the single entrance into the Entomology department, she took the Professor's straw boater from his head.

'You won't be needing this,' she said, turning around and skimming the hat through the opening and into the dust and detritus. Once through and ensuring both herself and the Professor were safe, she returned to the part-fallen column, and with a single swift shove, it buckled, crashing down before her, taking the ceiling and support with it. The only entrance to them was now blocked and for all intents and purposes, all that was left to the outside world of herself and Professor Malcolm were the crushed remains of a red-ribbon straw boater.

Chapter 6
Gideon

After withdrawing back into the room even further, Aggie was sure she could no longer be seen in the shadows as she observed the passers-by way down below. Peering through the window at the empty street below, she stared and took in as much information as she could. The slim perspective she was afforded offered a view of several houses and what looked like a small store, but from her position within the tall building, the tiny writing could not be seen clearly. Turning her neck in all manner of angles and twisting her body from left to right she only managed to flit her vision from the church steeple, to the street. It was useless. There was nothing she could garner from here.

As she observed the street below, a dark figure, cloaked in a long gown – black or maybe brown – the type very much like a friar or monk would wear, briskly walked uphill with their arms interlocked within their own sleeves, headed towards the rear of the church, and vanished out of sight.

Aggie returned to the bed and lay down. Why, oh why, hadn't her captors made themselves visible to her? By her own reckoning, she had been here at least twelve hours. She was so hungry, so thirsty. Rationing had made everyone hardier since the war had begun but she was light-headed and weak. The pitcher and goblet now looked like a good prospect, and even if it was poison what horrors lay in store for her now anyway? She turned and grabbed the swan-necked terracotta jug and poured the transparent liquid into the pewter drinking vessel. She stood there for one last moment, pondering her fate. If it was to be a slow agonising death, at least it would be over soon enough and she would soon be with her great aunt, and finally meet the parents she had never known. That was, of course, if Florrie had passed away. That doubt still niggled at her.

She snatched at the goblet and raised it to her lips. It was heavy, not only due to its age and metal casting but it was weighted at the base. She couldn't lift it easily. She squatted down and there, underneath, it was tied to an almost invisible line of thread. It was catgut, fishing line. What on

Earth was going on? Aggie took the line between thumb and forefinger and followed it around the room. It ran at the base of the wall and along into a corner before splintering onto two pulleys. One ran directly downwards and through the floorboards below, while the other ran along the far wall and behind the mirror that covered it. Having noticed the footprints across the rug, which ran to and from the bed, she looked down and once again traced them as they disappeared into the huge mirror. It was quite obviously the entrance in and out of the place but she did not wish to venture down the dim passageway beyond.

As she peeked through the worn edges the distant glow of torchlight could be seen but this time growing stronger. Someone was coming. Aggie scoured the room once again, the only thing she could find to use as a weapon was the swan-necked pitcher. The goblet was tied to the fishing line and she couldn't move it. The mirror was not obviously hinged, and since she couldn't determine which way it would open, she just had to wait, weapon drawn. Whatever her fate, she would make sure she went down fighting.

Aggie composed herself, waiting for the mirror to move. She backed away to allow herself time and space to react once she knew which way her captors would be coming in.

First came the scratching of the key entering the lock, then the clunking of the unlocking itself before finally the squeal of an unoiled handle hinge. Her heart was beating faster and faster as she waited for her moment. She waited patiently but then the noise of the opening door came from behind her, she turned quickly, and the small oak door, which was no bigger than a child, was beginning to open. She raised the pitcher, holding the neck as if wielding an axe.

As the door began to open, she glimpsed the fedora from her kidnapper's head. At the same time, the mirror slid open behind her, she had to choose one or the other. The Fedora man was closer and his entrance was at such a level that if Aggie connected with her target, she could cause some real damage. No time to think otherwise.

She took a mighty swing towards the opening in the oak door. Almost immediately, she heard a cry from behind her.

'NO!' came the gruff lady's voice.

Agatha's blow missed her intended target and met the door, the flint wall, and the guarded forearm of her captor before she was bundled from behind and onto the floor. She kicked and punched for all her worth but the woman attacker held her in a vice-like grip and wrestled her to the floor.

As Aggie lay there with the remains of the jug in her hand, exhausted, tears of anger ran down her cheeks. The tall man pulled himself up through the tiniest entranceway, dusted himself down and crouched behind her. The young girl just stared into space. Removing his trademark hat, he tapped the female assailant on the shoulder and she loosened her grip on Aggie. Aggie crawled into a foetus shape and began sobbing.

The gentleman placed his hand on her head and gently stroked it.

'I'm so, so sorry, my lovely,' he whispered softly in her ear.

Aggie's steely blue glare lasted momentarily and then a sudden rush of anger and adrenaline combined so quickly that she turned furiously with her clenched fist and caught the Fedora man square in the chin.

He slid back and clicked his jaw into place.

'I'm so sorry, Aggie. There really was no other way,' he apologised.

Aggie burst into tears and collapsed into his arms, sobbing.

'Uncle Gideon, is it really you?' she asked through streaming tears. 'I can't believe it's you. I really don't know what is going on!'

'I can explain everything,' her uncle replied, cradling her tightly towards his chest. 'But first, we need to get you fed and watered. It's been days, you know.'

'I've been here for days?' Agatha questioned, looking up at him.

'Oh, a couple at least.' He nodded.

Agatha was stunned, truly stunned. The confusion contorted her face. Gideon sensed the anxiety and pulled her closer.

'You must be hungry, my love?' he whispered, cradling her. Aggie nodded in response.

'Let's eat, and all will be explained'

The sense of relief lifted through her body as she stood up, and followed her uncle down the hidden stairwell before all of a sudden, the very terrifying thought entered her mind once again.

'I think Florrie's dead!' she blurted out.

Gideon turned around and looked back at her on the stone stairs. He took her hand within his and cradled it gently. They stood almost touching noses as his height from the lower stairs, in comparison to hers, drew them level. He lent in to her ear. At first, Aggie thought he was going to peck her on the cheek and embrace her again but instead he whispered very softly and reassuringly, 'Oh no, she isn't.'

Aggie pulled back slightly and was just about to ask another question when her uncle pursed his lips, drew his index finger to them, indicated silence, and winked.

'Sshhhh!' he smiled. 'That's our little secret!'

The stone stairs descended sharply in a tight spiral towards an adjoining tunnel. Every ten feet or so, small torchlights cast dancing shadows from within a wrought iron basket. The flames were lit with wick and wax just as they would have been for their forebears. Again, it reminded Aggie of a medieval ruin, such as The Tower.

'These corridors were not built for the likes of me,' said Gideon as he took one of the torches, crouched, and then squeezed his way through the winding passageway.

'How do you know?' Aggie replied.

'Well, they're several centuries old, and our relatives were much smaller back then,' he replied.

'No, not that. You know what I am asking. How do you know that Florrie's alive?' Aggie responded, curtly.

Gideon paused, twisted himself around and surveyed the tunnel behind, raising his index finger to his pursed lips once more. There was no one there. The thickset lady who had wrestled Aggie to the ground had closed the passageway door behind them had left the room by the mirrored entrance.

'We need to be careful. Not all is as it seems. I know you have many questions but you need to trust me just for a few moments longer. Please?' her uncle responded in an assured, comforting tone.

Aggie nodded, and they navigated the serpentine passage until it widened into a fork with two options to take.

'Left is rest and right is flight!' Gideon announced pointing out the two options. 'Heaven forbid you should ever have to take flight, my love, but if you ever do, place a torch on the opposing alleyway; it will mask the other alleyway into darkness.' Her uncle duly demonstrated placing the torch on the right-hand side of the left passageway, the light shone down it and cast a shadow against the fork in the wall, duly obscuring the neighbouring passage.

Through several twists and down at least two more sets of steps Aggie faithfully followed her uncle until they finally came to a door. It was small and similar to the one connecting her former room to this. Gideon peered through an almost invisible knothole before opening the doorway. He gestured Aggie inwards. It was a dark box, almost coffin-like. He helped her in, and then followed into the tight space. Once in, he closed the door and then pressed his ear to the other side of the panelling. Confident he could not hear anything, as he expected, he then slid the wooden panel sideways, revealing another large box space. This was different; there was a rail, and clothes hanging down from it. Gideon encouraged Aggie as she climbed inside and through what was surely the world's largest wardrobe. She shoved the doors open and in streamed a crisp autumn sunlight that speckled dust around the sumptuous room.

Aggie was aghast. She stepped out of the wardrobe and revolved on her heel almost a full 360. The wardrobe she could not recall, but the huge Georgian sash which let in so much light was familiar to her. Beneath it was a small writing desk and to either side, children's toys just as she was beginning to recall. To the right-hand side, a wooden rocking horse with a red leather rein, and white and grey patina. To the left-hand side, a dollhouse the size of an adult. It was built to represent a property three storey's high with a dark brick facade, elevated stone steps with wrought iron railings and a prominent white front door, tiny brass knocker in the form a lion's head and with '1a' in bold type on the front. It was an exact replica of the house she now found herself in. She opened the sash on the second floor of the model and inside was a wooden, patina rocking horse with a red leather strap that sat within the palm of her hand.

'Do you remember?' Gideon enquired tentatively

'Of course, I remember,' she said as she smiled and as tiny tears welled up in her eyes.

'Now, about Florrie,' Gideon said.

Her uncle sat down side-saddling the large double brass bed. He patted the green velvet down that draped over it, and Aggie sat beside him cradling the toy horse in the palm of her hand.

Aggie had spent summers in this house, several years ago now. She remembered the long days spent with Uncle Gideon, playing in the fields and orchards. It was when she had just been a small child yet the room seemed so familiar still as if it hadn't been touched since her last visit

'On the night of the attack,' Gideon began. 'Word from Florrie had reached me some days earlier, asking if you could be evacuated to the countryside and come live with me.' He reached inside his breast pocket and produced a small telegram.

'Here…read it,' he said, ushering the paper into her hand.

DEAREST G (STOP) LONDON TOO DANGEROUS FOR A (STOP) REQUEST EVACUATION (STOP) F (STOP)

It was a brief and concise message, Aggie thought. Without knowing who G, A, and F were, it would not make much sense to anyone else and was no doubt part of Florrie's plan. Knowing her great aunt as she did, she knew the wily old lady was obviously worried as the message was so succinct.

'Ok, so she was scared,' Aggie responded. 'The Thunder Machines are menacing, Uncle, and they are not exactly fussy about which homes they decide to destroy,' she explained in expressive hand gestures.

'True, Aggie, very true. But I think you already know that on that night, something more sinister was afoot and I need you to tell me what you can recall.'

Gideon had always been a very subtle presence in Aggie's life. He wasn't always there day-to-day, but he never missed a birthday, never missed Christmas celebrations, and as far as communication was concerned, he wrote to her almost weekly from wherever his adventures took him or whatever business he was on. He was quite secretive at times but he had never treated her with anything but love and adoration.

Aggie, in her heart of hearts, really could not piece anything together that had happened in the past few days. How had she managed to arrive in the safety of Ambledown and Gideon's care? The more she knew, the more she realised something was missing. The kidnapper, the men he had shot in Florrie's doorway, and the train journey. How on earth had she ended up here?

'I need you to think, Aggie. Tell me exactly what you saw and how everything happened.'

Composing herself she started from the very beginning; the Thunder Machines overhead, the 'thunder-and-lightning' game, the fact it was her missing gas mask that had meant Florrie had succumbed to the noxious fumes, the two men with the peculiar markings on their faces shot dead by the assailant, and, of course, the killer himself. Aggie described at length how sinister he was, how he had crept up from behind and restrained her with such force that she could not struggle or warn the two home guards who he then brutally murdered. His snakelike skin, and his asthmatic wheezing; all-in-all, a monster of a man in every sense, and he told her she was going to die.

Gideon listened intently and nodded in recognition as she explained.

'That's good. Your memory seems fine,' he said.

'Well, why wouldn't it be?' she questioned.

'You were poisoned,' Gideon replied as he watched his niece's face change to a state of alarm.

'Poisoned?'

Her uncle was slightly hesitant before his response. 'Gas poisoning. Strange toxic fumes that we did not understand at first. They made you quite poorly and you were hallucinating, seeing all manner of weird and wonderful things, and screaming for several days. That's why we kept you high up in The Keep and out of sight of nosey local eyes.'

Aggie was relieved to understand that not everything she had seen or sensed had been true. Lord knows she could not make head nor tail of half of what had gone on in the few days past.

'So,' she quizzically engaged her uncle. 'I wasn't kidnapped at all?'

'You were not kidnapped, Aggie, per se. It was a friend of mine sent to protect you.'

'I don't understand?' she frowned.

'It's complicated,' Gideon said, exhaling a deep breath. He took a moment, drew in another lung full of air, and began to talk once more. 'The two men that came to your door that night, for all intents and purposes, were random home guards just checking and helping the neighbourhood, right?'

Aggie nodded, but she began to doubt herself as she recalled the markings on their faces.

'Well, although your induced hallucinations presented many strange visions that night, I can actually tell you that those were not one of them. Those markings you glimpsed were real,' Gideon explained.

'Real?' Aggie responded, alarmed for the second time in mere minutes.

'Yes, unfortunately,' Gideon confirmed uncomfortably.

'I'm sorry, Uncle Gideon, but I really do not understand what you mean.'

'It's probably too much to take in for one day but I need to show you something in my shop,' he replied.

Aggie had forgotten about the shop. Gideon was first and foremost an explorer, adventurer but he funded his exotic trips through his antiquity dealing. If she recalled correctly, the shop was just next door. It sat on the ground and lower ground floor of the Georgian house that was conjoined to the one she was currently in. A wave of excitement came over her as she recalled the exhibits and peculiarities she would gaze on or play with when she was much smaller.

'But before we do so, we need to get a few facts straight, OK?' Gideon told her in a stricter tone.

Aggie nodded silently back at him.

At that moment, there was a knock at the bedroom door and, soon after, the broad woman, who had wrestled Aggie to the ground, entered. She was carrying a tray with a large mixing bowl within which was a pair of scissors and a black tar-like substance.

'This is Nan. Not your grandmother obviously, but Nan, my housekeeper,' Gideon explained. 'You may recall her from years ago. Anyway, for the time being, you are not my niece. You are just an evacuee from London, OK?'

'Why?' Aggie asked.

Gideon exhaled a loud puff of air again. 'I just need you to trust me, Aggie, please? People cannot know we are related. There are many reasons.'

Aggie was becoming more curious and confused. She had no reason to distrust her uncle but why was he being so secretive? For the time being she agreed to go along with his plan and nodded.

'And we need to cut your hair.' He smiled

'No, why?' she asked angrily.

Gideon briefly held his head in his hands deciding how best to explain everything to his young charge. He leant into her and smiled.

'If you let me cut your hair, I will talk to you about Cairo!'

Aggie leant backwards and paused. Goosebumps pimpled her arms as a chill spread across her body.

'Cairo, really?' Her lips quivered as nervous tears welled up in her eyes.

Gideon passed his right arm across her shoulder and cuddled her as Aggie found her head now bowing. The tears trickled down her cheeks and turned into a sob. Cairo was not a word that was used in Florrie's house. The unwritten rule was that Cairo was a forbidden subject, a swear word.

Cairo was where her parents had been killed, that, Aggie was sure of.

Chapter 7
Lost and Found

Shattered mahogany boxes and glass scattered the floor as both Erket and Malcolm trod across the rubble. There was limited light in what remained of the Professors' beloved department. A few shards of daylight streamed through the tumbledown walls and exhibits that he had spent so many hours dedicating his life to. The ceiling reminded him of an emaciated ribcage that had now decayed and was at the mercy of the elements.

'Oh, my goodness,' the Professor exclaimed. 'What on earth is that dreadful stink?'

There was an ungodly smell that emanated from deep within his laboratory. It was a foul stench reminiscent of rotting meat. Whatever it was, both Erket and Malcolm held their hands over their faces trying not to gag. Occasionally, the Professor would squat and retrieve a half-intact exhibit, a presentation glass of moths or butterflies, the occasional rock of natural amber and it's preserved fly inside. It was difficult in the darkness for him to orientate. The distraction of the smell did not help either. As complex an environment as this now was to the Professor, to his subjects, the darkness and decay were paradise.

'It's funny,' he chortled. 'While outside a human war of devastating impact continues to rage, in here, an epic battle of indigenous species would have fought and likely succumbed to foreign invaders.'

Sabine Erket smirked and inquisitively cast her glance towards him. He couldn't see the look upon her face but she wondered if he knew more than he was letting on.

'Here we are,' Malcolm said, stopping at a large piece of furniture. He ran his fingers across the top of the desk. The green velvet baize that had decorated the top, was torn and his once immaculate set of tools, magnifying glasses, and embalming flasks were now scattered and shattered around it. He reached inside his trouser pocket and pulled out a small set of keys. He then fumbled away at the drawers beneath until he found the lock. Presenting the key and turning clockwise he was able to open his drawers and sift through until he found what he was looking for.

'Do you mind holding this for me, Ms Erket?' he asked. The Professor handed her the chrome tubular torch, stood up and removed his white linen blazer. As he was doing so, he turned it inside out so his outstretched arms now held the blazer in front of him like a large white flag.

'Shine the light directly at the blazer,' he proffered to the now accommodating Ms Erket.

As she turned the torch on and directed it, under his guidance, the devastation of the department became more apparent as the light-filled beam caught the desolated remains of the world-renowned facility. Sabine focused the torch on the white blazer but after a minute of pure silence, she grew impatient.

'What are we doing?' she asked.

'Shush!' the Professor curtly replied.

After another minute or so, a slight droning noise could be heard. Not as loud or as terrifying as a Thunder Machine but definitely something circling in the air. She could sense excitement from 'Meticulous' Meredith Malcolm. First, there was a single drone-like noise and the gentle sound of tapping against objects as if a wasp trapped within a shop window that infinitely exhausted itself was trying to exit through the glass. First, there was one, then maybe two, but before long a small army of drones hovered overhead until the first of many tiny thumps hit the blazer. Ms Erket looked on as insect upon insect began to land on the Professor and his perfect linen suit.

'Fascinating, isn't it?' he giggled. 'I expected the moths first, but just look, look at the beetles and look there, upon my moustache,' he concluded with a cross-eyed glance.

Sabine looked to see a large green insect with an inverted triangular head, sitting upright on the end of his moustache preening its spindly arms.

'A female praying mantis!' he exclaimed. 'They are known to devour their mates you know, post-coitus.' The Professor chuckled.

'Fascinating,' Sabine sarcastically responded.

Juggling the torch, she took another cigarette from her scorpion-embellished case, inhaled deeply, approached the Professor, and purposely blew the smoke towards his nose.

'So, Professor you are going to help me – YES!'

'Yes,' he replied and lowered the blazer while squinting directly towards the beam.

Sabine Erket then switched off the torch. As the darkness descended once again, the wing cases opened and with a swift flap and flutter, the bugs disappeared once more into the pitch black.

A moment of silence fell. Then, taking the Professor by surprise, Sabine Erket produced another torch from within one of her deep coat pockets. On illumination, this was not the white light they had just used. It was a violet colour. Its beam did not attract the common insects towards them. Instead, it caught the ethereal movement of her cigarette smoke as it danced and tumbled as soft as a cloud on the slightest of breezes. As she scoured the room, the Professor suddenly shouted out.

'There!' He pointed. 'Over there!' His index finger directed the path to follow. A throb of glowing green, luminously exposing their owner against the dark camouflage, lit up just several yards away.

'If I'm not mistaken, that's bio-luminescence?' the Professor announced with authority.

'Part of t*he Wolf Pack*!' Sabine Erket laughed.

Moving discreetly towards the illuminating little monsters, several minutes later, several more venomous arachnids shone through the darkness. The closer they moved towards them, the wretched stench of rotting meat grew ever stronger. The Death-stalkers were not the only creatures to light their own way. An occasional metallic beetle with blue-hued antennae would pass, or even the showcasing of yellow leg joints from an Orb spider, which adorned the arachnid-like exotic nylons, would make themselves visible via the torchlight.

'What are you looking for?' the Professor asked.

'Scarabidae,' Erket responded.

'I wasn't aware the humble dung beetle offered up any luminosity?' the Professor questioned.

'There are over 30,000 scarab species, Professor. Did you know that? I'm sure you did,' Sabine Erket advised him.

For once, 'Meticulous' Meredith Malcolm was impressed with someone else's knowledge.

'The Hercules Beetle, The Goliath Beetle, The Rhinoceros beetle…' she reeled off. 'Of course, they're the supreme specimens; the gladiators of their world. I don't know all 30,000 by name. Most of them we classify as dung beetles; those that feed on carrion and waste,' she continued. 'But there is one special lady I do know of and, unlike yourself, sir, I know she offers up a polarising display of colour!'

The professor racked his brain. Had he ever heard of such a creature? To the best of his formidable knowledge, he had not heard of scarab beetles beyond that of nature's rubbish collectors and processors of waste. So why now would this strange lady be searching for one?

Sabine Erket paused for a while as a broad smile came across her face. She crouched down and directed the light towards the concentration of the scorpions that had gathered to feast. The reek of rotting flesh had now reached its pinnacle. Professor Malcolm was half-excited and half-trying not to wretch at the deathly stench engulfing them. Sabine momentarily turned the torch off.

'Listen, Professor,' she urged him.

From below them came the tiniest macerating sounds of hundreds of tiny insects gorging themselves on the rotting carcass that had been presented to them just two weeks previously. It would not be long until they stripped the flesh and muscle down to bone. Switching the light on again, illuminating the scorpions and their fellow luminous counterparts, many more undetected insects scurried and scrambled to dine at the top table. Sabine scanned her torch up and down. What had been unclear to the Professor minutes before was now a ghastly reality. The feasted upon-carcass was that of a human torso. No one would have been in his laboratory the night the bombing raid came and Collingdale's security would have never allowed anyone to enter without express orders from Meticulous himself. So, who was this poor soul?

As Ms Erket ran the torch across the cadaver's chest, the emaciated face bore luminous blue symbols where flesh was still intact. The rest of it was a collection of roaches and scarabs devouring what remained. As she followed the top of the shoulders, with the torch, the victim's outstretched arm led to a skeletal hand that grasped a spherical object. Ms Erket peeled the fingers back one by one. One cracked and broke off as she did so, sending shivers down the Professor's spine. Once she had retrieved the object, she then firmly fixed the torch beam into its centre.

There, from within the frosted tomb of the stone, where it had been embedded for several millennia, was a fossilised beetle. A large

Scarabidae. It was much larger than any other beetle specimen of that genus. Entombed for centuries it may have been, but as the torch's emissions were absorbed through the crystal surroundings, a small red ember emitted itself from its thorax.

'That's a fossil that's as dead as the ancient civilisation itself. How is that possible?' the Professor remarked.

'Ha! Call yourself a professor?' Ms Erket let out a loud laugh.

As the light beam focused on the Scarab, the red embers began to throb and grow, as if a filament was suddenly receiving a huge surge of energy. Sabine Erket switched the power off of the torch. In the darkness, there was no visible sign of the beetle or the radiant glow. When the torch was again switched on, the Scarab again began to emit its vivid red glow.

'May I introduce you to our most distinguished guest, Professor?'

Meredith gazed on in awe, confused between the light sources and what he had just witnessed.

'Professor Malcolm, this is the beetle Queen. Her Royal Highness, The Scarlet Scarab!'

Meticulous Meredith Malcolm was rarely impressed with a fellow human being but on this occasion, he succumbed to Sabine Erket's superior wisdom on this very specific matter. How was it possible that a beetle, fossilised for millennia, could emit such a splendorous display of colour and then only when exposed to very specific light conditions? How on earth had Ms Erket come to have known about this, and how on earth was she aware that he had such a prized exhibit? Until only moments ago, it had been a complete mystery to himself and, as far as he was aware, any prior or current contemporary of entomology had been oblivious to the beetle's hidden ability.

Sabine Erket placed the ball-size fossil into her pocket and then fumbled softly for her cigarette case as she held her violet torch and cigarette holder in the other hand. Meanwhile, Meticulous retraced his footwork and opened his desk drawer.

'What are you doing?' she asked bluntly as the darkness obscured her view.

'Re-homing my torch,' he responded quickly. 'I prefer your torch, and I prefer my belongings just so, as I believe you already know.'

Sabine Erket raised her eyebrows and pointed the ultraviolet beam towards the fastidious man. His moustache was twitching as he squinted into the desk drawer.

'Oh dear, where on earth are my spectacles?' he fussed. 'I'm quite blind without them.'

Ms Erket allowed him a few moments as she spiralled the torch beam across the room scanning for clues to their exit. It hit the occasional luminous emission from an unsuspecting bug or two, which ignited them like minor diodes across the laboratory. The Entomology department had been badly bombed, and within the darkness the fallen exhibit cases, books and rubble made for an awkward environment, but after several spins of her torch, she spotted what she was looking for. There, sketched roughly on the wall was a blue eye, unnoticeable until the beam struck it and lit it up. Its shape and the positioning of the pupil were an obvious sign to the mysterious blonde woman.

'This way!' she exclaimed.

The Professor was still hurriedly scrabbling around in his top drawer. She spun the beam towards him and in a direct and uncompromising tone shouted at the poor Professor.

'On the desk! Your spectacles are there, on the desk.'

'So they are.' He squinted, picked them up, and curled them behind his ears.

As Ms Erket led them through the department, following a steady flow of the eyes daubed on the walls. She failed to spot Meticulous Meredith Malcolm drop a single white envelope onto the desktop. The envelope sat there, in the dark, but would soon be sitting atop his dirty desk in plain sight. At least that was if anyone came to his rescue. Major Boyd Collingdale was certainly no guarantee. For now, the Professor was at the mercy of the mysterious Ms Erket.

Chapter 8
The Department

The rain had not been kind to the city that evening and lashed down mini torrents that washed water against the kerbs, scooping up the remaining autumn leaves until they found a suitable drain to block. An air-raid, hours earlier, had seen the streets evacuated and now the majority of the city huddled within frozen underground stations, and waited nervously for the signs that the bombs were no longer coming. The night was edging towards dawn. If you listened carefully choruses of birds began their cross-city correspondence.

Where Piccadilly and Leicester Square meet, Eros looks south towards Shaftesbury and that is where the Royal houses' preferred purveyors of tea and fine foods go about their business. Fortnum's, as it is known in such parts, has been supplying high-end produce and exotic blends of leaf to the well-heeled and aristocracy for generations. During wartime, you could still obtain such grand pleasures if you knew who and where to ask. '*Num's* the word' as they would say in these parts, with a wink.

The exterior of the building maintained its pomp even if inside and behind the secretive passageways, the supplies of ever-decreasing rations resembled Old Mother Hubbard's cupboard rather than such a renowned name of retailing. There was still a buzz and lots of comings and goings in the huge department store. Front of house was always spic and span, demonstrating its impeccable turquoise and gold livery, while behind the staff doors existed a labyrinth; corridors of concrete block, electrical wiring, and copper pipework. For all intents and purposes, this was the hidden world of the worker. Who would notice if additional pipework, soundproofing, or more than enough electrical cables were harboured here? No one would know. So, while on the surface this immaculate building maintained its appearance, behind closed doors it was a very different story.

To the rear of the building, where several tired signs pointed delivery drivers to the unloading bay, the alleyways were dingy, rat-infested, and smelt like a public convenience. That evening, the alleyways behind Fortnum and Mason lay dormant, albeit for a lone shadow, that made its way cautiously towards the goods entrance. Occasionally, the screech of a tomcat or the shattering of a misplaced bottle would break the monotonous deluge as the creatures of the night went about their business. This particular creature was being overly cautious indeed. The rain helped, drowning out any echo of his soft steps, as he limped several repetitive looping routes until finally arriving under one of the worn-out delivery signs. He stood subtly cloaked within a disused doorway and waited. Ten minutes passed without so much of a gust of wind for company as the rains petered out. He listened carefully, ensuring he had not been followed. He headed towards the clandestine entrance, passing several large steel refuse bins. A fleeting glimpse of a rat shot across his pathway. As he moved towards the final bin, an inebriated tramp lay against it, empty booze-bottle barely in hand.

'Oo ah you?' the vagrant asked as he staggered to his feet and began to square up to the cautious man.

'The Milkman,' he wheezed in response.

'Haa, ha, ha!' spluttered the tramp, laughing. 'In that case, a pint of your finest mother's ruin, sir!' simultaneously coughing and laughing at the second phrase.

For a brief moment the two men just stared at each other before the tramp stopped swaying, dusted himself down a little and stood to subtle attention with a smirk across his face.

'Good evening, sir,' the vagrant now replied, in a cut-glass accent.

The cautious man did not engage in an extended conversation, as often he did not, he just nodded. The young man with the now-impeccable accent let his shoulders relax and pulled the final bin so it swivelled forty-five degrees outwards. Beneath it sat two large oak doors, with impressive iron hinges cast into the ground. A previous cellar to an old alehouse, long forgotten. Initiating a singular large thump on the doors followed by two lighter knocks, signalling the Morse code for D, the men waited until a large wheel turned, unhinging the lock from below. The doors then opened slowly and a dimly lit subterranean walkway was revealed. The vagrant nodded to the cautious man as he then descended inside. Within moments, the doors were locked again and the bin wheeled on top as the vagrant took his position once more, into the sodden autumn's night, his booze-bottle cover just about in hand.

Only the faintest flicker from the candlewick offered light in the cellar passageway as the cautious man was guided through. They reached a studded steel doorway and after the same long thump, followed by two muted knocks, a viewing window slid open. The weasel face of a bespectacled man in half-moon bifocals stared outwards and then the window slid shut. Momentarily the limping man waited to be let in and then the hulking reinforced door swayed open.

The brightness inside blinded him. He held up his left arm shielding his scarred side from the fluorescent tubing that dominated the ceiling above them. Whereas the rest of the city was plunged into darkness, this place was lit up like Piccadilly Circus, before the war. The long corridors were partitioned with wood panelling and glass down each side, then sub-divided into smaller rooms that were all buzzing with activity.

The first looked more like a typing pool. Each person at a single desk, audio-set upon their heads. The clacking of typewriters was furious as bells rang here and there to advise a new line of cypher was required. As the typists deciphered and articulated their transcripts, the blinds were drawn shut as the cautious man was ushered along behind the man in the half-moons.

The next room was another telephony exchange; again, it was a hive of activity and again, the blinds were drawn as he walked past. As they continued so the same pattern continued, a brief glimpse of activity in the rooms and then shut out as to not discover too much. A map room, with replica battleships being manoeuvred with a large croupier's rake. As they approached the end of the long corridor a large oak door with a frosted window dominated by a large gold embossed letter D greeted them. The man in the half-moons turned the brass handle and marched straight in.

Inside the room, there sat a desk. A single plant and Newton's cradle were the only items that were upon it. Behind the desk, a library of books from floor to ceiling dominated the walls, which ran in a half hexagon and saw a flat back to the room with two angular sides. The weasel-featured man, he of the half-moon glasses, rounded the desk and took his place behind it. He sat there with his angular arms joining at the fingertips to form a triangle while tapping his index fingers together as if contemplating a chess move.

'So, you decided to come in at last, Nathaniel?' the weasel-faced man began, his tone was soft and subtle.

'How could you be sure it was me?' the cautious man wheezed.

'Well, I doubt very much the world's greatest prosthetic surgeon could quite replicate your grotesqueness, Nathaniel, do you?' He smiled.

Nathaniel smirked on his right-hand side, the burns scarring on his left-hand side had left neither muscle or nerve endings to replicate a smile across his whole face.

'Welcome to The Department,' the weasel man said as he gestured his outstretched arms.

'It's been a long time, Draper,' Nathaniel Noone replied, through his asthmatic breath.

Chapter 9
Serkets and lies

The 'All-Seeing-Eye' was lit up by Sabine's torch one last time as she and the Professor found themselves at the rear of the Museum. It had taken almost half an hour straddling and navigating fallen bricks, glass, and rows upon rows of filing cabinets of fallen exhibits. The inconspicuous plain oak door and its subtle brass ironmongery could have been an entrance to a lavatory or janitorial cupboard, it was certainly something you would not easily notice against the surroundings. Ms Erket lowered the lever and the door opened smoothly, untouched by the bombing campaign that had seen such destruction so close by. She extended her arm towards the room beyond, and Meticulous obligingly entered.

The stone building that sat to the west of the Museum, and just outside the official boundary, had been built to house a recreational room for guards and porters when the Museum was the thriving hive of activity prior to the war. It was now a mini treasure trove of the items those guards had kept and maintained, which previously the curators had wished to dispose of. A giraffe's head on the wall, but with only one eye, Victorian glass flasks full of formaldehyde and peculiarities from the deep, a broken tusk from a Narwhal, and even the top half of a skull belonging to a particularly large species of crocodile. It was a curious little place and even Meticulous had been unaware of its existence. Sabine crossed the room and gazed out from the window. A large black car waited outside, its engine revving, and exhaust fumes puffing smoke into the autumn chill. One quick flash of her torch and the chauffeur left his seat. The engine remained running, as he made his way towards the building. From the outside, this 'keepers' cottage maintained the same brick-and-stone feel of the mighty Museum but with ornate lattice ironworks adorning the entrance porch where on top there sat a slender stone cat. Not as large or as impressive as the sabre-tooth that protected the main building, but in its own mischievous and malevolent way equally as impressive.

Sabine Erket allowed the Professor to be guided to the car by her driver. It was a bright, crisp day and a far cry from the darkness and debris from inside the corridors of Entomology. Squinting, as the chauffeur forcefully led him to the already-open passenger side door, Meticulous turned and smiled one last time at the Museum. He wasn't sure if this was to be the last he saw of it.

Ms Erket approached him with her cigarette case open

'Smoke, Professor?'

Meticulous Malcolm Meredith moved his head from left to right, politely refusing.

'Shame,' she responded. 'It might have helped with the pain!'

The professor looked up stunned just as Erket pinched the pincer clasps together. The motion retracted the gilded scorpion sting and then clamped down onto the Professor's arm, piercing his linen suit and penetrating his skin. A small globule of blood seeped into the white fabric before the Professor swayed and took a stumble backwards. The chauffeur caught him as he fell, using his momentum to lay him into the back of the car. Through the windowpane, the Professor convulsed until he was left staring wide-eyed into space.

Ms Erket turned away as the car drove off without her. She re-entered the cottage and removed the long blonde wig that was now infuriatingly tight and sweaty. Her dark black plaited hair fell down neatly between her shoulder blades. She kicked off her shoes, unscrewed and discarded the heels, so her new footwear was flat and as prescribed by the government. The vivid tiger-skin coat was reversed and the outer layer torn from the inner to leave a pea-green regulation trench coat. She tossed the tiger skin across the room. It looked perfectly at home amongst the unwanted and damaged exhibits. Finally, she pulled out a pair of black, horn-rimmed spectacles, they were as dark as her eyes were bright. The distinguishing sapphire glare was now all that remained of Sabine Erket.

Discarding the blonde wig and remnants of her disguise behind her, she left the cottage and walked south to where she hopped onto the back of a bright-red double-decker. At the front of the bus, just above the driver's cabin, set against a black background and with white lettering, read 'Route 101 – Oxford Street via Piccadilly, Leicester Square and Shaftesbury'.

The Route 101 from Kensington to Shaftesbury was a swift journey of no more than ten minutes; little time for Ms Erket to compose herself. Being of significant height even without the heels and trying to blend in as swiftly as possible she undertook a stooped demeanour.

Her regulation pea-green coat, the thick prescriptive lenses that unnecessarily magnified her steely blue eyes couldn't be further away from the tiger-skin temptress she had been just moments before. Sabine now adopted her humble, timid analyst personality; Ms Jennifer James.

As she hopped off the rear of the double-decker, opposite the boarded over statue of Eros, she checked herself over one more time. Her identification card, accompanied with a few shillings and pence, being the only few obvious possessions she kept on her. Other than that, she was a regular worker in any office or shop anywhere across London. That is, with the exception of the unusual belt buckle she wore around her waist. It was jade with a gilded pattern that ran horizontally across the face. For all onlookers, it was a simple buckle; the size of a small cigarette case. It was attractive but not ostentatious. On the reverse, it hid its little secret. Two golden pincers intertwined, leaving just enough space for the belt to run through them.

Ms Jennifer James made her way to the turquoise-and-gilded facade of the shop where *Nums'* the word. Passing through the revolving walnut doors, she headed for the lift where all staff had to report. The lift itself also had a walnut surround where, via thick glass, an elaborate metal lattice could be seen straight through it. She pressed the arrow for downwards and waited.

The whirring of a motor and the creaking of cables could be heard as the lift slowly travelled upwards from the basement. Jennifer James studied the brass arrow and numbers that sat above the walnut doors as the arrow moved from B, the Basement, and then to G, the ground floor.

'Ding!' a crisp hammer on bell chimed. The concertina metalwork was pulled across and the doors were then opened outwards.

'Good Morning, Miss,' came a rasping welcome from within as an elderly gentleman in concierge dress greeted her.

He wore red tails adorned with exquisite brass buttons, tapered grey trousers, and upon his head a neat circular hat embossed with 'Concierge'. He couldn't have stood more than five foot high. He seemed to be the oldest bellboy there ever was, and Ms Jennifer James dwarfed him. As was protocol, and as he had done so for the past few months, he held out his left hand. Jennifer duly obliged him and placed her identification into it. He glimpsed at it briefly before handing it back. Then, reaching around her, he pulled the metal cage back until it crisply locked in place. With his right hand, he lowered a brass lever, and within moments, the motors began to whir, cables began to creak, and they were on their way to where secrets were kept deep in subterranean London.

Chapter 10
Cairo

Aggie's initial enthusiasm was quickly offset with scepticism as she left the bedroom so beloved of her earliest childhood memories. What little information Florrie had divulged to her about her parents, had never quite satisfied her curiosity.

She followed Gideon and Nan downstairs and into the lower servants' quarters. In the middle of the room was a solitary chair with several tea cloths scattered beneath it.

'If you don't mind,' said Gideon, and gestured towards the chair.

Aggie took her place as Nan removed the large shearing scissors from the bucket. They were much larger than conventional coiffing scissors and from the glint on the edging, they looked like they could slice through human flesh pretty easily.

'Don't move!' Nan ordered in her thick accent. Aggie wasn't sure but it could possibly be German or Polish. It had an authoritative monosyllabic tone.

Aggie was shaking slightly as the first huge snip lacerated her fine long chestnut curls from the back of her head. It felt as if she was being prepared like a convict as the shears made light work of many years of fine grooming. Florrie would have been horrified she had always insisted her niece took pride in her appearance.

Within minutes, the shearing was over. Where once well-kempt hair flowed freely and was in essence long with loose curls, it was now just above shoulder length. The bobbed cut was not straight and ran at an angle from an inch below her left ear to an inch just above her right shoulder.

'Thank goodness for that!' Aggie sighed. Though she was yet to see how she looked in a mirror.

'Not so fast,' Nan replied. She was stirring black tar within a large mixing bowl.

'Yes, sorry Aggie, we need to dye your hair too,' Uncle Gideon explained.

Aggie was not happy but sat there and endured it all the same. It was wretched. The tar-like substance smelt of boot polish and wax. it was vile. Again, after several minutes the ordeal was over.

'Am I free to go now?' Aggie sarcastically directed her remarks towards Nan.

'It will be set within the hour,' Nan replied sternly. 'Do not touch.' The older lady then squinted her eyes and removed all the objects, placing them into a large ceramic butler sink where the steam was evaporating off of the water.

Uncle Gideon helped her up from the seat and gestured with his head to follow him into the basement corridor.

'Here,' he said, offering her a small parcel wrapped within his handkerchief.

Aggie unwrapped it and there was half a pork pie. She looked up at him as if she had unwrapped the greatest Christmas present ever.

'Go ahead.' He nodded.

Aggie wolfed it down without so much as a breath. All of a sudden, her nostrils flared with a sharp burning and her eyes watered.

'Sorry, I forgot about the mustard,' said Uncle Gideon and laughed as he handed her a small bottle filled with an opaque cordial.

Aggie paused. she was beginning to remember he had played the same trick on her when she was very young and had stolen his beloved pork pie during Sunday tea. That time, the drink was soapy water and was to teach her a lesson. This time she refused.

'I assure you, it is not soap this time.' He smirked and took a swig.

Aggie smiled and took a huge gulp before finishing it with a second. Elderflower, her favourite. Far more palatable then soap. For the first time in several days, she felt relaxed but was still anxious to talk about Cairo.

At the end of the corridor was an unassuming wooden door with a light bulb just above her head height attached to the front. Gideon pointed to the bulb.

'If this is ever on Aggie, you cannot enter the room. It will be bright red, so you cannot miss it. Do you understand?'

Aggie nodded, still removing pastry crumbs from inside her mouth.

Gideon pulled a set of keys from his inside pocket. It was like a gaoler's set of keys; a round iron circle with keys of varying sizes and metals hanging off of their own metal bows. How on earth he had managed to keep them quiet and out of sight all this time was quite intriguing. He unlocked the door and Aggie followed him in before he locked the door swiftly behind them. It was as black as pitch. Not even the slightest chink of light to capture surface reflections could make its way inside. Once in there, Aggie heard Gideon pull on a suspended chain before a crimson-hued tube flickered and lit up the room into deep reds and scarlet.

Suspended across the room by string, and attached by small-hinged clips, were photographs of various shapes and sizes. There were lots of them and a great deal to take in. Aggie flashed her eyes around the room and saw images of what looked like aircraft, maps, even landmarks she thought she recognised. Though squinting and focusing as much as she could, it was difficult to fathom the images out in such peculiar light.

'This is my very *Top-Secret* work, Aggie, and no-one in this village needs to know, OK?' Uncle Gideon said directly to her.

Aggie nodded and then recalled a saying Florrie loved to use.

'Loose lips sink ships!' she said aloud.

Gideon looked her squarely in the eyes and smiled. 'You remind me of her so much!' he replied.

'Aunt Florrie?' Aggie questioned.

There was a brief pause. A tiny tear escaped from Gideon's eye. 'No, Aggie. I meant your mother.'

Aggie nodded humbly and then Gideon switched the light off, plunging them into darkness. She heard the jangle of the gaolers' keys once again before a doorway was opened and a muted light streamed in from a room at the opposite side of where they had entered.

This room was more like a carpenter's workshop. Pieces of wood lay scattered everywhere and a lathe was set up in the corner. Wire mesh and old newspapers were stacked up around them, and there was a long wooden bench, with a large vice attached to it, which had many drills, drivers, and files sprawled across it. The smell of fresh wood shavings was ever-present.

'This, Aggie, is my day-to-day work,' Gideon said without breaking stride, and headed for the small circular wooden staircase in the corner. 'This is what the village think I am and what I do. Come with me and I promise you that very shortly we can talk about Cairo.'

Aggie's anxiety was replaced with a keenness to understand exactly what her uncle was talking about and what he knew.

'Ding, ding.' The chimes of the church bells of St Joan's broke the morning silence, and from outside they could hear the congregation dispersing.

Gideon dashed up the stairs, closely followed by his niece. The blinds in the room were shut and only the faintest flickers of sunlight crept in between the gaps. Aggie looked around her and took in a deep breath.

'Wow! I remember this place now. I remember!' she said excitedly.

As Aggie perused her surroundings, Gideon peered out of the blinds and kept an eye on the crowd of people now filtering down the Steep.

She couldn't believe it. The room was still full to the brim with antiquities and curiosities. Quite how anyone could manage to move around the place or even know where to look for anything was beyond her. There was a fair sprinkling of dust across the many exhibition cases. A smile stretched across Aggie's face, for the first time in days, as she relaxed and found solace in familiar surroundings.

'Where is he?' Aggie asked after searching, pointing upwards, for something she so clearly remembered that used to hang there.

'Who?' Gideon responded with a mischievous look on his face.

'The giraffe. You used to have a giraffe's head. It sat right up there looking down on everyone. I remember it being ginormous.'

'Well, you were so small the last time you came.' He smiled. 'Alas, old Geoffrey has gone to pastures new.'

'I remember him because he only had one eye. You used to say he was winking at everybody and it used to make me laugh.'

The two of them chuckled. Then there was a banging on the shop door front. Several small shadows cast themselves onto the shop window from behind the blinds.

'Aggie, I need you to go hide in the back somewhere, out of sight. You can observe but don't let yourself be seen, OK?'

Reluctantly, Aggie agreed. Her hair still smelt like a tar bucket so she was relieved, to some degree, to hide herself away.

Gideon pulled a pair of round spectacles from his top pocket and placed them loosely over the bridge of his nose. He looked quite different from how Aggie saw him. Somehow, he seemed like an older professor or teacher and not the daring uncle she felt he had always been.

He released the blind from behind the shop door window but kept the closed sign visible. He looked over the eager crowd of small children that had gathered on his steps outside. What at first was a small gaggle had now manifested into a full-on herd.

He continued to peer over them as if they did not exist.

'Gideon! Gideon!' they all began to shout. 'Open up. It's freezing out here!'

Gideon then looked down at them and smiled. Opening the door, he was met with a wave of enthusiasm as several small children ran under his arms and into his shop of paraphernalia and delights.

Aggie hid out of direct sight behind a poor reproduction of a human-sized stone Sphinx and watched eagle-eyed as little hands rummaged everywhere.

With a swift clap, Gideon's enthusiastic class stopped and formed a cross-legged semi-circle around him on the floor or perching wherever they could find space. It was cramped and dusty but all of them managed to find a spot.

Reaching behind he pulled out an old box, covered with a filthy rag. He leant in and whispered quietly as his class paid absolute attention.

'Under this ancient cloth lies a creature that still resides, even now, in our rivers and waterways. Many people will say that these creatures are just myth and stuff of legend. But I can reveal to you now that I caught this one just days ago in the estuarial canal off of *The Downside* near the stone bridge over the Amble. Behold, the Mer-Monster! Raaargghhh!' he finished, whipping the room into sheer terror and revealing the mysterious beast from beneath the cloth.

Its mummified face and gnarly teeth stared viciously at the youngsters. Its ribcage seamlessly weaving into a fishtail to confirm the perverseness of the species.

Screams of terrified children rang out. Several fled the shop in a panic, but for those who were brave enough to stay, though some were crying, he sat them all back down and explained what it was. With its scaly tail like a fish and its human-like front body, this was considered to be a Mer-monster.

'If you believe in monsters, children, then I suggest you stay away from the Amble and its numerous canals. You never quite know what is down there. If you think this is a hoax and the imagination of a very clever taxidermist, then you should sleep well tonight. But if you do not and you still believe in magical beasts, do not worry as Mer-monsters never leave the water, so you should be safe in your beds. And who's to say they're not delightful little creatures behind that brutal facade!'

There were a few more smiles following that part of the story and as always Gideon rounded off his mini-performance by revealing a jar of American candy. Such a rare treat in these times. More than likely the majority of the children endured his tales just for their weekly sugar fix afterwards, but for some, it certainly peeked their imaginations.

'Just one each…' He laughed as hungry young eyes pounced upon him. The last of the children took their sweets and left his shop as he replaced the Mer-monster under its filthy cover and once more out of sight. He reached onto a shelf much higher up and brought down a dusty box that he blew over creating a puff of particles.

'It's apt you chose to hide behind the Old Sphinx.' He smiled, turning to Aggie, hiding at the rear of the shop.

'It's not very convincing. Is it?' replied the girl as she strode forward and patted the poor papier-mâché copy she had crouched behind.

Gideon roared with laughter. 'No, I suppose not. But you wouldn't believe what people will fall for with a damn good story.' He smiled back and sighed. 'The Mer-monster, for example, is half a pike and half a macaque, a small mischievous monkey,' he explained. Her uncle composed himself, still perching on his stool, encouraging his niece to come and sit next to him. 'This is for you,' he said as he passed the dusty box Aggie's way.

It wasn't clear who was more tentative. Gideon looked anxious while Aggie felt a sense of nervous excitement. Brushing the remnants of dust away, revealed dark blue velvet beneath. She slowly opened it. On the inside casing, a mother of pearl silk shone crisply clean, with the exception of a tiny dark scrawl. The silk overlapped like an envelope of fabric, where Aggie slowly pinched both upper and lower parts together between index and forefingers and pulled them in opposite directions. Beneath the fabric lay a perfect circle of silver. The silver was joined by a golden ball and clasped into an ebony handle. The handle itself had several sections and each spun independently of one another. In the centre of the circular silver ring was thick glass, tempered lightly towards the metal edges where it had been polished into multiple facets, reminiscent of the eye of a fly, and where it captured and reflected kaleidoscope images.

'You can take it out if you like,' Gideon offered quietly.

Aggie paused for a moment, placing the case delicately on her lap and removing the object from inside. Holding it up in front of herself, the glass brought items in and out of perspective. If she held it directly in front of an object, she could look at it in far more detail then with her normal sight.

'It's a magnifying glass,' she said, slightly mystified.

'Of sorts. A necklace magnifier I believe. You can wear it around your neck.' Gideon nodded and smiled back at her. 'Perhaps you should read the inscription?' he said.

Aggie opened the box once more and focused the magnifier on the writing within the case. The minuscule scrawl of calligraphy was faultless and she could now read the message clearly, which she read firstly to herself and then out loud to her uncle.

> *Dearest Daughter,*
>
> *You are such a revelation. I will love you forever.*
>
> *Mum x*

Aggie's head slumped downwards. Her skin covered with Goosebumps once more as a chill shuddered through her. Gideon was already shedding tears as he leant forward and embraced her. Both of them were now sobbing. She for the loss of her mother, who she had never known, and he for the loss of his twin which he had shared more than half his life with.

'Do you like it, Aggie?' Gideon inquired as he smoothed the tears away from his cheeks.

'Of course, I like it,' Aggie responded, sniffing hers away too. 'But why a magnifying glass?' she questioned.

Holding it up to the spectrums of light cascading through the window, she examined the handle in more detail. Seven separate ebony dials, of seven different shapes and sizes, spun independently of one another. On each face of a dial, there was a separate symbol.

'What do all these mean, Uncle Gideon?' she asked inquisitively.

'I'm not really sure and to be perfectly honest, I've barely looked at it since the day she gave it to me,' Uncle Gideon responded, intrigued.

Aggie looked up at her uncle's pallid complexion. He looked interested but most uneasy as he studied the magnifying glass. Perhaps it was the thought of his long-dead sister and his emotions catching up with him.

'Ouch!' screamed Aggie.

While distracted by the dials and their detail she had failed to see that the small streak of sunlight streaming through her magnifying glass had focused itself to burn through her dark woollen jumper.

Gideon leapt forward with lightning reflexes and patted the minor scorched hole to ensure any embers were put out.

'Are you Ok?' he asked.

'I'm fine,' Aggie replied. 'Are you OK?' she asked back.

'Of course, I am.' He smiled.

'Bang! Bang!' came a short-fisted thump on his shop door, breaking a momentary silence. Before Gideon could move towards the blind to see who it was, the door burst open sending the customer bell ringing erratically. As the door flung open, a grubby, pint-sized boy, much smaller than his mature face suggested, extended his arm inwards holding what appeared to be a very small penknife.

'Gideon! Giddy, are you OK?' he shouted aggressively.

'For pity's sake, Eric. What on earth are you doing? Put that thing away,' Gideon bawled.

Realising everything was fine, the boy withdrew his knife before removing an oversized flat-cap he was wearing and humbly offering an apologetic bow. Gideon pulled him into the shop by his collar and quickly shut the door behind him.

'Sorry, Gideon. I 'erd a scream and I fought you were bein' set upon,' came the boy's apology.

Gideon sighed and shook his head. 'OK. To work then, Eric,' he ordered.

Eric Peabody scurried away down the stairs to the cellar workshop.

Aggie watched him through the gap in the treads. He briefly looked back, caught her crystal blue gaze and then turned away smirking.

'I think it's time we ate,' Gideon suggested.

Aggie placed the magnifying glass back into the silk fabric and snapped the velvet case shut. Grasping it as if it was the only possession in the world she'd ever need, she followed her uncle out of the shop.

'Aren't you going to lock up?' Aggie asked as her uncle strode onwards.

'No need for that. This is Ambledown. Besides, I have a Peabody on guard.' Gideon smiled and nodded towards the cellar.

Aggie cast a perplexed frown. As if that boy was any deterrent at all.

Chapter 11
Silvera

The Professor, Meticulous Meredith Malcolm, awoke to dappled light shining through the rear car windows, casting speckled variations of the autumn woodland as it sped through the countryside. A small bloodstain remained on his immaculate linen suit. He tried in vain to remove it using his own saliva but it had dried. He had been unconscious long enough for that.

Composing himself, he sat upright, straightening his suit, adjusting his spectacles, and grooming his impressive moustache. After half an hour's silent observation of the flora and fauna passing by, he tapped the thick glass barrier that separated himself from the chauffeur who had so un-eloquently bundled him into the car in the first place.

'Are we on our way to the seaside?' Meredith Malcolm enquired.

It was a peculiar question to have asked his captor. Then again, Professor Malcolm was well-known for his eccentricities.

'It's just that…' He paused briefly. 'I notice the chalky soil. I am sure we passed blooming ragwort, which Culpepper himself may have used and what with the indigenous pine and oak, I strongly suspect we are heading south? High Weald, maybe? Sussex? Am I right?'

The chauffeur glared in the rear-view mirror at the Professor. He reached for a large red switch on his dashboard, and with a simple click, black glass rose from within the padded seats and created an impenetrable barrier between them.

Seconds later, the same thick glass shrouded the rear windows until Meticulous could no longer see anything and was surrounded in a subtle darkness.

Flicking a second switch, this one coloured blue, a small vent opened between the reading lights above Professor Malcolm's head and an ethereal violet gas cascaded downwards. The Professor reached for his handkerchief but the impact was immediate. The gas infiltrated his lungs first, swiftly followed by his bloodstream, until he slumped back into a silent slumber.

The car drove hastily onward. The chauffeur donned sunglasses as the car peaked over a hill and in the distance, the Sussex Downs met the coastline and the Channel rose into view. The crisp October day brought brilliant blue skies and piercing sunlight: a far cry from the bombed-out greyness of the city.

In the distance, the chalk cliffs reflected their brilliant white glare and there, just back from the cliff's edge and barely visible at this range, another vividly white reflection could be seen. What was it, a lighthouse?

As the immaculate black saloon reached the driveway of the large white building, it slowed down, allowing the sentry to raise the red-and-white-striped barrier towards the entrance. The silver bird shining upon the radiator reflected the brilliant autumn glare.

This wasn't the welcoming facade to the front of the building, which offered less security. This was the hidden, highly guarded, rear entrance. Standing an impressive four storeys high and an epic testament to modernist concrete and glass, the Silvera Institute had only just been completed twelve months before war had broken out.

The original patron and philanthropist, a wealthy local industrialist, had conceived the building to host concerts and exhibitions that would allow the world to still see how 'great' Britain was. Its curved main hall looked out over the cliff-tops and across the Channel. Where once corridors, painted to echo the surrounding chalk cliffs, had seen Turners and Constables hang, they now saw hospital beds in the convalescent wards. No more recitals or piano concertos. No more curators. In their places were wheelchairs, the stench of iodine, and the ever-feared matrons.

The chauffeur drove cautiously over the white gravel surface as it crunched underneath the wheels. In front of him, two large orderlies stood either side of a high-backed, padded, wheelchair. When the car finally stopped, the two orderlies opened the rear passenger door and unceremoniously dragged the Professor out. Hitching him up into the chair, they buckled several restraints across his body and a mask that covered the bottom half of his face and silenced his mouth.

Meticulous Meredith Malcolm was awoken as two huge orderlies manhandled him from the car. Looking up, and just managing to focus, he read a simple sign on the wall before him:

Dr Mialora

The Silvera Institute.

Meredith Malcolm was still struggling to focus his sight, shackled and bound to a wheelchair, as the orderlies steered him through poorly lit sandstone corridors.

'Welcome, Professor,' came the voice through blurred colours and hues.

The accent was not obvious; possibly Spanish, maybe Portuguese. Professor Malcolm could not be sure.

'You will be feeling quite queasy, but that will subside in due course. I am Silvera. Dr Mialora Silvera. I will visit you again tomorrow, but now I leave. Mr Louds here will help you with anything you need.'

Professor Malcolm's sight was still blurred as the first figure disappeared but was soon replaced by a second.

'I am Brian, Brian Louds. Pleased to meet you, Professor,' came the polite voice.

Professor Malcolm felt a strong grip take his own limp wrist and shake it vigorously as he unlocked the restraints.

'You'll want for nothing here, just as long as you play by the rules, sir. Anything you need, you just let me know. These are your chambers and your working quarters. I trust you'll find everything to your satisfaction.'

Professor Malcolm had heard every word but was not fully conscious. His eyesight slowly began to return but by the time he could focus at will, he was now alone, sat in a wheelchair in his new surroundings.

Taking a cautious observation of what was around him, he first noticed a glass prism situated twenty-five feet above the centre of the room and directly above him. Directly beneath, in order seemingly to make best use of the direct sunlight from above, and where he sat, a large, circular, mahogany desk surrounded him. It was unlike any other desk he had seen or worked from. It was as if the inner rings had been bored away from a mighty tree where the Professor could rotate and work from in 360 degrees, albeit for a sliced section to enter and leave. Perfectly ordered in ascending shape and size every phial, scope lens, specimen jar and magnifier he could have ever wished for surrounded the outer edge of the huge wooden work surface.

As Professor Malcolm's observations tentatively moved him on from the desk, he noticed that the walls sloped inwards towards the glass pinnacle, and each side served a particular purpose. The wall coverings were gilded in bronze leaf and helped the light bounce across the surfaces where it could.

On one wall surface, there was a perfectly crafted library where on approaching it, Professor Malcolm recognised prestigious works on flora, fauna, entomology, and natural science. On a second surface, there were rows upon rows of specimen boxes. Constructed in immaculate mahogany, all exhibits were expertly pinned and spaced, with their names neatly scribed in Latin and with the species running alphabetically from A-Z.

Continuing his cautious tour, the third wall contained numerous live environments for all manner of tiny bugs and creatures. Varying in size and conditions for the mini-monsters that occupied them, they ranged from full biospheres for cross-species habitation, to isolated glasshouses for apex predators of the insect world, which were cut off from but staring directly at their incarcerated prey.

The Professor could only take so much in at once. A sceptical excitement came over him. He immediately noticed the primary glass terrarium that dominated the living wall. It had a stripped-down skull of a cow in it and eager scarab beetles aimlessly pushing their balls of waste against the glass and making tiny tapping sounds at their futile attempts to push them uphill.

The fourth wall was the least exciting of them all. A simple panel door sat in the centre and two large mirrors hung on either side.

Professor Meticulous Meredith Malcolm, having surveyed the impeccable surroundings he had been left in, was both equally impressed and sceptical. The sanctuary of peace and quiet this place afforded him, combined with the sheer quality of equipment and specimens, led him to a single conclusion; whatever it was he was to be asked to do, it wasn't within the confines of legality. It most likely was treasonous and once he had completed his task his fate was surely sealed. The body in the Museum laboratory was evidence enough of Ms Erket's callousness.

A double knock on the door and Mr Louds, Dr Mialora's assistant, entered the laboratory. The surgical operating mask obscured his lower face. It was startling that he did not have a single hair on his head. He wasn't just bald, he had neither eyebrows or lashes. An ink line scribed on each brow was a crude attempt to conceal this fact but close up it was obvious.

'I trust everything is to your satisfaction, Professor?' Louds asked politely.

'Very much so,' Professor Malcolm responded eagerly.

'Is there anything else you should require, sir? Perhaps some refreshment?' Mr Louds continued.

'Tea, please. Honey, not sugar if you have it?' Professor Malcolm asked gleefully.

'Anything else, Professor?' Mr Louds concluded.

'I would like to know what you actually require from me?' Malcolm responded, smiling wilfully.

Mr Louds nodded and then exited the laboratory without a final response. Meticulous made his way to the long line of live exhibits, examining each case carefully. The largest enclosure was dedicated to a host of scarabs that were eagerly decimating the remaining cow's skull and aimlessly rolling their defecated balls of dung against the panes of glass. The professor removed his spectacles and pressed his nose against the glass. His breath misted the pane and with his index finger, he drew the 'All-Seeing-Eye' that Sabine Erket had followed to escape the Museum.

'Why are you so important?' the Professor whispered to the insects beyond the glass. He replaced his spectacles, rubbed away his misted doodle and began pacing the room, examining the library of books, and all the while grooming his impeccable moustache. 'What was it about Ms Erket and what was the importance of the Scarlet Scarab?' he pondered. Where did they sit in her plan?

Chapter 12
Secrets and Lies

Closing the door behind them as they exited via the shop entrance, Gideon and Aggie descended the half a dozen or so stone steps onto the mossy cobbles. They left Eric Peabody working in the cellar. After a few steps, Aggie turned around to take in a better view of Gideon's house. Its dominant black brickwork facade, accentuated with white flagstone edges, made it stand out against the castle ruins behind. Locally it had been known as the Gemini house, on account of its conjoined asymmetrical habitats. Together the residences were formally known as '1a' and '1b' – *The Keep*.

1a was Gideon's home. Aggie's room and its identical miniature version of 1a were on the first floor accompanied with a bathroom. Gideon's quarters, bathroom and reading rooms cum entertaining space, sat on the raised ground floor. Not to forget the developing room that ran as a subterranean passage between both properties and where Gideon performed his Top-Secret work.

1b, although identical in many ways, housed Gideon's business and was home to his vast collections and hobbies. On the raised ground floor, from where they had recently departed, the uniform Georgian window had been replaced by a carbuncle of a glass bay, which the adventurer used to showpiece his worldly finds. The locals had been horrified when he had installed it, just before the outbreak of war. One incensed resident referred to it as, 'A bulbous drunken nose on the face of a handsome Georgian gentleman'. And to make matters worse, Gideon had enlisted a local artisan to paint a garish red, blue and gold sign on top of the glass, which read:

'Curios, antiquities, and fortuitous paraphernalia'

It made Aggie chuckle as it was so out of place, and just how she remembered her uncle. Outlandish, boisterous, and quite the showman. Although not so much now. But what really made it stand out from the black brick was the backdrop of the old ruins behind.

The Keep, from where they took the name for 1a and 1b, sat just to the east, slightly back from the shop side. Even though it was many centuries old, the local flint and sand mortar still stood proud, unlike the ruins of the castle and the Priory just behind. The ground floor beneath *The Keep* acted as the gatehouse and passage through to the hill-topped grounds beyond. A reinforced hulk of a portcullis was suspended within the external wall but had not seen daylight for at least two centuries. Its only protrusions were the rusting gate teeth that were rotten and crumbling and scared many a small child into thinking the pathway was the mouth belonging to a demonic monster or even the gateway to hell itself.

'Come now, Aggie, much to see, much to do.' Gideon rushed her along.

'Much more to explain,' she responded, still clasping the velvet case in a white-knuckle grip.

Gideon looked down through the corner of his eyes and saw Aggie's piercing sapphire glare inquisitively awaiting a response. Her eyes were a constant reminder of his sister.

'Of course,' he replied. 'But just for today, I need to introduce you to Ambledown.'

He stood with outstretched arms, presenting the town as Aggie gazed down *the Steep* to the hodgepodge homes, stores and public houses that lined up unevenly on each side. As Aggie and Gideon strolled down *the Steep,* she was struck by how quiet it was. Admittedly, it was Sunday and most homes across the country would be embracing whatever meat or rations could be mustered for a post-service lunch.

Not only was it quiet, but it was also intact, unlike London and the streets surrounding Florrie's Marylebone house, Aggie's home, where roads were peppered with the brutal detritus and everyday reminders of the war that continued unabated and certainly didn't stop for Sunday lunch.

'It's quiet,' Aggie said. 'and it smells.'

'Smells?' Gideon laughed almost insulted by such a comment.

'Not in a bad way. Not really,' she responded. 'Just different from what I am used to.'

'That will probably be the brewery,' he said. 'I'll take you there as part of my famous Ambledown tour.'

As Gideon proceeded to point out Ambledown's finest landmarks – 'The Church of St Joan's', 'The Castle', 'The Keep' – Agatha felt an uneasy

66

sense that they were being followed or at least being watched. She would occasionally turn around, and it did not go unnoticed.

'Are you OK, Aggie? You seem agitated,' Gideon enquired.

'I feel we're being followed,' she replied nervously.

Gideon paused for a moment, scanned their immediate vicinity and then bent down facing her. Taking her by the shoulders, and with his eyes staring directly into her brilliant blues, he proceeded to reassure her.

'What you have been through in the past few days is not, for the want of a better word, normal. Rest assured you are safe under my stewardship. I will not let any harm come of you. As long as I am here, you have nothing to fear.'

Aggie had not anticipated such a response. It actually made her already inquisitive mind work even harder. Gideon was no doubt sincere and she wholeheartedly felt safe beside him. There was, however, an underlying menace that she could not articulate to him. She felt that he knew, that she knew, anyway. The stranger who'd kidnapped her, the mysterious train journey, nothing made sense. An explanation was still required, despite him skirting over it all.

As Gideon stood back up and composed himself, Aggie saw over his shoulder, the flick of a curtain in the upper room of a house behind him.

'There!' she shouted, pointing at the window and forcing her uncle to turn around. 'Up there in that window. Someone was watching us.'

Her uncle followed her protruding finger as it pointed sharply to the terraced housed behind.

'I've no doubt they were.' He laughed.

Aggie was not amused and frowned intently back at him.

'That's Mrs Parker's house. Old Nelly Parker. Care to guess her nickname around here?'

Aggie didn't care to at all and stared back just as intently.

'Well...it's Nosey. She is Old Nosey Parker.' He laughed again. 'Nothing gets past Nelly. Listen to me, Aggie. You will quickly learn that this place, like any place, is a cauldron of secrets and lies. It's terribly difficult to keep secrets around here but almost intrinsically simple to offer up a lie. Therefore, we must maintain at all times you are just another evacuee and most definitely not my niece. Understand?'

Agatha did not offer a verbal response, more of a sulky nod.

'Let me tell you about poor old Nelly. She was widowed in the Great War and left to bring up three young boys. All three sons went off to fight in this war. Two of them were killed; the twins, Ernest and Arty. Lovely, gentle men. But the other son, Thomas, is still missing in action. That's why you see her at all hours peering out from behind her curtain, longing for his return.'

Aggie could feel the tears filling up her eyes until one breached the lid and trickled southwards removing the dirt and dust from her cheeks. Gideon pulled out a handkerchief, wiped her cheeks clean and then handed it to her.

'Let's eat,' he said. 'I think you would feel better if you had something inside you. I know I would,' Gideon said encouragingly. And then, as if this was just a part of any other Sunday, Gideon continued to march on down the Steep, assuming Agatha would follow. After a few defiant moments, and urged on by her grumbling stomach, she did.

Chapter 13
The Compromised

Nathaniel Noone sat opposite Draper as if a staring contest was not beyond these two grown men. It lasted a minute or so before he broke his gaze and began to laugh. Draper laughed too and before too long they were far more relaxed.

'Why, Nathaniel Noone? Why after all this time?' Draper asked.

Noone reached inside his coat pocket and pulled out a brown envelope.

'Because of this,' he replied, throwing the envelope between them onto the desk.

Draper cautiously leant forward and pulled a photograph out of the envelope. He held it up in front of him. There, to the right-hand side of the picture, dressed in tuxedo and dickey bow, Draper saw himself. He was to the side of the picture and almost in the shadows, where he preferred to be. But on this occasion, he had been caught on camera along with several members of state and influential members of society.

'Good-grief. Where did you get this?' Draper asked, now curt and aggressive.

'I found it on a dead man, sir,' Noone replied.

Draper was not amused, but knowing Nathaniel Noone's reputation as he did, he sat awkwardly in his seat waiting for him to speak again.

'Would you mind dimming the lights please, Mr Draper?'

Draper rounded the table, leant past Noone and brought the lights down to as low as he could.

Noone reached into an outer coat pocket this time and pulled out a small steel torch. He struck the beam of it against the photograph and there, in brilliant iridescent blues, the picture was covered with ancient glyphs and symbols. As he turned the torch, they glowed a violet purple. Most of the people within the picture had some sort of mark across their faces. All but one of them were men. The remaining person in question was a lady much taller than all of them who seemed to have long pale hair and the most distinguishable tiger-skin patterned coat.

'Do you know who these people are, sir?' Noone wheezed.

Draper nodded, uneasily.

'Do you recall where and when this was taken?' Noone continued.

Again, Draper nodded.

'Good,' Noone responded. 'It's a start.' Nathaniel Noone stared at Draper. It was uncomfortable for anyone to stare directly back at him, considering the horrendous scarring Noone displayed. Not as uncomfortable as what the man had endured to receive it, but nevertheless, he was aware of how it reviled other people, and occasionally revelled in making them squirm. Noone subtly reached inside his pocket.

'This is most unusual, Nathaniel,' replied Draper as he calmly reached for the panic button immediately beneath his wooden desk.

'Come on, Draper. You won't be needing to do that.' Noone smiled, second-guessing his ranking officer's next move.

'I just need to show you something,' Noone reassured him. That was always the problem with spies. They trusted no one, least of all each other.

Draper eased himself out of his chair, rounded the desk and switched off the main light. The darkness was immediate. Easing the blinds a fraction to let peripheral light in, Draper then moved behind Noone who remained seated at the table.

Nathaniel held two torches in his hand. He switched the first one on and the white light beam shone brightly and directly onto the subjects of the photograph previously presented to Draper.

'What is the purpose of this?' Draper inquired.

'A photograph, sir. Records moments for posterity,' Noone sarcastically responded.

'I'm not in the mood for your wisecracks, Nathaniel, what are you actually showing me that I don't already know?' Draper's tone was curt.

Noone flashed the standard torch over the photograph revisiting several people, including Draper, who was just caught in focus on the periphery.

'Slightly out of the shadows there, sir,' Noone responded with the calmness of a professional card player. 'Now, watch this,' he finished as if revealing a full house.

As the first torch was dimmed, and a moment of darkness engulfed them, Noone moved to the second torch. This time the beam was a violet hue and did not light up the photograph as expected. It illuminated symbols that glowed over each of the subjects' faces as if they had been daubed with miniature masks at a masquerade ball.

Draper's face was covered with the symbol of what looked like a dog's head. Its muzzle was angular and the ears pointed skyward. The unknown lady within the picture had the symbol of an eye masking her face with a large curling eyebrow protruding from it. The remaining members simply had triangles framing their faces with the exception of one man, dressed in military uniform and displaying multiple medals, possibly a high-ranking commander. Above his left eye, there was a small crescent moon scar. On top of his face, there was the illuminated head of a bird, a hawk-like predatory raptor.

'Where was this taken, sir?' Noone asked.

'It was a fundraiser for injured officers.' Draper responded, agitated. 'I can assure you there were many more people there than this. Worryingly, many more important people than these,' he confirmed. Draper's furrowed brow emphasised an uncomfortable concern. He made his way back to his desk, slowly. All the while, Noone switched from the normal torch to the violet torch and then back again, trying to make sense of the symbols and what they could mean. As he did so, the gap in the blinds offered a meagre light show, as flickering white became darkness and darkness in turn became flickering violet light, repeated and repeated, again and again. It was subtle enough that no one would notice, not unless they were watching, which they were.

'Your thoughts Nathaniel?' Draper asked.

Noone took a momentary pause. He was sceptical at what Draper's response would be to what he was about to say and chose his words carefully. If, and only if, these happen to be glyphs –' Noone began.

'Not bloody Cairo again, Noone. How many times must we revisit this?' Draper interrupted abruptly.

Nathaniel was well aware of what people thought of his concerns about Cairo and the past he had left over there, with much of his arm and face, but unabated he continued. 'I cannot be sure what all this means, sir, but if and I repeat, only *if* these are glyphs, then you are either the god of the afterlife, which I doubt very much, or someone has put a price on your head. I believe it's the death-mark of Anubis.'

'Absolute tosh, Noone!' Draper exclaimed. 'I'm sorry, Nathaniel. I find this all a little farfetched. Where did you find this photo, really? Have you lost the plot? Creation of your own imagination, I mean. What is your obsession with Cairo, Nathaniel? I think you need professional help. Maybe Internal Standards?'

'You seem unnecessarily flustered, sir. It's just a theory,' Noone calmly replied. Noone, who had been focusing on the photograph, had failed to see Draper procure a small, hidden, firearm.

Draper rounded the table once more and, switching the main light on behind Noone, he directed the gun at his subordinate and moved back around to his seat. His finger paused over the panic button once again.

'I only came here to warn you. I thought, given our history, you of all people may understand,' Noone said. 'What's with the gun?'

'You've finally cracked, Nathaniel. I think you need help.'

Draper was within a whisker of pressing the panic button when a red flashing light lit up on his phone. Training the pistol on Noone with his right hand, he picked up the phone with his left. There was a long pause as he listened intently.

'I see.' Draper spoke into the phone, and then calmly placed the handset down.

Lowering his gun and his tone towards Nathaniel, Draper stood up abrasively. He walked towards the coat stand and donned a full-length raincoat and tweed flat-cap. He walked towards the bookcase, which stood directly behind his desk. Pulling a specific copy of Dickens' *Oliver Twist,* the book released a hidden lock from within the case enabling it to revolve upon a central axis.

'Come on, Nathaniel. I apologise. We must leave. We've been compromised,' Draper ordered Noone.

Glimpsing over his shoulder at the door he had entered by, to ensure no one was immediately coming for them, Nathaniel Noone stood up, placed the photograph and torches back into this pocket and removed his own hidden revolver. Following Draper's lead, he disappeared into the bookcase and the tunnel beyond. It was dimly lit with the occasional wall-light every twenty yards or so. After about one hundred yards, they climbed a circular steel stairwell on top of which was a brightly lit exit sign above a plain wooden door.

'We need to holster our firearms,' Draper advised Noone. 'Keep a grip on the trigger, Nathaniel, but hide it from view. I've been expecting this. Someone is corrupting the Department from within and I momentarily thought it was you. I'm sorry.'

Both men slid their hands into their pockets with fingers paused on triggers. Draper reached for the long brass exit handle and they made their way through it.

Squinting as they were greeted by the fluorescent tubing of shop light, they moved along the slender corridor to where a crowd of people had gathered. Draper did not pay any attention to the moans and groans of eager shoppers grumbling about the unavailability of the lift. Instead, he made eye contact with an older woman standing near the commotion, and who was supervising a cha trolley with a cigarette hanging out of her mouth. He approached her with Noone.

'What will it be, love?' she asked in her cockney accent, inhaling a huge drag of her Capstan full strength.

'Two teas, please,' Draper ordered.

'Sugar?' she asked.

'Not today,' Draper replied. He usually took three in his cuppa.

The woman poured two cups of tea and Draper paid her. Alongside the coins, which ricocheted into her tin, he subtly dropped a folded piece of paper. The cha lady didn't acknowledge anything out of the ordinary but did stub out her cigarette and marched off to the 'chinking' of teacups as she pushed her trolley forward.

Draper allowed her a few moments while he slurped his tea, before following the same route. It led them past several shoppers to a revolving door. He peered outwards intently.

'Count to fifty, Nathaniel, and then follow me out,' Draper ordered in a direct tone. 'Opposite Eros's fountain, there are two phone booths that sit back to back. I will meet you there. Make sure you count the full fifty.'

Nathaniel nodded, still confused, then nervously stood back from the doors and began his long count to half a century. Draper spun through the doors and alighted into the street outside. It must have been all of 7 or maybe 8 a.m. but it was remarkably busy for a Sunday all the same.

Draper bustled his way out. With a flat-cap and raincoat, he was indistinguishable within the crowd and disappeared within moments.

Nathaniel began to count out a very long and lonely fifty.

Chapter 14
Trinity

Gideon continued his brisk walk, pointing out random homes and shops during his unbreakable strides. Aggie tried absorbing it all but not without checking behind her, as she swiftly followed her uncle, scanning the properties and streets for signs of threat. There was an abundance of side passages and alleyways randomly scattered between houses. The shadows played havoc with her already fraught nerves.

'A sheer labyrinth of pathways, nooks and crannies,' Gideon explained. 'No wonder smugglers and thieves had adored this place for centuries.' He laughed.

The Steep itself ran downhill at a steady slant from The Keep, before splitting off around a circular stone cenotaph, commemorating The First Great War. At this point, the road diverged into two. Southerly it ran at an even sharper gradient downwards, still known as the Steep and from where it originally took its name. Easterly, the road continued on a less steep incline and out towards open countryside. To the locals, this was the Old London Road.

The cenotaph, with its great Archangel pointing skywards, had the names of all the Ambledown residents who had perished in the 'First' carved into stone ledgers that lay at its feet. All were expertly chiselled, alphabetically, by surname. Such was the volume of brave servicemen and women that half-a-dozen tomes were covered in their unfortunate names and where lichen and moss now resided.

Overlooking the memorial and marking the corners where the roads divided were three public houses. The Crown was a traditional coaching house, preferred by Ambledown's well-heeled, and peered directly down upon the steepest part of the hill as if peering down on the residents itself, as so often its clientele did. South-westerly to The Crown was The Poacher and Ferret. 'The Poacher' as it was known locally. To say this epitomised everything The Crown was not, was an understatement. Its perpetually shuttered windows served to keep prying eyes out. Inside, it was cloaked in darkness, criminality and mystery. Thirdly, The Hart.

Sitting almost opposite the Poacher and South-easterly to The Crown it was a fine public house; the common ground between Crown and Poacher. Not as snooty as The Crown or as intimidating as the Poacher, it was the popular haunt for most of the Ambledown residents.

Uncle Gideon paused at the stone angel. Aggie's eyes followed the course of his finger as it moved between the three alehouses. Several glances between establishments and she already preferred the look of The Crown, but it seemed very quiet. The Poacher's shutters were boarded up but it was still the noisiest of the three, while The Hart appeared welcoming and was loud enough to suggest a brisk trade. After a brief, calculated decision, Gideon romped forward towards the Poacher.

'You're kidding, right?' Aggie asked, surprised at his choice.

'Not at all,' her uncle responded laughing. 'Today is officially Sunday Harvest,' he continued. 'It's the only day of the year you really would choose to dine at the Poacher. It's Marsh Mutton Day and that's why it is so busy. Even The Crown will be missing a few regulars today.'

Aggie looked back at The Crown. If people were willing to leave the refined surroundings of the coaching house to venture to this wreck it couldn't be all that bad. But nevertheless, the Poacher looked squalid and uninviting.

'One thing,' Gideon explained. 'This is a hive of rogues and villains. Don't be fooled by the temporary shift in clientele. Stay close to me and do not talk to anyone.'

Oh great! Aggie thought. She had just explained to Gideon she was nervous and after her train ordeal was still seeking answers.

Undeterred at the expression she cast his way, her uncle bounded into the pub, but this time, for the first time since she'd arrived, grasping her left hand with his right as he did so. Sensing what he had just said could not be taken lightly, she thrust her right hand into the pocket containing the blue velvet case that housed her now most treasured possession – the magnifying glass.

Quite unexpectedly, the atmosphere inside the Poacher and Ferret was not as dark as the subdued candles and occasional bulb that lit it suggested. It was rowdy and it stank of the stale ale and tobacco smoke that smothered the air. However, there seemed a genuine good humour to the place. There were much laughter and the constant chinking of pint glasses followed by the traditional 'Cheers'. Admittedly, there was a fair share of dubious-looking clientele and unable men who were not off to war. But also many ruddy-faced older folk too old to serve in foreign fields, and most seemed very well-turned out and simply enjoying a libation or two to accompany their merriment.

Aggie felt less intimidated than expected as her uncle guided her through the first bar and its crowd of drinkers. Gideon seemed to know everyone. People doffed their caps to him, said hello, and occasionally shook his other hand. None of them so much as even glimpsed at her as she followed him. Through the initial bustle of the crowd, he made his way to an inner courtyard. It was dark enough for mischief though a few well-placed lanterns sufficiently lit their way.

There were men playing skittles, some men pushing pennies across a striped wooden board, a noisy card game was in full flow, and there was a very large man sitting in the corner on his own with his back to them. He was as broad as the table he sat at and tethered to the leg of his chair was a large grey wolfhound. The man was too busy devouring a haunch of meat to spot Aggie staring at him but the hound occasionally opened an eye to observe her.

All of a sudden, the men playing cards erupted into a fight. A stein of ale was thrown and it peppered the wall just above the large man who continued eating. Cards flew up in the air and the coins from the game were tossed violently across the courtyard. As the men threw punches at each other, other men scrambled for the coins.

Gideon stood in front of his charge to protect her as the scuffle broke out. Aggie was shaking. She had never witnessed such an immediate eruption of violence. Her uncle gripped her hand tighter as if that was somehow comforting. As the scuffle began to subside and the men scrambled to retrieve the money they had lost to the floor, a whoosh of wings flew past Aggie's cheek. A quick flash of black and white dashed to the floor before flapping upwards and landing on the large man's shoulder. The creature cawed at the man and tapped its beak on him.

The man had not stopped chewing his food or even offered a glance during the skirmish. He now turned his head to look at the large magpie that was dutifully looking back at him with an object glinting in its beak.

Aggie could now see the slightest profile of the man. Bearded and grizzled he sported a large tattoo of a teardrop beneath his eye.

'What's that you have there, my lovely?' he said to the bird, before offering an oversized finger to hop on to. Stroking its plumage, as he observed the coin it had produced for him, he pulled a wormlike string of mutton from his plate and offered it as a reward. The magpie, which was well-versed in such enterprises, dropped the coin, sending it spinning just in front of him as it took its well-deserved prize and retired to the rafters. His large hand slammed down on the coin with immediacy, stopping it in mid-spin. He paused for a while before sliding it off to reveal the treasure below.

'Heads, I win.' He laughed.

People laughed in response, except for one man.

'You know that's my farthing,' responded a much slighter man who had instigated and been embroiled in the fight.

'Really?' said the much larger man who, even seated, towered over the tinier rival. He turned around now to face his accuser. 'If that's so, which year was it minted?' he continued, squinting purposefully and observing the tiny details on the coin's tail.

The much smaller aggressive man scowled at him taking a step forward as he did so. There was a growl from under the table. The wolfhound's head was now up and its canines exposed. The slight man said nothing.

'Not even a guess, Lyle?' the giant of a man asked, staring down at his mismatched opponent. 'Finders keepers then!' the large man concluded before continuing his meal.

The troublemaker cursed once more and stormed out of the courtyard. He purposely bumped into people, spoiling for a fight, spotting that Gideon was clasping his niece's hand he tried to break their bond by walking through them.

Gideon rounded on him. 'Walk around us,' Gideon said with authority as he stooped and stared eye to eye with the little wretch. The little man did not fancy this adversary either. The man eventually strode around them but not without bumping into Aggie's right-hand side as he passed. He glared back at her but she didn't falter and remained next to her uncle, glaring back, still clasping her precious case within her pocket.

With a final curse and a smash of glasses as he left, the troublemaker was soon gone. It was just a momentary interruption. Soon, as if nothing had happened, everyone turned to their drinks and carried on with their gaming and eating.

'Good evening, Gideon,' the huge man said with his mouth now half full of the marsh mutton he had been devouring just moments before. Aggie was sure he hadn't even glanced their way but somehow he'd known they were there.

'Hello, Pop,' Gideon responded and then slid into the chair directly opposite him. Gideon pulled Agatha and nodded towards the spare chair beside him. Aggie was pre-occupied by the large dog that lay immediately beneath keenly observing her.

'She won't bite you, girl. Will ya, Luna?' the large man reassured Aggie before a soft sole towards the dog's rump forced the hound to move out from the table and behind him.

'Aggie, this is Pop Braggan. An old friend of mine,' Gideon advised.

Aggie stared at the giant of a man. His grizzled face scarred with many a battle and a single teardrop tattoo, she keenly observed. His impressive beard was harbouring a few recent gravy trails and crumbs from his dinner but the most outstanding aspect, apart from the man's sheer size, was the gold that adorned him. Many rings on fingers, a dozen or so individual gold chains and large studs within both of his ears. He was a walking jewellery shop. Pop acknowledged the young girl with the slightest of nods.

'You 'ungry?' he asked Aggie.

'Starving' she replied.

Despite his brutal presence, he had a calmness that enveloped them all. Gideon was at ease with him and with Pop Braggan, the gold-laden giant for a friend. it was very easy to see why.

'Gemima!' Pop called out. 'Two more plates, please.'

Aggie wasn't sure who he had just spoken to but within a few moments, a small girl , no older than seven of eight, appeared with two plates and set them down in front of her and Gideon. Aggie recognised her as the small girl that had peered up at the window while she had been imprisoned within The Keep. The girl didn't recognise her. No doubt her recent change of appearance was responsible, and, of course, it was some distance to recognise her through a slit of an archer's window. No sooner had Gemima left when an older girl appeared with a large steaming pan. She proceeded to ladle out a rich stew containing large lumps of meat, vegetables, and pearl barley. Aggie recognised her too, she was the one that had looked back at her and stared right into her eyes.

'Who's this then, Gideon?' the girl asked, trying to place Aggie.

'My new evacuee,' he replied.

'Got a name, has she?' the girl asked Gideon, staring directly at Aggie.

Aggie was just about to respond for herself when Gideon beat her to it.

'You can call her Agatha,' he responded.

'Hello, Agatha. I'm Elizabeth. Parents a fan of Mrs Christie?' Elizabeth asked.

Aggie smiled, impressed. Although obvious to her, most people just took that as her name and never enquired about the origin.

'I think it was my mother actually,' Aggie responded quickly. 'But as they both died when I was young, I never got to ask.'

The mood turned slightly sombre. Elizabeth had only been making conversation and Aggie's answer was completely unexpected. Gideon gave his niece a swift kick under the table as if to shut her up. Elizabeth, embarrassed by Aggie's revelation went red and quickly cleared away Pop's now empty plate. Pop pushed the farthing his magpie had procured earlier towards her. She thanked them and left, ruddy-faced and embarrassed.

'Eat Up,' Gideon urged his niece. He had already begun to consume his.

It was surprisingly good, and she too wolfed it down. Aggie was so hungry she did not pay much attention to Gideon and Pop's conversation. Something about blackberries being in harvest, fish swimming upstream, and a sunset over the cliffs. All very boring. What's more, the large hound was making its presence felt, whimpering at her feet for scraps. She was just finishing the last morsel on her plate when Pop let out a laugh.

'You *were* starving, girl.' He chortled, staring down at her plate, which was almost licked clean. 'Didn't even leave none for me poor dog. Orrible int she, Luna?' He laughed. Standing up and brushing himself down from the dinner he exclaimed to the whole pub, 'The Braggans' marsh mutton hasn't disappointed yet.'

To a round of applause, he took a small bow – well, as small as a man of his size could – with his arms twirling like a courtier.

'Be seeing you, Gideon,' Pop said, shaking her uncle's hand, which looked like a child's in comparison to Pop's bear-sized mitt. 'You too, Agatha,' he whispered towards her as he donned his hat to say goodbye, casting a smirk towards her uncle.

His huge hulk blocked out a great deal of the natural sunlight coming in as he strode outwards. A slight whistle from his lips encouraged the huge wolfhound to nonchalantly rise. It whimpered for a final time as it saw the starkness of Aggie's plate and as its eyes drew level to hers. It then shook itself down and followed Pop's path. As Pop was leaving, the whoosh of wings rattled from the rafters once again and flew a straight path through the pub, causing people to duck as it did so. As the door closed, 'Lady', the magpie, just managed to swerve through the threshold to perch on her master's shoulder.

Now suitably replenished with a fine mutton stew, Aggie smiled up at her uncle. He placed a caring arm around her.

'Right then, time to finish the grand tour. At least two more stops before we get you ready for school tomorrow.'

'School?' Aggie questioned.

'Yes, school. It doesn't stop for war so it's not stopping for you,' he replied.

'But Florrie always said I couldn't go to a normal school.'

Nudging Aggie to alight from her chair, he reached across to where Pop's empty plate was. She hadn't seen it but a tan leather ledger was laid out right beside it.

'What's that?' Aggie enquired.

'It must be Pop's,' Gideon responded, 'and I'm not leaving it here for any light fingers to take it. I know who to give it to.'

With that, both her uncle and she pushed through the remaining crowds. This time, he didn't feel the need to grasp her hand, instead, he clung to Pop's ledger. Just as they were leaving a voice came from behind the bar.

'Be seeing you around, Agatha,' came the welcoming girl's voice.

It was Elizabeth, the girl she had unintentionally embarrassed earlier. Aggie rose a half-hearted wave to her as they left.

Just after they left the Poacher, the grubby, ink-covered face of Eric Peabody appeared as the boy ran down the road.

'All finished, Giddy,' he shouted as he ran.

'Good lad,' Gideon responded with a smile, tossing him a coin.

Eric caught it in flight. 'I hope they saved some mutton for me,' the boy said as he flew into the Poacher. 'Lizzy can be a right cow to me sometimes,' he added before laughing and disappearing inside.

'They allow children in that place?' Aggie asked in shock. Not realising that it was true of her too.

'Much goes on in that place, Aggie, but serving children ale is not one of them. The adults wouldn't want to share it for starters. No, Eric lives in the Poacher with his older sister Elizabeth and younger sister Gemima. All three of them evacuees from London, a bit like yourself,' Gideon explained.

'Really?' replied Aggie.

'Yes, really. You'll have plenty of time to get to know them. At school, tomorrow!' he curtly responded back. As if Agatha had no choice in the matter and certainly no time to dispute it, Gideon began his briskest of walks down the sharpest descent of the Steep towards a shop that had a large black cat swaying on a sign that protruded just above its doorway. 'A little surprise for you.' Her uncle smiled, changing tone with his pace, as he walked beneath the metal feline. 'Le Café Chat Noir!' Gideon exclaimed.

Chapter 15
Eros

Nathaniel Noone watched out through the revolving door, counting to fifty as ordered by Draper, though it felt much longer. His hand still clasped the hidden pistol deep inside his coat pocket, trigger finger ready. In the other pocket, the photographs and the torches he'd used to light up the hidden markings.

On 'fifty', Noone rushed out of the door. It was as if the elements had been waiting for him to alight as just then a mighty crash of thunder came from the heavens. Screams rang out and people rushed for cover. The lonely night of the air-raid, fresh within everyone's minds, convinced the masses that the Thunder Machines had arrived again. Panic ensued and within the immediate rush, people pushed and shoved themselves erratically to find safety. Pushing became crushing and as people lost their footings, the very real threat of serious injury from themselves and not an air-raid was increasingly developing.

BANG!

The deafening volley of a gunshot came from across the road and it caused the crowds to momentarily pause and squat for cover. In that brief interlude, the heavens opened and the torrents of rain hammered down, saturating everything in their path. The cold from the teeming precipitation had stunned everyone into a brief sensibility. It was not a doodlebug strike. It was simply a thunderstorm. Nevertheless, a new scramble for warmth and cover broke out amidst the already-nervous civilians.

Noone managed to push his way through the crowds. Anyone daring enough to catch the full horror of his scarring soon retreated, allowing him a pathway to the memorial fountain. Nathaniel leapt upon the temporary wooden scaffold of the fountain to peer over the scattering pedestrians.

From the statue, he spotted the booths and rushed through the crowds hurriedly. As he met the roadside kerb from the pavement, a large black saloon thundered past him almost dragging him under within its slipstream. The shimmering chrome bird on the radiator blinded him as it caught the suns beams that were desperately breaking through the thunderclouds. Puddles of water were sent crashing towards him as the tyres spun away. Soaking wet now and enraged from his near-miss, he ran as fast as his lame leg would allow him towards the red boxes. Draper was nowhere to be found. Noone scoured the immediate area. Nothing suggested a struggle. Could Draper have hidden for his own safety's sake? He kept on looking, examining the floor for clues, thumbing through the catalogue of phonebook numbers hanging from the phone via a chain attached to its metal spine. Nothing. He went from one booth to the other, repeating his observations, still nothing.

'Damn it!' He shouted looking skywards into the torrential rain that relentlessly bore down on him. 'Think, Nathaniel, think,' he muttered to himself as he paced around the booths. He had failed to see a young newspaper vendor talking to members of the local constabulary just fifty yards or so and pointing in his direction.

Subtly walking towards him, the two policemen stalked up behind Nathaniel. One drew his truncheon while the other drew his cuffs. Without so much as a warning, the first officer struck him beneath the knee of his already lame leg, which made him buckle to the floor. As his face was planted into the miserable, damp paving, the second officer straddled his back and pulled his right arm behind him and up between his shoulder blades into a standard policeman's hold. Noone's left-hand side, the scarred side, was pushed downwards into the grit and the dirt.

'We have reason to believe you are carrying a firearm, sir?' the first officer explained.

'What?' Noone shouted aggressively, writhing on the floor.

The officer on top of him placed his full weight down to pacify him while the other quickly frisked him. From the left-hand pocket, he removed the photograph and torch. From the right-hand pocket, he pulled out Nathaniel's gun.

'Well, well, well,' the second officer said, and then blew his whistle out loud for immediate support.

Nathaniel Noone stopped fighting, exhaled, and lay there as the continuing torrent of rain soaked him through to the bone.

Having heard the whistle for help, several beat *'Bobbies'* came to the aid of their police colleagues. Taking Noone from beneath his elbow joints, they raised him onto his feet. A crowd of onlookers had now gathered despite the terrible weather.

'Good God!' one of them shouted and backed away.

Several people from the crowd gasped in shock. Nathaniel's scarring was exceptionally grotesque, as people's reactions often liked to remind him. Such horrors suggested to the onlooker he was indeed a monster. The policeman took a step backwards, and they all drew their truncheons as if Nathaniel posed a significant threat to them, despite the fact his arms were shackled around his back.

Just as Nathaniel's fate seemed inevitable, and he prepared himself for a beating, a large black saloon came speeding around the corner. It was almost identical to the one that had nearly run him down. The subtle difference was the winged lady that adorned the radiator, unlike the winged bird of the other vehicle. As it drew to a halt, two men in long dark coats and fedoras alighted from the rear. One of them made his way to the police officer standing behind Nathaniel manning the shackles. Noone could not see what was happening behind him as the man whispered quietly in the policeman's ear and showed him an identity card drawn from an inside pocket. The policeman did not seem pleased. The other man was talking to the other police constable, the one who had struck Noone with his truncheon. Again, Nathaniel could not make out the conversation but the constable did point to the street vendor who had accused Noone in the first place. As he was led away and ushered into the car Nathaniel Noone watched on as the second man made his way to the vendor, showed his ID and then took him into a nearby alleyway.

'Mind your head, sir,' the first fedora-wearing man said as he placed Nathaniel into the large black saloon.

Inside, the driver sat next to yet another man, who also wore a large black hat. The windows were tinted. You could see the outside world but they couldn't see you, and between front and rear passengers was a glass partition.

'You can un-cuff him now,' came a cut-glass accent, via a speaker, from the man in the front.

Duly, the first man removed Noone's shackles before closing the door behind him and disappearing into the crowd that had formed during Noone's assault. The second man returned and started a conversation via the front passenger window with the man who had just ordered Noone to be un-cuffed. Nathaniel couldn't hear a thing but a small flash of white stood out as he passed something through the window. Then came a photograph, a torch, and a pistol. The front passenger then looked into the rear-view mirror catching Nathaniel's single-eyed stare before ordering his driver on. Noone recognised his eyes. They had met briefly not long before.

They sped away as quickly as they had arrived but the journey was over in mere minutes. They were at the rear of Fortnum's once again. Several heavy-goods lorries were already there and men in brown overalls were removing items from the store. Everything was wrapped in brown post-office paper and everything was labelled with a coded luggage tag.

Nathaniel's door swung open and standing there was the young spy he had met the previous night. Only this time, his clothes were not rain-sodden or riddled with the stench of booze but crisp, fragrant and well-tailored.

'Hello again, sir,' he announced.

Noone finally realised that it was him, the vagrant from the night before.

'I'm Thompson, sir; Draper's deputy.'

The man offered his hand and Noone shook it tentatively. Directing an open arm towards the cellar door beneath the bin, where he had entered just hours previously, Thompson led the way. As they walked forward, Noone noticed two burly removal men standing on top of the door smoking cigarettes. Thompson nodded at them. They bent down and opened the large oak doors that revealed the subterranean entrance to The Department. Thompson descended quickly followed by Noone. The two men then locked the doors down again and carried on as if they really were two removal men on a fag break.

Through the long passageway, Noone followed Thompson until the dazzling fluorescent tubes that lit the labyrinth hit them. Where previously the rows of wood-panelled and neatly glazed rooms had seen a hive of activity they were on temporary lockdown. Armed guards stood at every doorway.

Thompson had not uttered a single word since they had descended into the secret depths. He remained silent until they reached the foot of a lift shaft where several nurses and a doctor were tending an elderly man in full concierge dress, sprawled out and unconscious in front of them. A saline drip ran from his arm. The doctor was raising each eyelid in succession and shining a penlight into each pupil.

'He's alive?' Thompson asked, quite shocked.

'Catatonic, but still breathing,' the doctor responded.

'We all thought he was dead. Thank heavens for that,' Thompson explained to Noone, then sighed with a sense of relief.

'What happened?' Noone rasped.

'Still putting the pieces together,' Thompson replied. 'Needless to say, we have been infiltrated somehow.'

'And Draper?' Noone asked.

'I thought you would answer that for me. Evidently not,' Thompson concluded.

'Sir,' came a voice from behind them. It was one of the men who had helped un-cuff Noone.

'What is it, Smith ?' Thompson replied abruptly.

'You need to come and see, sir,' Smith replied.

Thompson and Noone followed Smith back down a corridor and into one of the rooms where the cypher-interpreting team worked. Where this had recently been a hive of desks ringing with typewriter bells, it was now empty of people and all but one of the desks had been neatly packed away with boxes on top of them.

The single desk that remained had its headset hanging off of the chair by the elasticated phone cord, indicating someone had left in a hurry.

'Whose desk is this?' Thompson asked politely.

'Jennifer James, sir,' Smith replied nervously.

'Where is she?' Thompson continued.

'We're not sure, sir. But that's not all.'

Smith picked up the headset and passed it to his superior. The headset crackled with an inaudible static.

'One moment please, sir,' Smith said and left the room.

Several moments passed until the static Thompson could hear turned into sound. A brief crackle and Smith's voice could be heard loud and clearly

'Hello, London. Are you receiving me? Over,' came Smith's soft voice.

'Smith?' Thompson asked. 'Smith, is that you? Where are you?'

'I'm in the office, sir.'

'Which office, Smith?' Thompson enquired.

'*THE* Office, sir.'

Thompson's complexion changed from a confident blushed pink into a pallid sickly white. He dropped the headset and looked around at Noone.

'You need to come with me. I need to know everything that you discussed with Draper.'

Thompson and Noone left the cypher room and proceeded to Drapers' office where Smith was sitting at Drapers' desk. On Thompson entering the room, Smith shot up from the desk and stood attentively behind the chair.

'Where were you, Smith, when you just spoke to us?' Thompson asked.

'Just sitting here, sir,' he replied, tapping his fingers on the backrest of Draper's chair.

'Show me again and be careful to speak in exactly the same tone and volume. We have an intruder to find.'

Smith regained his seated position and repeated what he'd said. The vocal level Smith spoke in was not loud, so the device, the bug, could not have been set far from Draper's desk. Thompson moved silently around Smith. First, he felt under the desk edge and along its overhang. Then, he opened the drawers and repeated his silent search. Nothing could be found. The chair was examined too as was the underside of the desk and drawers. Still nothing. Draper kept a tidy and minimal working space. On top of the desk sat only four objects. The first was a silver letter opener, solidly cast. Thompson retrieved it, eyeballed it through a 360-degree rotation and then dismissed it. The second was a gold-plated fountain pen; an heirloom form Draper's father. Thompson carefully dismantled the casing, removed the cartridges and unscrewed the nib but nothing extraordinary existed within it. He then painstakingly put it back together. The two final items were the chrome Newton's cradle and the pot plant. Thompson pulled one of the suspended metal balls back and started the cradle's motion going. As its rhythmic clacking continued he stalked around it scouring around its frame as it reflected distorted images back. He could not see that this was the source of the intrusive device either, which left the plant. Thompson was interrupted by a knock on the door.

'Come in, Jones.' Thompson beckoned to the second man who had been on the scene to save Nathaniel.

Jones entered the room with a very nervous-looking member of staff.

'This is Ms Hilary Nevis,' Jones advised, introducing the timid-looking woman. 'She's a friend of Ms Jennifer James.'

Thompson ushered the short lady in. Ms Nevis was trembling.

'D-d-do you think something a-a-awful has happened to her, sir ?' she nervously stuttered.

'We're not quite sure what to think, Ms Nevis. We're doing all we can to unravel this. Perhaps you can help us?' Thompson asked kindly.

'I'll try,' she replied, sobbing into her handkerchief.

'We need to know everything about Ms Jones. Everything and anything about her. OK?'

Ms Hilary Nevis sat anxiously as Thompson, Noone, Smith, and Jones looked down at her. Her sobbing had reached an uncontrollable level. Not only had her best friend just disappeared but she was now set to be interrogated by four imposing men, one monstrously scarred and at whom she couldn't help but keep staring back.

'Smith, Jones, I'd like you to revisit the scene where Mr Noone was retrieved, and canvas more information from the policeman and any other witnesses,' Thompson directed. The two officers left immediately.

Sensing Ms Nevis's disposition – Nervous Nevis as she was already known within The Department – and the effect Noone was having on it, Thompson ordered a pot of tea be made and brought to *The Office*.

'Ms Nevis, I can assure you that you are in no trouble whatsoever. I hear you are a remarkable translator and have been instrumental in breaking cypher and code.' Thompson's tone was sympathetic and complimentary, and with just himself and Noone, the doe-eyed Ms Nevis steadied her heart rate and began to breathe more easily. Noone's scarring was distracting her, making it uncomfortable for all three of them.

'Shall we talk privately, Ms Nevis?' Thompson asked

'You can call me Hilary, sir,' she replied, nodding in reply to his initial question.

'OK, Hilary, no need for tears now. Let's discuss this just between ourselves. Let's go through this one final time, and then you are free to spend some time with your family.' Thompson said, reassuring the timid cypher clerk. Gesturing Nathaniel Noone to take his leave.

Thompson continued his light interrogation, repeatedly asking questions about Ms James, Ms Nevis's now-missing colleague, and any information that may lead them to both the disappearance of Draper and the increasingly mysterious Jennifer James. Thompson sat opposite Ms Nevis in Draper's office and so not to scare her or distract her in any way, the scarred and melted man, Nathaniel Noone, listened in from the cypher room.

'So, again, you both started on the same day approximately six months ago,' Thompson repeated.

'That's right, sir,' replied an exhausted Hilary Nevis.

'And you say she had gained somewhat of a rapport with Mr Draper.'

'I wouldn't like to gossip, sir, but they were friendly.'

'Friendly, how?' Thompson pressed

'Well, they would share the occasional cigarette, sir.'

'Share?'

'Well, not share the actual cigarette, sir, but spend the same time together. It's probably nothing, sir. Most smokers have spent time in each other's company as it's confined to a single room.'

'Quite right, Ms Nevis. I'm sure it was nothing.'

'She did buy him a birthday present, sir. That was a bit out of the blue, a senior officer being bought a present from his subordinate. The office did have a chatter about it. But Jennifer was like that; very, very kind. She was always kind to me.' Hilary Nevis sobbed into her handkerchief.

'Do you happen to know what the present was?' Thompson asked politely

'That,' Ms Wallis responded, nodding at the plant on Draper's desk.

'This plant?' Thompson responded with alarm.

'Yes, sir. It's a papyrus plant, sir. Jennifer told me that David, I mean Mr Draper, had spent time in Egypt. She thought it would be a lovely surprise.'

'Oh, did she now. Well. Thank you, Ms Nevis. you've been most helpful.' Thompson stood from the chair and escorted Hilary away from Draper's office.

Nathaniel Noone was already making his way aggressively towards them down the corridor. 'Papyrus grass, Egypt!' he shouted at Thompson. 'I bloody well knew it.'

Thompson raised his index finger to his lips. 'Shhhh,' he said softly into the hole where Draper's ear used to be. 'We can't talk here. Follow me.'

Thompson then left the room, the plant pot accompanying him under one arm.

Noone followed him through a sequence of corridors and tunnels to where a car was already revving up, waiting for them with its exhaust puffing smoke into the new dawn ready to whisk them away.

'Noone?' Thompson led with a question. 'Do you have level three clearance?'

'No,' Nathaniel Noone replied.

'Pity. I need several hours in Whitehall. Can you occupy yourself until I post instructions via *The Exchange*?' Thompson asked.

'I have things I can be getting on with,' Noone responded.

Thompson ordered his driver to detour via The Embankment and dropped Noone off near a waterside newsvendor.

'Grab a copy of the Times, in your name. It's already paid for,' Thompson advised before speeding off hastily to Whitehall.

Nathaniel Noone approached the vendor and was given his Times. Inside were a small envelope and cypher-decoding table. On the back of the paper, replacing the usual sports headlines was a half-page advert.

'Fortnum's apologises for the unforeseen closure of its Haberdashery and Drapery floor due to inclement supply line issues. All other floors are open as usual.'

He managed a half-smile at the subtle message to members of *the Department*. Now, what of Draper and the mysterious Jennifer James? Time to call in a favour from an old friend.

Chapter 16
Le Chat Noir

'How's your French?' Gideon asked his niece.

'Florrie makes me have lessons twice weekly,' Aggie replied.

'Care to translate for me?' he said pointing upwards to the large metal sign. 'And be sure to look closely at the tail.'

The dark feline silhouette creaked softly to and fro from the suspended sign just above the doorway. Above its head, the fluid writing of 'Le Chat' stood out in a vivid white. Written beneath the subject's paws and painted in vibrant blue, 'Noir' could be seen in a much bolder type. Aggie squinted her eyes to focus on the tail as her uncle had suggested. Not as obvious as the other words but still visible in a gaudy red, the word Café could be seen as the 'C' adopted the final counter-clockwise curl of the creature's tail and tailed off with it.

'The Black Cat – Café,' Aggie proudly announced.

'Excellent!' Gideon replied. 'Take a look through the window. Go on.'

Aggie could hear music from inside. It sounded similar to old records Florrie would play. Ragtime Jazz she used to call it; all banjo and brass. As the gradient of the Steep was at its sharpest on this stretch of the pavement, Aggie had to go on tiptoes to look through the window. She used the cuff of her jacket to wipe away the dirt and peered inside.

Like any café or restaurant, there were rows of tables and chairs. In Le Chat Noir, the tables were covered in bright, checked tablecloths and on each of them, a candle burned within an old, empty, glass jam jar. With its dimmed lights and vibrant music, Aggie couldn't wait to go inside. As she turned to her uncle to ask permission a black shadow landed at the window and startled her backwards. A guttural growl came from behind the glass. Aggie peered back into two large yellow eyes that had set upon her, as the large cat peered back at her without blinking. She put her hand to her chest that had momentarily increased its heart rate and giggled embarrassedly.

'Please, can I go in?' Aggie begged Gideon.

Her uncle looked up and down the Steep and through the barricades of wood and barbed wire that zigzagged downwards. In the distance, he focused on two automobiles that were parked beyond. One of them was a large ambulance truck, a familiar visitor on Sundays, and which dwarfed the much smaller roofless jeep parked opposite it.

'Uncle?' Aggie persisted, breaking Gideon's stare

'Yes, of course…' he replied '…but, just be aware, there are some men in here, that are, how do I put this? Wounded veterans.'

'OK.' Aggie smiled, thinking nothing of it. 'I'm only interested in the cat, to be honest,' she said as she pushed the entrance door open.

'Catsssss,' her uncle replied, accentuating the plural with a hiss.

A small copper bell that was suspended between threshold and mid-air, rang to announce their arrival into the café. Aggie was greeted by a large black moggy that slowly stalked her until it wove in and out of her legs purring loudly. The music was much louder inside, with even louder conversation heard in the background. No one responded to the chime of the bell that had rattled upon their entrance. Aggie bent down and began to fuss the large feline that had now completely succumbed to her and was rolling around on its back encouraging its tummy to be rubbed. Aggie duly obliged.

All of a sudden, another cat made its presence felt and jumped on top of Aggie's arched shoulders. It purred even louder into her ears before nuzzling into her neck. Aggie pampered this one too as it draped its tabby coat across her and flicked its tail into her bobbed hair. Then from behind the drapes of the front window, a small ginger tomcat dashed out to her. At this point, the large black cat threw itself up onto its paws and issued a defensive growl to its fellow creatures. The ginger cat dashed off immediately between chairs and tables. The tabby issued a slight warning back to her counterpart but then slowly slid off of Aggie and sauntered deeper into the restaurant. The black cat, fully regaining one hundred per cent of Aggie's affection, flopped childlike into her cradled arms.

'Giddy, Giddy,' came a sweet female voice as a slight lady wearing a slender black dress and white pinny danced her way over to Aggie's uncle.

Embracing Gideon with a tiptoed kiss to each cheek she then took his right arm and twirled herself around.

'You see? I am now very giddy.' She laughed through mild intoxication.

'Cecile, this is my n–' Gideon began, almost introducing Agatha as his niece. He paused very briefly and then continued, 'My new evacuee, Agatha.'

'Bonjour, Agatha.' Cecile said welcoming her in an almost French accent.

'I see you have already made friends with Malkin. You are very honoured,' Cecile said happily, pointing at the now sleeping fur-ball in Aggie's arms.

Aggie's attention had been so clearly focused on the cats that had greeted her and was now pampering Malkin so she really had not observed the full surroundings of Cecile's beloved café. As she looked up she was greeted by what must have been a dozen, possibly more, cats, parading around the café as if it was rightfully theirs. Certainly, they outnumbered the guests that were in there. To the right-hand corner were three guests deep in conversation, and cloaked in hooded Cossacks that covered their faces. Nearer to the bar were several servicemen. One had his back to her and was in full British uniform. The two others were loud and smoked large cigars as they laughed and drank with their British ally.

'Hey, Cecile,' one of them called out. 'Trois vin rouge, sil vous plait.'

Their enthusiasm was infectious and far from being rude their request was jovial. Cecile laughed on her way back to the bar and poured three large red wines for them.

'Will you be joining us, Gideon?' came the broad New York accent towards her uncle.

'Not today, gents. thank you,' Gideon politely declined

The British serviceman who had kept his back to them turned around and raised his glass to Aggie's uncle. Aggie unceremoniously dropped Malkin as she looked upon his face. It was scarred beyond anything she had seen before. It was horrifying. Where his ears once were there were now only holes and his eyelids and lips had melted into his face. His ghostly stare emphasised by the milky frosting of his eyeballs. She stared away but didn't say a word.

'Usually, people scream,' the serviceman said to Aggie. He then bent down and picked up Malkin before walking over and handing him back to Aggie.

Aggie wasn't sure what to say and just looked back. His opaque eyes stared towards her.

'Thank you,' she said, suspecting the dry gulp she had just swallowed was quite obvious to everyone.

'No, thank you, for not screaming,' the serviceman replied and then continued drinking with his friends.

'Cecile, as always, it's been a pleasure,' Gideon interrupted cordially and turned to leave.

'I'd like to stay for a little bit,' Aggie asked her uncle, unperturbed by the man's grotesque appearance.

The serviceman and his two American friends turned and raised a welcoming glass to her. Gideon cast a look towards Cecile who, in turn, returned a reassuring nod.

'You can help me feed the cats,' Cecile suggested to Aggie.

Gideon nodded in agreement and turned to his niece.

'Aggie, I will be two minutes down the road seeing my friend Tink. His shop is the one with the large wooden shoe outside. If you need me, run straight there.'

'We'll look after her,' Cecile interrupted, taking Aggie's hand and leading her behind the bar to a small set of steps that descended beneath the restaurant.

With a chime of the bell, Gideon left Le Chat Noir and headed south, down the Steep, weaving in and out the barbed-wire barricades.

Beneath the restaurant, flint and sandstone arches provided the cellar where Cecile maintained a small but impressive selection of fine wines. Very hard to come by in such frugal times. Cecile held up one of the jam jars with the candle burning brightly as they passed into the dimly lit subterranean passageway.

'Take this,' the restaurant owner said to Aggie, passing her a large ceramic bowl with a steel ladle. Cecile then poured a mixture of damp sloppy food from a sealed bucket in the corner. From within the darkness, the increased level of purring from several cats could be heard. It grew louder as the excitement gained momentum. From behind them, Malkin made his presence known with a small cat meow and following him down the stone stairs came the tabby, the ginger tom, and several others. Cecile raised the lamp and lit several candles along the wall. As each one lit, it illuminated rows of cat cubicles. Each cubicle had its own blanket or makeshift bedding and names were decorated on individual cat bowls that were uniformly laid out on the floor in front of the them.

'One spoonful per bowl, no more,' Cecile ordered and Aggie began to slop the food into them one by one. On hearing the chink of the ladle against the ceramic bowl, all the cats descended from either the restaurant or their darkened quarters in anticipation of the fare.

'It's not easy herding cats,' Cecile advised Aggie, smiling. 'It takes time, a lot of patience, but most of all ... food.'

Aggie filled each bowl, and a small legion of well-drilled moggies were now eagerly eating their food. Aggie counted that there were twenty cats in all. However, there were twenty-one bowls. Aggie grabbed the empty bowl and held it up to read the cat's name. Decorated in fine calligraphy and adorned with tiny fake jewels the pewter cat bowl read 'Purrsia'.

'Purrsia, here, kitty. Purrsia!' Aggie called out.

'Up here!' the scarred serviceman shouted.

Aggie skipped up the stairs with the bowl and ladle.

'He's over there with my friends,' the serviceman continued, guiding Aggie towards the three cloaked men in the corner. 'They won't bite,' he assured her.

Aggie took a few tentative steps forward them and there she could see Purrsia curled up into the Cossack on one of the men's laps with just his nose peeping out during his cosy slumber. As she approached them, the three men turned to look at her from under their hoods. All of them displayed burns scarring, much like the serviceman who had already made her acquaintance. The gentleman, whose lap was currently Purrsia's bed, sat in a wheelchair. Aggie had not realised this until she was up much closer. His legs were missing from the knees downwards.

'I wouldn't wake him,' he said to Aggie. 'He has a filthy temper.'

Just then the restaurant door opened with its customary bell chime and in walked two large thuggish men. Each was dressed in white overalls, one of them with a large gold tooth. Aggie noticed official-looking name badges that read 'Silvera'. Without so much as a grunt, they made their way to the wheelchair-bound man and began to wheel him out of the restaurant.

'Well I guess that means we're leaving then,' the serviceman shouted across the restaurant to ensure the two brutes heard him.

As the cloaked men upped and left, the serviceman Aggie had engaged with followed just behind. He too carried a long hooded gown but refused to wear it. He preferred his pristine uniform.

As the orderlies began to lift the wheelchair down Le Chat Noirs' steps, Purrsia awoke. People had forgotten for a moment he was still snuggled in. With an aggressive hiss, he raised his paw and shot a sharp-clawed blow across the large man's cheek. The man struggled to carry the wheelchair and maintain balance. He lost grip of the wheelchair and sent his colleague onto his backside, bumping down the steps as he tried to control the chair from falling.

Purrsia the cat now stood rooted in the road, spitting and hissing at the man at least fifty times his own size.

'What the hell is that thing?' the brute snarled, taking a sweeping boot at Purrsia.

Aggie looked out of the window in horror. The man's foot was just short of connecting with the cat's head. But he was right. The cat was odd. It was all wrinkly with folds of flesh exposed. It didn't have a single hair on its body. Perhaps that's why it preferred the company of the burned men in hoods. Nevertheless, Purrsia was smart enough not to wait for the next assault and scarpered up the Steep.

'Don't worry. I'll catch him,' Aggie volunteered and shot out of the restaurant and quickly up the hill.

'No, Aggie, no! Come back!' Cecile shouted. Chasing after her.

The tip of Purrsia's tail could just be seen as it entered the passageway adjacent to the Poacher. Aggie rushed up the sharp incline and rounded the corner. The pathway led into a dark, damp corridor of adjoining pathways as she called out to the cat.

'Purrsia! Come on, Purrsia. Here kitty, kitty,' she called, in-between pursing her lips and making kissing noises.

Winding along the alleyways and labyrinth of passages, Aggie continued calling out patiently for several minutes. She ignored the calls from Cecile in the background who was tracking her like she was tracking the cat. Finally, she was rewarded by a 'meow' from just around the next bend.

On turning into the bend, she was greeted by Purrsia the hairless cat who was being held aloft by the rump of flesh between its shoulder blades, desperately swinging its paws at the man holding him. Purrsia's captor was the small wretched man from the Poacher; the one who had tried, unsuccessfully, to challenge Pop Braggan earlier.

'Here kissy-kissy.' He laughed with his screwed up little face puckering towards Aggie.

'Give me the cat,' the young girl demanded.

'Of course,' he replied, holding Purrsia forward. 'If you give me whatever it is you are hiding in your pocket.'

Aggie had forgotten the blue velvet case and magnifying glass as she had transfixed her attention on the cats. Now reminded, she immediately placed her hand within her pocket and grasped it tightly.

'OK,' she said, removing the case and placing it on the floor in front of her.

'No funny business or the ugly moggy here gets it,' he snarled back. Holding Purrsia at arm's length he edged towards Aggie.

'That looks pretty. Such a beautiful-looking case, what treasures does it 'old inside. Pearls maybe? Is it pearls, girl?' he asked with a broad grin across his face.

'How did you know?' Aggie replied in a surprised tone.

Lyle, as the wretched man was known, awkwardly bent down, while keeping the cat aloft, and grabbed the blue velvet case. He was unable to unclasp it with one hand. So he handed Purrsia over. Aggie cradled the cat in her arms as he opened the case.

'Magnifying glass! A tiny bleeding magnifying glass!' he shouted up at her, incensed it was not pearls as he had just been promised.

'It's very precious to me!' Aggie shouted back.

'Well, I'll show you how precious this is to me,' he snarled, raising his boot above the opened case.

Aggie moved quickly and, using poor old Purrsia as a shield, she thrust the cat into Lyle's face. A bad-tempered frenzy of paws and claws tore into Lyle's emaciated cheekbones and eyelids.

'Aagghhhhhh!' he screamed raising his hands to defend himself.

Aggie dropped Purrsia and grabbed the magnifying glass and its case. She turned and ran as fast as her legs could carry her. Purrsia the cat hurdled a wall and Lyle pulled out a sharp fisherman's knife.

'I'm going to gut you and your cat,' he screamed chasing after her, blood streaming from his cheeks.

Aggie's heart was beating so fast she was sure it would jump straight out of her chest. She could hear Cecile's voice in the background and headed towards it but she was disoriented and, as her uncle had explained, the sheer labyrinth maze of Ambledown's alleys was easy to get lost within. As she took her third right-hand turn in a row, where she thought Cecile's voice was coming from, she hit a dead end. Almost instantly her foe caught up with her.

'Oh dearie, dearie me,' came the aggressive little voice behind her.

Lyle, who was adept as any smuggler at navigating Ambledown's mazes, had cornered her. A glint from the knife he wielded caught the last of the autumn sun as he relished a slow walk towards her. Tears streamed down her cheeks as she sobbed and closed her eyes and waited.

'Thwack! Thud.'

Aggie heard the two dull sounds as she waited for her fate. And she waited and she waited. But there was nothing. Perhaps Lyle was taunting her in petrifying silence before he struck. But the strike never came. She opened her eyes and there flat-out on the ground, sprawled in front of her, lay his pathetic little frame. His knife was nowhere to be seen. A bloodied lump of wood abandoned by the wayside. A shuffle of feet disappearing into the maze of twittens.

'Aggie?' Cecile's voice called out.

'Agatha?' then came Uncle Gideon.

'I'm over here!' she cried out

Gideon and Cecile arrived soon after, accompanied by the two American gentlemen. Gideon snatched his niece into his arms and embraced her tightly. Cecile went looking for her cat. One of the Americans bent down, and with two fingers under the wretch's throat, felt for Lyle's pulse.

'He's still alive,' he confirmed.

'We'll take it from here, Gideon,' the second American said.

Gideon acknowledged their help, picked up his niece, wound through the passageways, and started the steep climb back up to 1a The Keep.

'Trouble finds you, young lady. Just like your mother,' he whispered into her ear. 'I do hope you can stay out of it at school tomorrow.' He laughed

'Seriously?' she frowned at him, casting her sapphire-blue stare at his.

'Seriously! About time you mixed with other children,' he replied seriously.

Chapter 17

The Imposter

During her influential exchange with Major Boyd Collingdale Ms Erket and Professor Malcolm had disappeared without a trace. Along with the Major's recollection of events. An entire day had passed since the Amazonian figure draped in tiger skin had clip-clopped her way swiftly in and out of his life. She'd preferred the company of Professor Malcolm though, which had been met with somewhat incredulous disbelief by the army veteran.

On this day, in fact, the annual Sunday Harvest that everyone throughout the country would be enjoying, the Major had insisted his staff work until midday. And so, like every day before it, at 8 am sharp, the stout, balding man with flamboyant facial hair and splintered bamboo cane directed his staff, quick smart, on his daily rounds of the Museum of Natural History. Passing such rare and exotic creatures that had taken centuries to collate, was now commonplace to them all as were the daily altercations between the Professor Meticulous Meredith Malcolm and Major Collingdale.

At 8:05 am, as the entourage rounded the familiar mahogany-cased exhibits, the moustache on Boyd Collingdale's face twitched in anticipation of a verbal altercation with the adversarial professor. Much to the Major's surprise and those who shuffled behind him with their notepads and pencils drawn, the Professor was not there as he consistently had been. Perhaps he had taken the day off for the harvest? The Major considered it but he wasn't convinced the Professor would ever take a day off and continued his military march towards the cordoned off Eastern Quarter.

As he passed the recently assaulted taxidermist triumph of a fully grown ostrich, a crunch came from beneath his foot. Peeling his immaculately polished, government issued, black ankle boots back from the stone floor, the blood and guts of a crushed arachnid revealed themselves. The pincers and unfurled sting were still intact but its abdomen now succumbed to the imprint from the toe end of his size ten.

'What an abomination of a beast!' the Major exclaimed, desperately trying to scrape intestines and blood from his sole.

'Sir,' one of the actuaries said, raising a hand and pointing into the rubble at the foot of the cordon.

The Major's gaze, directed by the pointed pencil of the actuary, focused on the red ribbon, a protruding ember in the dust and debris surrounding it. Stepping over several rocks and squatting on his heels, Collingdale removed the straw boater from its crushed, stony grave, and dusted it down. Looking up at the red-and-white cordon tape, he noticed that it was covered in more dust than it had previously been covered in, and the pillar that had dissected the entrance by forty-five degrees and had acted as the remaining support to the Entomology department's gateway was now broken and scattered into pieces around him. From the mouth of the opening rock, rubble and plaster had been spewed out from the guts of the Professor's department.

'Oh, Meredith. What on earth have you done?' he whispered under his moustache before taken a moment before addressing his staff. 'Gather round,' Collingdale announced to the men and women he had mustered. 'Approximately twenty-four hours ago, Professor Malcolm was last seen in this exact spot. This morning we found this!' he exclaimed, holding up the battered straw boater.

Anyone who had spent more than a few days on duty at the Museum knew of the natty professor's dress sense and the Penny Farthing he rode to work every day. The rich crimson ribbon of his straw boater was his trademark attire.

'By the looks of that hat, he's probably been crushed, sir,' came a voice from the back.

'"*Probably*" doesn't cut the mustard here!' the Major yelled back. 'So, unless we find evidence to the contrary, our primary goal is to clear all this detritus and seek out our friend.'

Mumblings rippled around the staff who had never seen the Major or Professor exchange pleasantries, but as Boyd Collingdale stood there with the Peacekeeper eager to start thrashing, all staff began the arduous task of removing each rock and fallen joist of timber hand by hand.

'Oh and just a polite warning,' Collingdale announced, pulling up the end of his cane and placing the remains of the crushed Death-stalker on the end of it. 'There may be more of these illustrious little beasties to contend with. Be cautious and be careful. Carry on!'

Immediately, everyone took a step back and started patting themselves down.

'What on earth are you all playing at,' came the booming Major's voice. 'You have just under four hours, by my calculations, to clear a path. That's if you wish to have your Sunday Harvest lunch with your loved ones and not with the Professor's pet monsters.'

The itching stopped and people cautiously, carefully, and with utmost efficiency began to remove the mountain of rubble in front of them. No way they were missing Sunday Harvest.

*****

Professor Malcolm Meredith awoke from a light slumber. His head was resting on Culpepper's *Everyday Medicinal Fauna*, having fallen asleep at the huge desk. It was just one of many rare and exceptional scientific books and journals in the library that the mysterious Dr Mialora had created for him.

A subtle tap from the doorway, which was flanked by two full-length mirrors, announced the entrance of the politely accommodating Mr Louds.

'Good morning, Professor,' he said courteously, from beneath his ever-present surgical mask. 'I trust you slept well.'

Meticulous Meredith Malcolm, who had managed forty winks with a book for a pillow, smiled back politely. Following Mr Louds were two large men who pushed trolleys covered in different fabrics. The first man wheeled his fare towards the Professor's workbench. He smiled back with his golden tooth. Withdrawing the muslin cloth, he presented a slender swan-necked silver vessel that had steam escaping from the spout and accompanied with a rack of toasted bread and a jar of amber liquid.

'Tea, with honey,' Louds advised. 'As requested. We also provided toast, in case you were hungry.'

The Professor thanked him and made an eager flit to the trolley. He didn't think he'd eaten in the past twenty-four hours, and keenly tucked into the food and drink offered to him. Mr Louds directed the second trolley into the centre of the room and then ordered the two orderlies to leave.

They did so, dimming the lights down low as they departed.

'I must apologise, Professor. Dr Mialora had hoped to be here to present this to you himself. But he remains in surgery,' Louds said respectfully.

Meredith Malcolm, who had been busily gorging on the sustenance provided became increasingly attentive as Mr Louds unfurled the silk cloth covering the second trolley. Beneath it, bound each end in leather tubing topped off with golden domes, were three separate scrolls. Each scroll had two sets of tubing so in front of them sat six, golden-domed, tanned leather tubes. Two pairs of white cotton gloves lay beside them. Mr Louds donned the first pair and then passed the second to Professor Malcolm.

'These scrolls are millennia old,' Mr Louds explained. 'They come from a recently discovered burial chamber of one of the most powerful Pharaoh's that ever lived.'

'Pharaoh?' the Professor mumbled in excited amazement through a half-full mouth of food. Professor Malcolm accepted the white gloves and slowly put them on, ensuring a snug fit finger by finger. Approaching the trolley behind Mr Louds, his nervous excitement, though non-vocal, emitted tiny beads of sweat from his brow.

Mr Louds moved to the first scroll, which sat to the right-hand side of the trolley. With his right hand on the farthest tube, he steadied the scroll, and with his left, he gently brushed its partnering leather tube sideways, which helped them to slowly unwind counter-clockwise.

Inside the thick leather binding, which indeed looked old and well-handled, was a membrane of much older parchment. This membrane then housed flaps of soft vellum that were so thin and stretched, they were almost transparent. Beneath each swatch of vellum and protected by an ancient amber varnish were scraps of papyrus. Each scrap had been painstakingly put together from an initially shredded jigsaw of parts and was now bonded so as to form larger tableaux to these intricate puzzles. Where the amber bonding met the edges, between paper and animal skin, the darker veins emphasised the joins. The sepia hues of the brittle amber made everything look an aged orange but on closer inspection colours sat suppressed beneath it, amongst the darkly outlined hieroglyphics.

Professor Malcolm looked on in awe like anticipation.

Mr Louds then unfurled the second and third scrolls. The three scrolls were laid out in front of Meticulous Meredith Malcolm for him to examine. What immediately became apparent to the Professor was that each scroll was divided into three separate segments. Some of the frayed edges of papyri would join up and, therefore, they had been taken, or more realistically copied, from a single stone. Each of them was now separated to contain a detailed hieroglyphic for each element of that stone. Each of them, that is, if they had been complete. Of the supposed nine segments that they looked upon, in a matrix made up of three by three swatches, only one glyph existed in the centre of the first row. In the second row the middle and right-side segments were present and in the last row, the first and final segments remained. Of nine potential images, only five, just over half, were present. It resembled tic-tac-toe but with ancient messages, riddles, rather than noughts and crosses, filling the grid.

Professor Malcolm examined the five glyphs. In the centre, a large scarab dominated the central triptych and was accompanied to the right by female servants who knelt worshipping the beetle with an offering of some ancient plant or grass. Above the scarab, the symbol represented a half-crescent moon that ran horizontally with a sun dominating it from above. Below to the bottom left were three simple lines that traditionally depicted water and then following the gap and the final piece of this most ancient form of messaging, was the half-man, half-dog image of the ancient Egyptian lord of the underworld, Anubis.

'Where did you get them?' the Professor asked excitedly.

'We purchased them from an unlucky tomb plunderer,' Mr Louds responded. 'People believe them cursed and, well, let's put it this way, it didn't end well for him.' There was a sinister undertone from Mr Louds, part-threat and part-lesson to be learnt. Meticulous Meredith Malcolm chose not to react.

'Where's the rest of it?' the Professor questioned.

Changing subjects hastily, Mr Louds reached inside his operating gown and presented a small silver pillbox. It must have been no bigger than one-inch square and half an inch deep.

'We also purchased a relative quantity of this,' Louds advised, opening the small container and revealing a powdery violet substance.

Walking towards the glass and mahogany cabinet teeming with scarabs that were being eagerly looked upon by their voracious scorpion neighbours, Mr Louds lifted the lid of the enclosure and removed a live scarab, its six legs writhing aggressively as it was lowered to its doom amongst the formidable arachnids. Placing it amongst the Death-stalkers it was a matter of moments before a swift lash of their venomous stings rendered a lethal paralysis and moments before they set about devouring their prey, limb by limb. It was both uncomfortable and fascinating for the Professor to watch, yet no real revelation to him.

'Pass me that silk,' Louds ordered Malcolm, pointing to the light fabric that had been used to cover the scrolls. Placing the silk over the scorpion enclosure, so that it was almost pitch black, Brian Louds then opened the tiny pillbox. He pinched a snuff-sized thumb and forefinger of the violet powder inside. He ordered Professor Malcolm back and to cover his nose and mouth. Turning his back on the Professor and being careful not to inhale the substance himself, he raised his surgical mask for a brief moment and blew gently, as if blowing the flowers of a dandelion into a gentle breeze, over the unsuspecting Death-stalkers. Waiting a short time he then repeated the process of removing a scarab and placing it within the scorpion's tank. This time however he revealed a tiny pencil-sized torch that he then shone down on the insects. The luminous stripes of the nocturnal beasts lit them up like mini-dodgems on seaside illuminations, as they scurried throughout their enclosure bumping into one another. This scarab, unlike the specimen prized from the dead man's hand, remained its dark blue-black metallic self. The beam, which was violet, not white, passed over the mini-monsters. Previously eager to devour the scarab, the beam drew the predators away. A small, tiny circle of violet light, directed in their paths and the scorpions were powerless to resist and followed it around the enclosure guided by Mr Louds hand.

'Goodness me.' Meticulous exhaled in complete surprise.

'Centuries of human endeavour to domesticate lay animals such as the pig, cow or dog , Professor, but just look at what our ancients already knew. From this simple understanding, they could influence the most chaotic of creatures. The most primeval of instincts. No wonder they worshipped the humble scarab so much. The only problem is, the person who discovered this little trick is unfortunately dead, and with them, I believe, the ever-fading papyrus puzzle.'

Having been passed the pencil-thin torch from Mr Louds, Professor Malcolm studied the scorpions under the dark silk. Even when he pointed the beam directly onto the scarab the scorpions did not attack. They were entranced by the beam.

'Professor, may I ask you, can you recall how you actually got here?' Louds enquired.

Professor Malcolm stopped for a while, thought through his answer, and then responded as he shook his head from left to right. 'Not fully,' the entomologist said. 'I remember the Museum. I recall waking up in a car, dappled light, and the bright horizon of the coast. I seem to remember arriving. But for the best part that's about it.'

'So, I think you understand what this tiny pinch of powder is capable of,' Mr Louds responded. 'It is very important to our organisation we find a way to replicate this discovery.'

Professor Malcolm began to make sense of what had happened to him but could not contemplate the enormity or potential of what he was being told. Just a pinch of this influential dust and you were the master of the inhalant. The possibilities were huge. The possibilities were both magnificent and terrifying.

What purpose was it that the mysterious Dr Mialora and his ever-pleasant man-servant Mr Louds were pursuing?

'It is a complex conundrum, Professor. We have the words of a thief, a tomb robber, four parts of the story missing, and even then if we had all nine parts to look upon there are surely thousands of possible combinations. We need you to help us, Professor. We need you to replicate the possibilities of what I have just shown you.'

Professor Meticulous Meredith Malcolm felt the crushing anxiety of the task ahead of him. No doubt the scarab and influence of the fauna presented in the glyphs were part of this ancient recipe for influence. His doctorate in entomology and Botany were surely why they had chosen him in the first place. But how on earth could he start to understand the relationship and missing elements of such a puzzle? Let alone why they wanted him to replicate it. For surely, if their intentions were noble, why were they so secretive in the first place? They could have just sent a car.

'What is your master's purpose, Mr Louds?' Professor Malcolm asked nervously. 'And what if I refuse?'

Brian Louds remained effortlessly calm through the conversation. No emotions visible, just facts provided to his captive. 'I can see you require convincing, Professor. I can see the manner in which we whisked you away has no doubt cast considerable doubt in your mind. And I apologise for the nature of that escapade. However, there are factions at work that would move to steal our secrets. We live in a time where 'loose lips may sink ships', as you might say, but as for this specific secret, there are forces at work that would use such power for their own evil pursuits. So, please, follow me so I can convince you otherwise, and to allow you the courtesy to see for yourself the real purpose of our ambitions here at the Silvera Institute. Please, after you.'

Brian Louds directed Professor Malcolm towards the large doorway flanked by two mirrors. As they approached the door, it opened and the two huge orderlies stood like footmen on either side. Ahead of them was a dimly lit stone tunnel, stretching into darkness.

The stone corridor, lit from wax and wick, was more temple-like and in complete contrast to the illustrious laboratory Dr Mialora had provided to his guest. Professor Malcolm followed Mr Louds, flanked by the two burly guards. He couldn't see what threat he posed to such men but having just witnessed the extraordinary potential of the violet drug he fully understood what was at stake.

As the narrow perspective of light gathered into view and each spot of small, flickering flame passed them by, the passageway drew to an end. Mr Louds removed a full set of gaoler keys and unlocked a stone door entrance. One of the orderlies, muscle-bound and with strength in depth, pushed with his might to grind the door open. The immediacy and brightness of light pierced straight through and in contrast to the subterranean thoroughfare that joined the laboratory, Professor Malcolm was now greeted by the glare of white concrete, steel and glass. What's more, the perfectly framed view of the English Channel, albeit with its overcast autumnal day, provided infinite views of tempestuous seas that were silenced by the protective glass of the Institute.

'Please, this way, Professor,' Mr Louds said as he guided them onwards and down a sloping walkway.

The building was built on an ever-decreasing helix. The subtle gradient allowing nurses and their invalid patients a stair-less means of mobility. It had originally been intended as a gracious ascent to study modern masters and observe symphonies against the backdrop of seasonal skies. Now, however, it served a greater purpose to provide ground-breaking medical convalescence for the unfortunate forces injured overseas. The gilded frames of the previous pictures remained, but alas, the paintings did not.

As the smell of iodine wafted through his impressive moustache, the Professor felt a sense of calm come over him. There was a busyness of more people as they descended to the next level down. Nurses wheeled combat-weary soldiers around. Bandages covered a great part of many of their faces, and some had lost limbs. But in such extraordinary cases, they were going about their business. Playing card games, listening eagerly to the wireless for any combat updates but most importantly being nursed back to fuller lives.

'Professor, have you ever been inside an operating theatre before?' Mr Louds asked.

Meredith Malcolm took that to mean two very different things and cautiously frowned back.

'As an observer, of course,' Louds continued, sensing the Professor's next set of questions.

'No,' came the short reply.

'It can seem somewhat disorientating,' Brian Louds confirmed. 'But do not fear. Your two bodyguards will catch you if you faint.'

'Faint?' Malcolm questioned.

'I'm sure you won't, sir,' Louds concluded, before guiding them all through yet another set of locked doors with a large green light illuminated above.

The corridor to the operating theatre was clinically spotless. Large ceramic sinks sat at the entrance. Hanging up in uniformed order were clinicians' pristine white overalls, surgical masks, and hats.

'Please, wash your hands and put on the surgical clothes, Professor,' Mr Louds said.

Professor Meredith Malcolm had achieved a first-class doctorate but was in no terms a man of practising medicine. He was, however, a huge fan of pristine white garments. He removed his outer linen suit jacket, the one which had been spoilt by the single droplet of his own blood, and replaced it with a surgeon's set of overalls.

'One last item, Professor. Please, wear this at all times,' Mr Louds ordered. He presented him with a gas mask. It was like any other gas mask, only the glass was tinted with a violet hue.

On entering the corridor of operating theatres, the lighting and mood were completely different from the stark clinical white of the institute's primary corridors and convalescent wards. His surroundings seemed pink, not rose-tinted by any means, but almost like that of a fuchsia.

The low drone of repetitive conversation crackled through amplified speakers in each room. The light throbbed to a slow and constant rhythm. It was as if the world had slowed down. The Professor felt nauseous and his immediate reaction was to remove the mask. The orderlies restrained him from doing so as Mr Louds pointed through a window to a man who was sat upright. He was completely conscious but having skin cut away from his inner thigh and then grafted onto his severely scarred face.

The doctors and nurses all wore gas masks and with the exception of light and sound, it could have been any normal operating theatre. It was, however, the most peculiar and alarming site. The patient did not seem distressed in the slightest as intricate scalpel-cut after scalpel-cut layered small squares of living tissue onto the patient's lower jaw and cheekbones, which had been the product of a lost aerial battle with a Messerschmitt. The brave pilot was chatting away as if simply visiting a GP, not having major surgery.

Mr Louds monitored Meredith's every move. As he watched the Professor wince at the operation, he decided the Professor had seen enough and guided them back out of the operating area.

Removing his mask and taking a few small pants of breath, like an over-exhausted pup, Meticulous Meredith Malcolm promptly bent over and vomited the tea and toast he had so keenly devoured earlier. Louds was eager to reassure him.

'Come now, Professor. We wouldn't be human if what we had just been witness to didn't revile us and wasn't fully explained. I was terribly sick the first time it happened to me and what's to say a little "Ether" did not creep in when you tried to remove your mask.' Taking the light-headed Malcolm by the elbow he sat him on a long white chaise. 'The skin is a living organism. Once exposed to the elements, the capillaries, the blood cells, all begin an internal battle to stop any alien invaders getting in and wreaking havoc. The downside is that this inevitably kills off the exposed skin and tissue, resulting in scarring, scabbing and the loss of feeling.'

The professor listened intently but any medical reference, such as blood, or scab, resulted in him retching. Louds chose his words very carefully.

'Our pioneering skin-grafting process, as unpalatable as it may seem, actually eliminates the risks of those losses and unlike traditional medicine and experimentation, it eliminates infections too. Just imagine the possibilities.'

The Professor composed himself. 'I imagine there are many people who would not use it in such a way. More likely it would be used to more sickening extremes. Just look across Europe now. How many millions of lives are already lost due to some misguided ideology?' Meredith Malcolm exclaimed.

'Dearest Professor. I understand. I really do. My people have been persecuted for millennia. But we have never been able to use the Ethereum for any extended period. Certainly not long enough to control any volume of people through misguided doctrine. To the contrary, it has its limitations in operating, and beyond a few hours its effects wear off,' Louds responded tolerantly.

Professor Malcolm shook his head in disbelief. There were far too many risks as far as he could see it.

'I'm sorry, Mr Louds. I cannot help you,' the Professor replied.

'Very well. If that is your final decision.' Louds nodded forthrightly. 'Escort Professor Malcolm back to his laboratory. He is free to go once he has his things.'

The two hulking orderlies stood either side of the Professor and walked him back up the incline, past the picture-less frames, through the long, stone passageway, and into the unique laboratory that Dr Mialora had curated for him.

'Hello, Professor,' came a pleasant female voice as he entered. She was admiring the Death-stalkers in their glass cabinet. 'I, am Jennifer James. Dr Mialora's personal assistant.' She beamed.

'I'd like to leave now,' the Professor responded, unimpressed by the assistant's charms.

Exhaling the smoke from her slender cigarette that matched her slender and elegant height, she turned and glided over to him. 'Are you sure you wish to leave, Professor? Just look at everything you could have here. Dr Mialora is a very generous patron.'

'Positive,' the Professor responded curtly and beyond hesitation.

'But such a riddle, Professor. Such an opportunity to prove yourself.'

An intimate drag on the cigarette and Jennifer Jones exhaled a wisp of violet vapour that danced through the Professors moustache and was inhaled through his nose.

'You want to leave. NO?' she asked again.

'NO,' he responded after a slight delay.

'You'd like to help us. YES?' she continued.

'YES,' came his lethargic answer.

'Very good, Professor. Why don't you get some sleep and in the morning we can make plans,' she finished.

Professor Malcolm began to yawn. He now felt sleepy. The orderlies took him under each arm and dragged him by his toes to a small bed that had been made up in the laboratory's corner.

Jennifer James smiled with satisfaction. 'He must be monitored at all times,' she ordered. 'Not from within the laboratory. We need him to believe he is isolated. You must document and monitor his every finding, his every move,' she insisted.

The two orderlies nodded in compliance.

Professor Malcolm snored effortlessly in the corner as Jennifer James left the laboratory and disappeared from the Silvera Institute and into the cold autumn night to initiate her plan.

*****

Midday had come and gone hours since. Only a tyrant would've kept his soldiers and staff working into the late hours on Sunday Harvest, and since they had worked so diligently to remove the rubble and debris from the Eastern Quarter, Major Boyd Collingdale had allowed them to leave on the stroke of twelve. He'd remained to pursue his own efforts to find the Professor, toiling through dust and sweat to clear a path.

The pillar, which had run at an adjacent forty-five degrees, was now completely clear, and where the broken and battered supporting foundations had capitulated during the airstrike a fortnight previously, his team had come up with an ingenious way to support the walls and joists.

Where concrete and clay once stood, now a tunnel of wooden and glass exhibit stands lined the corridor. How fitting such a peculiar entranceway could've been built to welcome everyone into the Professor's beloved Entomology department. On one side were primates, mammals, and predators. On the other side, birds and reptiles lined up in expressionless taxidermy to welcome the Major in and out of the Professor's lab. The job was not complete, just the opening into the bomb site had been finished. This still left the department's many exhibits, both live and dead, shattered and scattered in what remained.

The Major had a severe dislike for anything that demonstrated more than four legs, and as afternoon cast a shrouded loneliness into the cavernous Museum, each lamp he had set up to navigate into the darker confines of Meredith's world was now targeted by the creatures of the night. Whirring and buzzing busily above him, undertaking airborne battles and reconnaissance of their prey before landing for respite on electric lamp or gaslight before they reached out again. Boyd had tired of his futile attempts to thrash the bugs away with the Peacekeeper and instead made a carefully trodden methodical path, stepping in and out of the shadows of the light where the insects now congregated.

The terrible stench of rotting and decay was ever-present as he feared for his colleague's fate and the inevitability of the cadaver he would stumble upon soon. Only occasionally lighting up his battery-powered torch he would focus on an object or obstacle to navigate. As the batteries tired and the bulb flickered and failed, the Major stumbled over a heavy object underfoot. The torch fell from his grasp and he was plunged into darkness. His vision now impaired but his hearing heightened he sat there as he heard the tiny macerating sounds of a league of creepy crawlies working over a human carcass. Something crawled across his arm making him jump and shudder. He stood to his feet and scratched himself down from head to foot. His eyes, now adjusting to the enveloping darkness, caught the corner of a large desk. Pigeon-step by pigeon-step, for fear of risking a similar stumble, the Major edged towards the desk space until finally his outstretched arm clung to the corner. Placing his hand on top and feeling across the torn, green velvet baize, he felt amongst the dirt and tiny rubble rocks to where several ink-pens, pieces of paper, and envelopes lay. Something cold peaked his touch and made him jump. Thankfully it wasn't moving. It was actually metal and, on closer inspection, was a small set of keys. Perhaps, he thought, Meredith kept a pipe lighter or even a small torch within the desk drawers. Fumbling away, key by key, into the challenging tiny lock holes he patiently tried each of the keys one at a time before finally, the first drawer unlocked. His hands felt around inside. The coldness of a cartridge pen, the solidity of an inkpot, the sharp sting of a drawing pin until finally the pleasant rattle of a small cardboard box. The red phosphorous and powdered glass that made up the rough striking side of the box confirmed to Major Collingdale he had found matches.

The first match struck effortlessly and the sense of relief sent a warm glow over the Major before a minute's worth of flame burned itself out. Realising there were limited matches to strike and limited time to use the light once struck, Collingdale reached across the desk and procured a piece of paper. This time he struck the match and lit the paper. The light was far more ferocious as was the burn time and in those precious few seconds he spotted a stubby wax candle, the one Meredith would often use late at night, which had toppled off of the desk and was now on the floor. Searching across the desk once more for an object to light he fumbled a sealed envelope. Unable to pay any attention to its cover, he lit the corner and moved over to the candle. The envelope corner burned quickly but as soon as the candle was lit the Major blew the envelope out and tossed it back on to the desk. Now with more time, at the expense of the slowly reducing wick, Boyd Collingdale held the candle in front of him as the hot wax trickled down his wrist and bonded them together.

At first, he thought it had been the shadow of his own but a second glance through the flickering candlelight produced the shocking image of a grasping hand reaching out from a fallen exhibit case. The Major moved swiftly towards the claw-like hand and inadvertently to the source of the stench where he crunched insect after insect underfoot.

'Oh, good God.' He sighed under his moustache. 'I'm so sorry, Professor.'

In front of him lay the body of a man dressed in faultless linens, though now filthy and neglected. His face lay planted into the floor below and his body was overrun with creepy crawlies and critters. Perhaps this was how he would've wished to have gone, Collingdale considered. As he took a minute to step back from his colleague's corpse, he slipped on a crunch of material underfoot. Pulling it out and dusting it down, it was another straw hat.

'That's strange, why would he have two hats?' Collingdale asked himself. But then again, Meredith Malcolm was quirky and strange. Holding the candle aloft, he ran one last look over the Professor's body. He didn't have the strength to lift the exhibition case crushing it from on top. Linens from top to toe and from beneath the face on the floor a moustache presented itself. What was he thinking? Of course it was his old adversary. His hand outstretched in a final desperate cry for help. But what was that reflecting back, a gold band on his ring finger? Boyd hadn't known the Professor was a married man. How could he have not known that?

The candle wax ran its last drips down the Major's hand. He had no intention of spending the remaining hours of that night next to a corpse. For fear of creating another catastrophe, he moved across the broken glass and exhibits back to the safety of the desk just before the wick danced its final death. There he would wait until he could seek out light in the dawn.

Chapter 18

Sunset and dawn

Sunday evening had come swiftly in Ambledown. The excitement of pastures new and the accentuated fear from Lyle's attack had exhausted and petrified the young teenage girl, who had just days before been unceremoniously kidnapped from her loving Aunt Florrie in London.

Physically stuffed from the sumptuous marsh mutton stew she and her uncle had consumed in the company of the man-mountain Pop Braggan, Agatha was now safely tucked away in the drawing-room of 1a The Keep. Uncle Gideon as her guardian was now ruing his decision to leave her for a few moments in the company of Cecile and the serviceman at Le Chat Noir.

'It was a foolish, foolish thing to have done, Aggie,' Gideon said.

'I'm sorry, Uncle. I didn't mean to run off. Purrsia the cat just broke free and before I knew it I was ... well ...' Aggie began to cry, recollecting the vicious little wretch Lyle and his attempts to attack her.

'I didn't mean you, my love. It was foolish of me to have left you. No matter how much I trust Cecile. I'm truly sorry. Your mother would have killed me.' He shook his head. Disgusted with himself.

They cuddled each other for a moment both tearful and tired.

'I think an early night is in order, don't you?' Gideon suggested.

Aggie nodded, much safer now in the home spent during fond holidays as a child. But nevertheless not as secure as she'd felt at Florrie's in London. Ambledown had so many secrets still left for her to discover.

'Tomorrow you will start school,' Gideon advised to much protestation.

'But what if Lyle comes back when you're not there again?' Aggie responded, frowning at her uncle.

Gideon, who was feeling guilty enough, offered as much comfort as he could. 'Lyle is nothing more than a pint-sized bully and the commonest of thieves –' he began.

'A pint-sized bully who carries a knife,' Aggie interrupted.

'I've never seen him behave like that before,' Gideon continued. 'No doubt it was the result of too much ale, and besides my friends have taken care of him. Pop Braggan is his uncle and word would have reached him already. Pop will not allow Lyle back to Ambledown while you remain here. You have nothing to fear.'

Aggie could not be convinced. She turned her head away from Gideon and just scrunched herself up into a ball across the chaise lounge in his drawing-room. She stared into the crackling logs from the fireplace. It reminded her of looking out on the fires of London just before this all began. Thoughts lent themselves to that of her dear old Aunt Florrie and the relief that she was alive. Gideon had so much explaining to do. She couldn't believe he was immediately packing her off to school already.

A knock at the door broke the unpleasant silence between niece and uncle, as Gideon left the room to answer it. She lay there gazing into a ballet of flames as the spitting log sap popped and whizzed, and ever so faintly she recalled the distant cries of fire-engine bells as Florrie's voice hurried her along out of the attic. Her eyes drew heavy and slumber began to ensue.

'If you're going to fall asleep there, perhaps you'd like some company?' Gideon asked. He had returned with a worn-out apple box filled with old newspapers and rags.

As Aggie was poised to express that she would prefer an evening of isolation and staying snuggled in front of the blazing hearth, a small bundle of cloth was placed upon her. It was wriggling and writhing to join her under the blanket. A deep purring woke her attention as the hairless cat nuzzled its nose into hers.

'Purrsia!' She smiled, embracing the feline lovingly.

'He has no hair so it was lucky someone found him and brought him here. He could've perished in tonight's cold,' Gideon explained. 'Furless cats like these often do.'

'What happened to his fur? Is he sick?' Aggie asked concerned for the wrinkly old cat now purring in its sleep on her chest.

'Nothing wrong with that cat. It's just how the Sphinx are bred. They originate from a warmer climate,' Gideon said.

Aggie thought nothing of it and closed her eyes, comforted by her feline friend, and fell into a deep sleep.

Chapter 19
A new dawn

The dawn chorus came outside of the Museum and not before time. Inside,
Major Boyd Collingdale had hardly offered up a wink of sleep as he sat in
the dark laboratory waiting for any ray of morning light. He'd been too
petrified to move, and had been hoping an attentive employee would break
through into the insect-ridden tomb of Professor Meredith Malcolm. His
night had been interspersed with the creeping and crawling of six-legged
beasts that used his brow as a landing zone for their aerial ambitions. One
unfortunate bug had entwined itself in his wiry moustache and met a
somewhat unceremonious doom. Across his clenched palms longer, multi-
legged mini-monsters had taunted him and flirted with The Peacekeeper as
he sought to protect himself in the darkness. His mind wandered back to
the large pincers and stings on the Death-stalkers and how long it would
be until one of them made this night his last. His poor colleague lay there
as an edible feast for such creatures and having spotted the ring on his
finger the Major knew he would soon have to inform the Professor's loved
ones.

It was highly unlikely anyone would be in early, not after Sunday Harvest
and the general gorging that would have ensued. His only chance of early
parole from this laboratory gaol was a bright autumn morning and a
cascading ray to help him navigate the myriad obstacles that used to be the
entomology and Botanical department.

As the minutes turned to hours, the slightest dapple of early morning
sunlight splintered the fractured joists and speckled the desktop in front of
him. Much to his relief, not a single insect could be seen. Their twilight
hours were now gone for another day. The light was limited but he could
just make out a few items on the desk. A spilt inkpot with accompanying
quill splayed out near him. A couple of half-spherical paperweights,
amazingly not with creatures entombed but bright flower heads. There was
also the quarter-burned letter he had used to start off the candle. The
corner was completely ruined, and just charred soot edging remained
where it once presided. It was odd that it was perfectly left in the centre of

the desk amidst such destruction, and almost impeccably intact. The Major unfurled and moved his hands into the subtle sprinkling of light to pull it closer for further examination.

The front of the letter had been addressed to the Professor but the name and address had been struck through messily with ink and quill – no doubt the one now scattered across the desk.

At the top of the letter, just above the scribbled-out line of the addressee: *Professor Meredith Malco* – on account of the burned-out corner, it now read, *Major Boyd Colling*.

It was missing the *dale* suffix but as childlike as the hastily scribbled writing was it was definitely re-addressed to his self. The Major was completely perplexed. Why on earth would the Professor re-address a personal letter to him?

Still, with little light at his disposal and time on his hands, he decided to open the letter anyway. The paper was folded into three and as it unravelled, it was evident the whole left-hand side had been a victim of the match strike hour's prior. The sender's address was all but vanished. The content, however, was relatively well intact.

Dearest Professor Malco....

I believe yourself or ....

in grave danger.

Please contact me at yo.. ....

Yours sincerely

Professor G Belch......

Collingdale drew a huge breath and read the letter over and over again. Its message was clear if somewhat missing the burned-away content, Professor G Belch, whoever that was, was warning the Professor. And now Professor Meticulous Meredith Malcolm lay dead just feet away from him. Perhaps it wasn't an accident after all. Coincidence, maybe? An airstrike that happened to cover a more sinister event? Surely not. No air force in the world could pinpoint such a strike.

The sunrise couldn't come soon enough. The visibility in the laboratory was still too poor to examine the letter and envelope in more detail. The addressee's details may have been missing from the letter itself but once in the true light of day, he could examine it in far greater detail. Who was Professor G Belch?

'Sir? Sir, are you still in there?' came the welcome sound of two actuaries with fully charged battery torches that shone beams of light into the remains of the laboratory.

A full cheek puff of relief exhaled through the Major's fine moustache, which had seen a few insect invaders during that long night, came at last.

'Here, at the desk!' Collingdale called out. 'Shine your light over here.'

Through the fractured joists and plasterwork, over the fallen glass and exhibitions, the Major trod a weary path as he could finally find his way back. Clutching in one hand the letter addressed to Professor Malcolm and in the other The Peacekeeper.

'Have you been in there all night, sir?' one of them asked.

A solid nod came from the army man with The Peacekeeper now tucked under his right arm as he opened and re-read the letter. Looking at the two staff who were now at his disposal, he quickly formed a plan.

'Divide and conquer today,' he announced. 'Two actions to be concluded by the end of the day.' Pointing to the first person, a slim man, he ordered him to direct all staff who came back to work to immediately make their way to the laboratory. 'I have unfortunate news. A cadaver remains within this dark cavern. I fear it is our Professor. All staff are to continue the excavation and supporting structure of this area to ensure we have smooth access to the body and to make more sense of what has happened here.'

The first actuary scribbled notes furiously, nodded, and dutifully made their way to the Museum entrance to start directions. The second, shorter man, waited with pen in hand for the Major's next order.

'I need you to help me understand the origin of this letter,' he advised, unfolding the paper burned down one side.

The actuary lent forward and held the letter up. The light was still too hard to read anything with clarity.

'Leave it with me, Major. I have a few ideas but need to get this into the light.'

'You lose that on pain of death. Do you hear?' Collingdale barked.

The short man nodded, all too well-versed in the Major's style, then light-footed made they made their way through the cavernous halls of the Museum together.

Collingdale, exhausted from his sleepless and foodless night, composed himself and marched towards his office. He rarely entered it and preferred much more to be hands-on but only in his office did he have the ledger of the next of kin. There he would find Professor Malcolm's address and spouse's name before he made a trip he did not wish to make.

****

'Rise and shine, sleepyhead,' Gideon's enthusiastic charms echoed into Aggie's room. They were wasted on his niece so early in the morning. Purrsia the cat offered a disapproving 'Meow' as Gideon entered and sat down beside them, disturbing their perfect slumber. Nan followed close behind carrying a breakfast tray that had the rare luxury of both boiled egg & soldiers with crispy bacon. Both girl and cat were lured out of the warm blankets by the overpowering smell of deliciousness.

'A treat for a unique day,' Gideon enthused.

Aggie, who had never attended school, not in the traditional sense, did not share her uncle's enthusiasm. For as long as she could remember, Florrie had been primary carer and governess. She had been a teacher who was strict but fair. Her schooling had been that of structured reading, writing, and arithmetic as most modern staples demanded, and would often last from post-morning breakfast to midday. Afternoons allowed her to pursue more practical matters. Now, this is where her great aunt was somewhat of a revolutionary. Traditionally, needlecraft and pursuits designed to improve 'One's posture' were considered ideal for the so-called fairer sex. Aunt Florrie couldn't agree less. 'Absolute poppycock!' as she would say. So, in her matriarchal single-mindedness, each day of the week had dedicated themes and dedicated visiting teachers. Five different governesses supporting Florrie for the five days of the week, excluding weekends – of course.

Mondays began with Governess Fairfax, where practical training and physical exercise were employed to blow away the cobwebs of restful weekends. Afternoons alternated between modern languages and physical education. Of course, Florrie was too old to exhaust herself but would instead employee wilful experts in their fields. An ex-military man to run Aggie through her paces around Hyde Park, a professional fencer to teach her to parry the foil. She even remembered a sparring bout with a boxer from Bethnal Green, broken-nose Barry, although Florrie herself had admitted she might have been a little too young for that encounter. There had been so many different experts, Aggie could not remember them all but what she had preferred out of everything were cross-country runs. They were a tonic to the morning teachings that could so often drag and become repetitive.

Tuesdays with Miss Grace were dedicated to science and again where appropriate, her great aunt employed professionals for occasional visits. Aggie recalled vividly a faulty Bunsen burner in the basement, which almost blew up the house.

Religious education, cultures of the world, art, and art history were the Wednesday preserve of Miss Woes. It had always struck Aggie how the two worlds of art and religion were so often inadvertently intertwined, regardless of faith. On Thursdays, it was geography with Miss Fargo. Map reading, orientation, capital cities, and very rarely a visit to the Maritime Museums of Greenwich to understand how centuries of stargazing and pioneer had allowed humans to navigate the globe.

Finally, on Fridays, Miss Lovegood, and a full recap of the past four days where she was tested by Florrie as the five tutors gathered altogether just on that day. She feared Fridays the most and, in particular, letting them down.

It was safe to say that despite being a bright and attentive student she longed for the long runs her aunt rarely afforded her away from the house. It was during these jaunts she thought long and hard about almost everything, particularly her parents.

So now, after all these years of almost isolated teaching, she was actually going to embark on schooling, with other students of her own age, in a strange village, miles away from home. What's more, Lyle could be lying in wait in any passageway.

'Don't look so worried, Aggie. It really will not be that bad,' Gideon reassured her.

Aggie wasn't easily convinced. Gideon had still not explained the cloak-and-dagger essence of her arrival, and last night someone had sought to attack her. She felt nothing else could be so bad. She longed to see Florrie and yet, again, Gideon would not divulge anything other than she was still alive.

'I have a surprise for you!' Gideon exclaimed, and briefly left the room.

'Please, eat. Don't let get cold,' Nan told her in her unusual accent. 'If you don't eat, I will eat. Eggs are very rare thing now.'

Aggie was all too aware of what luxury this breakfast was. As privileged as her life had been with Florrie, there was still rationing, and eggs, bread, and bacon commanded great prices. Particularly if they were procured on the black market.

Aggie dipped a soldier into the succulent deep yellow yolk and savoured its rich taste. Purrsia the cat had managed to snaffle a strand of fatty pork rind, and it hung like a mouse's tail from his mouth and whiskers.

'Here it is,' Gideon said enthusiastically as he presented a grey set of clothes in front of his niece.

'What are those?' she replied in a reluctant tone, mouth half full.

'What are these?' he replied indignantly. 'This is your school uniform.'

He held aloft the clothing for all to see. In front of him was a grey jacket, its lapels piped with a blue and white edging. The breast pocket had a dark shadow where once a school badge had been displayed but was now no longer present. A skirt, ankle-length, was also grey but just below the waistline, a band of elasticated blue ran around it. A white collarless shirt accompanied it, as did a straw boater that was frayed at the edges and had definitely seen better days.

'It's vile,' Aggie replied.

'It's Ambledown Priory colours,' Gideon replied defensively. 'I wore these colours, as did your mother. You should be proud.'

'She wore those colours?'

'Your mother wore *these* colours. That's right.' Her uncle accentuated the fact they had actually belonged to her mother.

Aggie paused. The light bulb suddenly flickered in her head while fear enveloped her. She started scrabbling around looking for the blue velvet box and magnifying glass it protected inside. The only item she had owned of her mother's she had forgotten about it for the second time in one day.

'Don't worry, it's safe,' Gideon advised his niece knowingly.

'I want it. It is mine.'

'That it is, but I think for today I will keep it safe. Can't risk losing it on your first day at school.'

'And what if I refuse to go to school?' Aggie argued back.

'Then I'll refuse to tell you where it is.'

'I'll go to the police.'

'And tell them what, Aggie? Your own uncle kidnapped you from bomb-ridden London and brought you to the peace and quiet of the country?'

'Mysteriously kidnapped me, more like. And if that's what it takes. After all, you don't even want people knowing we're related. Do you?'

'They won't pay any attention to you. There's a war on, child. Don't you realise?'

'Don't you realise all you do is treat me like a small *child*. I have faced air-raids almost every night in London. I'm not five years old!'

The instant agitated volley from the teenager was unexpected.

Gideon recalled how quickly his twin and himself would fly into sibling spats at the drop of a hat. His niece, orphaned and isolated with Florrie for so long still possessed her mother's unbreakable spirit and, unsurprisingly, after the past few days she'd had, was not in the frame of mind to be agreeable to his every decision. Gideon retracted from a full-on argument.

'I'm your guardian, Aggie. I'm just trying to protect you,' Gideon responded in a more conciliatory tone.

'How? By keeping secrets from me, and never telling me what is really going on?'

'It's compli–'

'–cated?' Aggie shouted, finishing her uncle's sentence.

A verbal joust with his niece who quite clearly was everything her mother had been would get him nowhere.

'Fine, you can have your precious box. If you lose it, then it's yours to lose. But I have important business to conclude and I cannot babysit you all day. You're right, you're not a child anymore. School will keep you safe. It's up to you.'

'I don't need babysitting,' Aggie instantly responded.

'That's absolutely fine. School it is.' He smiled back calmly.

Gideon left the room. Aggie pulled at her strange new haircut and let out a frustrated scream. Purrsia fled in fear.

Nan, who had sat back quietly during the entire remonstration picked up the school clothes and held them up in front of the adolescent girl.

'Your mother wear these. Her initials are inside.'

Aggie's temporary anger subsided as the housekeeper passed the clothes over. Aggie turned the jacket inside out and began scouring the labels for ink or stitched initials.

'Your uncle loves you very much. He lost his sister, he was her twin, and he had known her all his life. And he worries every moment of day he lose you too.'

Aggie was listening but not responding, belligerence being a common family trait.

'Perhaps you go to school? You be safe,' Nan concluded, removing the breakfast tray as she left the room.

Aggie searched in vain but couldn't find any initials inside the grey suit jacket. Instead, she decided to try it on for size. She wondered how old her mother had been when she had first worn it. By the condition of the hat, it had certainly been worn a lot.

Gideon was seated in his parlour. In front of him a series of cartographer's tools and ordnance maps were placed across the floor; far too big for any desk. Two taps came from the door.

'Come in,' he answered.

'How do I look?' Aggie asked.

'Apart from our attempts at a haircut, you look quite the part. You wear it well, Aggie. It suits you. Well, the cuffs are obviously too long, but apart from that, perfect.' Uncle Gideon approached his niece and helped turn the cuffs inside out. 'This is yours,' he said, handing her the blue velvet box she had coveted so much during the argument. 'Be sure to look after it.' He smiled.

'I will,' she replied before tip-toeing up to place a small peck on his cheek.

There was a double thud at the front door.

'Giddy, Giddy! It's freezing out 'ere. Urry Up!' came Eric Peabody's cockney chime.

'Your escort party has arrived.' Gideon squirmed at his niece

Aggie raised an eyebrow to her uncle as he proceeded to open the door.

Eric's exuberant face was already peering through the letterbox as the door opened. Eric, his older sister Elizabeth, and younger sister Gemima were huddled on the stairs, breathing into their clasped hands and trying to keep warm.

'It's brass monkeys out 'ere today. You got a coat?' Eric asked Aggie.

'I'm not sure. Have I got a coat, Uncle?' Aggie asked

'Let's just check. Sorry while I keep out the chill,' Gideon responded, closing the door to the freezing Peabodys.

'Charming!' Eric shouted from outside.

'Remember, for everybody's sake, I am not your uncle. Just your evacuation host. OK?'

'If you say so,' Aggie replied nonchalantly.

'Aggie, it's very serious. We have a lot of history here and I cannot risk some people knowing. I will tell you as much as I can tonight. I promise you. Everything will become clear and Cairo will be explained in full.'

Aggie welcomed the news but was nervous as to what Gideon had held back. Despite her years of demanding answers from her great aunt, who barely even acknowledged the facts, she had never really thought through the consequences of such revelations. For the time being, it allowed her to take her mind off of last night's encounter with Lyle and focus her thoughts on questioning Gideon after school.

'So, what's my surname? I'm bound to be asked my surname. It's a bit peculiar if we were not related but we had the same name,' she said.

'You're right. It's Chatsmore. Agatha Chatsmore. If you forget just think of all those cats from Cecile's. Lots of them – *More* – and the French for cat – *chat*. Chats-more. Simple.'

Aggie just smiled and opened the door. Wearing her mother's slightly oversized uniform and a long grey cloak her uncle had just provided her, she alighted the stairs to where the Peabodys were waiting.

'Urry up then!' Eric shouted. 'Don't want any of the Brothers to cane me for lateness. Again!' he laughed and skipped off with the eagerness of a young boy but the face of an adult man.

'Ignore him, Agatha. He's just Eric,' came Elizabeth's voice.

'And you're Elizabeth, right?' Aggie replied.

'Well-remembered. And this is our little Gem.'

'Hello, Gemima,' Aggie said to the much smaller girl.

As they descended the cobbled gradient from The Keep to the Steep, it was abundantly clear that the village of Ambledown had much more life in it as people went about their weekday business than the peacefulness of a Sunday after service. Although the Poacher had no doubt had a brisk and eventful Sunday, much in line with Aggie's recent misadventure, the rest of Ambledown were unlikely to have any idea what had transpired on the previous evening. Aggie was still sceptical of the village and glanced over her shoulders every few yards.

'Don't worry,' Elizabeth reassured her. 'Lyle has been taken care of.'

Aggie managed a superficial smile. Elizabeth must have the full confidence of her uncle if she was her lead escort and he had told her of last night's incident.

'To be honest, Aggie. Lyle is the least of your worries,' Elizabeth advised.

'I beg your pardon,' Aggie responded nervously.

'You're yet to meet the Huntington-Smythes. They make Lyle look like the wretched pickpocket he really is.' Elizabeth laughed humorously.

'I don't really understand. Why should I worry about them?' Aggie responded, this time less agitated and more intrigued.

'They're the true monsters of Ambledown,' Elizabeth concluded.

'They're yuk!' Gemima piped in.

'But don't worry, Aggie, you can decide for yourself now.' Elizabeth smiled.

They had stopped south of the Steep, past the Poacher, past Le Chat Noir and where the river ambled under a large stone bridge. In front of them was a gleaming white colonial manor house. It was so out of place amongst the scattered two-up two-down fisherman cottages it was almost as if it had been newly built overnight and from an entirely different country altogether.

'Voila, Aggie,' Elizabeth announced. 'The Schoolhouse, formerly the Bailiffs-court of the Huntington-Smythes.'

Aggie said nothing. Preferring instead to follow the girls up the stone stairs just as Eric pipped them to the post and rushed in before them.

'Prepare yourself for anything, Aggie. Never trust a Huntington-Smythe,' Elizabeth forewarned her.

Aggie just gulped. The first time attending a real school, and before her first lesson being warned of the terrible enemies to expect inside.

The schoolhouse still had black iron railings accompanying the stone stairs leading to its impressive oak door. Aggie thought all of those had been taken down to smelt in order to form munitions. Obviously not in Ambledown. They offered a frosty chill as she made her way up the stairs closely following the Peabody clan.

On entering the recently converted courthouse, she felt warmth from the heat inside, much to her surprise. She had sensed a level of trepidation and frostiness and expected the large building to be old. However, the entrance hall was floored with varnished mahogany and a large Aspidistra dominated the table at the centre of it.

Two corridors ran opposing routes left and right from behind the table and it's natural curve split the directions of boys and girls. Each entranceway to the corridors was manned with either one of the 'Sisters' from the local convent, in full wimple and shroud, they educated the girls; or a 'brother' from the Priory, fully cloaked in Cossack from head to toe, and they taught the boys.

'Surname?' directed the sister on duty towards Agatha.

'Umm Chatsmore,' Agatha responded, slightly delayed but no more nervous than any other new evacuee.

'And your first?' the Sister continued.

'Agatha. But I prefer Aggie.'

'Well, Miss Agatha Chatsmore, you are not on the register.'

'That's because she was only evacuated this weekend,' interrupted Eric from the boys' line before a swift hand from the duty brother clipped the back of his ear.

'Nevertheless. You must see the governess before entering class. We require only healthy children to attend,' the Nun finished and led her down the girls' corridor to a small waiting room.

Aggie frowned back at Elizabeth, who shrugged her shoulders. The room was relatively bare. It smelt of iodine and had the sterile chill of a tiny doctor's clinic. Two green plastic chairs faced each other in the centre but nothing else. There was a small window, no more then a letterbox-sized intersection honed from the wall. It allowed Aggie a glimmer of outside light while she sat and waited nervously.

Chapter 20
Crossroads

The stench of human effluence after a long night within the underground was enough to deter even the hardiest of vermin. Nathaniel Noone had lost many parts of his human make up but his sense of smell was not one of them. In fact, he often felt it over-compensated for his damaged ears and eyelids. He baulked at the smell as he descended to catch the Tube back to Piccadilly. Now, after the commotion of Draper's disappearance, he wanted to revisit the area again. But first, he needed an expert's assistance.

As he sat there, gently rocking to the roll and camber, the darkness and intermittent light jogged his memory to the photograph of Draper and the mysterious markings under the violet light. The train journey several nights earlier and the ancient chambers beneath Giza flashed images into his mind as the lights of the Tube stations hurried by. Whatever or whoever was at the heart of all of this, he was convinced it linked back to the tragedies of Cairo, fourteen years past. However, only one person might believe him. The majority would not. He was determined to uncover the truth.

Noone was a man who slept little nowadays but the exuberances of the past seventy-two hours had exhausted him. He rested his eyes and gazed into the dark shadows. As darkness encroached on his dreams, candlelight and flame lit up stone corridors. Masked men, cloaked in robes, danced in circles of fire. The fire grew and flames burned stronger until he bolted upright from his temporary slumber. A bead of sweat announced itself on his brow. His moans had attracted interest from strangers who discreetly stared between fingers and over papers upon the grotesque within their carriage. Moving along carriages, he finally found the darker confines of solitude. He was happiest in the shadows.

Figures in the darkness watched with intent as he dozed off once more into a nightmarish sleep.

*****

A stretched yawn welcomed Professor Malcolm back into the spanking new laboratory at the Silvera Institute. He had slept well but once he had fully come round, a form of selective amnesia would not allow him to remember everything from the past few days. He could recall the room itself and the excellent facilities bestowed upon him. He could also recall the influence that the violet beam had over the scorpions and their would-be Scarabidae prey. It was astonishing and still extremely worrying. He remembered the papyrus puzzle and the accommodating Mr Louds. He also remembered he had an important part to play in helping Louds and the elusive Dr Mialora.

The person who he failed to recall was the Amazonian figure who had initiated his journey and influenced his decision the prior evening. Sabine Erket had been kind enough to leave him a timely reminder, but it was unlikely he would join the dots.

On the table where he had spent the prior evening studying the amber-glossed papyrus, three new items were left to assist him. The first was the pencil-thin torch that Mr Louds had used to demonstrate the influencing beam of light on the arachnid subjects. The second was a small marble pestle and mortar, which had a selection of crushed, dried leaves within it. The third and final item was the large crystallised piece of glass. Inside sat the deep-red fossilised remains of the large Scarlet Scarab. For a brief moment, a definitive image of the Scarab glowing as hot as fire burned brightly in his mind. The supercharged filament throbbing, pulsating. Then the image was gone. It was dreamlike, almost like sleepwalking, the item prompted the recollection, which his mind wasn't fully in control of.

Grabbing the torch, he focused the violet beam onto the Scarab, but it did not react. No ignition or spark of red light as he expected. He tried several times, each with the same result, before setting the fossilised rock back down.

'Well, that didn't work, Meredith,' he scolded himself, scratching his head. 'Perhaps you should focus on something you know,' he chastised himself politely.

Removing the pestle from the mortar he dispensed of the grinding tool so he could examine the leaves. Most people would have ground the leaves straight away but he did not fully understand their purpose so, if he could identify them first, it may aid with their part of the puzzle.

The sun shone brightly through the pinnacle prism above as Meticulous Meredith Malcolm began flicking through Culpepper's weighty tome of illustrated fauna. He was certain these leaves were not of any local species. As the beams of the rare British sunshine illuminated the laboratory it spread across gilded surfaces, absorbing into those that could be penetrated, illuminating the darkest corners.

*****

In his rarely occupied office, Major Boyd Collingdale discarded the paper bureaucracy that so often littered his in-tray and searched amongst ledgers for the *Next of Kin* portfolio. The leather-bound booklet, alphabetically documented by surname, weighed heavy in his hands. As he turned the pages to 'M', his thoughts turned to the fact that all the hours bickering and verbal butting with the Professor may have been better served finding common ground. It was too late now and soon he would be on his way to deliver the devastating news to Malcolm's spouse.

Malcolm, Meredith (Prof) – read the title in the ledger. Following his finger across the page, the Major passed over the Professor's address and to the 'Marital Status' column. 'Single, unmarried' it read. Collingdale squinted at the page. He then started over and re-ran finger form west to east. Single, unmarried, came the same answer.

'I say, you!' Collingdale shouted out at an unsuspecting actuary who was passing by. Thrusting the ledger forward, the Major barked his orders, 'Can you tell me Professor Malcolm's marital status?'

The actuary took the ledger and repeated the process the Major had already undertaken.

'It's single, unmarried, sir,' came the response.

'And when was this last updated?' Collingdale asked once more.

'There's a monthly census on personal details, sir. No more then three or four weeks, I would say.'

'Very well, carry on,' Collingdale concluded, which was almost as much as a thank you from the military man.

'Curiouser and Curiouser,' he mumbled to himself stroking his moustache.

'I beg your pardon, sir?' came a voice back, causing the Major to jump.

It was the short actuary he had sent off to examine the letter and envelope earlier.

'Don't people knock anymore?' the Major shouted back, still musing on Professor Malcolm's marital status.

'Sorry, sir. I just thought you would be interested in this. I believe I have located Doctor G. Belch.'

'Already? That's quick work,' Collingdale responded positively.

'Quite the coincidence, sir, in fact.'

'How so?' questioned the Major.

'Well, the nature of the letter suggested he knew the Professor or at least had an understanding of him.'

'Yes, yes,' Collingdale interrupted.

'So, I checked the register of incoming correspondence and any donations made to the Museum.'

'Yes, and…?' Collingdale replied already impatient.

'It seems a Doctor Gideon Belchambers donated a giraffe's head to the Museum only recently. Dr G Belch…you see?'

'Bit of a leap, isn't it?' the Major questioned.

'I would agree, sir, if I hadn't spotted this,' the actuary replied, holding the envelope to the light. Where the fold of the envelope had been gummed to the underside, he raised the paper flap. The light pierced a watermark only just visible to the naked eye.

The Crown Inn, Coaching House, Ambledown, Sussex.

'Dr Gideon Belchambers, Ambledown, Sussex. Sir, that's what the register of donations reads.'

'More than a coincidence indeed,' Collingdale agreed. 'Get him on the wire,' he then ordered.

'I'm afraid neither the doctor or the inn are contactable, sir. I've tried several times already.'

'Sussex, you say?' the Major asked.

'Just over an hour or so by car, sir.'

'Very well. With me then.' Collingdale donned his peaked cap, placed The Peacekeeper under his right arm and began his quick march to Entomology. 'Now, listen up!' he boomed to all the workers who were busily shoring up the joists and beams of Professors Malcolm's beloved department. 'You have four hours until my return and by then, this area must be safe. Electrical lighting must be available to illuminate the area but do not touch or move the corpse you will inevitably make an acquaintance with soon enough.' Then, with an about-turn and stomp of his right foot, he marched down the corridors of the Museum to commandeer a vehicle. 'With me, soldier,' he shouted at the actuary.

'I'm not a soldier, sir. I'm a clerk.'

Collingdale rolled his eyes and strode forward.

Chapter 21
Priory Colours

Aggie had waited almost half an hour and exhausted all avenues exploring the small cupboard-like room with the two opposing green plastic chairs. The letterbox window offered nothing more than a grubby, oblique, view of the sky. Finally, the door swung open and in came an older gentleman, half-moon glasses, balding and with a stethoscope around his neck. He looked slightly dishevelled and smelt of a previous night's indulgence of alcohol.

Accompanying him was a much younger woman, in her early twenties; at least that was Aggie's estimation. Her blonde hair was pulled back into a bun and round spectacles rested across her lightly freckled nose. She was dressed in a high-collared white blouse and ankle-length black dress. Not dissimilar to Florrie's daily attire – 'Victorian governess' style as Aggie nicknamed it. Her welcoming smile was the opposite of the nasal grunts from the older man.

'Good morning, my dear,' she said brightly. 'I am Miss Dove, Priory governess and this is Dr Beckworth.'

The doctor was coughing and spluttering so much he was more likely to infect his patients than do any good. Aggie recognised him as one of the ruddy-faced barflies from the Poacher the previous evening. Miss Dove seemed far too young for a governess. She had always imagined them as gnarly old spinsters, battle-axes, matron types. Having not attended a 'real' school, perhaps they were different. Miss Dove had a perkiness to her, a certain warmth, that Aggie felt she could trust. Not as she had imagined at all.

'Dr Beckworth just needs to check you over for any sign of illness. I'll stay with you for the examination,' Miss Dove explained.

The doctor hocked an ale-smothering breath on his stethoscope before proceeding. The chill of the metal made Aggie flinch.

'Breathe in,' he spluttered. 'Breathe out,' he spluttered again, and then repeated. 'Chest is fine,' Dr Beckworth announced. Turning Aggie around, he repeated the process on her back. 'Lungs seem fine too.' He coughed and wheezed. 'But what's this bruising?' he asked, pushing his glasses fully onto his nose to focus. 'Have you been beaten, young lady? Suffered a fall maybe?' he enquired.

'Pardon? No!' Aggie responded with incredulity. Although she had seen her fair share of conflict within the past few days, she couldn't remember anything specific in reference to her back and was not going to divulge how she came to be there.

Miss Dove's curiosity peaked. She stood behind the doctor who was examining between her shoulder blades.

'I don't think that's bruising, Doctor,' Miss Dove expressed. 'I believe it's a birthmark.'

'I didn't know that I had a birthmark!' Aggie said, surprised.

'Just here, between the shoulder blades, a small purple crescent. Like a smile,' Miss Dove explained, running her finger along it.

It was not a pronounced mark, nothing like a mole, and even if it had been, the position between shoulders is too awkward to easily run a finger over. It was practically impossible to see in a mirror unless you had an owl's neck to rotate almost one hundred and eighty degrees. No wonder Aggie was unaware. Florrie had never mentioned it either.

'I never knew,' Aggie concluded. One more question for Uncle Gideon, she thought.

'OK, Dr Beckworth. I assume that's a clean bill of health?' Miss Dove ushered.

The doctor nodded as he finally directed his splutter into a handkerchief.

'Agatha, you can follow me to class. Doctor, thank you for your assistance,' advised Miss Dove, politely directing him out.

As Aggie and her new teacher saw the doctor to the Aspidistra in the entrance lobby, an elderly home guard hobbled into the doorway.

'Dr Beckworth, you are needed down at Braggan Brook. There's a body been found.' The man wheezed, short of breath.

Aggie looked nervously at Miss Dove, all memory of her near-miss the previous evening flooding back to her. The colour drained from her face.

'Are you OK, Agatha? You look most peculiar,' Miss Dove enquired

'I've come over a little strange, Miss.'

'Would you like a cup of tea before I introduce you to the class?'

'Yes, please.' Aggie nodded and followed Miss Dove to her quarters.

'Do you take sugar, Agatha?' asked the accommodating Miss Dove.

'Two, please.'

'What is it, dear? Did you hear the gentleman mention a body?'

'Yes, sort of,' Aggie nervously replied.

'Don't worry. I'm sure it's nothing to concern yourself with. The brook runs into the River Amble and it's estuarial,' Miss Dove reassured her.

Aggie wasn't really sure what that meant and gave a perplexed look back.

'It means the tides drive the waters up and down. All sorts of items get washed up into Ambledown. That's why the smugglers used to love it. Last year, an unexploded bomb made its way all the way up. Imagine the palaver that caused at the time,' said Miss Dove as she finished with a smile.

Aggie managed to smirk, but the mention of a body only managed to remind her of recent perils.

'Is there something you'd like to talk about?' Miss Dove persisted.

'I'm fine,' Aggie responded.

'You can always talk to me anytime anything bothers you, OK?' Miss Dove reassured her.

'OK,' Aggie replied.

'In that case, you better drink up and we'll meet your new classmates.'

Aggie finished her tea and followed Miss Dove back down the corridor leading to the girls' wing.

'Take a deep breath,' Miss Dove advised. 'The sisters usually insist on parading you at the front of the class on your first day. But don't worry, you'll be fine.'

Aggie inhaled through her nose and filled her lungs.

Miss Dove opened the door for her.

'Ahh. Miss Chatsmore. Do join us,' came the authoritative voice from the nun at the front. 'Full bill, I take it, Miss Dove?'

'She's very healthy, Sister Harvey,' Miss Dove responded although the nun and the teacher strained politeness to one another.

'Thank you, Miss Dove,' the nun curtly acknowledged. She then quickly closed the door on her colleague and beckoned Aggie to the front of the room.

Not a lot of love lost there, by the looks of things, Aggie thought to herself.

'I see you are sporting *Priory* colours, Miss Chatsmore, if what, somewhat, old,' the nun continued, pointing towards Aggie's blazer.

'My…umm…host gave them to me. I wouldn't really know,' Aggie said quietly. Remembering not to divulge any family ties.

'And who is your host, may I ask?' Sister Harvey persisted.

For a moment Aggie had to stop herself leading with the word uncle and it seemed so peculiar to add his surname.

'Gideon Belchambers,' Aggie said.

A small round of oohs and ahhs came from the girls. Aggie looked around at the commotion, catching Elizabeth's eye. The frown that came back suggested she kept quiet and didn't really react.

'Quiet!' Sister Harvey exalted with a thundering clap. All the girls sat bolt upright.

Aggie, meanwhile, was observing the class. It was a mix of ages and maturities, five-year-olds through to mid-teens, as well as a mix of those in the local Priory colours and those without. There was distinct segregation of the Priory locals to the left-hand side, from the teacher's perspective. Uniforms pristine and coordinated. Elizabeth and Gemima Peabody sat on the dishevelled right amongst other girls whose makeshift uniforms and mismatched socks were as much at odds with one another as they were their Priory peers.

From the left, an immaculately dressed young lady placed her hand in the air.

'Yes, Ms Huntington-Smythe ?' Sister Harvey asked.

'Sister,' she started in an assured manner. 'As our newcomer, Miss Chatsmore, is sporting our colours, will she be placed amongst the Priory girls?'

Aggie looked towards Elizabeth with a puzzled look. Once again she was met with a negative frown and subtle head twist suggesting it was not wise.

'The choice is simple,' the sister replied. 'There are two spare seats and Miss Chatsmore can decide for herself.'

Aggie felt the eyes of the class all burn into her at once. From the left, the flattering debutante lashes and glinting pearly whites beamed back at her. From the right, Elizabeth and Gemima looked on like eager, doe-eyed pups. The rest looked angry as if revenge for the wrong decision was more important then the decision itself.

Had Elizabeth not warned Aggie on their morning journey she was sure she would have yielded to the flattery from the Priory girls. The evacuees, to be frank, were unappealing. All dirt and malnourishment. However, Gideon trusted the Peabodys and, therefore, her decision was made.

Walking down the centre of the class, she approached Miss Huntington-Smythe and held out her hand. 'Thank you,' Aggie said and was met with a huge beaming smile from the ladies on the left. 'But I do not originate from Ambledown. So perhaps I should sit over here.'

Miss Huntington-Smythe spited the handshake and looked forward smiling. The Priory girls swiftly followed suit as if Aggie no longer existed.

Aggie, awkwardly, made her way towards Elizabeth and took the chair that sat adjacent to her.

Under her breath, Elizabeth whispered to her new friend, 'You've just made a huge enemy.' Elizabeth giggled. 'It was the right choice, believe me. But watch your back. We'll be watching it too.'

'Quiet!' came the thunderous voice and clap from Sister Harvey as she approached the chalkboard to recommence her lessons.

Aggie glanced sideways at Huntington-Smythe whose stone-cold glare met her halfway. Day two in Ambledown, enemy number two confirmed.

Chapter 22
Friends and foes

The corridors of Whitehall allowed only those with level three clearance into their privileged confines. Thompson, by default of Draper's disappearance, was now allowed such privilege. Clutching the papyrus plant in one hand, he left the black Rolls Royce and entered via the fortified sentry from Downing Street.

Number Ten was the well known and obvious address bestowed on the Prime Minister. Number Eleven the Chancellor. But who knew of Number Seven?

On entering 'Seven', he was subject to the customary pat down, identity check, and had to relinquish any firearms. However, the small pot plant, which by any standards was a peculiar item to be carrying around in wartime, was not subject to scrutiny. A quick once-over and it was dismissed as non-threatening. Assumptions that it was harmless, perhaps due to its organic nature, may have contributed to how it had penetrated *the Department* in the first place. It proved to Thompson one thing. How easy the infiltration had been, and it was time to demonstrate this to the senior ranks.

'Enter,' came the gravelled voice from behind the polished wooden door.

Thompson was gambling with his career as he prepared for his next stunt. He drew a large breath and then exhaled with gusto before entering *The Master's* office at Number Seven, Downing Street.

Cupped within his right hand, he carried the papyrus plant hidden behind him as he proceeded. His first observation of the room was that it was dark. The walls were covered in padded burgundy leather and once the door closed behind him, he could not distinguish the entrance from any other part of the room. There were no windows, just a single reading light with emerald Bakelite shade that shone down on the writing desk. A brass nameplate, the only other item to keep the light company in the stark room, simply read, W. Waverley

Sitting within a swivelling chair, their back turned to anyone entering through that threshold, was Draper's superior, The Master. A wispy thread of cigarette smoke presented itself and danced vertically just above the dark head of hair only just visible from the large reclining chair's back. It was well-hidden against the dimly lit office.

'Afternoon, sir. I'm Thompson,' he said nervously. He stood with hands behind his back, masking the pot plant.

There was no immediate response. Thompson surveyed the room while the silence oppressed him. He scanned for the quickest exit. There were no windows and, on the face of it, there were no obvious doors, apart from the one he had just entered through – if he could find it again – but no obvious means of escape.

'I'm sorry to tell you this, sir. Draper is missing,' Thompson continued.

An ambitious individual, he had hoped that meeting a senior ranking officer would have been in more positive circumstances and not to tell them he had misplaced his superior.

Several minutes passed and Thompson's patience wore thin.

'Mr Waverley?' Thompson asked.

There was still no response. Just another plume of cigarette smoke discharged into the air.

'Wink? Wink Waverley? That is your name, isn't it? Draper told me that you would be reassured if I knew your nickname and it could've only come from him, sir.'

A coarse laugh followed and stunned Thompson. Then calmly W. Waverley responded, 'Wink is indeed my nickname.' She laughed, exhaling the final cigarette smoke. 'But rarely does one hear it to one's face. Although technically you're talking to the back of my head.' Wink Waverley spluttered and laughed at the same time.

Thompson rolled his eyes; luckily she wasn't staring right at him, as she would have seen his skin turning as burgundy as the surrounding walls. Draper had never explained Wink Waverley was female. What a fool Thompson now felt, having referred to her as 'sir' several times already.

'I'm terribly embarrassed, ma'am,' Thompson declared apologetically.

Wink Waverley, still very much amused, spun around and edged her face into the light. 'By the looks of your face, Draper failed to mention my missing eye too.' She smiled back at Thompson's horrified face.

Draper *had* failed to mention that too. Wink was an awful nickname. Who on earth thought that was a good idea? Fortunately, the void and its imitation glass eye were currently covered with a black leather patch. Something she shared in common with the recently encountered Nathaniel Noone.

'But Wink? As a nickname, seriously?' he thought to himself. Did he really know Draper at all? His right-hand still clutched the papyrus. He removed his hat and ran his left hand through his hair. Wink Waverley in the meantime meandered around the desk, grabbed Thompson assuredly with both hands and stared straight up at him. There must have been a foot in height between them but he was clearly the subordinate.

'For pity's sake, Thompson. I was just beginning to like your rare honesty.' She addressed him in an authoritative tone, no longer laughing. 'If this gets you hot under the collar then Draper may not have chosen his successor wisely.'

'I see,' he replied. Then regretted his choice of words. Taking a moment to compose himself, Thompson stepped forward and placed the papyrus pot plant under the beam of the desk lamp.

'I hope that's not a gift.' Wink smirked. 'I hate plants.'

'It's a gift of sorts, ma'am. Or it can be a spy,' Thompson advised.

Wink's ears pricked up. 'Really. A spy?' she responded interestedly. 'And you thought to bring it in here?'

Thompson was just about to reassure her that it posed no immediate threat when the wall to the left of the desk turned on its axis and in strode a man in full military regalia.

'Maam, I need your signature and support on these papers,' he bellowed as he strode. He hardly took a second glance at Thompson and left as soon as he had placed the folder with the papers in it upon Wink's desk. The briefest recognition between himself and Wink took place before he was gone through the door wall and the room was enclosed in padded burgundy leather once again.

Thompson, on the other hand, had paid much more attention to this interruption. The man had a small crescent-shaped scar above his left eye. He had seen him before in a photograph, just hours earlier.

'Who was that?' Thompson enquired.

'You've never met Commander Malling before?' Wink asked.

Thompson shook his head.

'He has the unenviable task of managing all the air-raid warning systems and ensuring Britain blacks out at night. Poor Malling.' She coughed as she spoke. 'One hell of a responsibility.'

At that moment he wished he had confiscated Noone's photograph and torches to present to Wink Waverley. Though he wasn't sure who he could really trust.

'So, Thompson, tell me about our little green spy,' Wink said, sparking up another cigarette.

'If you tell me about your eye,' he countermanded.

Emboldened by the fact that Malling could be the key to Draper's disappearance, he now questioned the entire situation he was forced into. Scepticism was the spy's favourite ally. The problem with espionage and spying is that trust was imperative and spies rarely trusted anyone. A simple paradox.

'Why? And be honest,' Wink asked.

'I need to know if I can trust you,' Thompson replied.

'You couldn't possibly know that,' Wink replied unreservedly. 'That's all part of the cycle of deception and lies we tell ourselves. You know that as well as I. So, I will tell you how I came to lose my eye and you can decide to trust me or not. I will, in turn, understand if you are very smart or very stupid.'

'Very well,' Thompson agreed.

'I was nine years old and on a hunt with my father,' Wink explained.

'You were shot?' Thompson interrupted

'No, I wasn't shot. The horse I was riding was spooked when a pheasant flew out from the bracken. He bolted. I was thrown into the hedgerow but unfortunately for my eye, it met with a Hawthorn bush. Pierced it through to the cornea.'

'Good grief. That must have been agony,' Thompson said sympathetically.

'Excruciating. The irony was the look upon my father's face when he found me. It was far more painful for him to see his little girl in such distress. God bless him.' Wink Waverley's voice lowered a little and her shoulders slumped.

'And you don't mind the fact people call you Wink?' Thompson asked.

'My first name is actually Winifred, you imbecile. I was nicknamed Wink and had perfect twenty-twenty long before that damned bush took my eye,' she replied angrily, sparking up another cigarette. 'I'll be damned if a plant was to define me.'

'Sorry,' Thompson apologised.

'So, you believe me?' Wink changed tone, suggesting she may be lying. 'Are you actually going to show me this plant?'

Thompson was convinced the emotions he had just witnessed could not be improvised, no matter how deceptive a person could be.

'This is a papyrus plant,' Thompson began. 'A gift from a colleague to Draper. Only this plant has ears, and I believe it may be able to talk too.'

Wink moved closer towards the green leaves under the light on the desk.

'You sound insane. Do you realise that?' Wink laughed.

'Well, I am an imbecile, ma'am.' Thompson smirked.

Wink Waverley then took and smashed the plant pot on her desk. Within the soil, a sequence of small electrical wires ran outward like artificial roots with smaller circuits of metal with plastic at the end. Thompson was no expert but had taken time to examine it during his journey to Whitehall.

'I assumed that was a battery ma'am. I disconnected it en route,' he advised, pointing to a metal disc. 'And I believe, by watering the plant it somehow empowers the circuit. Not sure how the wires work but no doubt a microphone and audio device of some description'

Wink Waverley pulled out a drawer from her desk. Inside was a telephone. She picked it up and dialled a single number.

'All plants to be removed from all parliamentary offices, departments, war rooms, and areas of special interest. Today!' she barked.

And with that, wheels were set in motion across the country to execute Wink's order.

'I think we'll have to send this to the boffins at Bletchley to look at. If it is what you say it is, they will uncover its secrets. Now, tell me about Draper; the facts of what happened and the circumstances surrounding it, including any of your own theories.'

'I'll start with Jennifer James,' Thompson began

Chapter 23

The body in the brook

No sooner had Sister Harvey's lesson reconvened than battle had begun. Henrietta Huntington-Smythe, to give her full name, glared at Aggie and with her followed the Priory sisterhood.

'Ignore them,' Elizabeth offered.

'I intend to,' Aggie whispered back.

The attentive Sister Harvey had ears like a fox and rarely did anything escape her attention.

'Miss Chatsmore,' she said, still scribing on the board. 'It is common courtesy in my classroom to pay attention and refrain from idle gossip.'

Smythe and her cronies giggled a little, but it was hardly worthy of note. Aggie was amazed that the ageing sister could've heard her in the first place.

'This morning, Class, we have a simple assignment. Weights and measures.' The sister punctuated the weights and measures as she underlined the words on the board.

The class looked abundantly confused at each other.

'So, quite simply, this is a lesson in mathematics,' the sister continued. 'I would like you all to write down what you had for breakfast this morning. From there, we will determine the weight of each item and thus calculate the costs using the imperial rationing standards.'

'What's that?' Aggie mouthed to Elizabeth.

Elizabeth responded with a nod towards a very large table that hung next to the board from where Sister Harvey was providing her teaching sermon. It was suspended on the Priory side of the room. Aggie then noticed there were charts and tables hung around the entire classroom. She could easily spot a periodic table for chemistry, a list of capital cities of the world; times tables, up to and including twelve, dominated the wall to the rear of them as well as many smaller charts she could not focus on from distance.

'You are allowed to confer within your respectful table groups. Older children, please assist the younger children if you can and be sure to explain rather than just do. You have thirty minutes to complete your task. Begin!' the sister ordered, more sergeant major than teacher. And with that, Sister Harvey produced an alarm clock that she set to half an hour and the countdown began.

'Did you understand that?' Elizabeth Peabody enquired as she turned to Aggie.

'I understood that we are to calculate the cost of our breakfast. But why?'

'Search me. They're always harping on about rationing and how things are getting worse. Children cannot possibly understand adult affairs. Blah Blah Blah. So I guess this is a lesson in mathematics and humility,' Elizabeth explained.

'First of all, we need to make a list, right?' Aggie replied.

'Shouldn't take long. Hey, Gem?' Elizabeth smiled at her little sister.

Aggie looked over and on both of their papers, they had already written "porridge". Although Gem had spelt it *Porrij*.

'Just porridge?' Aggie asked. 'No jam or honey?'

'Jam or honey?' Elizabeth sarcastically laughed back. 'We live with Mrs McGregor.'

Aggie sensed she had inadvertently offended what was possibly her only friend in the entire world right now.

'I'm sorry. I didn't mean anything by it. I'm not used to being away from home.'

'How about we take a look at your list instead?' Elizabeth asked, accepting Aggie's conciliatory effort.

Slightly embarrassed, Aggie passed over her scrawled list. Elizabeth read it to herself and then stared jealously at her new friend.

'Eggs, toasted soldiers and bacon!' she exclaimed.

The Priory girls may have missed it, they were too busy wallowing in their own privilege and discussing the merits of smoked kippers, but the evacuees certainly did not and enviously presented their papers towards Aggie. Half the class had misspelt the word but porridge, in its various forms, was held up on their papers in front of her.

'I'm sorry,' Aggie said to them all humbly.

'You don't have to apologise to us,' Elizabeth replied. She was obviously their nominated leader.

'I feel bad I gave some to the cat.' Aggie cringed.

'You might have to apologise now,' Elizabeth replied. She grabbed the paper Aggie's writing was on, folded it up, and stuffed it inside her cuff. 'Why don't you pretend you had porridge, without jam or honey, like the rest of us?' she advised Aggie, assertively.

'Why?' Aggie questioned.

'It's easy to work out, I already know the answer, which we can all use and we don't have to cross over to Priory's side for bacon and egg prices,' Elizabeth rebuffed her seriously. 'And because it's in your best interests to do so,' she whispered in Aggie's ear.

Aggie looked up at the surrounding eyes piercing back at her. She had chosen the evacuees over the Priory and now it looked like she had made friends with neither.

'Write down porridge and this answer,' Elizabeth ordered, explaining the paltry cost of the oat staple the evacuees ate most morning. Aggie stared back at her, confused.

*****

On this unsuspecting day, the torso was found face down having been exposed, overnight, in the waters of Braggan's Brook, a tributary that ran off the River Amble and notorious smugglers route. A quirk of natural design often threw up unexpected arrivals from the larger waterways. Several local men, including the town Sheriff, Wilson Bott, were trying their best to fish the victim out. Bott had been a capable policeman when a younger man. Much older now and riddled with gout, he limped around the dewy bank, careful not to slip in.

Within the brook, chest-deep in fishing waders, there were three elderly locals steadying the body and attaching a rope around the upper torso. Good men were hard to find. Young and fit ones even more so.

'That's secure now,' one of them announced, huffing and puffing as the buoyant cadaver slipped and bobbed in the cold waters.

On the count of three, more men and women on the bank began to heave the sodden body onto dry land. The ropes were hitched under the arms and the dead weight drove a flattened passage through the bull-rushes as they heaved it up.

'Turn it over,' Bott ordered, and with that, the dead man's torso was unceremoniously bundled over. On its face, a crab had begun its unpleasant dissection of the nose flesh. 'Oh, good heavens,' Bott shouted and kicked the crustacean far into the brook. 'Couldn't have travelled far as that's an estuary brown-backed crab. Does anybody know this man?' Bott asked aloud.

'Looks like Lyle Braggan,' came a solitary response.

'Oh, that's all we need,' Bott huffed under his breath. 'Are you sure?' he questioned.

The assertive nod confirmed the corpse's identity.

Word spread about the body around the village quickly, as it so often did, and the ever-inquisitive residents of Ambledown had come to see who it was.

'He had a run-in with Pop in the Poacher only last night,' Shouted out a well-meaning bystander.

Bott held his head in his hands. 'Braggan versus Braggan, a recipe for disaster,' he thought.

'I heard he had a run-in with the good Doctor Belchambers too,' came another voice.

'Gideon?' Bott questioned.

Wilson Bott ordered the men to lift the body into the horse-drawn funeral wagon that had arrived just moments before. On top, in charge of the reigns, sat a stout man in tweed with a squashed nose splayed across his face. Following the wagon but keeping their distance, were two American soldiers in their open-top jeep, slightly worse for wear from their previous evening at Le Chat Noir.

They looked at the lifeless body of Lyle Braggan before looking at one another and making a hasty exit out of Ambledown, trying their hardest to keep the previous evening's dinner down.

Watching from a distance, as they liked to watch through knotholes in fences or from the shadows of the smuggler-ways that peppered Ambledown's streets, a lone figure hid. They were cloaked in the long grasses of the marsh.

'Get word out to Pop that I need to see him. That's if he doesn't already know,' Wilson Bott announced. 'And, if anyone bumps into Doctor Belchambers, ask him to come and see me too. I am headed to the funeral parlour.'

*****

'And that, of course, is the cost of my morning breakfast initiated with kippers, followed by bacon, sausage, black pudding, toast – two slices with butter, of course, and sweet tea,' Henrietta Huntington-Smythe reeled off proudly, accentuating every last morsel of food as her foes across the room salivated enviously.

Sister Harvey congratulated her on an admirable calculation and hoped she had enjoyed such a feast. Her opposing classmates looked on reviled. The evacuees, however, had successfully calculated the cost of a bowl of porridge, particularly as it was made with water and not milk. The latter revelation causing much amusement for their rivals, the girls of the Priory.

'You have a fifteen-minute break now. Be back on time,' Sister Harvey said as she dismissed them from the classroom and readjusted her alarm clock.

The evacuees bolted out of the confined room as if the air oppressed them like calves off to market. Aggie followed Elizabeth and Gemima closely through the threshold.

'Miss Peabody senior,' Sister Harvey called out. 'Please, stay behind.'

'Shall I stay too?' Aggie said to Elizabeth.

'No, you shall not,' the Sister interjected. 'Run along, Gemima. Show Miss Chatsmore what's what, will you?'

Gemima smiled and took Aggie's hand. The door closed behind them.

'The playground's this way. I like to play hopscotch if the Priory aren't on it. They're usually on it. Do you like hopscotch, Aggie?' asked Gemima's innocent voice.

'I suppose so,' Aggie replied, looking back over her shoulder at the closing classroom door.

As Gemima guided her through several corridors, they finally alighted into a chilly autumn day and a small rear courtyard. It was full of children and not just the girls. The boys had been let out too but a consort of nuns and brothers divided the courtyard down the middle. Just as they had been divided into two distinct groups between Priory locals and evacuees, so too had the boys decided to segregate themselves. Same colours, same crested jackets, only the Priory boys wore caps and not straw boaters. As Aggie observed them on the male side of the human fence, engaging in active brutality towards one another under the guise of sport, she couldn't help but notice Eric was alone staring into the corner of the boundary fence, quite happily talking to himself.

'He's always put there. Every break!' Gemima told Aggie. 'He just can't behave himself. Mrs McGregor tells us that trouble finds him.'

Aggie smiled and recalled the exact same expression her uncle had recently bestowed upon her and how it likened her to her mother.

'That's your five minutes, Peabody,' came the booming voice of one of the Brothers.

Eric turned around, pulled his wooden spitfire from his pocket, and ran around the playground imitating gunfire. He coursed his fighter dangerously close to the dividing line of grown-ups, peppering nun and brother with invisible ammunition. As he neared the end of the partition and just opposite the on looking Aggie and Gemima, he feigned a stumble and then flung himself flat-faced onto the ground, sending his beloved plane skimming across concrete and onto their side. Losing a wing in the process, it skidded to a halt at their feet.

'PEABODY! Shouted the same brother, grabbing him up by his ear.

'It was an accident, Brother, honest. Look, my plane, my poor plane. It's crossed over into enemy lines. Permission to rescue it, sir?' Eric asked as he stood to attention and saluted the brother.

The bloodied-knee plea from Eric's urchin face was enough to allow the nuns to break from their male counterparts and allow him to cross over into 'enemy lines'. His large boyish eyes that belied his aged face were rapidly urging Aggie to join him at the broken spitfire. She strode forward, picked up the single winged plane, and marched towards him. He held his hand out as she placed it into his palm. At the last second, he retracted his fingers and screamed out loud forcing her to spill the pieces onto the floor once again.

'Ow, watch them splinters!' Eric cried out.

'Sorry,' Aggie responded.

They almost clashed heads as they both descended on the toy.

'Lyle Braggan is dead. Thought you'd like to know,' he whispered in her ear, just before the brother whipped him away.

'Right, Eric Peabody. In the corner for the remaining ten minutes of break,' came the authoritative voice.

Aggie rose up slowly, Goosebumps mottled her skin.

'Did he just say Lyle Braggan was dead?' came a voice in her head. 'I need to tell Elizabeth right away,' her thoughts continued.

Ten minutes can seem an awfully long time when you're anxious to talk to someone. It can seem even longer if you're staring aimlessly into the corner of a playground fence. Eric Peabody amused himself by happily chatting away in the corner. No one was paying attention. Eric was always talking to himself over there, and they were too busy bruising each other in boyish games. Agatha paced around like a caged animal, unaware the Priory girls were sizing her up, as a predator would stalk their prey.

*****

At the Funeral Parlour of Closet and Cleave, the sorry sight of Lyle Braggan's emaciated face, complete with claw pinches gouged into his nose, stared expressionless on the back of the horse-drawn wagon that Wilson Bott had summoned just over two hours before.

'Closet and Cleaves' respectful parlour for the deceased' sat at the pinnacle of the Steep, just south of the cenotaph. It was a torturous ascent for the poor shires that often made the hill-climb but Mr Closet refused to move his premises on account of its proximity to the trinity of alehouses and from whence most of his customers came. Closet was beanpole thin. Six foot to a man and always attired in a black three-piece with top hat. A silver timepiece's chain glinted from his waistcoat pocket and even in summer, he wore fingerless woollen gloves. Mr Cleave, on the other hand, was five-foot-tall, if that, barrel-chested and preferred a gentleman's two-piece Harris Tweed. It was unlikely a waistcoat could match the demands of his simian chest. His nose was flattened from years of amateur pugilism and the parlour's embalmer, the man who removed the organs and cut open the bodies. 'Mr Cleav-er' – as Eric Peabody had nicknamed him and relished in telling the younger evacuees.

Closet was the businessman, although Eric also said he was the seamstress and his real name was 'Close-it' on account he stitched the bodies up. That's why he wore those grizzly little gloves. They helped him find the perfect stitch as well as count the money. Nevertheless, Closet and Cleave's was the only funeral parlour in the village.

'You're already several shillings to the good Mr Bott.' Mr Closet told the law enforcer on account of the cost of the horse.

'How do you propose we finance his burial?' Closet enquired, examining Lyle's gored nose under his half-moon spectacles.

'I've sent word to his kin,' replied Bott.

'I hear he is a Braggan,' Cleave popped up with his gravel tone.

'That's right,' Bott replied.

'Nephew to Pop Braggan, I hear,' Cleave continued.

'Right again,' Bott confirmed.

'The gold-laden giant, Mr Closet!' Cleave informed his partner, beaming from ear to ear.

'Very well, Mr Bott,' Closet confirmed reaching for a luggage tag. 'He is now on account with Closet and Cleave. Do you have a name?'

'His name is Lyle Braggan,' Bott advised.

Mr Closet wrote Lyle on the front side of the tag and Braggan on the reverse.

'If you would be so kind, Mr Cleave,' Mr Closet said.

Cleave unlocked the solid iron bolts and released the sidebars of the wagon. Lyle Braggan's lifeless body was small and wretched, and underdeveloped for a young man, making it easy for the muscular, barrel-chested man to heave him up.

'There's not a lot of weight to this one, Mr Closet, though he is soaked through. Less timber for the casket, I would say,' Cleave advised.

'Place him on a slab, Mr Cleave, and we'll begin,' Closet ordered his partner.

'We will have to wait for Doctor Beckworth,' Wilson Bott interjected.

'Do you suspect foul play, sir?' Cleave wheezed as he waddled through the parlour, cradling Lyle like a child.

The freezing morgue sat behind the moth-eaten velvet drapes of the front quarters.

'I'd just prefer the good doctor to provide his opinion,' Bott responded.

'Is it OK to remove a single shoe?' Mr Closet asked. 'We must tag his toe.'

Mr Bott rolled his eyes, it wasn't as if there were innumerable numbers of dead bodies overcrowding the parlour morgue, but he agreed nevertheless. 'Very well, Mr Closet, if you must,' Bott confirmed.

Lying there on a cold marble slab, Lyle Braggan's body still retained its mysteries. Mr Closet gave the nod to Mr Cleave who approached Lyle's feet end. His right-side shoe was riddled with holes, damp cardboard that had been used as a temporary barrier to patch the sole now allowed the remaining brook water to drip outwards. The left sole was completely intact, new in fact.

Mr Cleave weighed up the options and a partially protected foot that had spent the night suspended underwater and one that was open to all types of intruders easily gave him his answer. He unlaced Lyle's boot and from the left ankle wriggled the foot free. There was no sock and more than likely the brook had given the body a far better wash than the recently departed man. The toenails remained uncut and ground in with filth and grime. Using his little finger Mr Closet daubed two small smears of embalmers' salts under his nose, to ensure he smelt nothing of the corpse, and then attached the tag to the big toe. Cleave meanwhile poured the water from the recently re-soled shoe. As he held it up at forty-five degrees, as if dispensing a carafe of wine from a great height, a soft thud presented itself on the floor. At first, all three gentlemen thought it was a rolled-up sodden cotton insole. As Cleave bent to clear it away, he looked up in shock.

'Well, I never,' he said, taking a gasp. 'Mr Bott, I do believe Mr Braggan here will be able to more than afford the funeral himself.' Holding aloft in front of the dim mortuary lights he removed an elastic band holding the roll of wet paper together and fanned the bills inside. 'Dollars, if I'm not mistaken. United States Dollars,' Mr Cleave announced. 'At least fifty, I would say.'

*****

Aggie and Gemima were following the evacuees back into the schoolhouse when two Priory girls muscled their way in front, isolating them from the group.

'Hey!' Aggie shouted.

'Hey, what?' Henrietta asked from behind.

Aggie and Gemima turned, twelve or so girls outflanked them. Henrietta Huntington-Smythe stepped forward into Aggie's space and sniffed her up and down.

'I'm so glad you realised you were not a Priory girl. I wholeheartedly agree with your decision.' She smiled.

At that moment, Aggie understood her decision had been the correct one too. At least they agreed on one thing.

'I mean, who in their right mind would deface the Priory crest?' Henrietta continued, poking Aggie's top pocket consistently where a dark shadow of her mother's crest once rested. 'If that is a true Priory crest?' Henrietta questioned in a spiteful undertone. 'I mean, how old is that moth-ridden rag?' she persisted, poking Aggie until her chest grew sore. Whether it was the physical jabbing or the insult about her Mother's old uniform or simply the stress of the past few days something just snapped in Aggie.

On the following pass, she grabbed Henrietta's forefinger and bent it immediately backwards. Crack!
'Ahh!' Henrietta screamed before attacking Aggie with a claw-like hand.
Aggie blocked the incoming arm and delivered a swift blow on to Henrietta's nose. That too cracked and began to stream with blood. Without thought, she channelled her inner boxer from Bethnal Green. Expecting a flurry of blows she curled herself up and held up a defensive guard.
'Aaaaghhhhhhhhh!' twelve girls cried out at once. 'Aaaghhhhhhhhhhh!' the screech continued and was deafening. Arms flapped around in the air. No attack just the sheer horror of Aggie's short-tempered pugilistic blows sent them into a frenzy.
'ENOUGH!' came a higher-pitched screech over them. Two whips of a cane sliced through the air. It was enough to cause everyone to pause on the spot.

Miss Dove strode across the playground and through the sea of female bodies surrounding the commotion. Her voice and demeanour were not the same as the teacher who had acquainted herself with Aggie that morning. She looked upon Henrietta's bloodied nose.
'Who struck you, Henny?' Dove enquired.
Henrietta Huntington-Smythe looked back at Aggie. It was such an obvious glare no teacher could fail to observe the accusation. However, she took the unwritten Priory code very seriously and being a snitch was not one of them. Instead, she just pinched her nose, wincing with pain from the cracked finger, to stop the bleeding. Revenge could wait for another day. It was always best served cold.
'Very well,' Miss Dove said, calming down. 'Every girl here must attend detention.'
The dissatisfied rumblings came from all of them, except Aggie who couldn't quite believe Henrietta's silence. The Priory girls were incandescent with Aggie and a little with her adversary too. She calculated the wrath of twelve of Ambledown Priory's finest might outweigh that of the previously contrary Miss Dove.
'It was me, Miss,' Aggie confessed. 'I hit her.'

'Whatever for?' Dove asked back.

'I'm not really sure, Miss,' Aggie hesitantly replied.

'Very well. Chatsmore and Smythe you are to report to me after school. One hour's detention.'

'I cannot see that's fair. And it's Huntington-Smythe,' Henrietta argued back with bloodied cotton tissue now inserted into her nasal passage.

'That's two hours physical detention for you both,' Miss Dove replied, upping their evening sentence.

Henrietta did not answer back again. She elbowed past Aggie back into class. Followed by her gaggle of followers.

Aggie and Gemima were the last two pupils to enter Sister Harvey's class.

'Detention!' Harvey called out with her back turned and was scribbling on the board.

'To add to the two hours I already have tonight,' Aggie replied sarcastically, much to the amusement of her side of the classroom.

'Join the club,' Elizabeth mouthed to her.

Sister Harvey turned around and looked down her nose at Aggie. A quick flash to Huntington-Smythe, still nursing a bloody nose, and the sister had already answered the question just about to roll off of her tongue.

'Very well. Miss Dove can deal with you all. That includes Peabody senior too. You never know, you may learn something.'

Aggie sat down, whispering Eric's revelation of Lyle Braggan into Elizabeth's ear.

'That's not good news,' Elizabeth whispered back.

Aggie now sat in a constant state of agitation, picking at her fingernails and scratching one calf muscle with the other foot before repeating over and over. The lunch bell couldn't come quickly enough as she intended to make a swift visit back to her uncle.

Day one at a real school. Enemies made; teachers included.

*****

Dr Beckworth announced himself at Closet and Cleaves with a lung-retching cough and splutter.

'Afternoon, gentlemen. Who do we have here?' he enquired.

'Lyle Braggan,' Wilson Bott confirmed bluntly.

'Lyle eh? I saw him in the Poacher just yesterday evening. Had a bit of a to-do with old Pop.'

'Really? What kind of a to-do?' Bott questioned.

'Cards were involved. Lyle is terrible at gambling. No doubt Pop taught him a lesson or two. Needless to say, Lyle left in a foul mood. He spilt my pint on the way out.'

'Should I consider you a suspect too, Doctor?' Bott amused himself at Beckworth's expense.

The doctor ignored him and started over on the body.

'So, you do suspect foul play?' Cleave interrupted.

'Doctor,' Bott began, composing a more serious tone. 'Any reason why I should consider foul play?' he asked.

Examining the dead body up and down and squinting in and out of his half-moons the doctor couldn't be sure. 'He's terribly bruised around his head and neck. Could have been struck or could have fallen from a height, considering the blunt trauma and bleeding to his skull,' Doctor Beckworth advised. 'I dare say his neck was broken as a result.'

'So you cannot determine either way, Doctor?' Bott pushed for an answer.

'Inconclusive,' Doctor Beckworth replied. 'You could, of course, ask Dr Belchambers for assistance. He is qualified in pathology, you know.'

Wilson Bott did know. In fact, it was ancient pathology. However, the inclination he may be involved in a minor capacity was peaked when the crowd had gathered earlier.

'I hear Gideon was also in an altercation with Lyle in the Poacher last night?' he posed to the doctor.

'Nonsense,' Beckworth responded. 'Lyle tried bullying his way through a crowd and Gideon told him to mind his way, that's all.'

'Right, very well. I'll speak to him myself,' Bott concluded and wished Dr Beckworth a good day.

Chapter 24
The egg thief

It had taken closer to two hours than just over the hour advised by his staff but Major Boyd Collingdale had finally arrived on the outskirts of Ambledown. The map showed the simplest route via the Old London Road. However, as they did not have a formal address for Dr G. Belchambers the Major had opted for the more challenging route via the foothill of the Steep. The incline was such that the large green military lorry he had commandeered revved aggressively and faltered, liable to conk out at any time. Coupling that with the village barricades of wood and barbed wire that zigzagged and snaked up the hill, making the path almost impenetrable, the Major knew immediately the decision had been wrong. Nevertheless, he soldiered on regardless.

A small posse of helpers he had mustered took it in turns to move wire and wood barricades where they could, as he barked at the driver not to stall the vehicle on the treacherous climb. Highly revving it coughed out clouds of black smoke as it nudged up the gradient shaking the cobblestone pathway of the Steep, having barely made the narrow bridge crossing that bestrode the Amble. As it reached the peak of the climb, it passed a blinkered Shire horse tethered to a cart.

'Halt!' Collingdale cried out.

Atop of the steepest part of the hill, where the road divided into three and masked just behind the large stone monument for Ambledown's fallen, the Major spied the fine coaching house The Crown. Engine still running, he descended from the raised passenger seat, placed his peak cap on his head, secured the Peacekeeper beneath his armpit and strode towards the inn.

A forthright palm on to the bell at the reception of The Crown Inn awoke the snoozing owner with a jolt. A successive volley of them, when he hadn't responded quickly enough, announced Major Boyd Collingdale's arrival.

'Alright, alright. Keep your hair on!' came the awakening voice of the innkeeper, Benjamin Paine. As he yawned and rubbed the sleep from his eyes, he focused on the stout bald man aggressively rocking on his heels at the reception counter. He soon regretted his words moments prior.

Benjamin was usually timely, articulate, and well-turned out but the previous night he had snuck to the Poacher for the seasonal mutton and inadvertently consumed ample amounts of Amble Ale, much to the displeasure of his wife who was the true proprietor of The Crown. Luckily for him, he had missed the Huntington-Smythes who had dined there the evening before that.

'Is this your establishment, sir?' Boyd barked.

'It is,' Paine replied cordially, now awake but nursing a hangover.

'I need your assistance regarding a delicate matter,' Boyd whispered

'I see,' Paine replied. 'Is it a mistress, sir?' he whispered, moving over the counter closer to the Major's ear.

'What?' Boyd exclaimed incredulously. 'No, it is not a mistress. How dare you!'

'Apologies, sir,' Paine replied, half-bowing and retracting backwards.

'I require the details of a former guest,' Boyd angrily volleyed back.

'I'm afraid we do not give our guests details out, sir. We pride ourselves on discretion,' Paine snivelled.

'Listen to me,' Boyd directed at Paine, pointing the Peacekeeper under his chin. 'I am a serving major in His Majesty's army. I have very little time and a friend who has passed in suspicious circumstances. Your guest wrote him a warning letter. What does that say to you?'

'That he knew it was going to happen?' Paine gulped.

'Precisely. And how would you feel if it turned out you were harbouring such a person. Interfering with a murder inquiry? So, please can you find me this guest's contact details?'

Paine adjusted himself and walked to a large cabinet that stood behind him. The thought of The Crown's reputation and utmost discretion played over in his mind. 'What would your guest's name be? The date he resided here perhaps?' he responded to the Major.

'I'm unaware of the date but the guest's name is Dr Gideon Belchambers,' Boyd Collingdale replied articulately.

Paine paused, turned around, and then laughed uncontrollably.

'What's so funny?' Collingdale asked.

'Gideon isn't a guest here. He's a resident,' Benjamin Paine replied.

'Guest, resident, makes no odds to me. Tell me which room I can find him in,' Boyd continued.

'No, I mean he's a resident of Ambledown. He lives just up the road at The Keep. Not sure why you ever thought he would be a guest here. Let alone caught up in a murder.'

'Because of this,' the Major responded holding up the letter with the watermark of The Crown just visible.

'That bloody Belchambers bugger!' Paine excitedly replied. 'I knew he'd been stealing stationery from me. Now I can prove it.'

'I'd recommend discretion, sir. You may have harboured a man with knowledge of the killer,' Collingdale replied acutely, amusing himself. 'The Keep you say?'

'Y-Yes. Take a right out of the door, just in front of the Castle. You can't miss his shop or his home.' Paine was now bowing and subordinate to the army man.

And with that, Major Boyd Collingdale donned his peak hat, made an about-turn, and set a quick pace yomping uphill. Paine, on the other hand, was eagerly considering the news about Gideon. 'Gideon Belchambers, murderer's mate?' he contemplated.

A crunch of gears later and Boyd's entourage of men followed in the van behind as it chucked out dark clouds of regurgitated diesel.

*****

Wilson Bott, who had been observing the large van from the inside window of Closet and Cleaves, continued to watch it slowly chug uphill before stopping just south of The Keep. He required Gideon's assistance and wondered what business the army had with him.

It wasn't unusual for Gideon to have vans delivering and collecting his antiquities and curiosities, but Wilson Bott had never before seen one that had an old sergeant major eagerly proceeding in front of it. He was just about to alight from Closet and Cleaves when the shadow of a man bore down the Steep and cast its all-encompassing shadow on the pavement outside. He stepped out of the funeral parlour to be greeted by the giant.

'Where's, Bott?' came the deep slow voice.

'Now, Pop. You can't be seeing him just yet,' Wilson Bott replied to the man-mountain in front of him.

'I'm kin and 'e ain't got no farva. 'Is bruvver is far away. I'm the only family 'e 'as,' Pop Braggan replied. The wolfhound on the leash looked like she would make light work of any man that got in Pop's way. The magpie on his shoulder cawed in support.

'Pop, we have witnesses that say you two had a fight,' Bott replied nervously.

'Wot rubbish. 'E was like a son to me, that boy,' Pop snarled back. 'Sure-nuff, I 'ad to put 'im right last night. Been drinkin' 'e 'ad. But I'd never 'urt 'im.'

'Sorry, but I can't let you in, Pop,' Bott insisted.

The man strode forward and placed the dog's leash in Bott's hand. He then bent down and removed his cornucopia of gold chains from around his neck and placed them over Bott's much smaller frame. The weight was enough to render him static.

'Right, I need just five minutes wiv 'im. Luna will look after you and the bird will look after me gold,' Pop told Bott.

And with that, 'Lady' landed on Bott's shoulder acting as an avian sentry while Pop Braggan removed his hat and entered Closct and Cleaves. Bott prayed that none of the feline residents of Le Chat Noir made an appearance that would see the hound drag him face-first down the Steep.

*****

The lunchtime bell finally rang and relief spread across Aggie's face as she vacated quickly from the classroom.

As she maintained a swift pace through the small corridors, Elizabeth struggled to keep up.

'Agatha, wait,' the senior Peabody called out. 'Aggie!'

Agatha rounded the corner to where the Aspidistra dominated the entrance lobby. Miss Dove was in a heated discussion with a portly woman who was remonstrating with her. She noticed Miss Dove hand over a pile of papers. They looked like the 'weights and measures' task the students had carried out first thing. She stood back observing them, obscured by the large green plant.

Elizabeth came hurtling around the corner, clattering into Aggie, exposing them both to the two women in deep discussion.

'Chatsmore! Peabody!' Dove shouted over.

Aggie and Elizabeth dusted themselves down and stood in front of them with their heads bowed. It never failed to amuse the governess how teenagers believed themselves invisible to the adult world.

'I might've known a Peabody was involved,' came the sneering leer of the woman Aggie wasn't familiar with. 'And I hear you like to talk with your fists,' she continued, pointing at Aggie.

'Lady Smythe, I will be dealing with this myself, after school,' Miss Dove announced.

'It's Huntington-Smythe!' she snarled back. 'And make sure you do, Dove! Or there'll be no peace around here for you,' she ordered before slamming the entrance door behind her.

'What are you doing here, girls?' Dove asked.

In all fairness, Elizabeth was just following Aggie but knew Aggie was making a beeline back to 1a The Keep.

'Agatha, I mean Miss Chatsmore, has a medical condition, Miss,' Elizabeth improvised.

'Really?' Dove responded swiftly. 'I cannot recall you mentioning that this morning during your meeting with Dr Beckworth.'

'I forgot. I was nervous,' Aggie added quickly. 'I need my pills, Miss. I struggle to breathe sometimes. I get anxious during air-raids and I believe that van noise triggered it.'

Miss Dove's sceptical frown surveyed the two nervous students for a very long minute. Aggie began a subtle wheezing and feigned pains in her chest.

'Very well. Be sure to be back within the next half hour. I would hate to extend the detention from just this evening to the full week. I'm locking the door so ring the bell when you return.'

'Yes, Miss,' both girls responded before sprinting out of the schoolhouse and north towards The Keep.

*****

'Mr Braggan, I presume?' wormed Mr Closet as Pop Braggan made his presence known in the funeral parlour.

'Take me to 'im,' Pop ordered.

Lyle was stretched out on the mortuary slab. His eyes peered soullessly at the dim candlelight that illuminated him from above. Pop's thumb and forefinger stretched across the dead man's face and softly closed his eyelids. Reaching inside his pocket he pulled out two silver pennies and placed them over Lyle's eyes.

'They're for the ferryman. Not light-fingered funeral shop owners,' Pop said, cracking his knuckles as a warning to Closet and Cleave. Once he had mumbled a few words to himself he then started searching inside Lyle's pockets.

'A-hum,' Closet coughed disapprovingly.

Nevertheless, Pop continued. Once he had gone through every pocket, he turned to the shoes. He examined the shoe still on Lyle's foot. The one that had holes in the sole. He then looked at the two funeral directors who were nervously observing him from behind the moulding mortuary drape.

'Oh, yes, of course, Mr Braggan,' Cleave announced, in a higher tone than usual. 'We are in care of his monies.'

'What d'ya mean?' Pop asked back.

'The monies he kept in the shoe you are looking for.'

Pop then looked down on the men from his towering height and slowly performed a single-handed clap with his right hand.

Closet stepped forward and presented a small purse from where he removed the still-damp US Dollars found in Lyle's shoe.

Pop then turned around and left the funeral parlour.

'You 'av this,' Pop said to Wilson Bott handing him over all but one of the US bills. 'Make sure 'is funeral costs are covered. Then you settle with me when I return.'

The money was more than sufficient to cover the burial, casket and generous wake.

'And by the way, Bott, 'is inside breast pockets are lined with wool. It runs down behind his jacket. I can feel damp bird shell in there. 'E was an egg feef, so you must ask who pays such monies for such prizes. He rowed wiv me over a farvin in the Poacher. Wouldn't 'av risked that if he 'ad so many dollars at the time. So, who offered so much that evening and who 'ad dollars to offer? That's wot I'd be asking.' Pop then bent down and relieved Bott of his horde of gold. Wilson stretched with relief after the weight had been lifted. Taking the hound's leash, Pop then sauntered down the Steep. Lady the magpie flew off, ever the inquisitive one.

*****

Gideon Belchambers was high up in The Keep when he heard the backfiring military vehicle pull up opposite. At first, he feared gunshot but the black puff of smoke allayed those fears. As he spied the top of the Major's hat moving towards his shop, not his home, his immediate concern was whether Eric had successfully finished the business he had employed him to complete on Sunday. For what other reason would the military come knocking? The previous evening's events had deterred him from checking on Eric's latest masterpiece so he was cautious not to let them into his business premises.

Descending via the stone staircase and following the route recently disclosed to his niece, he lit the candle where the tunnel divided. 'Right for flight' he considered for a couple of moments. However, with his niece now fully under his stewardship, he couldn't just run away. Instead, he made his way through the secret wooden panel and via the humongous wardrobe, into Aggie's room. Being sure to close all doorways behind him, he made a final survey of the room and offered an attentive pat on the doll's house chimney. On the final descent of the staircase, the shadow of Major Collingdale's cap now presented itself through the frosted glass at the top of the front door. Several knocks on the chrome lion's head knocker outside made the Major's presence felt.

'Coming!' Gideon shouted with a muted undertone, imitating he was at a great distance from the door. He was stalling the military man while he wrote out three letters.

A few moments passed and three hard knocks spurred his furious scribbles onto paper.

'OK, OK, I'm coming,' Gideon replied, as he opened the door.

'Doctor Belchambers, I presume?' came the authoritative tone of Major Boyd Collingdale.

'That's right. Whom am I speaking to?' Gideon asked back.

'I am Major Boyd Collingdale.'

'Pleasure, sir,' Gideon interrupted, offering him his hand. 'Are you buying or selling?'

'What?' Collingdale asked slightly surprised. 'Neither, man. I am hoping you can help me with a peculiar puzzle,' Collingdale replied.

'Oh, I see. How so, sir?'

'You wrote a letter to a colleague of mine, Professor Malcolm.'

'Professor Malcolm…' Gideon responded. 'I'm not familiar with any Professor Malcolm within the forces, sir.'

'What I meant was former colleague at the Museum for Natural History. I am in charge of securing and transferring the exhibits. Professor Mal–'

'Ah, of course … Meredith Malcolm …' Gideon interrupted, again. 'World-famous entomology professor and, not known to many, noted taxidermist. How is he? How's my giraffe?'

'Dead,' the Major informed him, pulling no punches. 'The Professor that is, not your giraffe.'

Gideon's complexion changed immediately, the colour drained from his face and he looked noticeably shocked.

'Good grief. That's quite a shock.' His tone was subdued.

'Did you know him well, Doctor?'

'Not particularly. We met on several occasions. I was trying to procure his services to value a collection of rare insects I am purchasing. And, of course, I donated the giraffe to him. Who was also dead, last time I looked,' Gideon replied.

'Well enough to send him this warning letter though?' Collingdale said inquisitively, producing the half-parched correspondence.

'Let me see that.' Gideon requested, again stalling for time. He read it to himself.

Dearest Professor Malco….

I believe yourself or …. ………. ..

in grave danger.

Please contact me at yo.. ……. ……….

Yours sincerely

Professor G Belch……

'I remember now and I can see why you would have thought it was a warning.' Gideon offered up a small chuckle.

'The missing words are 'at least your reputation'. *I believe yourself or at least your reputation to be in grave danger.* It was following a difference of opinion on a species of Scarabidae I had recently been sold and had asked him to value.'

Major Collingdale stretched a forefinger under his collar, an obvious admission of embarrassment. All this effort based on a hunch and the presence of a ring finger on an unmarried man. He had assumed the letter a foreboding but hadn't stopped to consider more obvious options. He still could not understand why Malcolm had left it re-addressed to him.

'Tell me, Doctor. Did you know him well enough to know if he was married?'

'Meredith was definitely not married,' Gideon replied immediately.

'You're sure?' Boyd questioned

'Positive, why?'

'On his ring finger, he had an entwined gold and silver band. Most unusual. Perhaps he was a mason, bit bloody strange for a mason though, incorrect finger too.'

Gideon was beginning to sense all was not quite as it seemed and the Major was not letting on everything. 'May I ask you, Major, who identified the body?'

'I did. Well, what I could see of it in the darkness.'

'Sorry, I don't follow,' Gideon said, confused.

'His body was, is, under a large exhibit case. Crushed after an air raid. His hat was just next to him. I could just see his moustache protruding from beneath, his perfect linens all dirty and dusty now. Poor fella's hand was reaching out claw-like from beneath the rubble. As if he was trying to clutch to life itself.'

'You haven't seen his face though? You couldn't positively identify him, not one hundred per cent?' Gideon continued to question.

'To the best of those circumstances, I could,' the Major responded defensively. 'Anyway, I doubt there'll be much of his face left to look at once all those beastly little monsters have devoured him. I wager one of those abominable scorpions has stung him too.'

'Scorpions?' Gideon asked, surprised. 'He kept scorpions?'

'Those bloody Death-stalkers or that's what he told me they were.'

Gideon now realised all that he had feared had come to fruition.

'Major, I am a doctor of archaeology, antiquity and also ancient pathology. I believe my latter skill, albeit this cadaver is much fresher, may help determine what happened to our dear friend. That is if you suspect foul play. He definitely was not married. I know him well enough to positively identify him, if you would like a second opinion.'

'Very well. If you can spare half a day,' Collingdale replied. 'I'll be waiting in the van.'

Gideon hurried to collect several items that he placed into a leather Gladstone bag. He went back to the three notices he had left. One was for his housekeeper Nan, the other two were for Aggie. The first of Aggie's he ripped up and discarded onto the floor. The second he re-read to make sure it made sense.

Dearest Aggie,

Business takes me to London. So much to tell you still. I shall return this evening. Nan will take care of things in the meantime.

The Peabodys are your friends. They will help you where they can.

Remember this, trust No one!

Love

G x

*****

'What's that pulling away from your uncle's?' Elizabeth pointed out to Aggie as the two girls looked up the hill.

The large green automobile wobbled from side to side and coughed out another plume of acrid smoke. Aggie's sense of urgency increased as she left her friend lagging behind. Breathless, she reached the foot of The Keep as the van disappeared into the distance.

'Why didn't you wait for me?' Elizabeth panted, now drawing level.

Aggie's mind was singularly focused on Gideon and her need for his protection right now. She stumbled up the flagstone stairs and engaged with the lion's head for three solid knocks. She began clicking her fingers nervously in anticipation before engaging the knocker for several more quick bursts. No one answered.

'Haven't you got a key?' Elizabeth asked.

'It's in my cloak pocket. I've left it at school.' Aggie sighed, lashing a kick at the door.

'We need Eric,' Elizabeth replied.

'At your service, ladies,' came the welcoming voice of Eric Peabody.

'What are you doing here?' Elizabeth asked.

'Charming, Lizzy. First, you wish for your knight in shining armour only to question him when he doth appear,' Eric replied with his mischievous tone, bowing towards them both.

Aggie smiled. Twice already he had helped her today, much to his own detriment.

'Didn't see ya at lunch. Gem told me you'd both got past Dove. I wasn't missin' all the action. So, what's going on?'

'I need you to break in,' Aggie ordered.

'Whoa! I ain't smashin' any of Mr Gideon's windows. What d'ya take me for a common criminal,' Eric responded with a categorical denial.

'Come on, Eric. You must have some sort of way in?' Elizabeth asked.

'Turn your backs and close your eyes.' Eric smiled.

'Eric! It's not a joke,' Elizabeth informed him in her serious voice.

'Turn your backs and close your eyes,' Eric emphasised the second time.

Aggie and Elizabeth duly did as they were asked. They listened intently as Eric scrambled around the foot of the stairs turning stones and cobbles over.

'Just pick one, Eric,' Aggie ordered him impatiently, waiting for the inevitable smash of glass.

'Yes, Eric, just do it. Time is ticking,' Elizabeth agreed.

'Da daah!' Eric shouted out, bowing in front of the now opened door.

'How did you do that?' Came the question from both of the girls in unison.

'A gentleman never tells.' Eric winked back, his arm directing Aggie to enter.

Eric and Elizabeth stood on the step outside while Aggie entered.

'Gideon!' she called out. 'Gideon? Are you in here.' There was no response. Nan wasn't there either.

Spying the letters on the table she reached for the one addressed to her and unfolded it. She read through the message and tried to digest it. *The Peabodys are your friends* – that was good. *Trust No one* – that was confusing. At least she would see him tonight to ask him what he meant. Eric and his sister all the while remained outside but he was nosing about nevertheless

'What's it say?' he shouted over.

'Eric, it's none of your business,' Elizabeth reprimanded him with a nudge.

'It's OK,' Aggie called back, now walking towards them with the letter. 'Gideon's in London on business. He'll be back later.'

'That's a relief,' Eric sighed. 'Thought the military police had nabbed 'im. Or those Yanks.'

'Why would you say that?' Aggie enquired.

Elizabeth was quick to interject. 'You should know what he's like by now, Aggie. A boy with a wayward imagination!' she said, semi-scolding her brother.

'We best get back to school. I'll be joining you for detention for sure. Don't fancy a week though,' said Eric, as he ushered the girls down the stone stairs.

'Close your eyes,' he said again. 'Don't want you knowing my little secret.'

Aggie and Elizabeth turned their backs and began walking downwards as Eric closed and locked the large door of 1a.

'So how did you get out of the school, Eric?' Aggie asked as she walked in front of him.

'I climbed the fence. My fence, as everyone now calls it.'

'Don't lie, Eric Peabody. There's a ten-foot drop, at least, straight into marshland.'

'Honest, cross my heart,' he continued, imitating a large cross across his chest. 'It's only a small drop when you know how.'

Both girls looked at each other confused but laughing never the same.

'If you say so, Eric,' they replied together, making their way back down the Steep towards the new schoolhouse.

Perhaps two hours detention was a good thing. Gideon would not arrive home until later that evening and her only trusted friends in the world right now would be spending it with her. *Trust no one,* she thought. Not even Eric and Elizabeth?

As they reached the cenotaph, she noticed more people. It was certainly busy, particularly surrounding the funeral parlour. There were much talk and whispering of the body in the brook, Lyle Braggan. 'Foul play,' and 'Murder,' she heard as she passed the large Shire horse outside Closet and Cleaves.

'According to Mr Cleave,' she overheard as she passed by. 'He had a large sum of American currency upon him.'

Her thoughts flashed back to the previous evening. The men in Le Chat Noir were American! They had offered their services to Uncle Gideon and now Lyle was dead. Perhaps it was them, disposing of Lyle in a way they saw fit. But that didn't make sense. Why would Lyle have their money?

All this information, but no answers. She really did require her uncle to explain everything and not just from last night. The remaining afternoon of school and two hours detention seemed like a lifetime away. Peering down the Steep, where the bridge crossed the Amble, she looked at the wooden shoe that hung outside of the cobbler's shop. 'Tinks' if she recalled her uncle correctly. Beneath the shoe sat Luna and upon her head, the Lady was randomly cawing out.

Chapter 25
Illuminating

Professor Meredith Malcolm had an encyclopaedic knowledge of insects. Botanicals he was an accomplished expert in too but would admit it, himself, it was second to his passion for all things that crept and crawled.

The leaves that had been left in the pestle were dry and had not made his investigations any easier. His first attempts to examine one had resulted in a crumbling of dust and he now had only a few well-worn samples to investigate.

Returning to the scrolls, he examined the reliefs below the amber varnish that preserved them. His first challenge was to ensure the paper jigsaw of papyri bonded below, could be properly observed. The dark veins that separated the pieces made the job intrinsically difficult and he needed to remove a sliver of the amber to be sure of what lay beneath. It may even provide further clues to the true pigment of the plant. The laboratory had every type of instrument he could have wished for. In this circumstance, a small magnifying glass fixed to a steel rod served as his observation tower, while a tiny pinhead pick would act as his etching tool.

Softly and steadily, he made his first incision into a corner of the amber covered-paper. The immediacy of his actions took him by surprise. Like a slingshot stone shattering a plate-glass window into innumerable pieces, the fracturing impact of the small metal pick shattered the amber, splintering the image below into a thousand minuscule pieces, turning it to dust.

The professor pulled back from the small magnifying tower he had created for himself and just sat there in shock. Why on earth would the amber varnish react in such a manner?

Just then, the door to the laboratory opened and in strode Mr Louds dressed in the customary facemask and surgical scrubs. There was no hiding the Professor's alarm penetrating from his eyes.

'I see you too have fallen foul to the secrets of the scrolls,' Louds directed towards him.

'I'm lost for words, Mr Louds. I – I apologise,' the Professor expressed, genuinely alarmed.

'Can you smell that, Professor?' Louds said, sniffing the air.

Meredith Malcolm's large moustache always obscured his sense of smell. He could not detect any change in scent.

'Don't worry Professor, those who have failed before you only ever got as far as this point too. Why is it, do you think, we can smell citrus every time one of the tableaux disintegrates?'

Professor Malcolm, who was now pre-occupied by what had happened to those who had failed before, took his time considering his answer. 'Citrus?' he questioned Mr Louds.

'A distinct lemon smell, come.' Mr Louds picked up a thumb and forefinger of the dust and imitated inhaling a pinch of snuff. Professor Malcolm followed his lead.

'Go ahead, Professor, take a good whiff,' Louds encouraged.

Being careful not to ingest the powder, Meredith Malcolm held his moustache down with two fingers from his left hand while in his right hand he held the particles and inhaled a deep breath. Sure enough, there was a strong smell of lemon that permeated through.

'Lemon?' he mumbled to himself. 'Why lemon, Meredith?'

'A very good question to ask yourself, Professor,' Louds agreed.

The Professor then took the tip of his tongue and tasted the dust.

'Professor, what are you playing at?' Louds called out.

'It's sweet, not bitter or sharp,' Malcolm explained. 'You can taste the lemon but there is an overwhelming sweetness. See for yourself,' he explained, offering a finger of dust to Mr Louds.

Mr Louds was not following and was in no mood to indulge the eccentricities of Professor Malcolm's dust consumption. Although unsure what it meant, the Professor approached the scrolls again. He sniffed them over and over as if a bloodhound securing a scent before the hunt. Sure enough, he smelt the fragrant citrus, as subtle as it was. He lifted the vellum swatches guarding them and took a deeper inhalation from the protected drawings. Then, taking Mr Louds by complete surprise, he licked one of the varnished glyphs as if it was a lollipop.

'Good heavens, Professor. Have you lost your mind?' Louds alarmed.

Professor Malcolm began to laugh. It was sweet but he hadn't been able to determine it amongst the lemon-infused paper dust he had just tried. But, sure enough, as he had suspected, the varnish protection was nature's sweetest gift bestowed to us.

'Ingenious!' He turned to Mr Louds, laughing uncontrollably. 'Ingenious…it's glazed in …honey!' the excited Professor repeated.

'I do not follow, Professor,' Louds interrupted.

'Allow me to explain.' Malcolm smiled, using the point of his tongue to taste part of the ancient scroll one last time. 'Honey! The lacquer that protected the parchment and what we assumed to be an ancient varnish is actually brittle honey.' Professor Malcolm exclaimed, particularly pleased with himself.

'We have just lost another part of the relief. I do not share your enthusiasm, Professor,' Louds replied, angering.

Professor Meredith Malcolm had now switched his attention to the vellum swatches that acted as protective guards to the glazed glyphs. He sniffed them with a powerful inhalation to ensure the subtle scent penetrated his formidable moustache.

'Please, Mr Louds, smell.'

Brian Louds who was characteristically a calm man was beginning to lose his patience with the Professor. 'Will you please explain what you are doing. Why are you so excited?' he questioned Meredith.

'Lemon, Mr Louds, or at least an extract of citronella!' The Professor laughed.

A returning blank expression from Brian Louds finally drilled the message home to the invigorated entomologist.

'Have you tried photographing these glyphs?' Malcolm asked.

Louds nodded.

'And on the instant of the flash, the cracking and crumbling took place?'

'That's correct. How did you conclude that? Two of the images were lost and the exposure never developed.' Louds confirmed.

'Haha! I knew it,' Malcolm congratulated himself again.

Mr Louds listened on intently.

'When honey is mixed with lemon and some very basic ingredients, it creates a chemical reaction. The result is a glue-like compound. A bit like tree sap. Given the right conditions, it will set as if it were a varnish.'

'And so?' Louds sneered.

'It can become volatile. If there is too much of the citric acid, in this case, the lemon, it can cause it to splinter and break. Add that exposure to heat or light and it will expedite things. Then boom! Disintegration,' the Professor explained, crumbling a small amount of dust as he did so.

Mr Louds followed the Professor word for word and understood his very basic lesson in elementary chemistry. It was such a plausible explanation as to why their photograph was a disaster and why several attempts to extract the scrolls' secrets had ended up in destroying the previous reliefs. The pieces of the puzzle were unravelling.

'That's very helpful, Professor, but how does that help us?'

'Here in learneth the lesson, Mr Louds. I believe your thief made a copy.'

'More than likely,' Mr Louds agreed. 'The problem with a thief is that you are already dealing with someone in a position of distrust. But he's dead. I still do not follow.'

'In doing so, sir, he left his mark. Almost a fingerprint to ensnare him.'

Louds was very much confused but nevertheless allowed the Professor to proceed.

'Let us step into the light, Mr Louds,' Malcolm advised. Picking up one of the unfurled scrolls.

'Careful, Professor, you've already destroyed enough today. They are centuries old and must be handled with care.'

'I've no doubt the vellum and the parchment are of great historical significance, Mr Louds. But I reserve judgement on the hieroglyphics we see before us!'

Louds stood back, stunned. 'I had the scrolls corroborated by the world-leading expert,' Louds confirmed.

'As I say, the scrolls themselves are no doubt millennia old. But, please, follow me,' Professor Malcolm insisted, directing him under the light.

The two gentlemen stood under the emitting glare of the prism that had intermittently shone down on them reflecting the inclement British weather.

'Do you have a knife or scalpel, Mr Louds?' the Professor asked.

Brian Louds procured a sharp scalpel from a faultless array already on the Professor's laboratory bench. He suppressed the urge to pass over a bloody one hidden from beneath his clinical scrubs.

'Be very careful, Professor,' he urged. 'I would say at least one of your nine lives was expunged this morning. Be wary not to make that two.'

Taking the scalpel handle presented to him, Professor Meredith Malcolm scored the parchment, which had previously supported the varnished glyph. The one that he had inadvertently destroyed. Gently, with precision, he ran over the initial square with a deeper penetrative cut which released a window of parchment glued to the leather binding of the scroll.'

'And now, Professor?' Louds questioned.

'We look through the window.' Reversing the outstretched scroll and raising the missing square so that the light shone through it, he peered at the remaining vellum. 'Eureka!' he cried out.

'Show me,' Louds demanded

And there, just visible, was a perfect negative of an ancient hieroglyphic. It was far more intricate than the basic glyphs presented on the reverse side. Perhaps the thief really hadn't realised his efforts to dupe Mr Louds and the elusive Dr Mialora would be in vain and the true value of this artefact had finally revealed its secret.

'Well, well, Professor. You may have just redeemed a full set of nine lives,' asserted Mr Louds. 'I must tell the good Dr Mialora,' Louds said excitedly 'Continue to discover the secrets from our ancients Professor. Carefully, of course. I shall return in due course.'

'Of course.' The Professor nodded, humbly.

Louds was just exiting the room when he returned to his accommodating self. 'Would you like tea, maybe a cake, as some reward? I'll order you tea and cake. You British love tea and cake.'

'I'd prefer something slightly stronger,' Professor Malcolm asked.

'Very well, I believe we can celebrate a breakthrough,' Louds congratulated him.

'G&T?' Professor Malcolm replied.

'Ha, you British and your love of gin too. If you insist. My men will procure you whatever you like.'

Louds left the laboratory instructing the two guards to accommodate the Professor's requirements.

'Gin, London Dry if you have it, Indian tonic water, and a cuticle of fresh lemon, please,' Professor Malcolm insisted.

*****

The darkness of the District Line rewarded Noone with a few precious minutes of sleep before the Temple station flashed and slowed into view. His connecting ride was a short hop on the yellow via The Strand. His preference would have been to stay underground, out of the light, hidden in solitude if he could be. However, the pressing matter of Draper's likely kidnap remained his focus.

As he alighted from the steel Tube carriage and climbed the already moving escalator, two shadows continued to follow him. Safely at distance, their observations discreetly monitored his every move.

The brightness of a crisp October day caused his remaining eye discomfort as he strode out of Temple station and towards The Strand. On the corner came the familiar tones of a news seller:

'Standard! Get your Standard!'

That reminded him of Thompson's passing comments that he must purchase the evening edition for his next instructions. In the meantime, he headed down to the black tunnels of The Strand Tube and onwards towards Russell Square, where he hoped his friend would be able to help him.

With the darkness of dreams came the whirling men spinning fire. Men dressed in costume; men cloaked in secrecy. Hawks and hounds, serpents and crocodiles. Cairo, Giza, the living, the dead. A nightmarish cocktail of images that Nathaniel Noone sought to extract from his mind.

Waking with a cold sweat to the announcement, 'Russell Square', he jolted upwards and just managed to trap his arm in the closing doors, they re-opened and he stepped off on to the platform. From behind him, he heard two sets of footsteps alight too. Coincidence that someone else almost missed their stop too? Doubtful, he thought to himself.

Securing his black fedora and raising the collars of his mackintosh, he stepped onto an escalator and allowed the mechanical staircase to elevate him upwards. After thirty seconds, when he could be sure the two sets of footsteps had stopped and were following his path, he turned abruptly and stared at the couple below. He had expected two men in similar dark hat and coats but instead, they were a man and woman intently staring at the Tube map as if they were lost. As he reached the top he stared back again and caught the woman's eye. She smiled politely and returned to the map. Noone's scarring usually initiated a minimal flinch in response, even from the politest, this woman hardly acknowledged he was there. Approaching the barrier guard he took an about-turn and swiftly rerouted back down the opposing escalator.

A gust of air announced the next Tube train arriving. Rather than board it immediately, he stood discreetly hidden behind a concrete pillar. As the doors began to shut, the couple rushed onto the train. As it pulled away, he stepped out of his cover and waved them a sarcastic goodbye. Obviously, Thompson hadn't trusted him at all. At least he could respect that.

Noone was pleased to see that the huge pillars to the temple-inspired entrance had held firm despite the relentless barrage of the blitz. Across town, the Museum of Natural History and Science had suffered little in comparison but they shared a common goal to protect and extradite their exhibits to safer surroundings.

The British Museum had withstood the worst of all of the capital's bombings. It was beyond doubt that it was being purposely targeted by Fuhrer high command, and the surrounding Bloomsbury landscape looked more like furrowed fields of twisted iron and brick rather than their noble historical facades that had stood there long before the Thunder Machines had successfully visited.

Coils of barbed wire created a twenty-yard barrier between the entrance and they looped over five foot high. Security was far tighter here than at its sister museum across town. Several sentries stood guard and patrols were frequent. Having been the subject of Thompson's tails, his confidence to walk straight in waned. Nevertheless, what was the worst that could happen? Thompson would haul him back to Shaftesbury or whcrever The Department was now being deployed. Walking as fast as his limp would allow, he approached the guarding sentry. As always, his melted face, eye patch, and intense lidless stare sent shivers down the spine of the onlooker.

'How can I help you, sir?' the guard asked nervously.

'I'm here to see Soames. Nathaniel Noone to see Soames,' Noone rasped.

'Professor Soames, sir?' the guard responded.

'Of course,' Noone replied impatiently.

'Which one, sir?'

'There's more than one?' Noone questioned.

'Professor M or Professor–'

'M. Definitely M. Professor Montague Soames, please,' Noone interrupted, he didn't require any other options.

The guard surveyed the list up and down.

'I'm sorry but Professor Montague Soames is no longer with us,' the guard replied.

'Dead?' Noone asked, shocked.

'Says he's recently retired, sir.'

'What? That's impossible,' Noone argued in disagreement.

'If that will be all, sir, I'd kindly ask you to move along,' prompted the guard with reference to his rifle.

How could he not of been aware that Monty had recently retired? He'd only seen him months ago. Noone was furious with himself and even more so that he had hit a dead end on the photograph. He limped away slowly. His next course of action to wait for Thompson's encrypted message and the night final of The Standard.

'Sir, Mr Noone!' the guard called out.

'What is it?' Noone replied abruptly.

'I missed it initially, sir, but it says here, next to Professor M. Soames' guest-list, that anyone by the name of Mr N Noone is to report to the other Professor, I. Soames in M. Soames' absence.'

'Let me see that.' Noone snatched at the guard. 'Professor I. Soames? What's that stand for?'

'Isabelle,' came a female voice from behind. A voice familiar to Nathaniel Noone but which he hadn't heard in a long, long time. 'Though you may have required it to be a B.'

'Belle?' Noone turned around; not quite believing it was her.

'Belle with the bunches – if I recall?' she responded with a humorous smile.

Nathaniel Noone's emotions were rarely played out in public, but the smidge of a tear allowed him a subtle embarrassment in front of her.

'So handsome still, Nate.' She smiled, kissing him subtly on his scarred face.

'Always were a bloody good liar.' Noone laughed.

'Come on, let's see Dad,' she replied, grasping his fingers into hers and drawing him in towards her as they held hands and entered the Museum.

'He's here? The guard told me he had retired,' Noone questioned.

'Sort of,' Belle replied. 'You'll see.'

Rarely did Nathaniel Noone drop his guard but the sight of Belle, after so many years, the relief Monty was still at the Museum and the fact he may finally have some answers to the photograph he kept in his pocket, allowed him a brief moment of relief. Belle intertwined her fingers tightly into his, childlike, excitedly leading him towards her father's office.

Chapter 26
Theory

Thompson and Waverley sat in the darkened room. The dim light from the single table lamp accentuated them with gothic facial features. Wink's chain-smoking did little to help the poor airflow.

'Let me repeat that back to you to ensure I understand the sequence of events,' Wink began. 'You believe this Jennifer James had somehow befriended and duped Draper, leading to this plant being, well, planted – for want of a better phrase.' she summarised.

'That's correct, ma'am,' Thompson confirmed.

'Any idea on the length of this deception?'

'She provided the plant on his birthday. August 31st. Therefore, we should assume since then she has been privy to the inner workings of Draper's office.'

'And you believe the information could have been relayed both ways,' Wink continued with mild agitation.

'I believe it could have, ma'am.'

'So, she had more than a passing duplicity. She had control over him too?'

'We're still trying to find out. We're cross-referencing all his communications as we speak.'

'Let's assume the worst, shall we?' Wink affirmed. 'Sounds like quite the spy, this Ms James. You may have to turn her someday, Thompson, if we ever find her again.' Wink smiled.

Did he just hear that correctly? Wink had an obvious admiration for the person responsible for his superior's kidnap. 'Ma'am, the details of her escape are equally intriguing,' Thompson continued.

'Enlighten me,' Wink encouraged him.

'First of all, we believe she poisoned our concierge. Not sure how, not sure what with, but he has been left catatonic ever since.'

Wink Waverley rolled her singular eye.

'Then there was the escape with Draper. We have eyewitnesses that tell us Draper had his pistol trained on her. Then he simply let the round off into the air,' Thompson explained.

'That makes the least sense of all. Why didn't he just shoot her?' replied Wink.

'Therein comes the control theory, ma'am.' Thompson shrugged. They both knew the likely answer was Jennifer James did have the ability to manipulate Draper. He may have considered the crowded streets and the opportunity to kill or maim an innocent passer-by a risk but Draper was a trained soldier himself and it was unlikely that would have stopped him, considering all that was at stake.

'Seems you have your hands full, Thompson. Anything else before I inform *the Executive*?'

Thompson thought long and hard about Nathaniel Noone, and the photograph with the symbols, but he couldn't help but feel the knowledge of Malling's inclusion was the best-kept secret, for now, at least. But there was one last thing. One single item Smith and Jones had recovered from the scene.

'There is this, ma'am,' he advised as he pulled a small white card from his inner pocket. 'Discovered at the scene and possibly left by Draper as a lead.'

Wink Waverley took the card and placed it under the Bakelite emerald hood of the table lamp. Emblazoned in embossed red type the front read: Official, Society, Improvement, Rehabilitation, Injured, Servicemen. The reverse glinted as it caught the light and as Wink gave it the once-over.

'Seems like a fundraising society. I do not recognise the coat of arms, possibly Swiss, as let's face it, its type is in gold. R-A? Royal Academy possibly – no doubt, but it's not British,' Wink advised.

'Thank you, ma'am. I'll investigate it too.'

'Actually, leave it with me,' Wink replied, encouraging Thompson to hand it over. 'I'll have someone help.'

Thompson was curious as to why Wink Waverley would help on this particular item, but as he already had secrets of his own to keep, his boss to find, a spy to catch and Nathaniel Noone to wrangle, he accepted her help, cautiously.

'Thank you, ma'am,' he acknowledged with a courteous nod.

'Be sure to close the door on your way out, Thompson. Chop, Chop.' Wink clapped, returning to her relaxed posture in her chair.

He would be sure of that, once he could find the route, amongst the padded burgundy leather walls.

*****

'Dad, Dad? It's Belle,' Belle gently whispered in her father's ear before placing a loving kiss on his forehead.

Montague Soames remained wheelchair-bound and unresponsive. A tartan blanket was draped across his knees, to keep him warm, as he stared into solitude.

'You'll never guess whom I just bumped into?' she carried on, regardless.

'Hello, Monty, old friend,' Noone whispered. 'What the hell have you been up to, eh?' Squatting in front of the older man, not even Noone's monstrous face could stir any response from his former mentor's dilated pupils. Belle placed a second kiss on her father's forehead and beckoned Noone away.

'What happened, Belle?'

'Doctor's say a stroke. But he was terribly well, Nathaniel, extremely fit still, for his age.'

'Any reason to doubt otherwise though, Belle?'

'Not really,' she said, shaking her head. 'Sure, he may have had enemies in his time, but he's an old man and what with the war, no one would focus on him now. He's just an ageing academic, irrelevant really. He sustained a few minor cuts and bruises from the fall, no reason to raise any suspicions though. They found him in his study, he'd been there all night.'

Nathaniel Noone embraced her as she began to sob.

'Why were you coming to see him, Nate?' she asked with her bottom lip still quivering.

'It doesn't matter now. It was just business.'

'I know what kind of business you are in, Nathaniel Noone, don't forget,' Belle responded abruptly. 'Come, I'm the new curator now.'

'Seriously?' Noone replied in disbelief.

'How dare you, Nathaniel Noone,' Belle hit him with the back of her hand playfully across his chest. 'As I told you already, I am not that little girl with the bunches from all those years ago. Double first in languages, Oxford. First in modern archaeology, I'm not a freckle-faced teen anymore. Now come on, don't be shy. Why were you coming to see Dad?'

Noone relented and withdrew the photograph and torches from his pocket.

'I'm going to require you to dim the lights and draw the blinds, Belle.'

'Pardon?' Belle laughed, jokingly.

'I'm deadly serious,' Noone replied curtly.

Belle drew the blinds leaving a slender gap from an external window that highlighted the dancing particles of dust they shared their space with. Noone placed the photograph on a desktop and weighted it down in the corners. It was too dark to see the black and white original image in detail. Noone had decided to jump straight to the revelations.

'OK, show me,' Belle encouraged.

'Watch closely,' Noone advised, shining the violet torch beam onto the photo.

Iridescent shades of purple and blue illuminated the totems and glyphs in front of them.

'Goodness me,' Belle exclaimed in excitement. 'Show me again. Move over the images, but slower this time.'

Noone repeated the process over and over as Belle scribbled rough copies then returned to the window and allowed the light to flood back in.

'So?' Noone asked.

'Very interesting,' Belle replied. 'You see this symbol here?' she said, pointing to the sketch of the dog's head she had just made. It was the one that covered Draper's face.

'Is it Anubis?' Noone replied.

'Of course, Anubis. God of the afterlife. Always associated with death. But the fact it is face on suggests that it's a death mask opposed to a deity.'

'You're positive?' Noone asked nervously.

'One can never be one hundred per cent sure,' Belle replied 'But Anubis as a god is usually portrayed from a sideways angle. Much like the other masks in the photo. They are deities and followers of said deities.'

'Show me,' Noone insisted.

'This one with the spiral is likely to be that of a lesser god.' Belle pointed to the image covering the lady in the picture. 'I'm not sure which god. I'd need some time to research older records. I believe her to be considered a consort to the other.'

'Which other?' Noone questioned.

'Umm…this one. The falcon-headed man is a high-ranking deity. In any cartouche, this would explain the presence of greatness, extreme power. The bird represents Horus or even RA. It depends on the chronology, the Egyptian dynasties chopped and changed them over millennia and we are constantly learning. In any case, he's high ranking. The God of light,' Belle explained.

'OK,' Noone responded, trying to make sense of the markings. 'And the eyes. I've seen them before, daubed on men, doors, and trinkets. What was that you said, *followers of some kind?*'

'The all-seeing eye of RA; if on a person, it's likely to mean they are the workers or followers of that God or master, very common back then. You must recall the many knick-knacks from vendors in Cairo? Used as protective spirits placed above entrances to family homes,' Belle continued.

Noone resisted the opportunity to discuss his current theory.

'It's even been considered that the great pharaohs may have daubed or tattooed their slaves in such markings,' Belle concluded.

'Thanks, Belle. You've been a great help.'

'Just let me see that photo again. I'd like to see the mark of the one I could not identify. I'm sure I can, given a moment,' she said, snatching it from Noone. Belle was just about to draw the blinds again when surveying the photo for the first time in normal light she paused in shock.

'What is it, Belle? You look like you've seen a ghost,' Noone enquired.

Belle turned to her old friend in shock. 'I recognise two of the people in this picture,' She replied.

'What? Who?' Nathaniel Noone followed up with a concerned eagerness.

'This man and this lady; the one that lights up as a hawk and the one I'm yet to confirm. The consort. The gentleman is Commander Malling, for sure.'

'Malling? I'm not sure who he is. What about the woman?' Noone probed.

'She had a peculiar name. I remember Father laughing but not letting anyone else in on the joke. I missed it at the time, as I was late to the conversation. Father didn't even introduce me, treated me like his secretary. Anyway, she was Swiss I think, her name was … Serena or something like that? They were both part of a fundraiser for injured veterans.'

'When was this?' Noone asked

'I remember it well because it was the evening before they found Father. We thought it might have even been the stress of allowing them to host it in the chamber of Mummification and Egyptology that brought on the stroke. He was so annoyed and agitated that day.'

Nathaniel Noone was staggered at the coincidences. No such thing as coincidences, Monty would have told him, if he could.

'I need to see your father's diary,' he asked.

'We couldn't find his diary,' Belle replied.

'That's odd?'

'Not really, Nate, no. I mean look at this place. Organised chaos, Dad called it. You know what he's like.'

'I do, Belle,' Noone agreed, bending and filtering through the many documents scattered over the floor.

Noone couldn't be sure, as Monty had always been a bit of a hoarder and came across as a complete scatterbrain, but it was all an act as Monty had a photographic memory and knew where everything was. The way the documents were bundled together, fanned out as if someone was looking for something specific, he was sure the room had been tossed. Monty was the best of the best. He had recruited half of them from university. If his old quartermaster had suspected something was afoot he would've sent correspondence, for sure.

Think, Nathaniel, think, hc told himself. Exhaling deeply in and out of his nose.

'What about yourself, Belle. Do you keep a diary?'

'I'm the opposite of Dad. I have a meticulous bent.'

'Can you show me?'

'Of course, I can. But you're worrying me a little, Nate. Should I be concerned?'

'I'm not sure,' Noone said trying to reassure her, suspecting the answer was yes, and hoping his wily old mentor lived up to his reputation.

Belle's office was adjacent to her father's and only a quarter of the size. For every inch of mess her father's was, Belle's study was meticulous in comparison. Orderly, arranged, and no doubt, a reverse product of the chaos that life with her father had etched on her. Belle removed a singular steel key and from a locked drawer inside of a locked cupboard, removed a bound book with a singular crimson elasticated band.

'My diary, Nate.' Belle said handing over the tan leather journal.

'Is that the only key to the cupboard?' Nathaniel Noone asked as he took the diary, Belle nodded her acknowledgement.

Looping the band through his index finger to open it at today's date, he noticed on each side of the pages the indices would allow entries for birthdays with a specific margin line that separated the column from the main body of writing space. Thumbing the pages back to the night of the injured serviceman's fundraiser he read Belle's entries out aloud.

'Anything suspicious, Belle?' he asked.

'Nothing obvious to me,' she replied.

Reading the diary entries over again, he couldn't fathom any relationship or message he had suspected may have been left for him.

'Do you really believe Dad's accident was anything but an accident?' Belle asked, staring into Noone's eye.

'It's too much of a coincidence that the night after this photograph was taken, your father suffered a stroke. A week later I am back in London at the request of a mutual friend. He knew something, your father that is, or stumbled across something he shouldn't have. I'm sure Cairo brings it all together.'

Waiting on a sceptical sigh from Belle, as so often he received from his peers, Noone placed his head in his hands. The criticism did not come. Instead, a comforting hand on his shoulder reassured him. Besides, why were the mysterious markings based on ancient glyphs and symbols?

'Perhaps he has left us a clue, Nate. Draw the blinds. Give me that torch,' Belle insisted.

The room darkened as the blinds descended. Belle lit up the torch. There was no writing in the diary space but as she shone the precise beam over the birthday index, a scribbled sentence announced itself in violet.

'At the centre of end, we redefine the middle'

'What on earth does that mean?' Belle asked, turning to Nathaniel.

'It means your dad's stroke was definitely not an accident. Our fears are confirmed,' Noone replied. 'Whatever this is, whatever it means, your father is key to unlocking the mystery.'

'*At the centre of end, we redefine the middle,*' Belle pondered, circling the room.

'He did love a riddle,' Noone remarked.

'Does, Nate, he's still with us. He loved a cryptic puzzle as much as he loved language and grammar. Look at the first part of this message. *"At the centre of end",*' Belle expressed enthusiastically.

'What is the centre of the end?' Noone replied.

'Well, you've just confirmed my suspicions on this clue. It's not 'the' end. It just says 'end'. With his attention to detail, I doubt that was simply a hurried mistake.' Belle responded.

'And so … the centre of end … is?' Noone questioned.

'N. the letter "N" is the centre of end,' Belle replied. 'I believe the answer is absolute.'

'OK, Belle, if it makes sense to you. So, how are you going to *"redefine the middle".*'

Belle reached towards a succinct collection of books next to a typewriter on the desk. She thumbed the Oxford Dictionary quickly to the M section. Speed-reading the description, she placed it back in its perfectly organised gap and grabbed the Thesaurus. Repeating the process, she skimmed the pages to the M section and focused on Middle.

'... average, between, betwixt, equidistant, mean, medial, median, medium, middle of the day … ' Half mumbling and talking to herself she read the list of associated words. 'Middle of the day? Why is that so specific in the list,' she called out.

'Middle of the day?' Nathaniel laughed.

'What's so funny.'

'Oh, come on, Belle. You can't be serious.'

Belle took a step back and cast a frown at Noone. For a brief moment, she couldn't see the wood for the trees.

'Noon! But spelt differently, Belle. N-Noon, your father is referring to me.'

The light bulb finally struck and she returned to her journal forwarding the calendar pages to July 1, Nathaniel Noone's birthday.

'You know my birthday?' Noone asked, surprised.

Belle blushed, very briefly, before moving over to draw the blinds once more. Lighting the torch and its ethereal violet glow she shone it over the diary page dated July 1.

'The wily old fox.' Noone laughed.

Lit up in purple scrawl was Montague Soames' handwriting, again. *'In plane sight!'*

'So much for old Monty being a stickler for spelling and grammar.' Noone laughed once more.

'That's definitely not a spelling mistake, Nate. Call yourself a spy,' Belle scolded him subtly. He knew already that Monty was directing them towards answers.

*****

The subtle majesty of the Museum of Natural History and Science came into view after a bone-rattling two hours in the company of Major Boyd Collingdale.

Gideon struggled to separate which element was worse. The uncomfortable seat, the smell of the engine, or the noise of the Major himself, who could drown out a faulty eight-stroke engine without a smidgen of effort due to his formidable military lungs. It was a welcome relief to finally stretch his legs as they pulled up past barricades of barbed wire at the impressive stone entrance.

'We want you!' Pointed towards him from the famous finger of Kitchener as his eyes bore down from the famous first world war image that now covered the corridors of the Museum and many of the billboards throughout the city.

On entering the intricately carved threshold, two orderly lines of staff had lined up to greet the Major on his return. Those who had worn them doffed their caps as a mark of respect for the Professor's passing. The opposing lines of staff created a pathway to where the entrance of Entomology once stood. A herculean effort had ensured that all manner of rubble and debris had been removed in the hours since Collingdale's reconnaissance and acquisition of Gideon.

'Major Collingdale,' came the voice of the actuary in charge of clearing the way. 'We've secured the area and it is now fully lit. We have removed the offending cabinet but everything else remains untouched.'

A rare acknowledgement of gratitude from the Major towards the man followed as he nodded then removed his peaked cap and began the quiet walk to where the dead man lay.

It was eerily quiet, unlike the usual hive of activity with the booming orders from Collingdale's mouth to keep everyone on their toes. The Major was unusually subdued. Gideon approached the Entomology entrance with a sense of anxiety but nevertheless impressed by the corridor of wood and glass exhibits now labouring under the monolithic weight of the Museum building. The Major and Gideon entered the area, alone, lights strung every few yards illuminated their way.

'Prepare yourself, Belchambers. This will come as a shock,' Collingdale advised.

The Entomology department had metamorphosed since Collingdale had spent a long night in the darkness. The desk, his refuge during those long hours, sat in the centre, almost impeccably cleaned with the exception of tears across the green baize. The linen-dressed Professor was not far beyond. A crushed boater lay by his side. His face was crumpled into the ground but his arm stretched out with a grasping claw at its end.

'Listen,' Collingdale instructed Gideon, pointing his ear towards the floor. 'Can you hear them?'

Following the Major's lead, Gideon bent forward, turning his head to hear the tiny macerating sounds of feasting insects. A random bluebottle whirred and made an occasional attempt to land on the cadaver but each time spooked itself with the presence of the advancing men. The department was well enough lit that the night time creepy crawlies had retreated to the sanctuary of the dark.

'Which way shall we roll him, Dr Belchambers?' Collingdale asked.

Gideon studied the outstretched arm. Rigor mortis was going to make the process awkward. As he stared at the grasping metacarpals, he noticed contusions running from the palm outwards. Whatever he had been clinging onto, it had been torn from his hand post mortem.

'I think we roll him using the arm as leverage, Major,' Gideon advised 'To me then, on three. One, two, three.'

With a heave and the countered weight of the arm, the two men managed to roll the body over.

'For heaven's sake!' the Major bellowed, as a mini plague of beetles and roaches scattered over his boots to find shade.

'Don't move, Major,' Gideon ordered him. 'Stay perfectly still.'

'What? What is it?' came the nervous reply.

Gideon made a quick search of the surroundings and found an empty inkpot. Spying the quill from the inkpot, he procured it quickly and returned to his comrade, crouching just beneath his knee.

'I wouldn't look down if I was you,' Gideon suggested.

It was too late. The Major had seen the undeniable sting of the Death-stalker as it stood there motionless on its eight legs just above his ankle. A woollen sock the only barrier between himself and a deadly encounter.

'What are you going to do with that feather, tickle the damn thing?' Collingdale critiqued through gritted teeth.

'That's exactly right,' Gideon responded.

'Whaaa–'

'Ssshhh. Stay very still,' Gideon ordered the Major before another bout of his shouting was unleashed. 'The hairs on its legs are sensitive to movement.' Gideon gently brushed the feather against the arachnid's legs. It slowly turned around as he coaxed it into the container. 'That was close, Major. A sock away from instant paralysis.'

'Or death,' Collingdale concluded.

'Oh, these can't kill you. They can sting you so badly you may wish you were dead though,' Gideon continued, securing the scorpion in the pot.

'Enough talk, Doctor. Shall we attend to our friend?'

Gideon took a deep breath and finally drew up to the dead man's face. Disfigured as he was from the impact of the cabinet, his eyes remained unmistakable. As green as envy itself. He would recognise them anywhere.

'It's not him, Major,' Gideon advised.

'Are you sure? Here, let me look.' Collingdale crouched closer and squinted. His eyesight was ageing, as he was.

Gideon scanned the face once again. They were excellent disguises but the hairpiece and moustache were fake. He gently teased the moustache before a tiny ripping sound tore the gummed adhesive from the wearer's upper lip.

'Good grief. An imposter,' Collingdale announced. 'But why?'

'I've no idea, Major,' Gideon replied. Knowing full well he was lying.

'I knew it. I knew he was a bachelor. That's not a wedding band. Is it?' Collingdale asked, seeking closure.

Gideon looked closer. The band was actually two separate rings interlocked in a serpentine pattern. It was familiar to him.

'I'm not sure where this leaves us,' Collingdale expressed.

'I would say that Professor Malcolm is now officially a missing person,' Gideon answered.

'I must inform the authorities of this at once. Hold fire here, Belchambers. Shan't be long,' the Major ordered.

As he slipped out of view, Gideon knew he had only minutes to secure what he suspected was there. The make-up gum that held the fake moustache in place was peeling at the edges of the cadaver's face. Ensuring he wasn't being watched, Gideon slowly removed what remained attached. Post-mortem rigor mortis stopped any bleeding but the occasional tearing of skin sent shivers down his spine. On removing the facial hair, he then set about the hairpiece. It too had been well set and offered a surreal identity to the man that lay beneath it. A few rips of glue from skin were inevitable but once removed his fears were realised. The bald man with the piercing green eyes he had known as a good friend all those years ago. It had only been weeks since he had re-entered his life. But this time without any subversion of the truth, Gideon had identified him as a considerable adversary. His foreboding was coming true. Gideon had been wise not to have trusted him.

'I tried to warn you, Ilya,' he whispered, shaking his head disapprovingly. Gideon began to search around the remaining area next to where the cadaver was lying. The pathway to it had been cleared but beyond it were the bare bones of the department in wreck and ruin. Ilya's grasping hand offered up no more clues but Gideon was sure he would not have arrived empty-handed. Kicking through rubble and dust, he approached the shattered window of the large exhibit case that had crushed his acquaintance and killed him. At the bottom of it were many smaller cases, some intact some decimated but all of them having harboured hundreds upon hundreds of pinned beetle exhibits. The dust and debris formed a blanket of coverage at the bottom of the case. Gideon focused on anything peculiar, anything that was out of place, well, as out of place as it could be in such mayhem. Glass, wood, thorax and abdomen of insect samples were commonly visible. Then he spotted it. A small handle, canvas, possibly beige or white, certainly not something you would find when the exhibit was intact. He grabbed at it but the satchel it was attached to was jammed beneath a layer of broken box glass. He kicked the rubbish out of the way until he gained leverage and was able to free the bag from below.

Double-checking the coast was clear, and that Collingdale was still occupied informing the authorities of Professor Malcolm's mysterious disappearance, he rifled through the bag. There were many documents he would have to look at once time permitted but the cold cylindrical barrel of steel was the first object he felt worthy of further examination. Removing it and looking it over it was identical to the one he had seen just weeks prior. Eric had procured it. 'Borrowed it,' Eric would have said. Tink had made him as good a copy as he could and now, he was looking at it again. He switched it on but in the white light of the lamps that were illuminating the laboratory, it bore no impact. He stepped over the fallen exhibits, the distorted web of twisted joists and plaster until he found darkness. He lit the beam and its violet presence cut through the shadows catching the occasional illumination of a previously camouflaged insect or two. He scoured the walls until he saw it, or it saw him.

The 'All-seeing eye' glared back. Its pupil directing him further into the recesses of the laboratory where it was at its darkest. Directing him to where more secrets lay waiting to be discovered

Chapter 27
Detention

As uneventful as the afternoon algebra lesson had been, Aggie still had two hours in the company of Huntington-Smythe and Dove following the final bell. Luckily for her, Elizabeth and Eric would be there too; although it was likely the Brothers would have a far more brutal punishment for the boy.

As Sister Harvey's private classroom alarm rang out, the metallic clang of the actual school bell echoed through the schoolhouse in unison. The evacuees were acutely tuned to the sound more than their local rivals and vanished without a second's thought. The Priory girls patted their cohort on the back as they left pronouncing that their 'Parents will hear about this,' and 'Surely an assault is a criminal offence worthy of gaol?'

Henrietta Huntington-Smythe acknowledged their sincerities but outnumbered by at least two to one for the next two hours she was smart enough not to make any signs of a fuss until she knew just how she would be spending the detention time.

With a customary glance of disapproval, Sister Harvey looked down on her charges and with a silent nod, bid them a good evening. Miss Dove, who had been waiting for her colleagues' departure then entered the room.

'Today, I have been unfortunate enough to witness lying and violence in a school which should never endorse such behaviour,' Dove scolded them. 'It has been necessary to alert the authorities in this instance.'

A collective gasp united all three pupils; two of them in fear, the other in anticipation.

'Why?' Elizabeth and Aggie expressed together.

Henrietta was smiling, smugly.

'Why did you try and conceal your breakfast from us Elizabeth? Why lie?' Dove asked the older Peabody.

Elizabeth hadn't expected that question. She thought Aggie's punch to Smythes' nose had trumped her unsubtle sleight of hand. 'I'm not sure, miss,' she replied. Caught off guard, she hadn't had time to prepare an answer.

'Seems a little odd, doesn't it? Do you wish to conceal what you actually had for breakfast? Bacon, eggs, toasted soldiers? Very tasty, a rare treat I would guess. So why lie? Lying just highlights a greater act of criminality does it not?' Dove summarised contently.

'You thieving Peabody!' Henrietta snarled at her. 'It was your lot all along.'

Elizabeth didn't respond. Aggie was confused by the accusation and Huntington-Smythe looked on with a snide vulpine leer.

'Do come in, Mr Bott,' Dove announced, beckoning the shadow that was waiting patiently outside of the classroom door.

Wilson Bott's day was busy enough without the misdemeanours of school children occupying his diary. A dead body in the brook was enough work for anyone to attend with but under the insistence of the Huntington-Smythe family, and the suspected revelation he was about to receive, he had made the short trip down the Steep. It was a welcome relief from an afternoon in the mortuary with Messrs Closet and Cleave.

'I need you to come with me, please,' he asked Elizabeth. Beckoning with a small hand gesture towards himself.

Elizabeth who knew of Mr Bott as the local law enforcer and regular unwanted guest at the Poacher gave an alarmed look towards Aggie. This was far more serious then she had imagined. Aggie who had no idea who the man was, or why he was even summoned just for the small note of breakfast written on paper, could only garner the seriousness by her friends' startled face. Come to think of it why had Elizabeth concealed the truth anyway? Elizabeth followed the Sheriff out of the room leaving Aggie outnumbered with Dove and Smythe.

'Miss Dove, what has Elizabeth been accused of?' Aggie asked concerned for her friend.

'That, Chatsmore, is on a need-to-know basis,' Dove curtly advised her.

Meanwhile, outside of the classroom and via the school corridors, Wilson Bott led Elizabeth to the governess's office. Lady Huntington-Smythe, with her stubby pointy nose and index finger surveying the sill for dust, lay in wait. Opening the door with his young female charge, Bott presented her to Lady Huntington-Smythe.

'Ha!' she clapped in a congratulatory tone. 'I told you it would be a Peabody, Bott. I'm surprised it's not that street urchin Eric, but not surprised at all it's a Peabody.'

'I'm not even sure what you are accusing me of,' Elizabeth angrily answered back, stepping forward.

'Quiet, Peabody! I'll be asking the questions around here,' snapped Lady Huntington-Smythe.

'Actually,' interjected Bott. 'I will be asking the questions around here, so if you could both calm down, we will discuss this in an orderly manner,' Bott said with authority, sensing a verbal and physical impasse between the two as he moved to stand between them.

Lady Huntington-Smythe held up a small handwritten piece of notepaper to Elizabeth. Dove must have informed her earlier when Aggie and herself observed them arguing in the school entrance.

'This was found on you by Sister Harvey this morning, was it not?' the Lady questioned Elizabeth.

Elizabeth nodded, recognising Aggie's handwriting and list of breakfast items.

'I knew it. Proof if ever we needed it, Bott,' she said, punctuating the desk with a rigid index finger.

'Hold on one moment,' Bott said calmly. 'Lady Smythe–'

'It's Huntington-Smythe, thank you,' she reminded him angrily.

'Lady Huntington-Smythe. You called me here advising you had apprehended a suspect in the robbery of Huntington Hall, correct?'

'Correct,' she responded quickly.

'And this note is your evidence?' he questioned.

'Yes, yes. Do keep up, Bott,' she said sarcastically.

'It's Sheriff Bott, thank you.' He took glee in reminding her of his position. 'And I am not sure I am keeping up. Please, explain.'

'On this vagrant's note,' she continued accentuating with malice. 'It quite clearly expresses the indulgence of bacon and egg,' Lady Huntington-Smythe responded, overly pleased with herself, laughing as if the Peabodys could ever afford such luxury.

Elizabeth listened on bitterly.

Bott still looked on puzzled.

'Good grief, man. No wonder the smugglers and rogues love this village so much,' continued Lady Huntington-Smythe criticising the Sheriff. 'When our stately home was broken into a fortnight ago, we recorded the breaking of our safe, the removal of several highly valuable personal items and –

here lies the rub, sir -- the theft of dozens of eggs and several sides of pork from our stores!'

Bott's face suggested that he finally understood the cloak-and-dagger approach Lady Huntington-Smythe had taken. As a minor revelation finally expressed itself across his face. It was incredulous that first of all, she had demanded his immediate attendance of the school and now the suggestion she had actually apprehended the culprit.

'I see, ma'am,' he replied unable to conceal an underlying tone of amusement.

'What's so funny, Bott?' the Lady angrily inquired.

'Sheriff Bott,' he reminded her again. 'I wish you had explained your theories to me prior to your insistence of my presence.'

'I do not see why that was necessary, Sheriff Bott!' she replied with her voice increasingly getting louder. 'You know how tongues wag in this village. I wanted to get ahead of this family of thieves before they concocted false alibis.'

Bott knew all too well how quickly tongues did wag in Ambledown and the irony that the lady herself was the biggest source of malicious gossip was not lost on him.

'This morning, as you may be aware, we pulled a body from Braggan's Brook,' he began to explain.

'And … .' the Lady interrupted impatiently.

'And.' Bott composed himself. 'It appears we may have found your egg thief already,' he replied confidently.

Lady Huntington-Smythe, whose personal dictionary did not contain the word apology, simply turned her nose up and looked away from both Bott and Elizabeth. Once more she ran her finger across the sill for dust.

'He had the means to steal eggs and conceal them. He also carried a large amount of money about his person. Ill-got gains I would say. That's little more than a coincidence, Lady Smythe, wouldn't you?'

'It's Huntington-Smythe, how many times must I correct you,' she said becoming increasingly frustrated.

'Which leaves me with a dilemma,' Bott calmly expressed. 'If this person was responsible for your break-in, and it's increasingly looking likely he was, and then suddenly washes up dead, what conclusions can I draw?' he asked.

'We were not responsible for a dead Braggan!' she shouted. 'I wish.'

'Oh, I wasn't aware anyone had been informed it was a Braggan.' Bott smiled.

'Well, it's hardly a secret when the giant clan leader leaves you outside Closet and Cleaves with his mutt, vermin bird and covered in his gold. Is it?' she snarled.

Admittedly, Bott knew that people were already gossiping. News, particularly bad news, always spread like wildfire. Even from the moment Lyle had been pulled from the water the whole of Ambledown would be aware within a few hours. Pop would be one of the first to have known and also the Huntington-Smythes.

'I think, considering what we currently know, Miss Peabody has nothing to answer for. Do you?' Bott suggested, offering a slight wink to Elizabeth behind the lady's back. 'In fact, where were you last night Lady Smythe?' Bott questioned, almost knowingly goading the lady

Huntington-Smythe didn't respond. The incredulity took her by surprise. Bott took her unacceptable silence as confirmation Elizabeth had done nothing wrong and showed the elder Peabody the door, following close behind and away from Lady Huntington-Smythe's imminent fury.

'Tell me, Elizabeth,' Wilson Bott asked 'Was that list yours or not?'

'Why does that matter now?' She replied quickly.

'I understand. You've nothing to prove to me,' Bott concluded. Leaving Elizabeth in the schoolhouse corridors while he headed back to the funeral parlour.

Elizabeth should have followed him out but concern for Aggie led her back to Sister Harvey's room. She had promised Gideon to look after her. The room was empty. Dove, Aggie, and Henrietta were gone. She continued scouring the corridors until a whisper greeted her along one of them.

'Pssst, Lizzy,' came the familiar voice of her younger brother.

'Where are you, Eric?' she replied looking all around her.

'I'm in the ceilings above,' he said and laughed.

Gazing upwards she could just make out an eye from his mischievous little face through a knothole as it peered down on her. 'What on earth are you doing up there, Eric?' she said, concerned.

'Dove's got the girls dusting down and cleaning out lots of old school mem'ribilya. I'm the lackey fetching it from up 'ere. It's brilliant; treasure everywhere and I can spy on nearly every room,' he enthused.

'Keep an eye on, Aggie. I don't trust Henrietta one inch. I best be getting back or McGregor will have poor old Gem trying to lift barrels.'

'Right-O!' Eric replied, a wink just visible through the dark opening above.

'Oh, and Eric, Henrietta's mother is in Dove's office. Be sure "not" to scare her.'

'I'll definitely "not" do that.' He laughed as he scurried away making ghostly noises above the ceiling.

*****

Gideon directed his torch, and contorted his body in and out of the tumbledown debris, following the occasional illuminated eye that guided his path to a plain wooden door. It glided open easily, unaffected by the surrounding chaos and devastation that had brought down the majority of the eastern quadrant and had ultimately stalled Ilya's plan, whatever that had been.

The room he entered had windows on several sides and was on old storage and porter's room. It was well lit in comparison and full of outcast exhibits. Bell jars with part-stuffed animals, half-jawed skulls of large reptiles, and a large broken tusk of a Narwhal dominating the space. Its primary resident he knew all too well.

'Hello, old friend,' Gideon mused, staring up at the one-eyed giraffe he had donated to Professor Malcolm to resurrect.

'Don't suppose you can tell me what went on here can you?' he said and laughed. A dumb silence from the forlorn creature greeted him as he began to investigate the room.

The violet torch beam was not as prominent in the subdued natural light but he rotated it around the room nevertheless. The exit door had the final mark of the eye. There was no doubt in Gideon's mind this had been Ilya's route in and out. The chaos of fate had dealt the crushing blow to stop him in his escapade. He stepped across scattered exhibits and stumbled as he caught his foot in the tiger skin that was strewn across the floor. He wouldn't have given it a second look considering the surroundings but his foot was caught in what appeared to be a sleeve. That's odd, he thought as he unravelled the material that was wrapped around his foot. He held up the skin and immediately it draped into the bedraggled form of the long garment that it actually was. Why would a tiger skin coat be left here? He asked himself. Surely, they were rare and extremely expensive not some throwaway exhibit from yesteryear. He had seen one before, recently in fact. He rifled through the pockets. There was nothing much to show in any of them. Just the quarter-end stub of an unfinished cigarette. He looked closer at it. The filter end had scarlet lipstick on it, no surprises that such a fancy coat belonged to a lady who would wear such rouge, however the filter itself had a small thread of violet silk that ran around the circumference. He took the torch beam and shone it over the end, using the cup of a hand to shroud it in darkness for optimum effect. Within the cigarette tobacco small emissions of light, as if minuscule diodes, sparkled and illuminated as they reacted to the ethereal effects of the violet beam.

'This is no coincidence,' he thought to himself.

'Belchambers!' came Collingdale's booming voice from the distance of the Entomology department. 'Where are you, Professor?' the noise continued.

Gideon paused for a while and gathered his thoughts. He did not reply to the Major. Instead, he opened the door emblazoned with the 'All-seeing eye' and had a decision to make. Should he take flight or stay and make things right? Should he stay and confess everything of what he knew to Major Collingdale. It would be a lot for the belt and braces man to digest. He paused for a while as Collingdale's voice disappeared once more.

He looked down at Ilya's satchel. 'So what secrets are you willing to reveal to me?' he spoke softly to himself.

*****

199

Half an hour had passed as Aggie and Henrietta scrubbed filthy furniture, frames, and pictures at the bequest of Governess Dove.

'Why I should be punished after such an attack is beyond me,' Huntington-Smythe complained.

'Insubordination, Henrietta!' Dove confirmed. 'And I'll have less of it.'

Aggie was warming more and more to Dove. She kept her head down and cleaned away.

Aaagghhhhhhh!' came a mighty scream from the governess's office.

'What on Earth is that?' Dove said, alarmed. Leaving the ancillary room to investigate. Leaving her charges alone.

'Oh, look at this one, Chatsmore,' Smythe said and laughed. 'It's so old they have the same shaped crest as your moth-eaten rag,' she concluded by throwing the old glass photograph so that it smashed just at Aggie's feet, splintering glass up her leg. Aggie clenched her fist, ready to fight her opponent.

'Whoops!' Smythe said bluntly. 'Silly me. I do apologise, Chatsmore.'

The door then swung back open and it was Lady Huntington-Smythe followed quickly by Dove.

'Hen, are you OK, my love? Has this girl attacked you again? I heard a crash.'

'She threw it at me!' Smythe feigned, forcing tears from her eyes.

'No, I didn't,' Aggie contested.

'I bet you did,' Lady Huntington-Smythe snarled back.

'Oooh noooo she didn't,' came the ghostly pantomime voice from above the ceiling.

'Aghhhhhhhhhh!!!' came the simultaneous scream from all four of the ladies in the room.

'I told you this place was haunted!' Lady Huntington-Smythe protested towards Dove. She grabbed her daughter, defied the detention, and left in a hurry.

Aggie was left shrugging her shoulders innocently as Dove stared upwards. 'Leave the attic space at once, Eric Peabody!' Dove shouted towards the ceiling.

Eric's laughter was heard before silence descended on the governess and Aggie who were left alone.

'I have had quite enough for one day, Chatsmore,' the governess advised. 'Can I trust you to clean the rest of these old school photographs, unsupervised, in the remaining detention time you have?'

'Of course, miss,' Aggie said and nodded assuredly.

'Very well. I shall return in just over an hour.' Dove left, locking the door behind her.

Moving to the shattered frame on the floor, she scooped up the glass and rubbed the photograph over with a damp cloth. The image was intact and beneath the photo it had initials of all the pupils and the teachers. She stared at the innocent smiles of the children gazing back at her. There was a mixture of ages but the majority must have been only six or seven years old. The class was only fifteen or so in numbers and a mixture of girls and boys though two-thirds were male.

'Ambledown Priory Preparatory 1907-1908' read the title underneath. True to Henrietta's observation, the crest, which adorned all of their breast pockets, was the same shape as Aggie's, albeit Aggie's was now a darker faded grey where the crest had once resided. It was possible, she thought to herself, that her mother and Uncle Gideon could be amongst these children or at least some of the photographs. She eagerly emptied the boxes in front of her and spread them out in chronological order. She wasn't exactly sure how old Gideon was but she had a rough idea and could look through them all cross-referencing the initials GB and CB, Gideon and Charlotte – the Belchambers twins.

'Eric? Eric are you still up there?' Aggie called out in a muted voice.

'Noooooo!' came his laughing ghostly impersonation.

'Before you leave can you find any old photos and bring them to me.?'

'There's loads up here, Aggie. Too many to count.'

'Can you find any from nineteen hundred to nineteen twenty?' Aggie asked.

'Me reading ain't too good, to be honest. I'll do me best tho,' Eric replied.

'I know, Eric. Look for anyone in the photos who has the same shaped crest on their jackets as I have … well … did. The old style,' Aggie requested. it was easy to distinguish old from new.

'OK, I fink I know which ones. Must go now,' Eric's voice disappeared as he crept as quietly across joists as he could.

Chapter 28
Revelations

'Gin, London Dry. Tonic Water, Indian. Lemon, and Mr Louds insisted you had ice too,' advised the golden-toothed orderly in uniformed fashion as he presented Professor Meredith Malcolm with his reward.

The Professor who was anticipating his libation with an excited preening of his moustache, sat down and began to prepare his drink. Two cubes of ice chinked against the tall glass tumbler. He cut a slither of lemon, executed with the kind support of a sharp laboratory scalpel and placed it neatly next to the glass before applying the alcohol. A generous glug of gin came next and was topped with Indian tonic water. Finally, a squeeze of fresh lemon juice followed by the spiralled zest he had neatly carved and set aside.

'Very good form. Thank him for me and, please, inform him I will have completed these revised works by nightfall,' the Professor advised taking the slightest sip of his drink.

The orderly left, leaving the Professor with his reward and allowing him to continue his works alone.

The intricate nature of removing the squares of parchment to reveal the hieroglyphic negatives could not be done so under the influence of alcohol. As soon as the orderly was out of sight, Professor Malcolm spat his sip back into the glass and continued with his work.

*****

Returning to Montague Soames' chaotic office, Belle and Nathaniel were convinced now, more than ever, that his missing diary entry was no mistake. It was true that the Professor and old spymaster insisted in a disorderly environment as that way any secrets or lies he had to maintain could not be easily deciphered. Nathaniel began to stalk the room for any signs from his old friend's latest clue.

'*In plane sight,*' he repeated and muttered as he stepped across documents and paraphernalia.

'You know, Nathaniel, this could all be a ruse and we're playing right into someone else's hands,' Belle suggested.

'I don't think so, Belle. It had crossed my mind but you said so yourself that no one else had a key to your cupboard, let alone knew of your diary's existence. I suspect your old man knows far more than we are giving him credit for. For starters, how could he predict that this torch would unravel the clue, the hidden messages, or even the fact I would come? How could he be certain? I don't think he could have. However, he saw a pattern, something rang alarm bells, and he hedged his bets he could rely on his puzzle being solved.'

'If you say so, Nate. So, "*In plane sight*" … what can we find amongst this mess?' Belle searched the bookshelf. Typically, it was as disorganised as the rest of the room. Belle searched through the bindings one by one. She procured a book on gliding and one on aircraft engineering. There were no messages attached. She fanned the pages holding them upside down for any notes to descend and float downwards, but nothing. She dimmed the blinds and re-fanned the pages slowly with the violet torch beam but absolutely nothing jumped out.

It remained a frustrating few hours. Outside, the evening was drawing in, Nathaniel and herself needn't draw the blinds for darkness anymore as the nightlight curfew was upon them and all blinds were closed as due course. Nathaniel Noone paced the room over and over like a caged animal just waiting for that clue to set him free.

'Your bloody father, Belle. He never made it easy. But it will be here. We're missing the obvious.'

Belle didn't like to hear her father and cursing in the same sentence but she shared the frustration of his former protégé. 'Let's forget about, '*In plane sight*', just for a moment,' she suggested. 'What do we know about Dad and what looks out of place.'

'He was a disorganised old bugger, so that discounts nearly the entire room,' Noone replied sarcastically

'Exactly. Now, what wasn't he – tidy, organised? Anything look out of place now?'

Nothing appeared organised to the untrained eye. Everything was in disarray.

'Wait, did your father ever wear a hat?' Noone asked Belle with an air of anticipation.

'I don't think he ever wore one. Not even in the midday heat of Egypt as you may recall. He was more likely to wear a headscarf to keep out the sun.'

'Exactly!' enthused Noone, stepping towards a set of coat hooks adjacent to the entrance door.

A black fedora was neatly presented on one of the hooks while beneath it on the floor were a few bundled coats and scarfs that looked comfortable in the jumble that surrounded them. Stepping around them, Nathaniel Noone removed the hat from its hook.

'Well, I never!' Belle exclaimed.

'Devious old bugger but a genius never the less,' Noone said and smiled.

Hanging from the hook and concealed by the hat was a rosewood-and-steel wood plane. The rounded handle and grip were suspending the tool downwards where its guiding site focused towards the pile of clothing on the floor.

Both Belle and Nathaniel scrambled at the clothing below, almost clashing heads in their eagerness to retrieve what was underneath. The disappointment was obvious on Belle's face as she retrieved a wire waste paper bin from beneath. It was full of ripped up papers but there was nothing on them.

'Oh for pity sake!' she shouted in frustration, turning red.

Noone began to laugh. He was sniffing the wastebasket like a hound detecting a scent before the hunt. 'Can you smell that, Belle?' he asked.

'What?' she looked on confused.

'Lemons,' Noone said jubilantly.

'Lemons?' she asked, still confused.

'It beats the effluence of the underground, I can tell you.' Nathaniel laughed, removing the pieces of paper and holding them up to the single dimly lit bulb that now illuminated Monty's study.

*****

An hour had passed quickly when the lock of Miss Dove's office clicked open and she entered to find Aggie enthusiastically polishing the final few photo-frames.

'My, my, you have been busy, Miss Chatsmore.' Dove smiled on entry. 'Perhaps this is a better example to set?'

Aggie smiled back. There must have been thirty frames laid out in front of her. The years of attic dust now a distant memory, all gleaming and set out in chronological order.

'I don't suppose you know when the crest changed do you, miss?' Aggie asked, gesturing to where hers should be.

'I'm sorry, I really don't know. I'm a relative newcomer to these parts compared to the likes of Sister Harvey. Sister Harvey would know. Or that lady in the village, Mrs Parker, I think. She was school secretary for many years.'

'Nose ... I mean ... Nelly Parker?' Aggie asked, correcting herself as she did so.

'That's her,' Dove confirmed. 'Why are you so interested?'

Aggie could not divulge she was looking for a picture of her mother when she'd attended the Priory. 'I'm just interested to know who may have worn this jacket before me,' Aggie replied.

Miss Dove cast her a curious look. 'OK. Well, as I say, Sister Harvey or Mrs Parker might be able to help. You're free to run along now.'

'I'd like to revisit these photos once I know,' Aggie said.

'Of course. They'll be in this room. Now, I must insist you leave for the day. A two-hour detention on your first day is some feat. I am sure Professor Belchambers will be wondering where you are. And, Miss Chatsmore, may I suggest your second day be far less extraordinary than your first.'

Aggie nodded and flitted out of the governess's room. Grabbing her cloak on her way out as she passed the large Aspidistra, she entered the cold and dark evening. She was expecting the Peabodys to be waiting for her but they were not. The confines of the school had offered her comfort and protection. Now that she had stepped back on to the Steep all alone, her anxieties greeted her again. Lyle Braggan was dead. She had no reason to worry about him, but she couldn't help but feel she was being followed, being watched.

Why weren't the Peabody's there to greet her? Aggie wondered. Gideon had reassured her they would act as her escorts and protectors. Something must have happened. She exhaled a cold breath and began the sharp incline towards home.

'Aggie! Aggie,' came a familiar female voice. 'Are you walking home alone?' she asked.

'I guess so, Cecile,' Aggie replied, turning to greet the restaurant owner and her effervescent smile.

'Where are Elizabeth and Eric?' Cecile questioned.

'I'm not sure,' Aggie replied, casting a perplexed glance her way. 'How did you know they were supposed to meet me?' she asked.

'Gideon asked me to keep an eye out too. Shall I accompany you?'

'Yes, please,' Aggie confirmed.

'Purrsia has gone missing again. He took a real shine to you. Perhaps we will find him on our way.'

Aggie's anxieties surrounding her lone trip home were overtaken with a desire to find and protect the cat. Its furless body wouldn't allow it to be exposed for long as the coldness of an Autumn night set in.

'Here, kitty,' they both called out, puckering and kissing the air as they passed the many alleyways on the way uphill.

Aggie was so lost in their search that they reached The Keep in no time at all. Nan was peering out from the raised ground floor window, anxiously surveying the cobblestone road in front of the building. On seeing Aggie, she rushed to the front door.

'Where you been? I worried sick!' Nan shouted.

'She was helping me,' Cecile defended.

'Night, Cecile.' Aggie waved as she climbed the stone steps. 'Good luck finding Purrsia. If he turns up here, I'll be sure to keep him safe.'

'Thank you and goodnight, Agatha,' Cecile responded before continuing her search for the bald moggy as she made her way back downhill.

'Is Gideon back yet?' Aggie asked.

'Not yet. He still in London. Come, I make dinner,' Nan replied bluntly.

Aggie closed the door behind them but not before one last look down the hill. A shadow disappeared into the darkness and her nerves peaked again but there was nothing to fear as two light wardens chatted with one another as they made their rounds. Sporting gas masks around their necks, enamel hats on heads, and waterproof sou'westers.

'Be sure to pull those blinds shut, miss,' one of them called out.

'I will,' Aggie acknowledged, closing the door quickly behind her and bolting it tight.

From a distance, the two men looked remarkably like the two men when this had all started, back at Florrie's. But they were dead. The scarred stranger who had tried to take her had made sure of that. The vivid image of blood trickling from the gunshot, central to the luminous eye that covered their foreheads, came flooding back to remind her.

Florrie, I wonder how Florrie is? she asked herself. Uncle Gideon still had a lot of explaining to do. Once he returned from London.

*****

Gideon Belchambers could not make sense of the tiger-skin coat at all. The cigarette he found in the pocket linked it directly to Ilya's strange violet torch, unquestionably, but it was too long and too feminine for the Russian and, therefore, the owner of this coat, whoever it was, was complicit in his plan. Sensing that Major Boyd Collingdale would not be able to navigate the Entomology department as swiftly as he had, after all, he did not have the torch beam and all-seeing eye to guide him through, Gideon took stock and began sifting through the contents of Ilya's crushed satchel.

The dust had settled, indiscriminately covering all the documents inside. He emptied the entire contents in front of him and began to remove the dirt. Scrolls and papers tightly bound together, which he would have to view in a safer place. There were also three identically sized envelopes. The first was written in Cyrillic, which he could not read or was likely to understand. He placed it within an inside pocket. The second one was written in English and addressed to Montague Soames.

'What the Devil?' Gideon spoke to himself. Opening the letter, though it was not addressed to him he read it out aloud:

Dearest Montague,

If you are reading this, I am dead. If you are dead too, I will see you for my judgement on the other side.

I am hoping you are alive and accept this as my apology for leading them to your door. If, as I suspect, they have found what they need then you will require the anti-venom I am in supply of and which accompanies this letter.

I bequeath all antiquities due to me from the tomb to your Museum, hoping one day you may make more sense of them than I.

Seeking your forgiveness in the afterlife,

Ilya Debrovska

'Good God, Ilya. What have you done?' Gideon questioned, searching through the bag for the anti-venom. At the bottom, beneath yet more papers and maps, he fumbled for a tiny bottle, still intact, with a flat cork stopper plugging the thick glass. He held it up to the light. Its liquid green transparency still allowed the fluid inside to be seen. The fluid ebbed from left to right as he rocked it slowly. On the front was a tiny black-and-white label showing a scorpion.

'Monty?' his thoughts turned to his old quartermaster and friend. 'I must get to Monty as soon as I can.'

'Professor Belchambers?' came the Major's repetitive calls.

No time to worry about Collingdale now. I'll return and explain to him one day, he thought. He placed Monty's envelope and the third envelope, which was not addressed to anyone, also within the inside pocket of his long coat. It would have to wait until later. Opening the exit, Gideon Belchambers alighted from the porter's lodge. Looking up into the dark sky and sighing a chilled breath, he spied the stone cat standing guard above.

'You're supposed to be a symbol of prosperity and luck,' he said to it. 'It appears you didn't waste any on the dead man inside so let's hope you favour me instead.' Taking the set of keys he had found in Ilya's pockets, he began his search for his ride across town to the British Museum.

*****

Nan was an excellent cook. An excellent housemaid, now Aggie came to think of it. The home was always warm, spotlessly clean and welcoming. Despite the chaotic jumble Gideon would set out on almost a daily basis. Any guest of Gideon's was always well looked after, spoilt in fact. Aggie was nothing less than royalty as far as he was concerned so Nan made extra effort to please her.

'It's getting late, Agatha. You go bed soon,' Nan advised.

'I'd like to wait up for Uncle Gideon, if that's OK?' she replied and was met with a disapproving frown. It was ten o'clock and way past Aggie's bedtime. It was also way past the several hours Gideon had expected to spend in London. He had not returned. Aggie worried he could have been caught in an air-raid and was, therefore, holed up somewhere. It was likely, as they were frequent and unrelenting in the capital. Ambledown, by contrast, was quiet and unscathed. If she listened carefully, the last of the summer crickets could be heard chirping before they hibernated or died.

Sleep was beginning to defeat Gideon's young charge. Nan brought in blankets and hot milk as she lay there drifting in and out of sleep. Nan dimmed the nightlight and left Aggie alone with her thoughts while she retired to her quarters.

Aggie wasn't sure how long she had dozed for when she heard a repetitive clack at the window. At first, she thought hailstones were falling but there were too few noises. She turned the light off fully so there was just darkness and crept on all fours to the window. There was a splinter of moonlight between the blinds that she peered through. Hiding out of sight of the main street but visible to her from the window was the mischievous smile of Eric Peabody. He was hopping lightly from foot to foot and breathing hot air into his hands in an attempt to stay warm. Once he spotted her, he made light work of the stone steps leading to 1a. Aggie made her way to the front door to let him in. His fingers had already poked their way through the letterbox and he was shoving an envelope through.

'SShhhh!' he whispered. 'Don't unbolt the door or nuffink.'

Aggie took the large envelope he was softly posting through.

'I got as many as I could with the old crest. But I'll 'ave to get 'em back tomorrow. D'ya 'ere.'

'Of course,' Aggie whispered back. 'Thank you!'

'Welcome,' he replied.

'I was expecting to see you all after detention.'

'Yeah ... Sorry 'bout that. I've been in the attic all this time, sifting through all the treasure. And Gem went an chopped 'er 'air off, didn't she? McGregor 'it the roof. Lizzy couldn't risk leaving her alone. She said Cecile was told. Didn't she turn up?'

'Oh, yes, she did. Poor Gem. Hope she's OK.'

'Apart from looking ridiculous, she'll be fine.' Eric laughed and sauntered back into the shadows as shrewd as a scavenging fox.

Aggie made her way back into the living room. The fire was almost out but its subtle embers provided enough warmth for an hour or two yet. She re-lit the nightlight, but kept it low, and began to deal the photos out from within the envelope as if she was playing a huge game of patience. She ran them vertically to represent each decade and then horizontally to represent each year. Eric was right, there were lots of them. Before 1900 and just up until this current war. There was forty years' worth at least.

'I'm thirteen,' she said to herself, beginning to count backwards on her fingers. 'It's 1943 now so that's right, 1930, the year I was born.' She picked up all photos after 1930 and placed them back in the envelope. 'They had both been to university before Egypt and it was several years after when Mum fell pregnant with me,' she spoke to herself, confirming her mother's and Gideon's history to herself. 'That could be anywhere between twenty or even twenty-five years,' she confirmed to herself in a whisper.

Once again, counting backwards, she eliminated any photos prior to 1905.

'I doubt they started school much before seven or eight,' she continued, removing a few more years. Re-arranging the remaining photos into a single timeline, she then began to work across the images, waiting to see her mother and uncle smiling back at her – from carefree children through to moody teenagers.

She spotted Gideon at once. Firstly in 1919. He was so slender, about twelve years old by then, beanpole thin and with his unmistakable flop of hair and foolish grin that spanned his face. He was broader now. His face carried more weight for certain but back then he was stick thin. It was definitely him. He was at the far-right end of the photograph. She scoured the girls who were fewer in number and placed either at the front of the photograph or to the left. The boys outnumbered them by about two to one so that should have made her job easier. Staring intently on the far left was a girl whose features mimicked Gideon's exactly. She was slender, tall, and with a foolish grin. It must have been her. Florrie had only ever had photos of her in her adulthood, her early twenties. Aggie was sure it must be her. She referred to the footnote below, which displayed the pupils' initials

Top Row L-R – C.S-M

That wasn't right. Her mother's name had been Charlotte Elizabeth Belchambers. She had never been married so it could never have been a maiden name either, and besides, her uncle was also a Belchambers. She looked across to the right-hand-side of the initials:

H.S-M

How could that be wrong too? Both of them had the same hyphenated surname, which was a peculiar coincidence, but their forenames were also wrong. It must be a clerical error she thought. Or she hadn't interpreted it correctly.

Aggie then proceeded to look at the surrounding years. Sure enough, there they were again, on the photo from the year before and the year before that. Same grins, but younger each time. Same positions and, much to her dismay, the same initials used. There was no chance it could have been wrong over so many years. She must be interpreting something incorrectly. She picked up the photo dated 1920. True to form, there they were; both of them bookends. But their smiles had been lost and a seriousness cast over their faces. Same initials, same confusion and then Aggie spotted the proof that she needed. Her mother, or at least she was ninety-nine per cent sure it was her mother, was wearing her blazer. A dark grey mark was present where once the crest had been but no longer was. It was her, it had to be. Aggie squinted. The age of the image and the size of the mark were not clear.

'Aggh, the magnifying glass,' she thought to herself. Making light work of the stairs, she bounded into her room and procured the worn velvet box and its precious contents from within the dolls' house where she had hidden it. She returned to the living room where the nightlight still provided her with enough means to look at the magnified image in detail. As she pored over the photograph, the opaque edges, those that looked like they had been etched to emphasise the design, cast a circular pattern of light as she focused the glass in and out. Aggie had seen children use glass, magnified and other, to burn ants using the heat from a strong summer sun but she wasn't aware that the small amount of light offered from her internal nightlight would cast any at all. It allowed her to target her mothers' jacket and focus on the crest. Sure enough, it was missing from her jacket.

Aggie fetched the blazer from the landing coat hook. She turned it inside out and began to look for the initials Nan had suggested were marked inside. It was so obvious to her now but having looked for CEB before, she hadn't spotted them. Drawn in an intricate calligraphy and intersecting each other like a Venn diagram the three initials presented themselves: CSM.

What did CSM stand for?

It was late now and her eyes grew heavy. She couldn't remember anything linked to the initials CSM. Perhaps she would have better luck in the morning when there was more light and she could focus. Surely Nan would know. She'd been around for as long as Aggie could remember, or perhaps Sister Harvey or Nelly Parker would know. For now, she snuggled up and fell asleep, downstairs, so she could greet her uncle once he returned.

Chapter 29
The Russian

He'd been there from the beginning. Mainly in the background, keeping a low profile. Adapting as best he could to the scorching Egyptian heat having journeyed from his arctic Siberian home via several years of adventuring. Fate had convened so his arrival was at a time of revelation in Cairo.

Carter, of course, would win all the plaudits after the most famous discovery of them all, Tutankhamen. Ilya Debrovska was there, patiently waiting in the background. He didn't seek the limelight. Quite to the contrary, his objective was to remain concealed. His fortune would be made by offering services to those who sought to ship and transfer the great findings of the time – through legitimate or illicit fortitude. That all changed after the accident, and several years later the second great war came.

What had brought him to a rural corner of the United Kingdom and a market town on the English coast couldn't be further away from the ancient monuments of Mesopotamia or the Pyramids of Giza. As he stood there, blanketed by darkness and a covering of famous British rain cloud, he waited patiently for the thunder to come and the torrential rain to conceal the intimate sounds of his housebreaking.

Though it was neither Sphinx nor Luxor's finest, Huntington Hall was nevertheless an impressive country pile. Its rambling grounds maintained pomp despite the challenges of war. Tonight, its mullioned windows reflected and refracted the palette of dark purple skies as they awaited the formidable rains that were coming.

Late August storms were common after the glorious blistering summer that this part of the British coast had been lucky enough to receive. Ilya waited at a distance under an ancient yew that offered shelter, protection, and a platform for covert surveillance. Peering through a single spyglass, dressed in black, a satchel tightly strapped across his torso while his face concealed by a balaclava accentuated those envious emerald eyes. Beneath his legs, at the foot of the ancient tree, was a sack of dead animals. It contained several corpses of roadside mammals that Ilya had gathered over the previous week. Its pungent odour was gut-retching to humans and at least a hundred-fold fodder for its canine targets. As its stench wafted through the night air, the Russian stood upwind as heavy, bell-sized blobs of storm water began to rain down.

This was not the first time he had been a hidden observer at the hall. He had waited weeks, lived isolated outside of the village where he would make his entrance when the time was right, assuming his hunches were about to come true. His accent and appearance would warrant too many unwanted approaches from the locals, including local law enforcers. So, for now, he exiled himself far away to a hidden woodland habitat.

A converted Rolls Royce Silver Shadow glinted against the moonlight and pulled up at the grand entrance. The driver disembarked, unbuckled two long wooden planks that had been customised to strap perfectly to the passenger side of the vehicle and placed them over the stone steps to Huntington Hall's entrance.

'Do hurry up, Henny,' the stub-nosed Lady Huntington-Smythe hollered through the door. A serving girl desperately tried to tiptoe with an umbrella followed close behind her predicting her whims and ensuring she did not get wet. 'And be very careful with him. He's terribly fragile.' The Lady switched her attention and was now asserting her position over several serving staff who were busily navigating an elderly gentleman in a convalescent chair out from the grand entrance.

Lord Huntington-Smythe was in his eightieth year, though surely, it would be his last. He was immobile and now reduced to a shaking skeletal form. The large wooden chariot, part-used to move him around and part-used to park him conveniently at a window for most of the day, had two large brass wheels at the rear. The transportable device was long enough to be a daybed and at its pinnacle, a much smaller and troublesome wheel sat beneath the volume of blankets used to warm the elderly aristocrat.

After ten minutes of negotiating the challenges of the chair, the staff had finally wrangled it and hoisted it into the prestigious vehicle. The front wheel-end hinged backwards and with intricate movement, the chair provided the impression that Lord Huntington-Smythe was sitting upright in the passenger seat of his prestigious automobile.

'We will follow on behind,' the lady instructed the driver as she did every Sunday evening. 'Enter via the rear of the building. They are waiting for us,' she reminded him, as she did every Sunday evening.

'Oh, I do hope The Crown has not overdone the Lamb, Mother,' Henrietta Huntington-Smythe said. She was dressed as if she was meeting the Queen and not going for dinner at The Crown, Public House.

'Rest assured, Mr Paine is aware of our reservation and he will endeavour for perfection, dearest Daughter.'

The Lady and Henrietta then took their ride, via chauffeur, in another Rolls Royce, and followed Lord Huntington-Smythe's car as it pootled at only five miles an hour through the long gravel driveway, past uniformed topiary and into the dark rural night.

If he hadn't had seen it himself, he could not have imagined the eccentric ridiculousness presented in front of him. If his plan worked, this would be a swift break-in and the most rewarding one of his career. He had spent weeks watching the Huntington-Smythes' routine, meticulously gathering information, months investigating what he believed was true, and now it was only moments away before he could uncover the answers that would offer him a far greater reward then he had first imagined.

Observing the luminous hands on his wristwatch, he recorded that it would be no greater than ten minutes once the cars had left, that the staff would enjoy Sunday Supper too. It appeared it was the only night of the week they received a break from the Huntington-Smythe family. Sure enough, within ten minutes the gatekeeper's steps could be heard crunching up the gravel and his shouts were heard in the great house.

'Dogs away!' came his voice.

The Huntington-Smythes kept several large patrol dogs on their grounds. Tethered at systematic posts they were an efficient deterrent to local vagabonds and thieves. On Sunday Supper, the handlers locked them away with the estate's pack-hounds so that they would not be disturbed during their dinner, drinking, and card games. It was a little reward from the employment of such a family. The dogs would be returned several hours later, and the Huntington-Smythes would be none the wiser.

Ilya waited. Patiently.

'All away,' came another servant's voice as the house staff strode across from the Hall and headed to the staff quarters where their favourite meal and time of the week was about to unfold. Their lapsed judgement of security was the real benefit to the on looking Russian.

Taking the sack at arm's distance, Ilya returned to his BSA motorcycle that was camouflaged by ivy close by, down a nearby track. The thunder echoed in the background.

'One, one hundred,' he muttered to himself as he began the thunder-and-lightning game with himself. It was important. A sheet of lightning could illuminate the estate and he couldn't risk even an observed silhouette to reveal him.

Kicking the starter motor and revving the throttle gently, the reliant dulcet tone of the BSA's engine fired up with ease. He tied the sack to the rear exhaust pipe and slowly began to accelerate down the pitch-black country road. For now, he kept his lights dimmed. He had walked the route a hundred times and was now accustomed to the road's idiosyncrasies.

Passing the locked iron gates with the intertwined 'Double H's', which protected the entrance to Huntington Hall, he smiled to himself. Shortly, he would have what he needed. He revved the engine a little and drove steadily downhill to where a cobbled-stone bridge met with a tributary of the River Amble. A subtle current was flowing steadily south and he knew as the rains became heavier, it would flow quicker. Lightning flashed. His silent count was over twenty so the storm was at least twenty miles away, as the crow flies, he thought. Plenty of time to remain concealed in the darkness. Stopping briefly, he unravelled the sack that was beyond repugnant and removed the remains of the animals' torsos with his bare hands. The remains of half of a fox and several decimated rabbits were unceremoniously scattered around and into the riverbanks. Their lifeless limbs and odorous bodies would soon travel downstream, attracting the right kind of attention far away from the hall. He entwined the sack in the rope and placed it within a plastic bag that he sealed and carried under his arm. Washing the remains of blood and guts in the stream he then replaced his leather gloves and dispensed of his overalls and watched them travel downstream.

Reversing the bike around, he drove slowly back to the hidden lay by to once more cover his getaway vehicle in the hedgerow of ivy. By foot, he wandered a short distance to where the brick fortifications of the boundary wall were at their shortest. It was still a good seven to eight feet high. From the satchel, a rope and grappling hook were hoyed vertically. Several tugs and the assurance the ageing stonework would not falter under his weight, and in no time at all, he had climbed and conquered the wall as his plan moved onto stage two. He reversed the hook and rehung the rope, leaving it suspended in situ. This would be his failsafe should he require it.

Another flash of lightning, this time forked, lit up part of the sky. The slow rumble of thunder in the background came again. 'One, one hundred,' he repeated as he paced the boundary wall back several hundred yards to the momentous iron-gate with the Double Hs. From the grounds' side of Huntington Hall, he then lifted the large iron latch bolt that secured the gate from the inside. There was no human alive who could manage the lift from the roadside, the iron bars made that too difficult, but from the Hall-side it could be achieved. It was heavy but he managed to lever it enough to swing the gates open. Removing the blood-stained sack from its plastic enclosure, he dragged it up the gravel pathway towards the grand entrance. The rain, which was descending ever quicker and in golf-ball-sized drops, masked his carefully trodden path. Lightning came again and he hid behind one of the many finally coiffed conifers that lined the driveway. This time he had counted to eleven. The eye of the storm was approaching faster but his plan was still on track.

Past the grand entrance and to the rear of the main house were the servants' quarters. He could hear the joviality and humour above the storm. 'Perfect,' he thought to himself. As with blackout rules across the country, the servants' quarters were shrouded in darkness behind wooden shutters. As he approached the point between their quarters and the kennels, he heard the dogs howling and causing a commotion. The storm always set the pack on edge. Moving slowly now, ensuring he was camouflaged in darkness for fear of a lightning strike revealing his identity to anyone who indirectly may spot him, he approached the kennel. The hounds must have sensed the scent of the decomposing mammals as they wildly upped their howling and flung themselves at the kennel door. He couldn't risk opening the door from the ground for being torn apart. Instead he tied the rope onto the large iron lever that barricaded the door and ascended the flint outbuilding to its roof. With a steady wrenching of the rope the ironwork lifted up and released the doors. He dropped the sack, sending it ground wards, with a subtle thud on the floor. At that very moment, an ogre's rumble of thunder bellowed into the night. The dogs' heckles were up and the pack howled wildly.

'Eight, eight hundred. Nine, nine hundred. T–' Ilya counted to himself before the heavens were ablaze with the summer storm that brought pyrotechnic sheets of lightning to the sky. It was so bright that if anyone at that time had gazed towards the heavens, the silhouette of a green-eyed gargoyle glaring from the roof would surely have caught their attention.

The extending creak of timber cracking under pressure was suddenly met with a ferocious explosion of forty dogs forcing their way out of the kennels. Light work was made of the sack as the pack tore it to shreds and ran off with the rope on the scent trail Ilya had set for them. Wild animals scattered and took cover in their burrows as the canine force thundered across the grounds. The pack was so loud that even the heavens themselves could not drown out their noise. Within a moment, the servants and staff at Huntington Hall had fallen silent, the dawning of the commotion and the escaping hounds triggered them into action. Alighting from their quarters they hadn't expected what was to happen next.

'Oh Christ, I think the main gate is down,' cried one man.

'I locked it. I definitely locked it!' shouted the gatekeeper back.

'The pack are getting further away. I can hear them. They're tracking something.'

'Everybody who can handle one – grab a shotgun or rifle. All others, grab leashes and low lights and follow me.'

Ilya had calculated at least twenty staff during his weeks of surveillance. Sure enough, he counted twenty-two as they were leaving the servants' quarters and chase the disappearing pack out of the grounds. He waited patiently for any more signs of life but Huntington Hall was eerily silent itself as the flashes of lightning and thunderous rain deluged it from the skies above.

Chapter 30
Pieces

'Lemons?' Belle replied, confused. 'No, not really.'

Nathaniel's acute sense of smell was certain that the sharp citrus undertones emanated from the remains of the papers that were ripped to pieces and lay in the discarded bin, disguised by the mound of coats on top of them. Removing several remnants, he held them aloft, one by one, to the dimly lit single bulb at the centre of Monty's office, as if he was surveying negatives in a lab. Squinting with his good eye, he focused intently on the paper.

'Help me, Belle,' he said. 'I'm not sure in this light my eye can focus as well as it would in the daylight.'

'What are we looking for?' she enquired.

'Whatever clues your father saw fit to leave us,' he replied. 'Inhale from the paper before you look. I guarantee you will eventually pick up a scent of lemons. We need to focus on the papers with the lemony smells first, which will give us the pieces of the puzzle before we put them back together.'

Belle duly copied Nathaniel, sceptical there was any scent of citrus at all. Then, after several pieces of paper, it hit her, a full zing of zest. 'What now?' she asked.

'Try and piece the torn segments back together. There may be dozens of them but once we are able to determine a single page the rest will follow.'

'Just like a jigsaw then, Nate, "Corners first?" as Dad would say and then all the straight edges.'

'Corners first,' Noone agreed.

They worked relentlessly into the night. Noone had wished Monty had been less aggressive in his shredding of paper but no doubt there had been good reason. The first piece of paper they were confident they had solved was stuck together hastily with Sellotape. The bonded edges coursing like veins across the paper jigsaw.

Belle held up the paper towards the low wattage of the pendulous office bulb. Sure enough, an image began to present itself. Concentrating in detail, the light revealed the negative lines of lemon that had been quickly transferred onto the paper in its transparently copied outline.

'It's difficult to catch the full image, Nate. You're right, the bulb is too dim. I think we need the daylight from the windows to see it for sure.'

'Let's carry on until morning. We should have resurrected all the documents by then,' Noone said and reluctantly sighed.

*****

Nightfall came before Professor Malcolm finally finished removing the parchment from the scrolls. It was too late to sufficiently observe them from the pinnacle window and via the natural sunlight that streamed through intermittently during the day. Instead, the Professor used a single candle, as he had employed so many times in his Entomology department back at the Museum, and moved from square to square to reveal the true images and negative impressions of the original glyphs. If this was now the true face of the original and which would lead to the code being broken, it would come to fruition with the sunrise. He turned to the untouched G&T, the ice now melted, and drank the clear liquid in one large gulp. He hoped it would help him sleep and postpone the decision he would need to take the following morning, but it did not work.

It would be hours until daybreak when he could truly look upon the ancient scrolls with revised wonder. He feared what they may reveal. As he searched for his spectacles, which were usually on top of his head whenever he lost them, he heard the tiny tapping of insects on glass. The noise was consistent and repetitive. Taking the candle that was now in the final stages of its waxy life, he made his way to the wall of vivarium's and enclosures. Fumbling the spectacles downwards on to his nose, he focused his stare onto a revelatory site. Each insect, be that beetle, scorpion, locust, spider, all species that were in the laboratory had all moved to their casings' edge and were directing themselves to a single point of focus. It appeared they were all moving in unison.

'Well, I never,' he whispered to himself, surprised. 'What are you all so interested in?'

He turned his back on the creatures and viewed the surrounding vista from their perspective. It seemed to point him towards the large laboratory table amongst the splayed-out scrolls. Tentatively, he paced towards the table. The wick was beginning to falter and the candle flickered a reminder of its final moments. Professor Meticulous Meredith Malcolm did not want to use up any more of his nine lives by blundering in the dark and damaging the ancient scripture, so he took stock and sat at the chair equidistant between the sentry of bugs looking on obediently and the mahogany exhibit table. The candle finally faltered and what little light he held in his hand was now gone.

As his eyes cast green negatives in front of him, pupils expanding to focus, the intermittent light of the moon between the clouds beamed through the prism pinnacle above and gave him the occasional chance to observe the room again. He scoured the table from where he was, between the changing night-time shadows, and there he spotted it. A tiny emission of orange light throbbed between the spread of scrolls. It was already receding, growing weaker with each throb, like a failing heartbeat in its dying moments.

'To hell with it,' he chastised himself and stumbled towards the small amber glow. Grabbing the palm-sized object he found draped in a dirty muslin cloth, its ember pulse like that of the last coals, the object, which appeared to emanate heat and suggested itself to be hot to the touch remained chillingly cool. Unveiling it slowly, one layer of fabric at a time, the light grew stronger as it unravelled. It must have been the dirt and grime of the well-worn muslin cloth that gave it an orange glow for as it revealed itself, the deeper red, an opaque crimson, penetrated through. Fully visible in its natural glory, he could now see the aptly named fossilised creature emitting its powerful stream of light from within its crystallised coffin. The Scarlet Scarab shone brightly.

'You are truly astounding. How come you are so shy in the daylight?' the Professor asked it.

As he carried the entombed anthropoid towards the insects, they followed its every change of direction. When the Professor moved the scarab left, the insects followed it left. He moved right and they moved right, like a cheap illusionist at a penny fair.

'Truly amazing.' The professor beamed.

The scarab's light began to fade. Mimicking an Indian summer sky, it turned scarlet to rose-pink and then to a light orangey-yellow before it stopped glowing. It was not the revelation he had quite expected. The professor's focus had been on deciphering the scrolls, which would now wait within the dawn.

Rewrapping the crystallised insect carefully, he placed it back on the table before walking pigeon-step by pigeon-step back to his chair. As if that was not enough for the Professor to absorb within one day, he took a final glance at the insects in their cases. Nearly all of them had returned to their normal evolutionary states. The mesmerisation had passed. All of them with the exception of the common scarabs, the scavenging dung beetles. Their iridescent shells had metamorphosed from a reflective purple-black to a palette of vibrant violet hues, which were now emitting a twinkling of violet light.

'I am lost for words, Meredith,' the Professor spoke to himself again. He would observe them for the rest of that night until daybreak as their micro-luminescence revealed their tiny travails as they scurried in the dark.

Chapter 31
The Russian Pt. 2

The hounds' barks disappeared into the distance as they followed the bloodied trail that would lead them towards the Amble. The chaos he had created at Huntington Hall would now allow the final act of his plan to be enacted.

Descending from the hidden safety of the kennel roof, the rains lashing down now as the angry heavens jostled in the summer's worst storm, Ilya Derbrovska took nothing for granted and crept in and out of the shadows. Camouflaged in black with those jaded eyes to guide him, he maintained the silent thunder count though it barely reached two now as the skies erupted in powerful lightning. During the chaos, the doors to Huntington Hall remained unsecured and he entered directly via the grand entrance.

Passing walnut-panelled hallways, multiple portraits of the ancestral Huntington's sneered down on him as he ascended the broad tread of the grand staircase where he had two rooms to conquer. The first room was where the family safe and their most valuable jewels were kept. In Lord Huntington's office, behind a decade-old portrait of the aristocrat, a two-inch-thick steel safe was set into a concrete wall. It was impenetrable to most men. The elderly aristocrat, despite his age and frailty, changed the combination weekly, always hidden behind closed doors. The Russian had neither the affordability of time or considerable skills required to crack such a safe. Instead, he pulled two sticks of explosives from the satchel and placed them specifically at the lock end of the safe's door. Waiting patiently, he peered out of the window. His thunder count had been reduced to two. As the clouds battled one another, and their guttural rumblings came again, he lit the touch paper and took cover. The lightning illuminated the sky and within seconds the explosion from within Lord Huntington's private office created the chink in the safe's armour he required. It was loud but not loud enough to alert anyone outside during the storm and amongst the cacophony of canine whelping.

The safe remained relatively intact, with the exception of a fist-sized hole where the lock had been. It was all Ilya required. Inside were a collection of jewels and gold worth tens of thousands of pounds. Each of them sat within leather or crushed velvet casings. Ilya began to fish each individual case out. What he sought most was the small blue velvet sack of diamonds, which were the last and most rewarding jewels he removed. They alone could fund his disappearance and place him firmly on the path to prosperity once this final adventure was complete.

The storm raged on outside. The count between thunder-and-lightning strikes now becoming greater as it began to move away. Ilya knew time was of the essence and the greater prize he sought just a room away. Tidying his tracks, trying his utmost to conceal the safe breaking, he tiptoed out of Lord Huntington's office delicately locking the door behind him. His next and final visit was the Lord's private chamber.

Now, while it was quite obvious families of such wealth would indeed maintain a fortified vault on their premises, the true treasure he sought was one that the Lord had hidden away privately and confidentially. But for a couple of solicitors and trustees, no one else knew. Lord Huntington knew that when his remaining days finally came, the vault would be the first place his grieving family would come to pay their respects. However, what they were not aware of was that he kept vital copies and details of his estate and final will under lock and key in a hidden panel of his private chambers. So secretive he had been over the past forty years that his own flesh and blood were not even aware. It was only Ilya's intricate observations that allowed him to stumble upon the routine. It was his patient peering through his spyglass over days and weeks that meant he now knew where to look.

Ilya rounded the corridor that led from office to chamber. The private room was locked. It took a minute for him to pick, although it was more complicated than he had thought. As he entered into darkness, a deep rumbling met him. It wasn't the thunderclouds outside since they had begun to draw away. The noise moved closer and with it an unnatural familiarity. Ilya desperately fumbled in his bag. The noise turned from a rumbling to a ferocious growl. It was still dark but the vision of the canines being borne and the pressure the hounds' jaws would crush down on him flashed through his mind. Retrieving his tiny flashlight, he shone it directly towards the beast. Sure enough, the snarling muzzle of a large male German Shepherd was just yards away as the light reflected the green eyes to mirror his own. As if the flash of light had been a starter's gun the animal bolted out of the blocks and launched itself skyward towards Ilya's jugular. The satchel was merely a paper shield as the Russian held it in front of himself, the dog making light work of piercing the leather with its canine protrusions. Ilya's hand was still inside fumbling around for a sharp object. The dog's impatience allowed a brief pause as it took breath before a second wave of attack. It was just enough time for Ilya to locate the object he was looking for. As the dog launched his paws forward, the Russian crouched into a ball and thrust the tiny syringe between front leg and rib cage, piercing the animal's fur and sending it whelping into a heap. It was almost instantaneous. The dog's pupils dilated, it slumped sideways as its tongue lolled out of its mouth, and it struggled to breathe. The tiny skull and crossbones phial had shattered, and Ilya, cut and bruised on his arm had been lucky not to ingest the poison into his own bloodstream. Taking a moment to compose himself, check the savaged satchel and its remaining precious cargo, the Russian ensured the dog was still breathing. It was too close an encounter than he could have wished for but an ironic sense of justification that whatever he now found was more precious than gemstones and gold.

Why else would old Lord Huntington-Smythe leave his most aggressive dog on guard?

Chapter 32
Night at the Museum

Gideon regretted not responding to the calls of Major Boyd Collingdale. Unwittingly, the army man had offered him his biggest lifeline in over a decade. But with so much at stake, Gideon's focus was solely on visiting his old friend and mentor at the British Museum. He wandered the surrounding streets with Ilya's keys in hand. Half an hour passed until there, with a covering of dust, a product from the recent airstrike that had sealed the Russian's fate, was the BSA motorcycle Ilya had hidden out of view.

Gideon dusted it down, engaged the throttle, and kick-started it at the first attempt. The low revving tone reminded him of the God-awful Thunder Machines so familiar across the capitals. He looked to the cloudless heavens above. He doubted such a clear night would warrant such an attack. The spotters would too easily observe enemy fighters and implement citywide protocols to protect it. As he pulled away slowly, he took care not to turn on his lights until he was at least half a mile away. He couldn't risk being stopped nearby. As long as he could navigate the frequent bombed-out ruins between Mayfair and Fitzrovia, it would be thirty minutes before he arrived near Russell Square where his old tutor could shed some light on Ilya's maps and papers.

It had been a while since Gideon had made the journey between Natural History and British Museums. Dawn was approaching and for once the city was eerily silent. Cascading colours were breaking through against the dark shadows of the barrage balloons that perched upon giant metal cables above the ground.

His preferred route was obstructed by devastation. Almost at every turn, he had to redirect himself because the destruction and collapse of waves of buildings were incomparable to the solitude and impeccably unscathed Ambledown. This new city vista served as a pertinent reminder as to what was at stake for the country. Frustrated after the now-complex navigation of bombed-out London, he ditched Ilya's beloved BSA near Bloomsbury and continued on foot. Ilya's torn satchel was firmly strapped beneath his long trench coat.

The British Museum, despite the decimated streets and tumbled-down buildings that presented their iron and brickwork souls, was proudly intact. Gideon looked upon its large Grecian pillars with relief and approached the sentries that stood guard amongst the wood and barbed-wire barricades. In the shadows from just across the street, two black sedans were parked. Their windows were masked in condensation.

'Who goes there?' the sentry shouted with his rifle sight pointed at Gideon's head.

'My name is Professor Gideon Belchambers. I have an urgent message for Professor Soames.'

'Which one, sir?' the sentry asked, amused.

'There are two?' Gideon questioned

'Montague Soames, sir, currently indisposed as I understand it, and his daughter. Isa–'

'Belle?' Gideon quickly interrupted 'Good grief, little Belle with the bunches?' He was both shocked and bemused.

'You're the second visitor to be as equally shocked today, sir.' The sentry smiled.

'Second?' Gideon asked, tentatively.

'Oh yes, sir. A terribly scarred man came earlier. I wouldn't have let him in; bit dodgy, you know, but he was on the list.'

Gideon knew exactly who he meant. 'What list?' he asked.

The sentry pulled a plywood clipboard with a steel bulldog clip holding several sheets together. There, each Professor or senior member of staff had a list of preferred guests. The sentry perused the list. From a distance, the occupants of the black cars lurking in the shadows looked on at the unveiling events.

'I'm sorry. No Professor Belchambers on this list, sir.'

'Well, that's because…' Gideon began and then paused. He could read the list upside down and Monty had not used his name in a long time. He wasn't on it. They had agreed never to meet in person. Not since Cairo.

'Never mind,' Gideon advised him. 'Tell me, Professor Soames – you said he was somewhat indisposed. What did you actually mean?'

'He was paralysed, sir. A stroke they say.'

'OK. Now listen very carefully. You have a job to do, I know. But what I have inside my coat may be a cure for his infliction.'

'A cure for a stroke, there's no such thing, sir. What's your actual business?' the sentry asked, raising his rifle abruptly.

Gideon placed his hands in the air. 'Please, if I had wanted to harm you or gain access there are many ways to have done so. I have nothing to hide and Monty Soames is an old friend of mine,' Gideon advised beckoning to the man to undo his coat and reveal the satchel.

'No funny business or I will shoot you where you stand,' the sentry informed him. 'Keep one arm raised and unbutton your coat.'

Gideon duly followed the orders. Not as easy as it seemed. Advising the sentry of the letters inside and the scorpion bottle he had found on Ilya earlier. The sentry was just about to remove Monty's envelope. As he momentarily lowered his rifle a voice came from the darkness.

'Lowering your rifle when on duty and faced with a potential enemy is a court-marshal offence, soldier,' came the gravelly female voice.

Gideon began to turn around but a barrel of a revolver was firmly thrust into his spine.

'I don't think so,' came the cut-glass accent of a man. 'Calmly does it, old chum. Now, turn around slowly,' the gentleman said to Gideon. 'Keep those hands where I can see them.'

As Gideon rotated, he saw the lady first. Short, smoking a cigarette, a leather patch over one eye. The man holding the gun in his long black coat and fedora was textbook Department.

'So, where's Draper?' Gideon asked.

Both of them glanced at each other.

'I'll take a leap,' he continued. 'I suspect this isn't the first eye patch you have seen today,' Gideon directed towards the sentry.

Not knowing who to point his rifle at, Gideon, or the man with the gun, the sentry simply lowered it.

'The visitor earlier also had an eye patch, am I right?' Gideon continued.

'How did you know that?' the sentry replied.

Gideon observed his captors, still with his hands in the air, as he weighed up their responsive body language.

'Assuming you are friends of Nathaniel Noone, allow me to present myself. I am Professor Gideon Belchambers.'

'Never heard of you,' the man said, intently pointing his firearm at Gideon's brow.

The eye-patched lady, on the other hand, drew a final drag on her cigarette before tossing it underneath her foot to be crushed.

'I, on the other hand, have,' she said, puffing a cloud of smoke as she exhaled. 'You may lower your weapon, Thompson,' she ordered, placing her hand on the barrel and putting pressure on it.

'Well, Professor Belchambers. I can call you that, can I not?' she continued, an underlying tone to her voice.

'Of course, you can,' he replied.

'This is Thompson and I am Wink,' she replied.

'Seriously?' came the surprised voice of the sentry 'Your name's Wink?'

With a click of his fingers, Thompson summoned Smith and Jones from the shadows who began escorting the young soldier away before Wink Waverley could court-marshal him there and then.

'Wait, the letter.' Gideon gestured towards the departing sentry still in possession of Monty's envelope.

Thompson opened it and read it first before passing it to Wink.

'Shall we … ' She pointed towards the Museum, allowing Gideon to walk ahead of them.

*****

Aggie struggled to sleep. Whether it was the couch in the drawing-room or the temperature that plummeted during the night, she didn't really know. She had tossed and turned for hours now and Uncle Gideon had not returned. What little, precious sleep she had been afforded had been interspersed with the recurring claustrophobic nightmare where insects crept and crawled over her body and animal masks whirled and danced hypnotically in front of her.

The mantelpiece clock chimed to inform her it was 5 am. Daybreak would be another couple of hours yet. She wrapped up tight in a patchwork blanket and revisited her mother's face peering back at her from the photo. Amazingly, the magnifying glass still presented a dim circle of light. Aggie moved it in and out until a small circumference perfectly surrounded the missing crest on her mother's Priory jacket.

'Why did you destroy it?' she asked her mother in the photo. 'What made you so angry you ripped the school colours from your very own blazer?'

Her mother offered little response. Aggie knew all too well of the anger and fury that would erupt in her. Throughout her short fourteen years, it had been suggested that it was proof she was her mother's daughter alright. Henrietta Huntington-Smythe was the latest to have fallen victim to it. But with good reason, she reassured herself.

'You wake already?' came the surprised voice entering the room. Aggie jumped and screamed in horror.

'Nan, don't do that. You made me jump.'

'I sorry. Did not mean it,' Nan replied 'You hungry? Come, I make breakfast.'

'Nothing from Uncle Gideon?' Aggie questioned her.

Nan offered a shrug and nothing more.

'Do you remember my mother?' Aggie asked, holding the photo aloft.

'I sorry.' Nan shook her head 'I come after your mother.'

'Miss Dove said that Sister Harvey or Nelly Parker may know.'

Nan laughed sarcastically.

'What's so funny?' Aggie enquired.

'Miss Dove,' Nan replied 'Oh, special Miss Dove. She be here five minutes and think she know everybody.'

It was a peculiar reaction, Aggie thought and pressed the housekeeper. 'Has she upset you?'

'No, she no upset me. But why Ambledown WI accept her with open arms? Residents of Ambledown only, they say to me. Miss Dove, here five minutes and she running WI.'

'Oh, I'm sorry,' Aggie replied. She could see Nan was upset.

'Bet she did not tell you Nelly's sister, Sister Harvey.'

'She told me they may know about my mother.'

'You have cloth ears, Nelly Sister, Sister Harvey's.'

'They're related?' Aggie replied, surprised.

'Exactly. Smart Miss Dove not even know that,' Nan confirmed.

'I see, how strange.'

'Been here five minutes and foot under tables,' Nan continued stomping around the place.

'Shall we have that breakfast now?' Aggie tried changing the subject.

'I cook special breakfast. Show WI what they missing,' Nan confirmed, stomping down to the basement floor.

I wonder why Dove did not know that? Aggie asked herself. How long has she actually been here? she wondered. As a school governess at her age, she must have come highly recommended. Without Uncle Gideon around, she would have to ask the Peabodys on their journey to school.

'Will it be special like the other morning?' Aggie asked.

'Of course,' Nan replied.

'Is rationing different here?' Aggie continued.

Nan refused to answer.

Chapter 33
The Russian Pt. 3

It had been the closest of shaves. Ilya had surveyed that room one hundred times. Little had he known during his surveillance that the Lord's most aggressive hound was poised out of sight to attack any intruder.

Ilya moved to the window. Situating his back against the windowpanes, positioning himself as if from the scope perspective, he stepped across to the opposite side of the room and counted the panels from right to left. Three along and two up from waist height, he mimicked the Lord's weekly routine. To the naked eye, the panelling appeared like a solid piece of workmanship, but subtle pressure in each of the corners sunk it, setting it back behind the surrounding panels. A smooth ball-bearing system allowed it to smoothly slide behind the neighbouring panel, leaving the hidden brass safe in the centre. This was not the appropriate time for dynamite and explosions. The storm had died and with it the cover that afforded him time and a cloak of isolation. He couldn't risk any shock that might draw attention to himself or the lifeless dog with venom coursing through its veins. Instead, he reached into his well-worn satchel for the final time that evening and pulled out a set of skeleton keys and metal picks. This had been his forte so many years ago and like riding a bicycle the skill had never left him.

Placing the main key into the brass outer, he rocked it with the tiniest of motions until a subtle catch of metal on metal clicked. Using a hooked pick, flat at one end, he then began to meticulously navigate the inner workings of the mechanism. Several, patient, minutes later and the flat metallic tool had connected enough for him to ease the lock anti-clockwise. It was an old and cantankerous piece of rusting metal but the Russian's skill remained undefeated as the safe finally swung open.

Before him were folios upon folios of papers. There were at least two dozen, varying in size and volume. Each of them was labelled on the spine and like a library of vertical, opposed to horizontal books, he read the titles on the bindings. Blueprints and plans of Huntington Hall, land registrics of his vast estate and property empire, *The Last Will and Testament* of the Lord himself, The White Star correspondence, and then one in a cardboard tube on top of a portfolio simply entitled 'Cairo'.

Time was ticking on. Pinpricks of light in the distance and the returning mewing of tired hounds grew nearer. He could not wait any longer. Carefully removing the tube and the folio named Cairo he placed them in the satchel. This is what he had been searching for and if he was right, he had found his Eldorado.

Removing the scorpion phial from his pocket he took a pinprick of the anti-venom inside and administered it in-between the dog's paw pads. He certainly couldn't hang around now. The dog had mauled him and his blood would leave a trail. He remained invisible in darkness until the dog caught his scent. He patched himself up as best he could. As soon as the dog awoke, he would undoubtedly be the new quarry. Ensuring his bounty was secured tightly, Ilya relocked the safe and replaced the panel as if he had never been there. Reversing the route, he had entered by, he smiled as he passed the portraits glaring down on him disapprovingly. Descending the stairs, he alighted through the stone threshold out of the main entrance. Slipping silently into the darkness and back to the rope and hook that would allow him an exit, Ilya was gone, into the calm after the storm.

Chapter 34
OSIRIS

Daybreak was steadily approaching. Nathaniel Noone and Belle Soames had briefly nodded off after completing their paper puzzles. Noone awoke with a jolt.

'Still having nightmares, Nate?' Belle asked.

'Sometimes,' he lied. They were more consistent than ever.

'How about a nice cup of tea as we wait for the light to hit the windows?'

Noone nodded cagerly and began to place the taped-together jigsaws onto the windows as he wiped away the morning condensation. From his initial examination, the papers were split into two sets. The first were pictures, images that looked, as much as he could tell at this point, like negative hieroglyphics. He would be certain of them within the next hour. The others were simply handwritten names, a list. The writing was far too small to observe under the dimly lit bulb.

A double knock on the door of Montague Soame's office and Noone turned the handle expecting to greet Belle with a pot of tea.

'Hello, old friend,' came Gideon's voice.

'What the hell are you doing here?' Noone responded surprised.

'Not exactly the greeting he was expecting, Nathaniel, but it will suffice,' came Thompson's voice from behind Gideon.

Entering behind them, the statuesque Wink Waverley made her presence known immediately.

'Nice eye patch,' she expressed in her gravel tone towards Noone.

'Likewise,' Noone replied.

'Nathaniel Noone, I presume,' she said, holding out her hand.

'And you are?' he asked.

'Wink Waverley. Of the Executive.'

Waverley didn't even bat her single eyelid. She just smiled, she liked Noone already. 'So, Mr Noone, what do you have here?' Wink continued.

Crash! An almighty shattering of teapot and china cups made them all jump. Thompson pulled his gun in nervous reaction and trained it on the door.

Belle was standing at the doorway, her feet spattered in boiling hot water and slithers of ceramic.

'Good grief, girl,' Waverley shouted. 'Haven't you seen an eye patch before.'

'Of course, she has,' Noone interrupted, sarcastically smiling beneath his own eye patch, pushing past them all to embrace her.

'It's ghosts she's not used to seeing,' Gideon interjected before taking a step towards Belle. 'Hello, Belle,' he whispered, placing a gentle peck on her cheek.

Belle looked up with tears flooding from her eyes and streaming down her cheeks. Noone and Gideon both took support of her under each arm and helped her to a chair.

'Hal –' she was just about to speak before Gideon placed his index finger over her lips.

'Shhhh,' he interrupted.

'Dad told me you were dead. You were all dead.' She sobbed uncontrollably.

'I will explain. I promise. Your father. Where's your father?' Gideon asked.

'He's in his private quarters, here, at the Museum.'

'The envelope – the one from the sentry. Open it and read it out aloud,' Gideon advised as he looked towards Thompson.

'Dearest Montague. If you are reading this letter then I am dead,' Thompson began. 'If you are reading this, I am dead. If you are dead too, I shall see you for my judgement on the other side.'

Belle sobbed in the background.

'Go on,' Noone encouraged Thompson, all the while offering a shoulder to Belle.

'I am hoping you are alive and accept this as my apology for leading them to your door. If, as I suspect, they have found what they need then you will require the anti-venom I am in supply of and which accompanies this letter.' Thompson stopped reading the letter and looked up.

Gideon was holding up the green glass bottle with the scorpion on it.

'That looks more like poison to me,' Belle stuttered through quivering lips.

'All the more reason to be cautious, my dear,' Wink interjected. 'Your father, I understand, had some form of stroke?'

Belle nodded.

'Unconfirmed though,' Noone interjected.

'And your man, Thompson … ' Wink continued directing her single glare towards her subordinate. 'The Concierge, that is what the doctor initially thought, am I right?'

'That's correct. He's been in a catatonic state since Draper's disappearance,' Thompson confirmed.

'Too many coincidences for my liking,' Wink said, shaking her head.

Clicking her fingers twice, a gentleman and lady stepped forward from their sedentary positions posted outside of Monty's office. Noone immediately recognised them as the tailing couple from the departing Tube several hours before.

'Miss Soames, these people will escort you to your father and will then take him to the Hospital of Tropical Medicine. Be sure not to break the bottle that Professor Belchambers is about to hand over to you. There, they may be able to cure your father. It depends on what is in that bottle,' Wink ordered politely.

Belle, who was drying her eyes on the cuff of her blouse, nodded in agreement and directed herself out of the room. Gideon duly handed over the bottle from Ilya's satchel, though he never took kindly to orders from someone who was yet to gain his trust.

'One thing, please,' Gideon added before they had left. 'At the Museum for Natural History, there are a number of Death-stalkers – the scorpions that may be the source of this venom or anti-venom. Should the hospital require more of them, Major Boyd Collingdale is in charge and if he hasn't trod on every one of them, he will be able to help. Tell him I sent you. And send him my apologies. I will see him again one day soon and explain.'

They acknowledged Gideon's information before a supportive confirming nod from Wink Waverley allowed them to depart.

'My, my, haven't you been busy, Professor.' Wink smirked towards Gideon. 'Resurrected from the dead by all accounts,' she continued, all the while observing Belle's reactions. 'And time to spare to visit two great museums in the dead of night,' Wink continued. 'What secrets you must be keeping.'

Gideon did not rise to her bait, or talk anymore on the subject. He simply handed the bottle over, brushing Belle's hands as he did so. He so desperately wanted to explain everything but he trusted no one. If as she had claimed, Wink knew who he was, she was goading him into revealing more then he would wish to and perhaps she knew more than she was letting on.

Belle briefly turned, smiling at Nathaniel. There was at least hope for her father now. Glancing at Gideon her facial expression turned from happily surprised to disconcertingly confused at the ambiguity of his reappearance. Even her father had confirmed he had died over a decade ago. She had even been at his funeral.

Dawn was breaking. The newcomers had not spotted the intricate paper jigsaws that were stuck to the glass waiting for the first rays of morning. Noone made no immediate efforts to direct their sight there. To the contrary he decided to conceal them for the time being. He would share the intricacies, should he believe them of benefit, on Belle's return. Instead, he drew the blinds for optimum darkness once more and pulled out the torches with the violet beam poised to go.

'I'm not sure how much information Thompson has informed you of, ma'am,' Noone began.

Pulling out the photograph that he had now memorised he placed it in front of them and lit up the violet hues that formed the masks and totems on top of the owners' faces.

'I assume you now know what these symbols mean, Noone?' Thompson asked.

'Belle was able to help clarify some for me,' he said, switching over to the normal torch.

'Draper's symbol is Anubis, god of the afterlife, but its forward-facing nature suggests a victim opposed to a helper or follower,' he explained.

'Well, thank God for that.' Wink sighed. 'Really wouldn't want one of my men to be the lord of darkness or whoever he is.'

'Any thoughts, Professor?' Noone asked his friend, continuing the pretence that they did not know each other. Gideon was transfixed on the woman in the tiger-skin coat.

'Who is she?' he asked with a pointed finger pressed down on her face.

'We're not sure. Belle remembers her here at the Museum, the night before Monty was taken ill.'

'What?' Gideon exclaimed. 'This photo was taken here, the night before his stroke?'

'That's right. Some fundraiser for injured veterans,' Noone confirmed.

Wink glanced at Thompson and clicked her fingers, to which he produced the card he had shown her in her office.

Noone grabbed it first before eagerly flashing it towards Gideon.

'Official–Society–Improvement-Rehabilitation-Injured-Serviceman!' Gideon shouted out slamming a fist on to the desk 'Bloody OSIRIS. How can no one see how this is all connected.' He was so angry his usual calm demeanour was fractured for the first time.

'You need to take a deep breath, Professor. No one understands what is going on here,' Noone encouraged him, shaking his head subtly from side to side to suggest he stops speaking now. They couldn't be sure who was friend or foe. Wink's obvious optical disability did not detract from her continued observation of the pair.

'Wait, Professor Belchambers, you need to slow down. You may wish to explain what you were doing there in the first place,' Wink advised.

Gideon paused and took a deep breath. Noone was right, no one could be sure who was friend or foe. It was almost as if Wink herself knew more than she was letting on and was subtly encouraging them to divulge everything for her benefit. She continued, taking a deep breath and moving centre stage.

'May I suggest to all that we take this a step at a time. Something is connecting all of these elements together. I feel each of us has a varying agenda but ultimately, we're on the same side. Agreed?' said Wink.

Several nods greeted her serious single-eyed stare. She moved over the room to switch on the dimly lit bulb of Monty's office.

'Very well, I will go first,' She continued, moving towards a blackboard that was covered in years of Monty's scrawls. It was a confusing jumble of information, representative of the man himself. She grabbed the discarded scarf from the pile of coats that had concealed the papers in the bin and rubbed the chalk into smudged circular patterns, like clouds.

'My immediate concern is for Draper.' She spoke like an authoritative grammar school teacher and wrote his name in a large chalk bubble in the centre of the board, punctuating the stop at the end of his name. 'Such a senior member of *The Department* being kidnapped should ring alarm bells throughout Whitehall. The information that passes through his team is paramount to intercepting and defeating the Reich. He is a large cog in an even bigger wheel. So, I, for one, would like to look at that photograph again. But under the normal light first. Not the pink light or whatever you are calling it.'

Nathaniel Noone passed her the photograph.

She examined it intently with her good eye. Holding it just an inch from her nose. 'This man, here,' she said to the room. 'Is Colonel Malling. He actually reports to me. So, what does the pink drawing on his head say about him.'

Noone switched torches and lit up the image so that the faintly visible head of a bird of prey appeared sideways on top of Malling's head.

'Horus!' Gideon said without question.

Wink squinted at him as if insult and answer were being thrown at her in one word.

'I agree,' came Belle's voice on re-entering the room. 'Its sideways presence suggests the deity as opposed to the follower or victim of such a god, opposite to that of the one of Anubis we just saw. The one on your colleague, Draper.'

'Agreed,' Gideon confirmed. 'This is *the* deity. The suggestion we can take from this is that Colonel Malling is very high up in the food chain, whatever it is.'

'And we do not know what "it" is,' Thompson interrupted.

'This woman, the one central in the photograph. I found a tiger-skin coat and blonde wig matching this picture in the Natural History Museum,' alerted Gideon. 'Definitely in disguise.'

'If we look at this literally,' Belle continued before Gideon could speak anymore. 'OSIRIS is usually considered the parent of the deity Horus. OSIRIS represents the afterlife, the underworld; it could mean transition, regeneration, or resurrection.'

'Or rehabilitation maybe? That makes perfect sense if they are aiding injured servicemen. Most of them burn victims or having suffered the loss of limbs, or certainly all three,' Thompson piped up.

'And what about Draper, a servant in the afterlife as his totem suggests?' Noone added. 'I doubt anyone kidnaps a senior civil servant during a war to help with raising awareness for injured servicemen. I would question whether this is a legitimate organisation at all,' Noone said beginning to become angry with Thompson.

Wink was trying to make sense of it all, scribbling the names onto the board with a flow of chalk arrows between them all.

'Your thoughts, Belchambers?' Wink asked. 'And please stop the pretence yourself and Mr Noone are not known to each other. I do know your history.'

'Show me the tiger-lady under the other light, Nate. The violet light,' Gideon said, smiling at Wink Waverley.

Nathaniel hovered the faint torch beam to reveal her duality in the various lights.

'Look at her markings. They are quite rare. Nothing you're likely to see as a main deity. They're not serpentine but they are similar. Belle, what do you think?'

'You mean some sort of secondary level god, a consort, or such like?' Belle answered, searching for the name she had been trying to think of since first casting eyes on the photo.

'Exactly!' Gideon exclaimed.

'Oh no. No, no, no, no, no,' Belle began to berate herself.

'Belle? What is it?' Noone asked, grabbing her shoulders.

'The woman's name. I recall it now. Sabine! How could I have been so dumb?' She continued to explain to an on looking and incrcasingly confused collective. 'No wonder Dad found it so amusing. That was her name. The woman in the photograph. Sabine Erket. S-ERKET!'

'I'm lost.' Thompson sighed.

'Me too,' Wink agreed, standing back to review the board.

'OK, Belle,' Gideon reassured her. 'You couldn't have known. But your dad saw through their plan, whatever it was. Waverley, write SERKET on the board,' he instructed with authority. 'She definitely links Draper and OSIRIS. She's most likely the poisoner of Monty and the concierge. Serket, for the less well informed, is the Scorpion Queen.'

'So, she may have poisoned Professor Soames senior and Thompson's man, this Scorpion Queen. If she is who we are believing her to be,' Wink suggested, standing up and back on point. 'Belchambers, you advised that the tiger-skin coat, one just like that in the picture, and wig you found at the Natural History, were coincidentally in the same place you happened to stumble upon the anti-venom.'

Wink's manner twisted the concept that Gideon's presence was anything but innocent. She scribbled his name on the board to the side of Serket. Thompson was already sceptical. Belle was certainly amazed at his reappearance after all this time. Nathaniel Noone, on the other hand, was doing his utmost to keep Gideon's secrets.

'If we take a leap of faith, and I believe this is not too great a leap, could it be that this woman is also the elusive Jennifer James you seek?' Wink asked.

'Likely, I would. Just thinking the same thing.' Thompson replied. 'Tall, languid appearance, but a black bobbed haircut, not long, blonde locks.'

Wink scribbled *Jennifer James/Serket* on the board.

'So, we may have a few leads now, people. But what exactly is their purpose?' the senior female spymaster asked.

Noone flashed a look at Gideon. Whatever brought all of this together one thing was for certain. Wink's priority was Draper. Their priority was Agatha.

'Miss Soames, you mentioned that your father believed something was awry. Perhaps, giving his history, he understood what this OSIRIS may represent. Care to share any thoughts?' said Wink.

'Well, I knew something was up when Father sent me on a false errand that day. He was agitated. He was excluding me from meeting this OSIRIS organisation and couldn't wait to get shot of me. Then he handed me an unaddressed letter, a blank envelope and expressly informed me to deliver it in person and not divulge the address to anyone. I memorised it and he made me repeat it back to him.'

'Where to?' Wink asked.

'Marylebone,' Belle advised

Gideon's head sank into his hands. He wanted to scream out loud but still couldn't trust anyone apart from Noone.

'I still don't understand,' Thompson piped up again.

'Continue the story, Belle,' Gideon encouraged her.

'I delivered the letter, as Father advised. Once the elderly lady understood who I was she invited me in for refreshments with herself and her great-niece. She seemed agitated but was very generous. Her niece, Agatha – I think, wanted me to stay but I had to get back. Then, when I returned in the evening Dad was more agitated than ever. It was like he had seen a ghost.' Belle flashed a look towards Gideon. 'He was furious at the use of the Museum and had stubbornly locked himself away in this very room. The next time I saw him, well he was …' Belle began to well up again.

Noone comforted her.

Gideon looked on in shock. *'Oh Monty,' Gideon thought to himself. 'You must have been desperate. What have you done?'*

'OK. So, for continuity, let's assume "tiger-lady" is both SERKET and James. She has kidnapped one of my main men, left two men close to death, but also masquerades as a charitable host. It doesn't add up,' Wink summarised.

'It doesn't add up if you believe the OSIRIS link is legitimate,' Gideon responded curtly. 'If she is using this organisation as a front, then, we must ask for what purpose?' he continued. 'The Egyptian links are more pertinent to myself, Nathaniel and Monty than this current war. The pseudonyms, the acronyms – why would they be used?'

'Misdirection maybe, Professor?' Wink responded.

It was no misdirection, Gideon and Noone both thought to themselves. Someone had recently tried to capture Florrie and Aggie. Whatever the underlying rationale, it harked back to the tragedies of Egypt, fourteen years ago.

'So, if that is the case, then we must assume they are working with the Germans. So again, we must ask ourselves, to what purpose?' Gideon replied.

'I'm not sure. There are a lot of ifs and buts in our theory. And we haven't even started on why you were even at the Natural History in the first place, Professor … ' Wink continued, plotting her own course of investigation.

Gideon felt uneasy the more Wink probed yet restrained himself from impertinent responses. If she did know about him, she knew about Cairo.

'But in the meantime, Professor Belchambers and Mr Noone, there is a man in this photograph that we can question for more information,' Wink advised. 'Thompson, ready my car,' she ordered. 'We are taking a trip to the Malling residence. Bring your men too. We may need them.'

Thompson's eyes rolled. Malling was a force to be reckoned with and an early morning alarm call would not be welcomed.

'Before I go, is there anything else you would care to share?' Wink asked.

Noone shook his head, Gideon shook his too, but the naïve Belle Soames jumped up eager to please.

'Nate, we forgot.' She smiled.

Noone winced as he knew what was coming next.

'Mrs Waverley – on these papers, written in nothing more than my father's hand and lemon juice are lists of names. They are difficult to read in this light but he wanted us to find them. Perhaps they may shed some light, forgive the pun, on OSIRIS or the night of my father's accident.'

'Thank you, Miss Soames,' Wink acknowledged. 'Slipped your mind who you are working for, Noone?' she then said, casting a penetrative stare at Noone. 'May I suggest we reconvene in Whitehall in twenty-four hours. Whatever secrets you gentlemen are keeping, whatever paths you are following, they must be divulged to me by then. Is that clear?' Wink ordered in a calm authority.

Gideon and Noone offered up the pretence of a lack of understanding as Wink began to leave, escorted by Thompson.

'May I?' she gestured towards the photograph in Nathaniel's hand. He was reluctant to hand it over. A subtle nod from Gideon encouraged him to do so. 'And the violet torch, Mr Noone, if you would be so kind.' Again Gideon's subtle agreement ensured Nathaniel passed them over. Wink Waverley's footsteps soon disappeared through the echoes of the British Museum.

'You're lucky she didn't probe you more about the Natural History,' Noone advised.

'Where do you think she's going now?' Gideon smiled. 'And *we're* lucky,' he replied, emphasising the 'we're', 'That I have these additional torches provided by Ilya.'

'She's not going to Colonel Malling's'?' Belle questioned. 'And who is Ilya?'

'Dearest Belle, never trust a spy. Particularly one so high up the tree. They don't get there by chance. She will be going to Malling's' for certain, however, she'll be confirming my recent visit to the Natural History first,' Gideon advised her.

'I gave up on spies a long time ago,' she responded, glaring at them both, but lingering a disappointed stare at Noone. 'And Ilya. Who is Ilya?'

'We, actually, I, owe you more than an explanation, Belle, more than an apology as your father will testify to. He will be OK, by the way. But for now, allow me to explain,' Gideon said. He pulled up a chair and took her back to the very beginning. Over a decade's worth of deceit ago. He was finally beginning to allow the weight off of his shoulders. Whatever OSIRIS was, whoever SERKET may be, he was sure the endgame was approaching, sooner than he had thought.

The beams of daylight were growing stronger and fractured sunshine splintered the blinds in Monty's office. Very soon the glyphs would reveal themselves to them all.

Chapter 35
The Marshes

'Good Morning, Professor,' Brian Louds announced from behind his ever-present surgical mask. 'Is your bed not comfortable as you seem to prefer your workbench?'

Meredith Malcolm slowly awoke with one eye open. The minimal amount of a single G&T to such a man of abstinence had left a hammer blow of a hangover. As always, he started his day by fumbling for the spectacles upon his head. His head was sore and aching.

'So today is the big day. The big reveal,' Louds said with a sweeping gesture towards the scrolls.

'Very true,' Malcolm acknowledged stretching and painfully making his way over to his recent works.

'It is early, Professor. The sun is yet to rise properly. I shall return within the hour for your presentation. Just wanted to ensure you were awake.'

Professor Malcolm, not looking particularly meticulous that morning, it has to be said, gazed upon the muslin-covered cloudy crystal that encased the revelatory Scarabidae. In daylight, there was no evidence of its ethereal glow. He glanced at the insect enclosures and there was no evidence they were behaving extraordinarily either. The iridescent purple and black depth of the dung beetles was as expected. There were no emissions of light. For the time being, this little secret would remain masked by the daylight.

'Of course, Mr Louds. I will be focusing my full attention on it,' Professor Malcolm confirmed.

'Very good. Now, enjoy breakfast,' Louds confirmed, clapping for the orderlies to enter. 'I hope you do not mind but honey will not be on the menu today. We cannot afford any more mishaps with the scrolls.'

The professor laughed in acknowledgement. As the orderlies placed the tea and toast down in front of him, they removed the G&T remains from the previous evening. He had been mindful to ensure that the wedge of lemon was obviously present to them and the observant Mr Louds. The tiny slither of zest he required he had temporarily wedged under his tongue.

'Tea,' thought the Professor, was the cure for almost everything. Certainly, for his dehydrated self after just a single swill of alcohol.

The light was beginning to stream through the prism at the top of the laboratory on this crisp autumn morning. He was able to securely suspend all three scrolls so light distributed itself equally amongst them. They may have been negatives but the citrus scrawl now allowed the papers to illuminate the lemon lines. Eureka, none of his lives would be lost for today. In-between the scrolls, he subtly moved the layer of muslin containing the encrusted scarab and allowed it to absorb the morning rays which began to beat down.

As each scroll contained three glyphs and working on the assumption that they were produced in the correct order on each scroll, the volume of combinations severely reduced from the tens of thousands to just six. It shouldn't take a genius to work out, he thought to himself. If the order of the glyphs could be read in their most simplistic form, then a beginning and end were all they required. The rest would solve itself. He was no expert but could offer Mr Louds a recommendation for further validation, since Louds already knew a world-leading authority. For now, though, he would focus on the detail of each one. He already knew that the peculiar leaves and fauna of a plant played a part on one of them and that would be his starting point.

In negative, the swatch containing the plants actually included the images of two females. The first was knelt down with a small bowl and tool, very much like the pestle and mortal presented to him. She was obviously crushing the plant leaves. The other female was stood behind presenting the plant as if she was gathering and supplying the ingredients for the other to use. The stem of the plant arched over and its leaves drooped like spines of an upside-down and inside-out umbrella, one that had succumbed to a gust of dramatic wind. Inside of those leaf fronds, the stamens were plentiful and tipped with large heads. None of this was in colour, just a faint negative outline. Nevertheless, the Professor was convinced, considering the subjects, that the plant must have been from the Nile delta or North African peninsular. Seeking an appropriate book, other than his beloved *Culpepper's everyday flora*, he searched the small, yet comprehensive library available to him and began to examine any plant or plant type from that region he could find, burying his head compulsively into the books.

'Have you ever noticed how quickly an hour flies by when what you really need is two?' Louds advised Professor Malcolm on his entrance to the room.

The Professor was so absorbed in his search for the correct plant he had not looked at his pocket watch once.

'Care to enlighten me,' Louds directed towards the scrolls and the glyphs.

'Of course,' Professor Malcolm said, accommodatingly. 'The light we now see penetrates the parchment and vellum so what we have is a perfect replica of the original but in negative. Where the ink, well, the lemon juice, is present, it is actually a line mark opposed to the negative it appears to us.'

'Oh, I understand that perfectly, Professor. But I was hoping for you to have deciphered and concluded the current conundrum by now. Instead, you appear to be searching for the intricacies within the puzzle itself and not solving the overall problem.'

Professor Malcolm who was fully aware that a certain fate had befallen his predecessors was on particular edge. 'My apologies, Mr Louds. I am not an Egyptologist, I do not understand all the symbols. I can only assume each triptych of glyphs is true to their order.'

'Good, then if that is so, the puzzle is far easier to resolve. Shall we take a look? Together? Perhaps we can take a leap of faith.'

Professor Malcolm dry gulped but, nevertheless, followed Mr Louds.

'Very interesting,' Louds pondered, looking at each square in turn. It appeared that he could read the glyphs like a book, an illustrated story. Whereas Professor Malcolm only concentrated on them frame by frame.

'This here,' Louds pointed out. 'This first Hieroglyph on the third panel, this is Horus, the falcon-headed Sun God, the bringer of light.'

The Professor noticed that the humble Mr Louds persona was growing more confident and his enthusiasm was increasingly gaining momentum.

'I doubt very much he would be the final piece in any puzzle,' Louds said, before examining the negatives again. 'And here, you cannot appreciate how this would look in colour. His flesh is green. The final square, on your first set of glyphs, this is OSIRIS. He is the God of the dead. He represents a plethora of differing ideology. Resurrection, regeneration and even life beyond the living world.'

Meticulous Meredith Malcolm was reminded once more of the Institute's ambition to rehabilitate the severely injured veterans. Perhaps this is what Louds was enthusing about. Perhaps he was, in a perverse manner, talking some sense.

'You know, dear Professor, I believe your focus may not have been wasted at all. The simplicity of this information, when faced with the images, suggests a very simple recipe for success.'

'Sorry, I'm not sure I follow,' the Professor replied.

'On the contrary, I believe you do,' Louds surprised him. 'I believe you understand most of this, my dear chum. So, let's call your current deception three lives lost. Dare you squander anymore?'

Malcolm was confused but dare not retaliate. He had no hesitancy in believing Mr Louds and Dr Mialora were capable of anything. They had kidnapped him in the first place.

'Then my apologies, Mr Louds. I do not wish to lose any more lives and ultimately not the one I cherish dearly,' Malcolm advised humbly. 'Having researched the plant, the one in the glyph of the serving women, I believe it is a rare marsh papyrus from the Nile delta. Here, look at this image I found.'

Louds took the book from the Professor and cross-examined it.

'You have excelled yourself, Professor.'

'And I thought you may wish to know that it has a very close relative in this country too.'

Mr Louds became more attentive.

The professor continued, 'papyrus are part of the Sedge family. This particular plant is aquatic and must rely on boggy and damp conditions. There is a unique sedge family but only found in marshlands bordering chalk cliffs relative to the English coast.'

'Then what a perfect coincidence we have, Professor,' Louds replied.

'I took the liberty of producing a handful of suggestions from the research books. Here's the list.'

He read through the list. One name stood out. Not many miles from here and well-known to his orderlies.

'Ambledown,' he muttered. Brian Louds could not disguise his happiness as a huge smile offered up a brief glimpse of his scarred face below the surgical mask. 'Ambledown, Professor. Tell me about this place,' Louds enquired.

Of all the luck in the world and but a stone's throw away. Ambledown was half an hour by car and Louds had numerous ambulances at his disposal. Professor Malcolm had certainly changed his luck and as his patients were repeat visitors to the market town their presence would not be a surprise.

'Well,' Meticulous Meredith Malcolm started. 'On the ordnance, you shall see that where the tidal estuary of the English Channel meets with the mouth of the River Amble there are salt marshes.'

Louds was not a great geographer and relied on the Professor's enthusiastic explanation to understand this great opportunity.

'These marshes are almost identical, in principle, to the Nile delta and the Sussex Sedge that grow there are a distant relative of the papyrus we seek.'

'Bravo, Professor. I will need you to instruct my men on exactly what it is you seek.'

Professor Malcolm looked upon the orderlies. He had only heard them grunt and wasn't sure they could speak.

'With all due respect, Mr Louds, these plants are delicate and easily trampled or mistaken for their sister plants. Such similar plants are toxic and I would be concerned we miss our opportunity so late in autumn. I am willing to accompany them and coordinate proceedings'

A long pause greeted Professor Malcolm. Brian Louds was perusing the scrolls and table once again where the scarab sat in full view of the light shining down from the pinnacle glass prism.

'Very well. But rest assured, Professor, should you fail to return, I doubt many of your lives will remain.'

Meredith Malcolm nodded in understanding.

Mr Louds then turned to leave the room with the orderlies. 'Prepare a list of anything you may need, Professor. My men will take care of everything while you are there.' And then he was gone.

*****

'Halt!' came the American accent, raising a pistol to the observer at the bottom of the cliff. 'Ahh, Pop Braggan!'

The gold-laden bear of a man was crouching down, examining the rocks and earth at the bottom of the chalks. Lady was swooping from observation point to observation point, and Luna the hound was dutifully standing guard.

'You shouldn't be here, Pop. The boundary of the brook is the water's edge and this is dry land. What do you want?'

'So glad you asked, boys,' came Pop's mumble. 'Me nephew Lyle was found dead in me brook.'

'We heard. We're sorry,' came their apologetic tone.

'Have you got something to be sorry for then?' Pop enquired.

'No, it wasn't meant like that. We're sorry for your loss,' the Americans said in a more conciliatory tone.

'Only I hear that you two boys were kind enough to escort him away from the Steep and onward to these cliffs on the night in question.'

The two men looked at each other and took a step back.

'Look, Pop, you really cannot be here, you know that,' one of them continued.

'Then make me leave,' Pop said inflating himself to his full stature and within a swift arm's grab of the two men. The Lady meanwhile had landed on his shoulder and was cawing at the men while his wolfhound was letting out an aggressive muzzle-sneering growl.

'OK, you wanna know what happened? We escorted Lyle to almost where you are standing. He had business, he said. We told him he had to move on. He knew the rules and we left him hurling expletives our way. We passed an hour or so later and we didn't see him again.'

'So, what's this on these stones?' Pop directed the men to the rocks at his feet.

'What do you mean?'

'These rocks and stones, look,' he said, holding one up. 'Brown staining probably used to be red. What does that look like to you?'

The men looked confused. They were not sure what he meant. They focused their rifles on Pop, no way that rock was being hurled their way.

'It's blood! Lyle's blood,' he said angrily.

'Hold on, Pop,' one of them replied. 'We don't know nothing about no blood.'

'No? Then what about dollar bills? I bet you know a thing or two about dollar bills. Don't ya?' Pop said, revealing the sodden dollars rescued from Lyle's shoe via the clutches of Messrs Closet and Cleave.

One of the men looked at the other. He lowered his gun and moved towards the giant hulk of a man.

'Show me the serial numbers,' he said, curling his fingers towards himself, beckoning the money forward.

Pop was not expecting that response. It confused him into complying. By now he would usually have expected to be brawling.

'You see this sequence of numbers?' the American said, holding the bill up to the Braggan. 'Each one is unique. However, servicemen overseas, such as ourselves, are paid in sequences which can be tracked. These notes here, your notes, are not typical army sequences, they are older and also larger denominations.'

'So, what y'saying, Lyle's money came from somewhere other than yours or yours barracks.'

'Probably. Most likely. Couldn't be sure but they look old. I doubt our guys hold on to theirs too long, let alone have larger bills to throw around.'

'So, who else has dollars round ere?' Pop barked.

'Your good friend Professor Belchambers deals in many currencies, my friend. We should know.' They smiled.

'Impossible, not Gideon. Who else?'

'Those guys from the hospital. The institute guys who look after the melted men. Silvera Institute. You know the two guys that drive the patients. One with the big gold tooth.'

'Not American though, are they?' Pop sneered.

'Definitely not. We agree on that one. Not even sure they're Spanish or Portuguese as their institutional name suggests. They speak a little English but usually just grunt and point but they do like to buy contraband using dollars. I've sold them American cigarettes myself.'

Pop stood there staring at the men for a while. 'What do you think, Lady?' he asked his feathered friend. If it had been down to the decision of his avian accomplice, he would have been embroiled in a fight with the Americans already. Instead, he turned around and guided his dog past the men and plodded back towards the Steep.

Pop Braggan made a slow saunter back to the stone bridge that straddled the Amble. It allowed him thinking time but nothing was clear to him as it stood. The large wooden shoe, which was actually a clog if anyone bothered to look, swayed on its squeaking sign that just about held it above the entrance. Pop Braggan was possibly the only man in Ambledown who could fill the large wooden shoe that acted as the sign for Tink's shop. 'Tinker the tailor and fine-shoe purveyor', to give it its official title, serviced the well-heeled gentry of Ambledown and surrounding areas. Or at least it had done so successfully prior to the war. Tink, as he was known to his friends and Tinks as his shop was less formally called locally, was not only an excellent tailor and cobbler but as his name suggested, could turn his hand to most things. His shop front caught the eye of every passer-by with its intricate models and tiny feats of engineering from the famous miniature buildings of the capital to replicas of Spitfires and Lancaster Bombers, which he suspended from the ceiling. All of them were made from old scrap food cans and disused matches. Eric Peabody was a particular fan and always found money to purchase Tink's latest aviation creations.

Pop encouraged The Lady to fly off and gather her lunch, while he left Luna unshackled outside. On entry, a discreet bell informed Tink he had custom as he whittled away in his backroom.

'Morning, Pop.' Tink smiled on greeting the Braggan chief. 'What news?' he asked. A humble man, considering his many abilities, he was dressed in a long brown overall with a dark tan leather apron. His fingers were muscular and gnarled with arthritis after many years at the flying stick and subsequently the cobbler's needle. Those hands that now kept him away from flying his beloved planes but allowed him the artistry of a double-breasted three-piece. On his head, he had temporarily placed his old fighter goggles. 'Much better than welding glasses,' he would always say and still a reminder to his glorious past.

'The Americans reckon Lyle was paid by someone other than the servicemen in the barracks. Somefink to do with sequences of dollars.'

'And you believe them?' Tink replied.

'Hmmm. Never trust no one is my motto,' Pop mumbled back, deep in thought. 'Said bills were old and asked me who might deal in them. Even said Gideon does.'

'Well, if that is the case, then that's very true. Gideon does deal in many currencies. However, he was looking after Aggie, Cecile will testify to that.'

Pop gave a sceptical squint. Tink and Gideon were as thick as thieves, always had been. But he really had no reason to suspect them either. They had always done right by him and his family.

'What d'ya know about the Silvera place?' Pop enquired.

'The hospital for recovering serviceman? Not a great deal, old chap. I hear rumours, mutterings that the place is pioneering surgery for burns victims and such. Though I've never heard it from the patients themselves.'

'Do you know some then?'

'Each Sunday a small group dine at Cecile's – you know The Black Cat. Anyway, they just talk about white corridors and odd picture-less frames from the time it was a gallery. They seem well looked after and relaxed but there's something incomplete about them. It may be my familiarity with them week in week out but they do not seem to be on the mend. That's my opinion anyway.'

'Sunday? The day it happened. Were they here then?' Pop asked, his interest piqued.

'Definitely. I know as Cecile's cat escaping was the fault of the orderlies throwing their weight around. That's what started it all, Pop.'

'OK. I might take a trip out to see this place for meself.'

'Be careful if you do. As fortified as any barracks by all account.'

'One more fing, Tink. When I saw you last, you told me Lyle's sole was re-heeled recently – the one which was missing.'

'As I told you, Pop, he wanted an extra-thick sole on it. Almost an inch or so larger than the other foot. I didn't ask questions. He was in a drunk and argumentative mood.'

'Could it have been for climbing?' Pop asked.

'Possibly, but unlikely. Unsuitable I would say. Why?'

''is jacket pockets was lined with down. I didn't mention it as wasn't sure, but he may 'ave been pinching eggs.'

'Well, I, for one, didn't line it, so cannot offer insight on that front. Eggs from the cliff you mean? Just gulls and the occasional birds of prey there. I doubt he was pinching any eggs. Too late in the season, Pop.'

'Perhaps it was the layers' of those eggs then,' Pop replied, his thoughts now on another plain.

'I'm not so sure there is the market for birds of prey anymore, Pop. Not while most men are off fighting abroad.'

'S'pose not. Not in this country, Tink, anyways.' Pop doffed his hat towards Tink and turned around, leaving the ringing chime of the bell echoing through the shop.

Tink composed himself and thought for a moment. If Pop was right, Gideon may need to know. Twisting the open sign to a closed sign, he locked up and pulled the blinds down. The whirring and subtle moments of his creations still projected animated shadows from his shop light onto the cloth rollers. Making his way back behind the counter and through to his workshop, he locked every door behind him. Once he was isolated, he opened up his large cabinet of haberdashery. Pots of pins and buttons, swathes of materials, and frilled refinery overflowing from inside. A neat row of tailor's scissors and fabric shears ran across the top shelf, each of them suspended on metal hooks. Tink simultaneously reached to the top left and top right, a full arms span for the man, and then pulled the two sets of scissors on the farthest hooks downwards in unison. A satisfying click from both of them allowed him to swivel the central axis until he had fully revolved the cabinet so that all haberdashery and tailoring had disappeared.

In front of him sat a single telephonic exchange machine. Several lights flashed red and white. A single earpiece of mahogany and tortoiseshell was suspended on a curling cord and in front of him, a circular wire mesh mounted on an enamel box. Tink flicked a single black switch beneath the mesh and waited.

'Good morning, sir, welcome to Fortnum's. You are through to Baker. How may I help,' came a sharp cordial man's voice.

'Baker, this is Tailor. I need to place an advertisement.'

'Very well, sir. Please, proceed.'

Chapter 36

The Blazer

Aggie had enjoyed a remarkable breakfast, courtesy of Nan and her anger expressed towards the WI. She desperately wished to keep all the photographs that included her mother and uncle. However, Eric and his sisters would soon be here and she'd promised to return them to him so he could replace them without raising suspicion. Aggie would keep the one with the picture of the missing crest. No one would miss just one, surely.

Fully dressed with an hour to spare, she sat at the window of 1a The Keep, hoping the Peabodys would arrive early. Hardly a soul had passed by in the crisp early autumn morning before she spotted an elderly lady walking up the Steep away from the village and towards St Joan's. The Lady was stooped over and pulling a tartan flanked trolley as she struggled uphill. Without much thought and with photo in hand she unbolted the door and ran after her.

'Aggie!' shouted Nan. 'Wait for Peabodys!'

Nan needn't have wasted her breath. Agatha continued unabated. Turning the corner, she saw the elderly lady disappear into the graveyard. The Steep, at this point, was moss-covered and slippery and she almost lost her footing as she continued at speed.

'Mrs Parker, is that you?' Aggie called out. 'Nelly, Nelly Parker?'

The graveyard was silent as morning mist engulfed her ankles. The dew on the grass glistened in the morning sun. The moss-covered gravestones were shrouded in a deep mysterious green. On the ground, the recent footprints and wheel-tracks the elderly lady had created, led up to the path and to the rear of the churchyard. Aggie followed them to a secret garden. There, kneeling next to three neatly kept graves, was the elderly woman. Aggie bowed her head. She couldn't interrupt her now, tending her husband and sons' place of rest. Aggie turned around and began to walk slowly away.

'What is it dear?' the elderly lady called out. Still focusing on the graves.

'Excuse me, I'm terribly sorry but are you Mrs Parker?' Agatha asked humbly.

The old lady turned, dark lensed glasses complimenting her headscarf.

'Yes, dear, I am. How can I help you?'

For some reason Agatha stalled, she thought it was insensitive to ask questions about her mother when Nelly was tending to those she had lost.

'Come, child, cat got your tongue? You wouldn't have chased me up the Steep if it wasn't important.'

Aggie smiled. Mrs Parker had heard her the whole time but had not let on. 'I'm Agatha.'

'Yes, I know. I'm not called Nosey Parker for nothing.' Nelly smiled, looking up at the young lady. 'You're Gideon's evacuee.'

'That's right. I was hoping you could tell me a little bit about this photograph.'

'Come closer over here then. They won't bite. Nor will I,' Nelly advised her pointing at the gravestones.

Aggie took a couple of cautious steps forward before handing the photograph over.

Nelly angled the edge of her glasses in order to see. 'I have a condition, dear. Daylight doesn't agree with my eyes,' Nelly explained. 'Well I never. They all look so young, so full of promise. It's such a long time ago.' Nelly smiled. 'So how can I help you, Agatha?'

'You can call me, Aggie.'

'OK. So how can I help you, Aggie?'

'In the picture, the girl on the end,' she said, pointing out her mother. 'The girl sporting the jacket without the crest … what was her name?'

Nelly peered for a moment and looked back smiling. 'Why do you wish to know that?' Nelly asked.

'Because I'm wearing her blazer.'

'So you are,' Nelly replied. 'Well, I remember she was a twin and at the other end of the photograph is her brother.'

'Really,' replied Aggie, feigning a response as if she didn't know.

'Really. You should ask my sister. She will know more. She taught them.'

'Sister Harvey?' Aggie asked immediately.

'Well, well. And they call me Nosey Parker. You've been here but a few days dear and seem to know a lot already. Yes, Sister Harvey is my sister.'

Agatha blushed, she felt Nelly could see straight through her.

'Best you be on your way, young lady. Miss Dove doesn't like latecomers and I'm sure the Peabodys are waiting.'

'Thank you, Mrs Parker.' She really does see everything Aggie thought.

'Call me, Nelly, dear. Most people call me Nosey, behind my back, but I prefer Nelly to my face.'

'Thank you, Nelly.'

'You're welcome. I'm here at this time most days if you ever need me. Tell me, do you like riddles, mysteries. Just like your namesake?'

'I suppose,' Aggie replied.

'Then try to solve this. If you take one from forty-nine how do you end up with forty-two? You may need my sister's help.'

Aggie was perplexed but smiled with an acknowledging nod to the eccentric old dear and ran back down the Steep to where the Peabodys were already halfway up to meet her.

'Where 'av you been?' Eric shouted

'Nowhere special,' Aggie replied.

'Give us the pics then,' he said, singularly clapping his right hand.

Aggie handed over all but one of them. Eric cast her a doubtful glare but then quickly made off to arrive at school early and repatriate them.

'I'm sorry about last night, Aggie,' Elizabeth apologised.

'It's OK. Cecile escorted me home,' Aggie responded.

'It's only, well – Gem, show her.'

Gemima, who had hidden herself behind Elizabeth, stepped out. Her hair had been cut to an uneven bob just above shoulder height and had been dyed as black as pitch.

'Apparently, accosting Huntington-Smythe has created you quite a following amongst the other evacuees,' Elizabeth explained.

Aggie was lost for words.

'Wouldn't get too close though. Gem stinks of boot polish. Don't you, Gem?'

Gemima bowed her head. No doubt the wicked Mrs McGregor would have made her evening hell. Luckily, she had Elizabeth to protect her.

'I don't think you should have done that Gem,' Aggie said towards the youngest Peabody, offering her a subtle wink in recognition.

Gemima beamed and led them with a spring in her heel back down the hill towards the schoolhouse.

'Do you like riddles, Elizabeth?' Aggie asked.

'That's a very odd question,' she replied 'You're named after the mistress of crime, not me.'

'If you take one from forty-nine how do you end up with forty-two?' Aggie asked her regardless.

Elizabeth just offered a blank stare back. 'Your uncle never used the word odd when he asked us to be your friends.' Elizabeth laughed as they continued jovially towards school.

'If you take one from forty-nine how do you end up with forty-two?' Aggie asked her again and again.

'No idea,' Elizabeth replied.

'Beats me too,' Aggie responded to Elizabeth. 'Sister Harvey is supposed to know though.'

'I'd tread carefully if I was you, Aggie,' Elizabeth advised.

'Why?' Aggie asked.

'Huntington-Smythe and her gang of Priories is more than enough to be contesting with. Don't upset Harvey too. She's no pushover and she does not care for Governess Dove, so you'll be without her stepping in if you choose a fight with a teacher.'

'I understand,' Aggie replied as they reached the school earlier than usual. 'Will you keep watch while I take a look around?'

'You haven't listened to a single word I've said, have you?' Elizabeth replied, raising her voice.

'I have, but I just need five minutes inside. Please?' Aggie begged.

'Gemima,' Elizabeth ordered. 'Play on the outside steps. Warn us if anyone comes. I'll wait in the foyer near the plant and will cough loudly if anyone does.'

'Thank you, Elizabeth. I owe you one.' Aggie smiled.

'You owe me more than that.' Elizabeth smiled.

Aggie was light-footed through the corridor and reached Sister Harvey's classroom in no time at all. Ensuring she was alone, she worked her way clockwise speed-reading anything she could find mounted on the walls. Harvey did not keep any pictures of previous pupils, as Agatha had hoped, but there were certain commendable works of poetry and art amongst the times tables and periodic tables that so dominated the wall space. Having made one circuit of the room in a hurry she slowed down and revisited everything again, but it was still no use. The seven times table was the only place the mention of '49' was apparent. Seven times seven equalled forty-nine. If you take away one then that was '48' how come Nelly had said '42'. Aggie could not understand Nelly Parker's riddle. The classroom would shortly be full of pupils and she so desperately needed to know. Working her way behind Sister Harvey's desk she took pen and paper from her top drawer and wrote her a letter:

Dearest Sister Harvey,

My host, the eternal prankster Professor Belchambers, has set me a riddle I have no hope of solving. He knows I am terrible at mathematics.

May I ask for your assistance?

Removing 1 from 49 = 42 – or that is where my riddle begins.

Sincerely

Agatha Chatsmore

Just as she finished writing, the sound of Elizabeth's cough echoed down the corridors. Agatha folded the letter into the top drawer, hoping Sister Harvey might oblige.

Gaggles of noise and lines clearly drawn between evacuee and Priory girl greeted Sister Harvey as she entered her classroom. It was the commonest of sights nearly every morning. Placing the work for the day on her desk just before she ordered its distribution, she noticed her drawer was slightly open. Immediately sliding it out, Aggie watched on with eager eyes. Elizabeth was reading her friend's body language while the rest of the class continued chattering. Opening and reading the note, Sister Harvey took stock for a while, did not make eye contact, then continued in her familiar tone.

'Quiet!' the sister bellowed and set her ticking alarm clock, timed to an hour and a half, on the desk. 'Geography!'

Henrietta Huntington-Smythe's hand shot up like a starter's pistol.

'Yes, Smythe?' Harvey asked although her back was half turned. She'd had a premonition about the forthcoming enquiry.

'Huntington-Smythe, Sister,' Henrietta corrected her. 'Maths is usually this morning's subject, is it not?'

'You're quite correct, young lady,' Sister Harvey agreed, scribing on the board, refusing to turn around and discuss face to face. 'But I have decided we will switch subjects anti and post meridian. All will be revealed.'

'My mother is a board member here, Sister, and it was agreed that routine was the best approach for all those children serious about maintaining their education despite the horrors of our country faces.' Henrietta, always prone to a monologue, was supported by her Priory girls as they falsely smiled across to the evacuees staring on in disbelief.

'Ahh, yes. Your mother. She is that, correct,' Harvey replied, not answering the question. 'You will be aware, therefore, that this evening, your mother holds her annual general meeting of her beloved Woman's Institute, right here, at the school.'

Henrietta looked back confused.

'So?' came the young girl's reply.

'It would be disappointing, therefore, to yet again detain you for insubordination. I doubt your mother would appreciate you disrupting her best-laid plans,' Harvey concluded.

The evacuees began to giggle, Agatha let out a huge laugh.

'Detention! Chatsmore!' Sister Harvey shouted, turning around and pointing at Aggie with a deathly stare.

Aggie was just about to issue a tirade in response but Elizabeth pinched her below the desk.

'Ouch!' Aggie jumped.

'Something to say to me, Miss Agatha Chatsmore?' Sister Harvey said, approaching her and eyeballing her nose to nose.

'No, Sister. Sorry, Sister,' Aggie replied dipping her head.

Henrietta Huntington-Smythe was cock-a-hoop that her current adversary had taken the detention when it was rightfully hers. No one messed with the Huntington-Smythes in Ambledown. Certainly not the nuns or vagabond evacuees, as her broad smile suggested.

'As I was saying,' Harvey began her lesson again. 'Geography,' she said and pointed to the board she had been busily writing on. There was a chalk outline of the south coast of England with wavy lines representing the English Channel beneath. London was labelled as a circle to the north. Dover and its famous white cliffs to the east. Several circles were unlabelled running along the coast marked A, B, and C.

''A' represents which coastal town infamously preferred by the Prince Regent?' Sister Harvey asked.

Eagerly all the Priory girls shot their hands up. Not so the evacuees. Scattered from all parts of the United Kingdom they were unlikely to know any of the answers.

'Anyone from Priory,' Sister Harvey encouraged them.

'Brighton!' came many voices in unison.

'Correct! Priory, take the lead,' Sister continued.

''B' – Need I ask you all?' Sister smirked.

Again, the Priory were all waving hands and gloating. A couple of evacuees thought they knew, including Elizabeth, but decided not to chance it.

'Very well – Priory?'

'Ambledown!' they all shouted, with much cooing and laughter.

'Of course, of course, calm down,' Sister Harvey said. 'Finally – 'C' – Our own famous chalk cliffs.'

'White cliffs of Dover!' shouted out an enthusiastic Priory girl.

'When I have that already written on the boards. Shame on you ,Miss Whychmore. You lose a point,' Sister Harvey mused.

Huntington-Smythe glared a visual scolding at her Priory alumni.

'Anyone *not* from the Priory care to guess. Let's face it you can't embarrass yourself as much as Whychmore just has,' said Sister Harvey uncommonly laughing to herself.

There was stony silence.

'Chatsmore, you usually have a lot to say?' the Sister directly engaged Agatha. Aggie had no idea and remained defiantly silent.

'It's the Seven Sisters!' Henrietta screamed out. The thought of not answering too much to bear.

'Very good, Priory!' Harvey concluded. 'You'd do well to pay more attention to the local ladies, Miss Chatsmore. You may even learn a thing or two.' 'Right – As Henrietta was so eager for maths, let us lead with the theme of seven! Lucky for some, but not necessarily for all you girls. Seven times tables out loud please, ladies.'

The class moved to their feet and began their rhythmic chanting of the times table as Sister Harvey moved back to the blackboard to orchestrate.

'Once seven is seven, two sevens are fourteen, three sevens are twenty-one,' they continued, the rules were such that once they forgot they sat down at their desks.

'Four sevens are twenty-eight.'

Several younger children were already out of step and sitting at their desks.

'Very good girls,' the sister said encouragingly. 'We shall stop at seven sevens.'

'Five sevens are thirty-five, six sevens are forty-two and seven sevens are forty-nine! Whoooooo!' The Priory girls finished with whooping.

'Forty-nine. Bravo, ladies,' Sister Harvey concluded. She walked over to the blackboard and underneath the letter C – where she had written 'The Seven Sisters', she wrote the number forty-nine.

'On my goodness,' Elizabeth said, whispering to her friend. 'She's giving you your first clue.'

For the first time ever, it had to be said that one child was looking forward to her detention.

Chapter 37

The List

'Do you trust a single word they say, ma'am?' Thompson asked from the front seat of the sleek black sedan as his superior sat in the back.

'Let's just say, I have my suspicions on the extent of their divulgence. They must not leave London, do you hear?' Wink replied through the cloud of customary cigarette smoke that followed her around. She had spent the past ten minutes turning the flashlight on and off so that the faces transformed from black-and-white smiles at a charitable fundraiser to glowing violet totems from a deceased civilisation many millennia past.

As they pulled up to the monumental stone building carved with mammal gargoyle's and testament to centuries of animal biology and botanic endeavour, she couldn't help but sigh at the sheer stupidity of placing army recruitment posters on the entrance to such a beautiful place.

'I'll be having words with Malling about you too.' Wink exhaled under her breath and pointing towards, mirroring Kitchener's eponymous index finger as she spoke to the poster.

'I'm sorry, ma'am, didn't quite catch that,' Thompson replied.

'Never mind, Thompson. Any luck with those papers?'

'There is writing on them, ma'am, definitely. They were not lying about that. I need a better source of light than intermittent morning rays if I am to decipher them all. I can confirm that Malling is on here, as assumed.'

'Colonel Malling, please, remember your position,' Wink fired back with authority as she continued to ponder the man in the photo. 'Now, Thompson, Major Boyd Collingdale is our man right? Tread lightly, to begin with. I'm not sure how much he knows of Belchambers or the 'tiger-lady'. If, Belchambers was telling the truth at all.'

Alighting the vehicle, Thompson was greeted by his number twos, Smith and Jones. Producing their identity cards and easing through the barricaded wooden sentry, they swiftly entered the Natural History Museum in their long black macs and fedoras.

*****

Sister Harvey's alarm, as always, ensured her room jumped to attention at the end of each lesson. Post the enthusiasm of times tables, she had distributed more complicated long division and subtraction that almost all evacuees had struggled with alongside most of the Priory girls.

'But what can she mean?' Aggie whispered to Elizabeth.

'Not a clue,' came Elizabeth's reply with a shrug.

Aggie made her way over to the teacher's desk.

'Sister?' she asked

'Not content with detention, Chatsmore, you dare interrupt my break time too?' Sister Harvey replied bluntly. 'We will have plenty of time to get to know each other after school, young lady.'

Huntington-Smythe cackled as she and her friends shoved past on her way out. Elizabeth grabbed her friend by the elbow and led her out.

'You need to learn to take a hint, Aggie,' Elizabeth advised.

'I don't understand,' Agatha replied, confused.

'Whatever it is you need to know and whatever it is Harvey may be inclined to divulge, she's not telling you in standard class time.'

Aggie huffed and puffed as they made their way to the playground.

'Perhaps I need *Eric's* help,' Aggie insisted, insinuating a preferential slur to his elder sister.

'Honestly, be my guest. If Eric can help you, feel free to ask him,' Elizabeth replied. Taking herself off on her own.

Eric, as quite often he was, stood isolated in the corner of the playground. Spitfire in hand, swooping and dive-bombing the invisible foe. No doubt another misdemeanour had encouraged the Brothers' penance. Aggie looked on at him, trying to get his attention but he was too busy chattering away to himself.

'Aggie,' came the soft voice from behind. Agatha turned to see the youngest Peabody, Gemima, staring up with her large doe eyes.

'Please, don't fight with my sister,' she said. 'She doesn't have many friends.'

'Oh, Gem, I'm so sorry. I didn't mean to be rude to her, it's just that I need–' she said, stopping mid-sentence.

'Need what?' Gem asked.

Agatha's attention was directed to a small group of Priory girls who were busily skipping. Two girls rotated the rope as one jumped in the middle until another girl would jump in and tag her out or she fell, whichever came first. The speed of the rope got quicker the longer they stayed in, all the while singing to a rhythmic tune.

'Agaathhaaa!' Gem said, extending her name and tugging at her skirt. 'Aggatthaaaaaaaaa!' Gem said as annoyingly as she could to gain Aggie's attention.

'Those girls. What are they singing?' Aggie asked, transfixed on the skippers.

'Playing, you mean,' Gem replied. 'It's called skipping. Do you skip where you are from?'

'I know it's skipping, Gem, and, yes, I can skip, but what is the song?'

'If you get a rope, I will get Elizabeth, and then all three of us will play,' Gem replied.

'OK,' Aggie agreed.

Gemima sprinted across to where a disused rope from the Priory girls lay discarded on the playground floor. She quickly swiped it and sprinted back again, grabbing Elizabeth's hand while leading her towards Aggie.

'You take this in one hand,' Gem instructed, handing a wooden handle to Aggie. 'And, Lizzy, you have this. Now start spinning.'

Both older girls did as they were told and began rotating the rope until they found a steady speed.

'Ready!' Gem shouted, running in and jumping. 'Shall I sing the song now?' Gem asked, panting for breath between words and jumps.

'Yes,' Aggie and Elizabeth replied together.

'There was once seven sisters from the Seven Sisters, forty-nine they called them. How about you? A gipsy curse upon them saw the youngest off to heaven. Take one away from forty-nine and you're left with forty-two.'

Both girls stopped spinning the rope. It caught Gem's ankles and sent her somersaulting over, cracking her head on the ground.

'Oww!' the young Peabody whimpered before her eyeballs rolled and the whites of her eyes disappeared into the top of her head.

'Gemima!' Elizabeth screamed diving down to her youngest sibling.

Blood had begun to run from a wound in her head. Aggie ran to get help. The nuns walked calmly over.

'For pity's sake, call for the doctor!' Elizabeth shouted at them, but they were still dawdling.

'Come on, Lizzy!' came Eric's voice as he broke ranks from the boys' side and grabbed Gem's legs. Elizabeth grabbed Gem's upper body and between them, they began carrying their youngest sibling out of the school.

Aggie followed them through the corridors, opening doors as they went. At the main door, Dove and Harvey were in heated conversation.

'Whatever is going on here?' Sister Harvey barked, observing the familiar face of the Peabody clan.

'Gem's 'ed's split wide open!' Eric shouted. 'Blood everywhere. Needs a doctor.'

Dove stood in front of them trying to get a better understanding of the wounds. Sister Harvey meanwhile had already unbolted the doors.

'Quickly then. You know where Dr Beckworth's surgery is,' Sister Harvey reassured them.

'Sister Harvey, is that wise?' Dove questioned.

'By the time we've sent word and old Beckworth has waddled down the street they will be there already,' the nun replied curtly to her teaching superior. 'Not you, Chatsmore,' she said, pulling Agatha tightly by the shirt as she tried to pass.

Agatha looked on helplessly as the Peabodys rushed their baby sister uphill. There was a loud screech of brakes.

'What on earth is that?' Dove shouted.

Dove and Harvey stepped out of the threshold and onto the Steep. Aggie stared out to see as much as she could between the two ladies. A large ambulance truck had swerved and was angled sideways up the Steep. Two large men were shouting angrily with indecipherable language at the Peabodys who were standing motionless in front of them having just missed being run down. Elizabeth took a breath and ordered her brother onwards. Eric took up the mantle and they continued to carry Gemima onwards to the doctor.

Moments later the commotion had passed. The men had managed to right the direction of the vehicle and it travelled down the hill, stopping not far from the school. Aggie continued to observe from inside the school's windows. The hulking men then left their van once again to help the cloaked men inside to find their feet, or if in wheelchairs to set them down safely. Most of the men were quick to head towards Le Chat Noir but she noticed a single forlorn figure being escorted by the orderlies away from the Steep and towards the river. He turned briefly. He was not burned, as far as she could make out, not like the men she had seen in Cecile's café. Instead, he sported a magnificent curling moustache. Aggie did not recognise him but she certainly recognised the much larger men. They were responsible for Purrsia escaping. That had led to Lyle's threats. Her heart began to beat fast again. Her anxieties multiplying as she stood there frozen, struggling for air. The bell rang and broke her temporary paralysis, the noise of girls rushing back in, singing the skipping song which had become infectious during the break and inspired, no doubt, by Sister Harvey's lesson.

'There was once seven sisters from the Seven Sisters, forty-nine they called them. How about you? A gipsy curse upon them saw the youngest off to heaven. Take one away from forty-nine and you're left with forty-two.'

'Miss Chatsmore,' came Sister Harvey's voice, breaking Aggie's concentration. 'Are you joining us or shall we make that double detention?'

*****

Belle was too shocked to respond. Fourteen years' worth of lies. Lies from those she held most dear to her; her father Montague and Nathaniel Noone.

'I don't know what to say to you both,' Belle spoke softly, stunned at the revelations.

'You cannot blame your father or Nate,' Gideon insisted. 'If you need to be angry with anyone, be angry with me.'

'I'm not angry. Well, maybe a little. No, actually, make that a lot. I am angry. My teenage years were those of nightmares. But I just cannot believe it is true,' Belle replied.

'Whatever anger you feel you need to let it out and direct it my way. Nate has suffered enough. Your father had found every day painful since.'

'Don't think so little of me,' she insisted. 'I do not blame you for wanting to protect her. I cannot blame you for your loss. I am no longer Belle with the bunches and a foolish teenage girl as I was back then. I blame the men responsible for where we find ourselves and will do anything to help you.'

Gideon embraced her. A tear trickled down his cheek. It prompted him to remember his niece.

'Nate, we need to find a news vendor,' he suddenly said of his friend.

'OK,' Noone responded, fetching his hat and coat.

'Be careful. We do not know if we are being watched by OSIRIS or Waverley for that matter,' Gideon explained.

'It's not Waverley I fear,' Noone replied with a smile.

'Don't be long, Nate, please,' Belle insisted

'I won't, Belle,' he said affectionately 'Or shall we call you Professor Soames from now on?'

'Belle's fine. But Professor Gideon Belchambers, what shall I call you?'

Gideon beamed back at her. 'You may call me Gideon for now, one Professor to another.'

*****

It had been days since Professor Malcolm had breathed fresh air. His clothes were filthy and he could do with a long soak in a bath. He was just grateful to be outside. The orderlies had organised a small group of men, consisting of those accustomed to Sunday visits to Ambledown and eager to escape the monotony of convalescing at the Institute Silvera. They were excited to soon be dining at Le Chat Noir and liaising with the feline residents.

'List?' the huge man with the glinting tooth grunted at the Professor.

'Of course,' Professor Malcolm replied in an accommodating tone, handing over his list of requirements.

'Wear,' came the second orderly's grunt, forcing a large dark cloak over the Professor before manhandling him into the van and onwards towards Ambledown.

The short, unusually silent drive from the Silvera Institute was that of country roads and coastal cliffs. Meticulous Meredith Malcolm recalled in fractured memories the dappled lights of the roads as he had first set sight on the white building rising up from the coast.

Arriving at the entrance to the market town he read it out loud, 'Ambledown.'

'Quiet. No talk,' came the familiar grunt from the driver.

Professor Malcolm had been warned not to converse or make eye contact with any other patient from the Institute. Several attempts had been made by them to start a singsong en route but the driver and his muscle-bound helper had slammed on the brakes and threatened the hooded figures.

As the van descended the beginning of a very long and winding hill, the churchyard and spire of St Joan's passed them on the right. Slightly south and opposite to the church a large black asymmetrical building came into view, set back from the road and dwarfed by the flint and mullioned Keep that ran alongside it. The van sped onwards until a fork in the road, overlooked by three alehouses and divided by a large angel monument, took their direction down a precarious moss-cobbled drove-way.

'Look out!' came a cry from one of the men at the back.

The driver slammed on his brakes and the van slid sideways. Two on looking children, carrying the limp body of a third, were frozen motionless as the vehicle careered towards them. Smoke exuded from the wheels as the tyre rubber screeched on the stone tiles. With inches to spare, the van came to a stop. The driver and his accomplice rushed out of the vehicle screaming at the children.

'Hello, old chap. I'm Goodfellow. Archibald Goodfellow,' came the voice from the cloaked gentleman next to the Professor holding out his hand. 'Who might you be?' he enquired.

At that moment, Professor Malcolm did not know who to trust.

'Don't be shy. We won't have long until the apes return.' Goodfellow chuckled. 'Come, let's have a look at you,' he said and began feeling the Professor's face.

Meredith Malcolm moved away from the stranger's advances. He then noticed that Archibald Goodfellow's eyes were clouded white. He was blind.

'Apologies, Mr Goodfellow. I am Meredith Malcolm,' he replied and allowed him to continue.

'My, my, impressive facial fluff, sir.' Archibald chuckled. 'So, if you are not burned on your face, I assume your lower body?' he suggestively gestured to the nether regions.

Professor Malcolm did not know what to say and became immediately embarrassed. The other men had been listening in and began to laugh.

'Don't worry, he's pulling your leg. He's off to see his fancy lady, Cecile.'

'Too right!' Archibald Goodfellow howled before starting off a rousing rendition of *Run Rabbit Run*.

'Mr Goodfellow, sir,' the Professor whispered while the others sang. 'Do you know of Professor Belchambers?' he asked.

'Cecile, my good lady, is a dear friend of his,' Archie replied. 'Why?'

'I need to get a message to him,' Professor Malcolm quickly said. 'Do you have a scrap of paper?'

'Not on me, I'm afraid. What is it? Just tell me,' Archie said just as the orderlies returned. Professor Malcolm had no time to answer.

'We say quiet!' they bellowed, entering the van cab as the hooded patients subdued their song. A crunch of gears and acceleration of speed saw them move on and park at the bottom of the Steep.

The journey was brief but, in that time, Archie Goodfellow had reached inside his wallet and produced a single pound note. He squirrelled it towards Meredith Malcolm who in turn covered himself with the hooded cloak and then returned the note to Archie. Only it was damp in places.

Archie could not see but a confused expression still peered towards the Professor.

The orderlies then manhandled the patients out from the van. Those able to walk were hauled out, those in wheelchairs unceremoniously heaved to the floor, and poor old Archie's head caught the doorframe as he alighted.

'You, come with us,' they ordered Professor Malcolm. 'Two hours!' they shouted at the other men, who were gesturing rudely as their backs were turned.

Professor Malcolm turned briefly to see the sightless figure of Archibald Goodfellow sniffing the pound note

'Be sure to have a wonderful afternoon, gentlemen,' Archie shouted sarcastically at the orderlies while brazenly waving the Professor's pound note in front of himself.

'I'll be sure to spend my pocket money with great zest.' He laughed before launching into song.

'Run rabbit, run rabbit, run – run – run!'

*****

'What took you so long, Nate?' Belle asked Noone as he finally returned from his paper run.

'Had to be sure I wasn't followed. You know, it's a beautiful day out there now,' he advised.

Belle moved to the blinds, drew them, and then looked upon the lemon negatives that she and Nathaniel had so painstakingly pieced together the evening before.

'Astounding,' said Gideon, moving closer to examine them.

'Extraordinary!' echoed Belle.

Belle and Gideon spent the next half an hour pouring over the glyphs and calling out names.

'Horus, RA, OSIRIS, deity, workers, scarab, smoke – no, wait, that could be water, no it's probably smoke, though, not sure. Anubis – agreed!' they spouted out names and references as they examined.

So much talking at speed and Noone was not keeping up.

273

'Even at our best guess, Belle, there are millions of combinations to their order,' Gideon suggested.

'We can at least take a stab. An educated guess at least. You know a scarab would not be a pre-cursor to Horus or the eye of RA.'

'You cannot be sure of that,' Gideon suggested. 'But you're right. Let us try and fathom this out.'

'Pass me a pencil, Gideon. Otherwise, we will be forever reliant on the light outside,' the pencil was passed and Belle began tracing the negative.

'If it's all the same, I shall read the paper,' Noone replied. 'I'll leave the Professors to it.'

He began reading the paper cover to cover; particularly the advertisements. He should have known to go to the back-pages first. While Belle and Gideon continued their massive task Noone completed his.

Fortnum's announcement: All departments now open and fully stocked! Remember – Num's the word!

'Gideon, take a look at this?' he said, shoving the paper under his nose. 'Do you think it is fake? Or do you think Wink is fishing for Jennifer James?' he asked.

'I can't be sure of that but look beneath it,' Gideon replied.

Under the dominant calligraphy of the Fortnum's advertisement, which represented four-fifths of the page was a dark black box with white writing on it.

Thought for the day from Gideon's bible:

Chapter 2

Nathaniel returned from the wilderness, ambled down from on high and bestowed his blessings to those that required his protection. All is not lost but the road that lay ahead will be fraught with dangers. 'Fear not for where there is darkness I shall provide the light'

'It's from Tink,' Gideon advised. 'He needs you for protection,' Gideon said, turning to his friend.

'Our protection. He clearly included you,' Noone replied, pointing out his friend's name in the title. 'Gideon, he wouldn't have sent it if it wasn't urgent,' Noone replied.

'I agree but I need Belle's help first. I will follow. I need two hours, Nate, please.'

Nathaniel Noone let out a huge disconcerting sigh. 'No,' Noone replied. 'This cannot wait. Trust Belle to solve this for you. All will be lost if "*she*" is lost.'

Gideon was torn. The answers may be right in front of them but if Agatha was in immediate danger he had to go. He turned to Belle.

'Professor Soames, dear old Belle with the bunches.' He smiled. 'Will you try to solve this for us? One of us will return as soon as we can.'

'Of course, I will,' she confirmed. 'Go, go on, go.'

'You take these, Belle,' said Noone. 'Handing over the torches and OSIRIS card. You never know what we may have missed. Something in "plane" sight probably.' He smiled.

'God speed, gentlemen,' Belle replied as she bid them farewell.

'If we are quick, Nate, the 12:03 from Victoria will take just over an hour to the coast.'

Chapter 38
Disorderly conduct

'I think it's your lucky day, Pop!' Tink said, peering through his shop window at the large black van that had ground to a halt almost opposite.

The large, gold-covered man, peered out too, dwarfing his counterpart as he crouched to look. He was just about to storm out of the doorway when Tink grabbed his wrist. It was always risky to manhandle a Braggan, especially their leader and sizeable adversary Pop could be.

'What, Tink?' Pop glowered.

'Softly, softly, Pop. I think we need to know their business here today. They never come into town. Sunday's being the exception. Something doesn't quite fit.'

'What ya finking then?' Pop asked, bearing down on Tink, before being greeted by a broad grin.

*****

'Help us! Somebody help us!' Elizabeth cried out, crashing through Dr Beckworth's surgery doors.

Eric was at the leg end while his older sister had her arms hooked beneath their younger sister's. Gemima was quiet and deathly pale, a steady stream of blood from her cracked skull now absorbed into a crimson bib around her throat.

'I say, young lady, you cannot just come crashing in here like this,' his secretary announced scowling.

'You stupid old bat, it's a bleedin' 'mergency,' Eric snarled viciously spitting through his teeth.

The Peabodys ignored the protests from the elderly patients waiting for their minor ailments to be attended to and burst through into the doctor's room.

'Doc, doc, please it's Gem, she 'it 'er 'ed,' Eric explained as quickly as he could, panting through his exhausted purple cheeks.

'Pop her up here then, son,' said the wheezing, kindly old surgeon. 'My, my that's a nasty cut. However, did that happen, hey?' Beckworth said towards Gemima despite her lack of consciousness.

'She fell skipping,' Elizabeth responded. 'It was all my fault.' She began to sob.

Simultaneously, the good doctor passed her a handkerchief and tended to Gem at the same time.

'Got anything stronger for me, Doc?' Eric chanced. 'I fink I'm having an 'art attack,' he puffed.

'How would you like a thick ear, boy?' the Doctor replied without even looking at him.

'Ummm. No, fanks.' Eric said, standing hastily.

'Suggest you run along, young Eric, and fetch me Mrs McGregor.'

'Oh Christ, no!' Eric shouted before a swift clip around the back of his head was dispensed by Beckworth.

'Blasphemy, child!' the doctor explained for his swift assault. 'Now, run along and fetch your guardian, please.'

Elizabeth gave him the nod and like a rat up a drainpipe, he shot off.

'Is it bad, Doctor?' Elizabeth tentatively asked, she too looking as white as Gemima laid out in front of them.

'She'll be fine, dear,' he reassured her. 'A bit groggy when she comes around, but I am sure she will be fine.'

'McGregor will not be happy with me.' Elizabeth began to sob.

'Now, now, dear. I only called for her so your fidgety brother could flit off. I need an adult to help you carry her over the road and confirmation we can administer a mild sedative. For both of you. You look in terrible shock too.'

'Beckworth!' came the loud shout of Mrs McGregor as she marched through the surgery.

'Ahhh … Millicent.' He smiled.

'Bloody kids.' She frowned at Elizabeth before plonking a bottle of single malt on the table for the doctor.

'That's very kind.' He smiled. 'Now, be sure they get their medicine, Milly. No work, just relaxation. Little Gemima may be absentminded when she comes around. If her symptoms deteriorate be sure to come straight back.'

McGregor snatched the prescription from Beckworth who was now salivating at the prospect of a dram before patients. She hoisted the young girl single handily over her shoulder. Gem was lighter than a cask of ale and no real effort for Millicent McGregor.

'Of all the days, Elizabeth, of all the days,' Milly moaned. 'My only evening out of that damn pub for a month and you kids have ruined it.'

'Oh no, is it the WI meeting this evening. I'm so sorry,' Elizabeth replied humbly.

'I'm sure you do it on purpose,' McGregor carried on moaning.

'I'm sorry. It was an accident, it was. You can still go. I'll hold the fort.'

'And have that drunk Beckworth berate me for not allowing you to rest?'

'The doctor has just been given a bottle of single malt, do you think he'll make it to this evening?' Elizabeth smiled.

McGregor almost smiled back. 'Come on, let's get Gemima settled. You're in charge of her for the rest of the day, do you hear?' McGregor told Elizabeth.

'What about school?' Elizabeth asked.

'How on earth are you and Eric related?' McGregor responded with a minor laugh. 'I can't imagine that question being in his vocabulary, can you?'

Elizabeth smiled as they entered the Poacher. Peering down the Steep, she saw the waif-like figure of her brother disappear into an alleyway opposite the school. It brought a smile to her face. And what was that he was carrying on his shoulder? Was it a black-and-white bird?

✳✳✳✳✳

Professor Malcolm was enjoying the fresh air and sound of the running water of the Amble, which passed under the cobblestoned bridge he had been marched to. As he looked at the course of the river to the south, it twisted towards the cliffs and back round again. One of the hulking men who accompanied him passed him the ordnance survey map and grunted.

'If I am not mistaken then that area over there,' Meredith said, pointing south-westerly, 'Is the marshland where we should find the Sussex Sedge. And here,' he continued, pointing westerly on the map to the top of the Steep. 'Is the farmland where the beetles should be found.'

'We need help,' the two orderlies replied.

'I most certainly think we do,' Professor Malcolm replied.

''elp with wot, fellas?' came the chirpy sound of Eric Peabody as he approached the three men, a black and white magpie perched upon his shoulder.

'You know marshes?' one of them asked.

'I am an expert on these marshes,' Eric replied. 'As I am expert in most fings round ere.'

'You boat us?' an orderly grunted again.

'Actually,' the Professor interjected. 'We need a boat and a guide as well as some help to collect specimens here and in the fields here,' he said, pointing to the map.

'Just so 'appens, gentlemen, you also need permission to journey on these marshes. Don't want to be caught trespassing on Braggan land.' Eric smiled.

The impact of what that might mean was lost on the two large men who just stared back at Eric.

'Tell ya wot,' Eric said. 'You show me the colour of your money, I'll get you a guide and all the 'elp you need.' Eric's gesturing hand encouraged them to pass over some cash and was met with one of the men revealing a large wad of American dollar bills wrapped in an elastic band.

'Ahh!' Eric replied. 'Bit of a tuff sell to me local lads but I'm sure the yanks will want 'em.' He smiled. Pulling a couple of the bills out he placed one in The Lady's beak and shooed her away. She swooped in a huge circle overhead before returning and landing just yards away at the cobbler's shop near the bridge. Where she persistently pecked at the door fame.

'That, my friends, has just secured you the best navigator and boatman of these marshes. He'll be along in a minute. Now, wot were we saying about the farmland?'

'I need to collect as many of these as I can,' Professor Malcolm replied, pulling out a small glass jar with a single scarab in it.

'Dung beetle?' Eric laughed. 'You want to collect these smelly little bleeders? It will be a princely price to pay to sift through all the crap for them. They'll be hibernating now.'

'A princely price indeed,' Professor Malcolm acknowledged, beckoning his captors to hand over a large swathe of cash. 'A dollar a beetle?' he suggested.

Eric stood in silent disbelief. That was a preposterous amount. Surely that was hundreds of dollars that had just been thrust into this hand. 'Blimey,' he replied, eyes wider than saucers. 'I'll need the whole school to help me.'

'We need today!' grunted one of the large men.

'Keep your 'air on. You'll get 'em today. Don't worry,' Eric reassured them. 'Must be proper posh beetles like those ones Gideon always goes on about.'

Professor Malcolm turned to him, took off his hood to reveal his hirsute features. 'Gideon?' he questioned, before a fist in the ribs shut him up.

'Yeah, Professor Gideon,' Eric replied, staring at the man who was not burned at all, as most residents of Silvera were but sporting a brilliant moustache instead.

'Someone order a ferryman?' interrupted the deep voice of Pop Braggan. He was no longer draped in gold, apart from the single solid bar that was secured across his right hand's knuckles.

'Show me man ere wot ya want,' Eric advised, pointing towards Pop. ''E'll row you to the best spot and I'll meet you 'ere this evening. With hundreds of those beetles.'

'Two hours,' one of the men grunted.

'No chance.' Eric laughed, running up the Steep as fast as his legs would carry him. 'See you this evening.'

'Shall we then?' Pop suggested, pointing towards the small slipway where a rowing boat was secured onto the Amble.

*****

'Can we expect a welcome party?' Noone asked Gideon.

'I'm sure Wink Waverley would have put measures in place to minimise our journey,' Gideon confirmed.

The escalator ascending the underground creaked and seemed slower than usual. Noone kept his head down. His scarring attracted unwelcome attention even at the best of times. Gideon continued surveying the area. There were innumerable people who could have been Waverley's men, or otherwise. As they reached the top, the crowds of people were being corralled into a single file. A man with a large acoustic trumpet was organising from the front.

'Due to an unexploded device between Victoria and East Croydon, we regretfully inform you there will be no services running directly to the south coast today.'

'You have to admire her efficiency,' Noone whispered.

'Should you require transport, a temporary double-decker bus has been supplied by the transport union. Please, ensure all tickets and identification are made available to the guards.'

'Change of plan, old friend,' Gideon decided, turning around and returning back down the escalator. 'Time to travel incognito.'

'Oh no, not again,' Noone replied.

*****

'Now, where on earth could he have gone?' Major Collingdale bellowed as the realisation Professor Gideon Belchambers was no longer in the Museum hit him.

'Excuse me, sir,' came Thompson's cut-glass crispness. 'Would you happen to be Major Boyd Collingdale?' he asked.

Collingdale eyeballed Thompson and his two subordinates over. Long black macs, and matching fedoras. This looked ominous, he thought.

'Official business is it, gentlemen?' the Major enquired.

'Afraid so,' Thompson confirmed.

'Best follow me,' Collingdale replied, directing them towards his office, back down past the innumerable exhibits of strange and peculiar beasts that were lined up and packaged to go.

'What do you know of a Professor Gideon Belchambers?' Thompson asked.

'I bloody knew it; knew he was trouble,' the Major hollered.

'Didn't say he was trouble, old boy, just what do you know of him? He advises us he was here only the other evening,' Thompson reassured him.

'He was, I can confirm that, but then he took off without so much as a by your leave. I thought I'd lost another one in Entomology; thought the corner rafters had fallen in and crushed him like the other fellow.'

'Which other fellow would that be?' Thompson questioned.

'Well it's not Professor Malcolm, that's for sure,' Collingdale confirmed.

'Sorry, I don't follow, Major.'

'I retrieved Belchambers myself from Ambledown, a small village on the coast, so he could identify the Professor. Only, it was an imposter.'

'Sorry, can you confirm that for me. Did you say Belchambers was brought here on your advice to identify a fellow of this Museum, only for it not to be that fellow?' Thompson probed.

'Exactly,' the Major confirmed.

'This is all too confusing. May we see this body, Major?'

'Of course,' Collingdale replied, showing them out of his office.

'Perhaps you can take a look at this photograph too, and tell me if you recognise anyone?'

Thompson handed the picture over. The tiger-lady was dominant in the centre alongside Colonel Malling.

'Of course, I do,' Collingdale confirmed. 'Malling! Colonel Malling. One of yours, isn't he?'

'Correct, Major. No one else though? Look carefully,' Thompson encouraged.

'No. Just Malling,' Collingdale reconfirmed.

'Thank you, Major. Now, shall we continue?'

As the Major began his hearty yomp through the Museum, Thompson's man, Smith, stayed behind to search his private office. Jones walked ahead on reconnaissance. The sentry of exotic animals and beasts greeted them to the well-lit and structurally secured Entomology department.

'This is where Professor Meredith Malcolm used to reside,' Collingdale directed.

'The man you thought was deceased?' Thompson asked.

'Affirmative, but, alas, it was not the Professor, but an imposter.'

'Doesn't it strike you as strange that someone pretending to be the Professor winds up dead on your patch and the real professor is nowhere to be seen?' Thompson questioned.

'Well, of course, it bloody does,' Collingdale replied with immediacy. 'The real Professor left me a scrawled note to engage Belchambers and that, sir, is what I have done expecting it to lead me to Meredith. It has, however, just raised more questions. And now you turn up.'

'Quite,' replied Thompson.

Ilya Debrovska's corpse was covered in a muslin sheet. The insect feast had not quite finished but Major Collingdale had tried his best to protect the man's dignity. Disturbing some debris as they moved, the repugnant sight of a scurrying scorpion flashed in front of them. The Major's army edition size nines were just about to come crashing down on it when Thompson stopped him.

'I am going to need all of those,' he said, pointing at the pincers and stings disappearing beneath the cadaver's sheet.

'Christ, man, why?' Collingdale replied.

'Could save a man's life,' Thompson replied. 'Can you have someone round them up?'

'They're not sheep, sir,' Collingdale challenged.

'Nevertheless, I need to secure them,' Thompson curtly stamped his authority.

A whistle from behind Boyd Collingdale's impressive moustache and several workers came running. Unluckily for them, they were now on scorpion-hunting duty.

'Sir,' came Smith's voice as he joined them around Ilya's body. He whispered in his superior's ear and placed a small white card in his hand.

'Are you sure you do not recognise anyone else in this photograph, Major?' Thompson asked again holding it up in front of him.

'Definitely not, sir,' Collingdale replied defiantly.

'And this? Recognise this?' he continued, holding up the white card that represented the organisation OSIRIS.

'Hmmm,' the Major pondered, racking his brain. 'I cannot remember who gave me that.'

'But it is yours?'

'Yes, old boy, it's mine but I do not recall who gave it to me.'

Thompson flashed Smith a confused look. Jones, meanwhile, returned from his search and held aloft a tiger-skin coat and a blonde wig.

'For the final time, Major. Do you recognise anyone else in this photograph?'

Collingdale's skin was turning its customary scarlet. 'And for the last time, sir, no!' he shouted back.

'In that case, I suggest you come with me,' Thompson advised him with a pair of pistols trained on him from behind his back.

'No need for that,' the Major replied. No doubt he could put up a good fight but he had no reason for that. As far as he was concerned, he was not guilty of anything. 'Quick march!' he ordered to himself, made an about-turn, and walked at a speedy pace with the Peacekeeper tucked under his right arm.

Chapter 39
Illuminated

Belle Soames had spent the best part of an hour ensuring the intricacies of each cartouche reflected as accurate an image of the hieroglyphics as if suspended in perpetuity from one of the chambers beneath the Valley of the Kings. It was her firm belief that each one began and ended as a separate set of instructions but what they truly meant, the content of such information when combined, eluded her.

The obvious images of Horus, the bringer of light; Anubis, the lord of the afterlife; and Osiris, death and resurrection himself, were ever-present in the hundreds of rubbings she had historically researched and recorded; as too the undeniable cye of RA staring back at her. The scarabs were also ever-present but their part to play clearly not understood. However, of the nine images that made up the three detailed copies, she was least sure of what the two serving women were actually doing. A plant in their hands and a vessel for grinding, if she wasn't mistaken. Could it be part of some ancient apothecary's task? She couldn't be sure but just footsteps away in the Ancient Hall of the Mummies she had ample exhibits she could use to find any historical links.

When Belle finally left her father's office to continue her investigations, the many workmen and women were already setting about their delicate daily tasks of preparing the removal and security of ancient artefacts. Akin to their sister museum across town, their challenges were monuments in stone opposed to taxidermy examples of gigantic mammals.

Belle cntered the Ancient Hall of the Mummies. She hadn't stepped in it since her father's recent accident. She wasn't sure who had actually trodden in its antiquated realm since the visiting organisation known as OSIRIS had left. Montague Soames had made it his pride and joy and people would not dare disrespect the revered Professor.

A cold chill sent Goosebumps up her arms as she entered the darkened room. The lights were set dimly to recreate the inner workings of a Pyramids tomb as well as preserve them from the damage of daylight. Intermittent electric candles flickered to mimic their waxy counterparts and illuminate their centuries-old subjects so visitors would have to move closer and examine them in great detail. Belle knew the route and sequence of the exhibits intimately and headed for the main sarcophagus of an ancient Egyptian priestess. Her obsession with this particular mummy was due to its revelatory hieroglyphics depicting everyday life. It was believed she may have been a doctor or physician to one of the great pharaohs, as her tomb had been found almost perfectly intact beneath one of them. Unfortunately, the light was so dim that the truly wonderful glyphs were masked in the shadows. Taking the standard torch left by Nathaniel and Gideon she began to project the steady white beam across the many images looking for any sign or relationship of the working women. There were hundreds of tiny markings and the task was infinitely laborious. If anyone had the tenacity to investigate then it was certainly Belle Soames. Ten minutes of focusing on torchlight and her eyes began to throb. The beam itself was growing weaker, the battery was running low. She laboured on as the light flickered and gave out a last final spurt before dying unceremoniously in her palm.

In her pocket, she still had the torch with the violet beam. She had little doubt it was next to useless in comparison, for this particular task anyway, but even the slightest advantage may allow her to spot the minimal of leads. With the beam lit, she moved very close to the glyphs so she could see the tiny hieroglyphics under the pink hue. Nothing. Not even during half an hour of intensive scrutiny could she find any similar images of the working women or the plant they tended. Belle had all but given up when she went back to the beginning just to double-check she hadn't missed anything. And there it was, missed by any standard light, but lit up in the same luminance as the totems in the photograph.

The curve of a line was as it appeared, to begin with. 'It's a circle,' Belle reassured herself, having followed the full line of the curve. At first, the crescent of luminous purple looked isolated, but once Belle had taken a short step back, she realised it was a great big oval she had stumbled upon.

'But what is it framing?' she asked herself. Using the violet torch once more, she began focusing on the glyphs inside the circle. None of them made much sense in isolation and the circumference cut through several cartouches to make no sense at all. 'That can't be it,' she spoke to herself once again. Stepping back even further, she shone the torch on the glyphs once more. Moving left to right the beam caught yet more of the illuminating colour, again another circle but smaller in size and a straight line heading upwards from its top-left curve.

'Oh!' came her amazement out loud. 'You're not ancient at all. Not in the same sense as the drawings.' She smiled. 'You're actually an "O", aren't you?' she continued, talking at the first luminous lettering on the wall. 'And your neighbour … is "b".'

Belle Soames was incandescent with the revelation, and somehow knew this was recent vandalism. As she moved the torch towards the right, two more letters jumped out from their illuminated state behind the sarcophagus. The next letter was 'e'.

'E for eureka!' she shouted out loud. She had to tell Nate and Gideon as soon as she could but she knew they were well into their journey by now. Whitehall, she must journey to Whitehall. She must find Wink and Thompson immediately.

*****

Aggie had waited nervously before finally, Governess Dove entered Sister Harvey's classroom.

'I'm pleased to advise that Gemima Peabody is now home despite nursing a minor concussion. A reminder to all of you ladies you must take better care when fooling around playing your games,' she advised.

'It was Chatsmore, Miss,' Shouted out Henrietta Huntington-Smythe, her arm lightning quick to be the first tell-tale from Priory.

Aggie was furious but controlled her immediate anger, not that she would jeopardise a detention she already had received, still, she wanted that time alone with Harvey.

'Thank you, Henrietta,' Sister Harvey interrupted. 'Chatsmore is detained with me this evening already. I shall deal with her then.'

Dove gave the Sister a peculiar frown. 'Be sure to have her gone before the ladies of the Women's Institute show up,' Dove advised her. Sister Harvey duly nodded.

It was a lonely lunch-hour for Agatha. No Elizabeth or Gemima Peabody to keep her company. The repetitive chorus of the Seven Sisters skipping song reverberating throughout her mind and the ever-threatening Priory girls who systematically stalked her as she tried keeping herself busy.

Isolated and alone in her thoughts, Aggie reminisced of Marylebone and the company of Florrie. Gideon would have no choice but to explain her missing aunt's whereabouts tonight. She would insist on that. While she walked repetitive circuits of the girls' side of the playground, she looked to Eric's corner but it was empty. Gemima was safe. She could take solace in that, and no doubt, Ambledown's sneakiest child was out causing mischief somewhere, which brought a smile to her face.

The clang of the bell ended that torturous hour. As she waited patiently at the very back of the line, a commotion broke out on the boys' side. In Eric's corner, a knotted rope had been hurled over from the side of the marshes. Several evacuee boys sprinted and made light work of the fencing. They were joined by local Priory boys too and, before too long, a few evacuee girls broke the boundary and had alighted from the playground. The Brothers and Sisters were taken by surprise. It happened so quickly. A dozen or so children had escaped to rounds of cheers, though the Priory girls, as always, offered a sultry disapproval.

'What on earth are you up to, Eric Peabody?' Agatha spoke to herself. 'It has to be you, Eric, no one else is that audacious.'

'Come along, Chatsmore. Stop gawping,' came the now-familiar authoritative tone of Sister Harvey. 'Only a couple of hours until detention.' She smiled.

Aggie smiled back with enthusiasm.

*****

'Do you think he will be receptive, considering recent events?' Noone asked Gideon.

'He's the more reasonable twin between him and Lyle,' Gideon said and smiled.

The unforgettable passageway they had just entered was moments from the checkpoints of Victoria. Its unappealing grime and detritus flowed into the street. Ensuring they had not attracted any unwanted attention, Gideon and Noone trod carefully amongst the filth as they approached a redundant ticket booth, knocking on the shuttered wooden boarding.

A letterbox peephole slid open and two familiar eyes stared back at them

'Well, well, if it isn't the Professor and The Melted Man. I thought I wouldn't be seeing you two again,' came a husky tone.

'Hello, Tate,' Gideon replied. 'I wondered if you could open her up for us.'

'Again?' Tate replied, already considering his price.

Tate Braggan's similarity to his recently departed twin was undeniable, albeit for a slight scar upon his lip. The pitiful waif was as scrawny and devious as his brother yet had twice the intellect of Lyle and already knew this was to be a generous payday as it had been just days prior.

'It's gonna cost ya, Professor,' Tate expressed gratuitously.

'No crew, Tate, no carriages. Just the engine and ourselves. And I'll double the last fee.' Gideon replied.

'You two going to shovel coal all the way then, after what happened last time?' Tate laughed, eyeballing Noone up and down.

'If that's what it takes,' Noone challenged back.

'Only I remember an incident with the flames, Mr Noone. Not sure you should be near the furnace.'

'He'll be fine. I guarantee it,' Gideon reassured Tate.

'Anything else I should know?' Tate smirked.

'Suffice it to say, avoid anyone you can. Particularly, any official types,' Noone interjected.

'Comes with the territory,' said Tate chuckling and shutting the peephole.

The sound of several deadbolts unlocked the door as the doorway to the booth swung open. Noone and Gideon crouched to enter.

'Follow me,' Tate directed, bolting the door behind them. Carrying a dimly lit paraffin burner, Tate directed them through the rear door of the tatty booth's interior as it descended via circular steps into a long winding corridor. Deep beneath the surface, where Wink's troops were surveying people above, Noone, Gideon, and Tate arrived at the tunnel entrance.

'Here she is, boys. I'm sure you remember how beautiful she is.' Tate smiled, greeting his steam engine as if were one of his offspring. 'Now, it'll be suicidal to leave before dark. Agreed?'

'Agreed,' Noone and Gideon replied. They had little choice.

'I suggest you get some rest then. You're gonna need it, Professor.'

*****

'My apologies, ma'am,' Thompson began. 'But we have reasonable doubt surrounding Major Collingdale's involvement. Swears blind he doesn't know tiger-lady, yet we found these, as Professor Belchambers told us we would. In the Museum.' Thompson held aloft the long stripy-skinned coat and the curled blonde wig.

'Ever thought he may be telling the truth and Belchambers is the duplicitous one?' Wink replied.

'Crossed my mind, ma'am, but we also found this,' Thompson said, producing the OSIRIS card. 'Admits it's his – well, we did find it in his office – but cannot for the life of him recall how he got it.'

Wink took a long drag on her continuing chain of cigarettes. She switched the light off from the panel in front of her, from behind the glass mirror where they were observing Collingdale, and switched another one on that lit up Colonel Malling.

'Interesting then that he too provides the same story,' she said, exhaling a large defiant puff of smoke as Thompson looked on, hidden from the two colonels.

'This isn't adding up,' Wink continued but was interrupted by a knock on the door.

Outside, the nervous Smith and Jones whispered into Thompson's ear as he opened it. He thanked them and told them to wait in front of the door. Revolving to stare directly at Wink his skin was pallid and beads of sweat were beginning to form.

'Good God, Thompson, it cannot be that bad, surely. Draper advised me you were made of sterner stuff.'

'Apologies, ma'am. Several worrying items of note to be aware of. These two men,' he said pointing at the now agitated Collingdale and Malling in their independent cells, 'are on the OSIRIS list and the majority of the additional fundraising attendees appear to work for them or have ties to them.'

'Enlighten me, Thompson,' she said.

'Well, this gentleman here, ma'am.' He pointed to one of the men in the photograph. 'He is the tower master of St Paul's.'

'And?'

'And this man here, ma'am,' he advised pointing to the second. 'He is man at arms at The Tower.'

'No time for riddles, Thompson. Spit it out.'

'Well, all these men are critical in air-raid protocols across the city. They control the safety of all the citizens. Hundreds of thousands of us.'

'Just these men?'

'Of course, not just these men, ma'am, but the list we found has the common denomination that the majority of them are somehow linked via Malling to the very heart of our security.'

Wink Waverley stopped puffing away. The reality of such an insurgency into London's safety left her as pallid as Thompson had been. If London fell, the war was lost, for sure.

'And another thing, ma'am. Draper is *not* on the list.'

'What!' Wink replied with incredulity.

'Not his code name, real name or any pseudonym I am aware of,' Thompson confirmed.

'Then what was he doing there?'

'Perhaps he is complicit, ma'am,' Thompson suggested.

'Or perhaps he had infiltrated them,' Wink replied curtly.

'Perhaps,' Thompson agreed humbly.

'May I suggest my men round up as many from this list as we can, ma'am. We need to isolate any suspects immediately and understand this scenario to the best of our abilities.'

'Very well,' Wink agreed. 'I will get to work on the two we have close by,' she said, pointing at the unaware prisoners behind the glass.

Thompson took his leave and was just departing when Wink questioned him one final time.

'Is there anything else you are not telling me, Thompson? You don't look your usual chipper self.'

'Of course not, ma'am. Just shocked, that's all,' he finished, leaving the room.

Ensuring he closed the door behind him he marched his men several steps from the observation room, informing them in a hushed tone, 'Smith, you take St Paul's,' he ordered. 'Jones, The Tower.'

'Is that it, sir? Is that all?' they replied together.

'Continue with your tasks. I must seek help on the coast and return tonight. Be very careful who you talk to and be subtle in your enquiries.'

'But what about the list? Surely, we cannot ignore–' Smith said before being interrupted.

'For now, we have to play along like nothing has changed. I don't know who to trust but, ironically, need you to trust me.'

Thompson looked down at the list of names in front of him. On the final page, having been executed in alphabetical order, one name stood out like a sore thumb: Winifred Waverley.

Chapter 40
The Crest

Professor Malcolm was surprised that the small rowing boat remained buoyant considering the weighty frame of Pop Braggan, accompanied by his wolfhound and The Lady, not to mention the hulking presence of the orderlies. The Professor sat in the centre of the boat while the finely counterbalanced men sat staring at each other from opposite ends.

'Got a picture of wot ya need?' Pop asked the Professor.

Meticulous Meredith Malcolm pulled a pencil sketch of the Sussex Sedge and passed it to the man. Pop gave a subtle grunt and his powerful forearms initiated momentum as he directed them towards the cliff bank near to where he had altercated with the American guards. Professor Malcolm saw the gold bar across his knuckles as it glinted in the sunshine. Pop ensured the orderlies saw it too.

'Why we head there?' the first orderly spoke. 'Men with guns, dangerous.'

'So, you been here before?' Pop enquired as his mighty barrel-chest exhaled and thrust them forward.

'We lose lots money,' the second one replied before the first one hushed him up.

'Oh yeah? I lost a nephew,' Pop replied, taking an oar in one hand and standing astride the boat. Luna was poised in attack mode.

'We not understand!' the two men shouted back.

'I fink you do understand,' Pop argued back, raising the oar to swing.

'We robbed. By little man with funny walk. He no deliver the bird but he take money.'

'Eh? Wot bird. Bird like this?' Pop asked, pointing to the cawing magpie on his shoulder.

'No, no. Prey bird, royal bird,' they replied acting out talons with their clawed fingers. 'He promise to meet us, not show. We trust him, due to cat.'

'Prey bird, like a falcon. Cat? Yer not making sense.' Pop replied.

'Yes, yes … he say pere … pere falcon.' The orderly was pointing up the cliff face, flapping his hands, mimicking the hovering style of the falcon.

'Peregrine falcon?' Malcolm interjected. 'Very rare at this time of year.'

'Not in Ambledown,' Pop advised. 'OK, you show me where,' Pop ordered them, lowering the oar and retreating his dog. 'And wot was that about a cat?'

'There,' said the first orderly and pointed. 'Up there!'

Pop looked up at the chalk cliff, almost vertical to the blood on the rocks he had found. He whispered into The Lady's ear and it flew off soaring in increasing circles until it landed on the cliff edge many feet above. It's jolty jumping from mound to rock in a nervous flapping manner created maximum attention.

'Your bird killed if falcon see her,' the smiling gold-toothed orderly warned Pop.

'We'll see.' Pop grimaced back.

The three larger men were intrigued and fascinated by the avian investigation on the rock face but Professor Meredith Malcolm had just spied what he had come for.

'Excuse me, boatman,' he interrupted. 'Can you row us just over to the rushes?' He pointed.

Pop sat back down, one eye on The Lady, the other on the two men. He heaved the oars through the marshy grasses. From above he then heard a large caw and a flash of black and white take off from the cliff face. Directly behind it, a flash of speckled brown was travelling at far greater speed. Gaining fast.

'Your bird not make it,' the orderly told Pop.

'You want to bet?' Pop replied ' I bet you this gold bar,' he offered, holding up his ham fists to show the size of the prize.

'I bet your nephew debt and that gold bar,' the second called back.

'Accepted,' Pop agreed. Crushing the man's hand in a handshake. Pop watched the now-black speck of The Lady being caught up. Seconds seemed like minutes in the intricate battle of the skies. The Peregrine's dive speed was twice that of a bird of carrion and imminently it would puncture his beloved bird's torso and return to its nest to feed. Just as the talons were touching her feathers The Lady expanded her wings and like a parachutist opening their chute the air inflated her instantly from a diving streamlined mass to a feathery black-and-white balloon, propelling her upwards. The falcon, who was untouchable at speed, could not swerve fast enough and was clattered by the larger magpie as if being hit by an airborne brick wall. It was sent spinning off-balance, almost dashing it into the rocks itself, before it righted and swooped down in an impressive arc just above the men's heads and looped the loop back to its hiding place safely on the cliffs.

'The fing is, a falcon will not take on a bird like The Lady in face-to-face combat,' Pop advised the two men who had lost their bet. 'Magpies, crows, jackdaws … it won't take on any of 'em unless at speed or unless they are protecting a nest.'

'A nest?' they replied, their interests piqued.

'So, ow much for two birds plus their chicks?' Pop enquired, removing his gold knuckleduster and getting down to business.

The orderlies smiled. This was a man they could do business with after all. Lots of money was to be offered if Pop could deliver on promises.

'Oh, and you mentioned cats. Lyle showed you a cat. I can easily get old of some moggies for ya. Cheap like.'

'Just special cat. Ugly cat. Cat no fur.'

'Never mind then, just the birds?' Pop grinned as the men shook his hand, weary not to get crushed for a second time.

'Gentlemen, quite when you've finished, can we concentrate on the task in hand?' Professor Malcolm interrupted holding up a perfect specimen of the Sussex Sedge.

*****

'Right, now listen up!' Eric Peabody shouted from the large oak tree stump, corralling the crowd like a masterful ringmaster. 'Oi, be quiet.' He whistled with four fingers thrust into his mouth. The crowd of gaggling and excitable schoolchildren soon stood still and paid attention.

'This is a scarab beetle, *Scaribidae*,' Eric said holding up a fresh specimen he had found and mocking a posh Latin teacher's accent as he'd done so to fits of laughter from the kids. 'We knows 'em as dung beetles. That's right, friends, dung beetles, and there is nothing they like more than a fresh juicy cow pat.' He smiled, as children stuck out their tongues to sounds of 'Urgghhh' and 'Yukk'. 'As a one-day special though, I am paying a penny a bug.'

'How much?' came an excitable yell-back followed by the stunned concentration from all the children in the crowd.

'A penny a bug, but they must be alive,' Eric confirmed. 'Now, it's as simple as that and it's a very smelly business, which is why I am most generous in my price. So, get going. It won't be long until the Brothers are upon us.'

The children looked at each other astonished. A penny was an absolute fortune to them. So what if they had to dig around in a bit of poo. As keen as mustard, they split in multiple directions and started scouring the fields for fresh and dry dung, rotting wood, and vegetation to capture as many as they could for their ample reward.

'If you get caught, or should I say, *when* we get caught, stay schtum and keep those bugs alive. I'll still buy them off of ya later. First one to return a full jar gets a shilling bonus.' Eric, impressed by his own industriousness, gazed on in wonder as his under-aged workforce was as busy hunting as the bugs were trying to avoid capture. Eric wasn't getting his hands dirty at all. He was keeping an eye out for the imminent entourage of adults, and besides, he couldn't count all of those dollars with dirty hands, could he?

*****

Agatha was the last to return to Sister Harvey's classroom. Eric's stunt had not only seen a fair number of pupils evade their God-fearing tutors and escape over the fence into the unknown wilds of the Braggan Marshes, but during the kerfuffle, many more had seized their opportunity to walk straight out of the unguarded front entrance as the Brothers and Sisters tried in vain to stamp their authority.

She took her seat, alone on the evacuees' side. No Elizabeth, Gemima, or Priory-loathing allies to stand by her side. Henrietta Huntington-Smythe and the Priory girls huddled around a desk as if a cackling coven exchanging spells around a cauldron.

'My, my, ladies. In all my years teaching at the Priory, I have never witnessed such disobedience. That Peabody family are a law unto themselves,' Sister Harvey announced on entering the room. 'Some people should care to choose wisely where their loyalties lie,' she remarked, aiming a glance over her spectacles towards Aggie, much to the Priory's amusement.

'My mother told me that a very disobedient girl once tried to burn down the school. She was crazy by all accounts.' announced Henrietta.

'That's not strictly true, Henrietta. But she did set fire to the Priory colours, was immediately expelled, and it is considered very bad form to discuss her,' Sister Harvey replied with a light scolding to Huntington-Smythe.

'Miss Dove and I,' the Sister continued. 'considering our concerns for all children's safety, have decided to have your parents collect you early so a hunt for Eric and his escapees can commence in coordination with the Brothers. While you wait, Miss Dove requires all Priory girls to aid her in preparing for the WI's monthly meeting.'

'That would be our pleasure, miss,' Henrietta smarmed on behalf of herself and friends.

'That leaves Chatsmore and me to fulfill our detention duties,' Sister Harvey said smugly.

The Priory girls erupted into sickly false laughter as they followed Henrietta out along the corridor to help the governess.

Sister Harvey watched her charges disappear out of sight. She slowly locked the door and turned to the nervous girl left all alone in her classroom. Removing her glasses slowly, she made her way midpoint between her desk and Aggie's and just stared into the schoolgirl's brilliant blue eyes. Agatha was already clenching her fist under the table. Should she have to embrace Bareknuckle Barry once more she would do so.

'Stand up!' Harvey ordered. Agatha tentatively rose under the instruction. 'Follow me.' The nun moved behind her desk and towards a cupboard on the Priory side. On opening it, stacks of aged notebooks tumbled outwards, scattering across the floor. There must have been several decades worth.

'Your punishment, Chatsmore, is to sort these books into chronological order. You do understand what that means don't you?' the sister asked.

Aggie nodded to confirm she had understood.

'And in absolute silence!' the Sister confirmed with a steely glare.

Walking away and unlocking the classroom door, the nun began a gentle whistle. Its tune echoed acutely through the corridor.

'There were once seven sisters, from the Seven Sisters. Forty-nine we called them, how about you?'

Aggie's ears pricked up as the tune repeated itself over and over in her head. Elizabeth's voice echoed in her mind.

'She's giving you a clue!' it reverberated.

Recreating the Patience game of cards, as she had done so with the photographs the prior evening, Agatha began to sort out the books into piles. Each year was systematically sorted. She wasn't even sure if the Seven Sisters skipping rhyme was that of her mother's or another pupil. She wasn't even sure why the initials C S-M were always represented in the school photographs, but it was unmistakably her mother; not to forget Gideon's grin.

On the front of each book, the surname led, the first name followed, and then the workbook year. There were so many degrees of legible and illegible handwriting across different age groups that some were consigned to the 'other' pile. An hour had passed quickly and the task was almost complete when she heard Miss Dove's voice. Aggie initially panicked, as if she wasn't supposed to be there at all but on turning around the room was still empty. Crossing the classroom swiftly, a quick turn of the door handle proved it was still locked from the outside. Yet, she could still hear Dove talking. It was faint and echoed subtly and it seemed to be coming from the base of the cupboard. Aggie emptied it of its remaining books and below them, she found an old brass draught excluder that looked like it had rusted over. The books would have hidden it and kept the room draught free but now uncovered after many years, it led through to a sister shaft into the governess' office.

Aggie placed her ear onto the metal plate and listened intently. There was a lot of crackling and interference. It reminded her of Florrie's half-working wireless. However, if she listened carefully enough, she could hear the soft voice of a man.

'Ault, Taube, nine,' was what she heard initially from the male voice. But it didn't make sense. Then there it was again. 'Ault, Taube, nine.'

'Ahh, sounds like October Nine.' Aggie realised, and that was but a week away. What was significant about that date?

Dove did not respond to the voice but it was obvious by her silence she was listening to it. Then, a solid knock came at her door. The noisy interference was immediately silenced then came the sound of an object moving, two clicks of locks and the squeal of rotating wheels. A momentary silence lingered before the governess spoke again.

'Enter,' Dove affirmed from her office a corridor away. 'Sister Harvey, what is it now?'

'I was wondering if I may take that picture from your wall?' she asked, pointing to a small wooden frame encasing a burned piece of fabric that sat behind the governess.

'Why?' Dove asked.

'A historical lesson on discipline for the class, following today's outrageous events,' the Sister insisted. 'Huntington-Smythe reminded me of it.'

Aggie tutted. It echoed back but was lost during their conversation.

'Well, if Henrietta has brought it up, let's do ourselves all a favour,' Dove replied, handing the small frame over, which Harvey duly acknowledged and left.

Aggie began scurrying around, knowing the sister was on her way back. She hadn't found what she was after. If Sister Harvey was giving her clues, why on earth wasn't she just telling her what it was and where it was to find?

The door lock disengaged slowly as Sister Harvey entered the room. Aggie went to speak but the Sister was pursing her lips with her index finger in front.

'Shhhhhh,' she whispered into Aggie's ear, before making her way over to the cupboard. She began to place the books back over the vent gently. Every so often, one book would be placed to the side until the tidy piles of Aggie's work were just bundled and toppled over each other again in the overcrowded cupboard.

Sister Harvey passed the small pile of half-a-dozen books or so to her and then signalled for her to leave.

Along the corridor, she tiptoed and out of the front door where Cecile was waiting again.

'Aggie, Aggie, Aggie,' Cecile said disapprovingly. 'You find more trouble than Eric Peabody.'

'I'm sorry. No Elizabeth again?' Aggie asked, desperate to read the books.

'Not after the accident,' she said, frowning at Aggie. 'You have to come to the café for supper as Gideon is still not back. Come on now, it's not safe.'

'Still not back?' Aggie said, fearing the worst.

Cecile had just bundled Aggie into Le Chat Noir and sat her away from the windows when a large black sedan cruised down the Steep and pulled up outside of the Priory School. The driver alighted, rounded the car, and opened up the rear passenger seat door. Sliding out smoothly, a tall, slender woman in a stripy fur-skin coat clip-clopped up the school stairs. The melted men who were still dining at Le Chat Noir, there since the morning, pressed their faces to the window for a second look. She was unlike anyone else from Ambledown. Aggie struggled to glimpse anything through the men as Miss Dove welcomed the woman into the school. Shortly after, a swift flurry of local women, all eager and overdressed, made their way into the school too.

'I don't understand all the fuss,' Cecile shouted at the gawping men. 'It's the WI.'

'Not her though,' one of them replied. 'She's the mystery woman of the Institute. Comes and goes as she likes. We've all seen her, lads, haven't we?'

A volley of agreement was met with the exception of one man, who slid into the seat opposite Aggie.

'Apart from me, of course,' came Archibald Goodfellow's voice, his ghostly eyes peering at Aggie and a mischievous laughter at recognising his own disability.

'Hello, again,' Aggie replied, smiling.

'Now, young lady. I understand from Cecile you are a guest of the good Professor Gideon Belchambers.'

'That's correct. He's my u … umm, guardian. That is, while I remain evacuated,' Aggie replied, concealing her identity as she was so often reminded to do.

'Would you be so kind as to give him this?' Archie asked, holding aloft the pound note. 'Only, a fellow Professor friend of his asked me to pass it on. He's at the Institute too.'

'I'll be sure to,' Aggie confirmed.

'And tell him that Archie said, "It's a little zesty".'

Agatha took a sniff and the faint smell of lemon was present.

Malkin, the robust black tomcat, made his presence felt by pouncing on the pile of books Aggie had sat down in front of her. Archie Goodfellow quickly removed himself as two books toppled down to the floor. As Aggie bent down to retrieve them the large cat insisted on her attention and splayed out over the other workbooks.

'You, silly cat.' She laughed. After a few minutes of fussing, Malkin was off pestering another patron. Aggie retrieved the two books. One had landed face up, presenting the work inside and was spread out by its bound centre. The other lay face down. The pages at the centre of the first were written in childlike handwriting. Aggie read through it, a child's memoir of what they wish to be when they were older, with plenty of misspellings highlighted in teacher's red pen. The second one, Aggie turned onto its cover and, there, in the same calligraphy as the inside of her blazer, were the intertwined initials L S-M. There was no other name on the front. It had been scribbled out.

She opened it up and skim read each page. She was nearing the end when she spotted a poem, entitled *Forty-Nine*, written in the centre of the pages in beautiful joined-up calligraphy. She read it carefully.

'There were once seven sisters of the Seven Sisters, forty-nine as known to some but not to me and you.

When the angels came a knocking, a death so heart-fully shocking, that sisterhood of support and love became known as forty-two.

When words were finally spoken and a promise eternally broken, the six remaining sisters vowed revenge for such betrayal.

Two children orphaned, forsaken. Their heritage stolen and taken. Curse you lords of Ambledown, remain cowed behind your veil.'

*****

Pop Braggan, Luna, and the remarkable falcon-dodging magpie 'The Lady' pulled up to the riverbank many hours after they had cast off. Night had crept in over them and only a few candles set in glass jars guided their path. The two large guards of the Institute sat at the opposite end, much more the happier now that Pop had struck a deal to replace the falcons, which his nephew had reneged upon. Professor Malcolm was also extremely happy as several large hessian bags had been stuffed with the Sedge plants he believed were a sufficient substitute to those within the cartouche.

'Evening all,' came the chipper tone of Eric Peabody.

'You stink, boy,' Pop informed him stepping back.

'That's cos dung beetles live in dung. Duh!' he lipped Pop, instantly regretting it and too slow to duck the clip behind the ear that immediately came his way. 'Good news is, though, I have these for ya! Da daahh,' said Eric enthusiastically, producing jars upon jars of wriggling beetles he had lined up on the cobblestone bridge lit by intermittent candles.

'You've excelled yourself, young man,' Professor Malcolm congratulated him.

Eric's broad grin accepted the praise un-modestly.

'Anyone fancy a drink to celebrate our new business deal?' Pop asked.

'We do not drink. Besides, we late already. Mr Louds will be very angry. We need get men back,' the orderlies announced.

'I'll join ya, Pop, but not the Poacher as Lizzy is running it tonight,' said Eric.

'Not at all, boy. Y' too young for ale and who's gonna let a stinky wretch like you in their establishment? The Crown and The Hart won't. So, where's Milly then, if Lizzy's in charge?'

'Mixing with the likes of the Smythes at the WI.' Eric grimaced.

'Beggars belief, boy. Milly?' Pop laughed 'Come on, let's go to the Poacher. I'll buy you a cordial, once you've washed.'

'Perhaps I should be the one buying.' Eric smiled fanning the dollars out in front of himself as he joined the giant man on a slow walk up the Steep.

'You need to be careful, boy. Plenty of folk shank you for a lot less around here.' He smiled with menace.

*****

'What did it all mean?' Aggie asked herself. Although the skipping and poem differed from one another, they were both based on the same poem. But what came first? The song or the poem? And C S-M, if that was her mother, what was her name?

'Aggie, you need to eat. Here,' Cecile told her, placing down one of her cassoulets. Soon the cats were all around her and on the table pawing for their share.

'Where's Purrsia?' Aggie asked.

'He never returned,' Cecile replied with a slight tear in her eye.

Aggie began eating as she turned her attentions to the schoolbooks. On every cover of each of the children's books, the ones Sister Harvey had given her, the names had been crossed out and were illegible. And it appeared it had taken place sometime later too as all of them were defaced in the same cartridge ink, which was peculiar in itself, and definitely different to what had been written beneath the scribble.

'Cecile?' Aggie asked. 'Do the initials C S-M mean anything to you.'

'No.' she replied shaking her head. 'Why?'

'They're the initials of a schoolgirl on these books. But I have no idea who she was.'

'Could try the graveyard.' Archie piped up. 'Anyone with Ambledown connections would have relatives buried there.'

'Don't be so morbid, Archie,' another melted man interrupted. 'Who'd want to visit a graveyard, particularly at this time of night to look for someone? If you ask me, the cenotaph is an easier starting place. Many lives lost in the Great War and all names in alphabetical order.' He concluded, before a heated debate with Archibald Goodfellow.

Aggie did not fancy either option in the dark. She could, of course, see for herself on the way to school in the morning. Nelly Parker would also know but she was making life about as easy as Sister Harvey; not very. Instead, she decided to read through the books for any clues she could find herself. Heaven knew where Gideon was. It could be a long night.

*****

'Welcome, Ladies.' Lady Huntington-Smythe beamed from ear to ear standing on a pint-sized temporary stage in the schoolhouse, erected by the Priory girls hours earlier. 'Welcome to Ambledown Woman's

Institute's monthly gathering.'

A brief round of sclf-congratulatory applause greeted her.

'I am pleased to introduce, not for the first time it has to be said, the outstanding fundraiser and campaigner for our injured servicemen – Miss Jennifer Erket.'

The tall slender figure of Ms Erket, Miss Jennifer Erket this time, made a short step up on stage to dwarf Lady Huntington-Smyth. Her prominent zebra-striped coat standing out against the backdrop.

'Ladies, without your kindness, support and contribution, our society OSIRIS, as we like to call it for short, would not exist today. Not only your donations but your time and influence are imperative for us to achieve our true goals.' She lit up her slender, purple-tipped cigarette with the elegance of a silent movie star and puffed intricate halos of smoke across her obedient crowd. Dove operated the projector screen as they dimmed the lights and began their show.

Chapter 41
The Formula

Belle faced a huge dilemma. Nathaniel and Gideon were headed for Ambledown. Wink Waverley and Thompson were much closer in Whitehall. There was no contest as to where her loyalties lay but as a prisoner of immediate geography, the safer bet was Whitehall. Belle felt sick to the pit of her stomach. Such talk of spies and trust had thrust her memory back over thirteen years. Back when she was Belle with the bunches, a freckled-faced redheaded teenager with daily crushes on the devilishly handsome charges of her father, Montague Soames. Professor, philanthropist, spymaster that he was. It was a feeling she remembered during those fractious days all that time ago. When they'd had to leave Egypt in a hurry, her father had been nervous and trusting of no one; where in Cairo tragedy had struck their closest of friends. Where she recalled dressing in black at a memorial service for the twins and the loss of the infant girl. A loss that had haunted her until now and the footnote of history rewritten on the vision of a single apparition who was now very much flesh and blood.

She would travel to Whitehall, despite allegiances. This information might expedite her own father's cure if indeed there was a cure and Gideon had been truthful. It was early evening now; she would leave at dusk disguised as a man in her father's clothes. Then one last check of the Mummies' chamber to make sure what she had seen could only mean one thing.

OBEY!

*****

The bell rang to announce the orderlies' entrance into Le Chat Noir. Aggie remained hidden back in the corner reading the books. Archie Goodfellow and his peers had spent many hours drinking and dining and had to be helped as they zigzagged to their waiting transport. Once they had gone,

Aggie peered out of the window to see Pop and Eric finish loading the van and walk towards her.

'Cecile. I'm going to ask Pop and Eric to escort me home. If that's OK?' Without waiting for a response, she picked up her books and left the café.

'Evenin', young Agatha. Should you be out after dark?' Pop greeted her and questioned.

'Will you walk me home?' Aggie asked.

'Course I will,' Eric replied eagerly.

'Course *we* will,' Pop corrected. 'Where's Gideon then?' he continued in his husky tone.

'I'm hoping he's back from London when I get home.'

'Wot business in London did 'e 'ave?' Pop asked.

Aggie just shrugged her shoulders.

The Lady, ever inquisitive, caught the shimmer of Aggie's necklace and flew from Pop's shoulder to hers. At first, playfully pecking her neck then making a quick jerk to steal the precious silver heirloom.

'Lady, no!' Pop shouted as he narrowly missed the bird with a backhand sending it flapping away.

The sheer look of horror on Aggie's face was as if she was facing Lyle again. She was petrified. Realising this Pop Braggan knelt down in front of her.

'I'm sorry, young lady. Us Braggans are a bad lot sometimes. Birds included. I assure you, my undying protection. You 'ave me word.' He crossed his heart as he finished.

Eric placed an arm around her to comfort her.

'Eric, you smell awful.' Aggie laughed.

'I smell of money!' He cheered, showing her a giant fan of American dollar bills.

'Wow!' Aggie replied.

'Wow to you,' came Eric's response pointing at her necklace. 'That's amazing. Can I buy it?' He smiled, producing a few dollars.

'Both of you hide your wares away. You never know who's watchin',' Pop advised them.

'It's not for sale anyway,' Aggie confirmed, looking down at the magnifying glass that was beginning to shine and glow the more that it took in the moonlight.

From an alleyway opposite stood the watcher, cloaked in a dark camouflaged Cossack, and continuing a vigil of observation. Stalking but not engaging the young lady with the dark bobbed hair.

The light of Aggie's magnifier travelled across the road as the watcher's eyes followed her and the accompanying friends uphill.

Always remaining out of their sight. The watcher's time would come. But not now. Those were the orders.

Aggie placed the necklace back beneath her blouse. After a while, the light faded, for now.

'Here we are then,' Pop Braggan announced standing at the side of the Steep looking upon the conjoined black brickwork of the Belchambers residence, dwarfed beneath The Keep.

'Eric, will you walk me to the door?' Aggie asked.

Eric beamed from ear to ear as he offered a linked arm to grab onto.

Pop Braggan rolled his eyes in embarrassment.

As Aggie then reached the bottom of the stone steps Nan was already unbolting the door. Aggie lent into Eric's ear to peck him on the cheek.

'Meet me here in an hour. Tell no one,' she whispered before planting a tiny kiss on him. 'And have a wash, Eric Peabody. You really do smell bad.'

Eric was powerless to refuse. He nodded as eagerly as a puppy. Flushed bright red he turned and bolted to catch up with Pop Braggan before Nan could volley insults his way.

*****

Belle was dressed in gentleman's trousers, shirt, and blazer, although all were baggy and ill fitting. She tied her flowing deep-red curls into a bun and hid them under an old Panama hat her father had not worn for years. When the time came to leave, she would place a gas mask over her face to conceal her identity.

Much darker since nightfall, Belle struggled to navigate the unlit corridors of the British Museum. Ghoulish shadows from the exhibits at the mercy of the shifting evening light took on a different perspective to the day.

The violet torch was all she had to help her. She lit it up intermittently, conscious of the batteries dying as they had on its counterpart. Her lonely echoing footsteps were soon joined by another pair. No one was allowed in the Museum past five, only her father and herself. She doubted very much the government had been that responsive in finding a cure and so she immediately hid, squatting behind a large stone carving of a giant scarab beetle.

The footsteps grew louder, clip clopping steadily towards her. A white beam of circular torchlight flashed across surfaces as if an anti-aircraft light was hunting its target deep beyond the clouds. It caught the corner of her foot that stuck out ever so slightly and was then fixed upon her hiding place. The shadowy figure moved closer step by step.

Belle jumped from her hiding place, lighting up the violet torch into the intruder's face, hoping it would blind them and give her time to run. The beam hit them right between the eyes but its glow incomparable with a harsh white light and it served little purpose in blinding them.

'Aagghhhhhhhhhh!' came Belle's blood-curdling scream.

Chapter 42
The Illuminant

Mr Louds was pacing up and down outside of the barricaded grounds as the black van approached the large white building. Usually calm, now extremely agitated, he wore a gas mask that covered his cheeks and jaw but still allowed his furious stare to be seen by everyone. The orderlies had given up on trying to maintain decorum in the vehicle as Archie Goodfellow and gang maintained a steady flow of army songs and high jinks throughout the journey. Perhaps it was Pop's offer to resurrect the deal for the birds of prey that saw the orderlies arrive in higher spirits than their master, Brian Louds.

'You can wipe those smirks from off of your faces!' Louds shouted as the van arrived and people began to filter off of the vehicle.
'That includes you too!' he screamed at the orderlies.

It was quite out of character and soon the drunken joviality had descended into a sombre march as the patients donned their Institute cloaks and began walking, like chastised Benedictine monks, to their hospital quarters.

'Good news, Mr Louds,' Professor Malcolm insisted, trying desperately to change his focus. 'We have all that we need.' He smiled.

Louds blink-less glare focused on the Professor and his dishevelled appearance as Meticulous Malcolm Meredith and the two huge men began to unload the bags of Sussex Sedge and the many jars of writhing scarabs.

'Do you think I am an idiot?' Louds aggressively rounded on the Professor.

'Nothing of the kind, sir,' Professor Malcolm replied.

'Then explain that!' he snarled, pointing towards the pinnacle of the building.

From a small triangular prism, indistinguishable in the daylight, a bright-red glow was being emitted. It was throbbing as if an electrical element had suddenly received a huge power surge. Had this been a night of an air raid it would have gained the attention of foreign invaders and would have been the object of an incendiary assault.

'Oh, my goodness!' the Professor cried out startled. 'It worked.'

'So, you did know!' Mr Louds accused.

'It, it, it was an experiment,' stuttered the Professor, struggling for an answer. 'I saw a flash of the stone's brilliance only briefly late last night but wanted to test a theory. Eureka!' He punched the air half-heartedly.

'Some cats lives can be extinguished in the briefest of moments,' Louds reminded him; furious he had not been informed.

The orderlies were keen to show Louds the haul and inform them of their new business partner.

'We manage to find new falcon, Mr Louds. Man has it in two days for us he says. Falcons and chicks.'

'You better make sure he delivers on that promise. No more mistakes or I shall inform Dr Mialora. Do you understand?'

The orderlies look terrified by the prospect, bowed and resumed carrying the sedge and beetles into the building.

'Mr Louds, if my assumptions are correct, then I have something more to show you.'

'It better be worth my while, Professor. No more failures, do you hear?'

'Loud and clear, sir. Loud and clear.' Professor Malcolm was excited as he led the way into the laboratory. The burning brightness of the Scarlet Scarab forced him to spread his fingers in front of his eyes before he could find the muslin cloth to cover it.

'Don't do that!' Louds cried out expecting it to catch fire immediately.

Instead, the muslin cloth muted the brilliant red, pulsating like molten lava, as the light below fought to get out.

'What on earth is it doing?' Louds continued in astonishment.

The Professor had passed the blazing, entombed insect and made his way to its living relatives. All other insects had forced their way to the edges of their glass tanks and were unified in a hypnotic state. The scarabs had once again succumbed to the influence of their scarlet peer and as with the night before, they had begun to metamorphose. Their shells had absorbed the illuminating light and they glowed a bright violet hue.

'Professor, what does this mean? Professor?' Louds asked.

Meticulous Meredith Malcolm gazed on in wonder as if a boy seeing his first tadpole sprout legs. What it meant to the Professor was an astonishing biological catalyst that the world had not seen before.

'Professor?' Louds shouted.

'It means we have solved your riddle.' He smiled broadly.

*****

The scream from Belle echoed through the voluminous halls and corridors as the shadowy figure was lit up in violet and purple. The figure grabbed her and clasped his hands across her mouth to muffle the sound.

'Belle, it's me, Thompson,' said the agent. 'Please, turn that thing off,' he asked calmly.

Belle looked beyond him, transfixed, maintaining the focus of the beam. She didn't blink at all. Instead, she pushed past him and walked towards the illuminated wall.

'What? What is it?' Thompson asked before turning around. 'Oh, my God!' he announced, his jaw aghast.

'Not your God, Thompson, but definitely *a* God!' Belle replied.

They stood there, sustained in observation of what they had just discovered. It must have been twenty foot in diameter and dominated the canvas of the huge wall yet no one would see it in daylight let alone darkness unless they used that very specific torchlight. Hundreds of people would have unwittingly walked past it day after day.

'It's RA!' Belle confirmed 'The all-seeing eye of RA. Observing, protecting, influencing his subjects.'

'May I?' Thompson asked for the torch. He took the focus of the beam and began to walk backwards so that the strength of the beam was diminished but its range expanded. 'Look, Belle, look there.' He pointed, just out of the circumference of the eye. 'What can you see?'

Belle walked towards the illuminated wall where, just legible, the words protruded outward like lashes from the eye. '*Believe*! This one says, *Believe*,' Belle confirmed.

Thompson redirected the beam around the edge and moved closer to Belle for a better look. They followed the light in a clockwise fashion as words flashed in front of them

Follow, Obey, Believe, Loyalty, Serve, Subject, Kill.

'I'm really not sure what all of this means,' said Belle.

'No one is, Belle.' Thompson replied, thinking for a moment. 'RA – where do I remember RA from?' he spoke aloud to himself.

'He's very famous, in Egypt anyway. You cannot go anywhere over there without spotting a totem or plaque above a doorway. People believe he will protect them from evil spirits'

'That's it,' Thompson announced, suddenly realising where he had seen it before. He fumbled inside his coat pocket and produced the white calling card from OSIRIS On the back he recalled the crest in fine calligraphy – 'RA'. He pointed the beam of light onto the card.

'OBEY!' was illuminated in front of him in bold. He flipped the card over to reveal 'FORGET'.

'I need to show you something else,' Belle interrupted. Taking the torch and Thompson's hand she navigated the dark Museum corridors to the hall of the Mummies. 'There,' she said, pointing upwards at the huge lettering

'OBEY!' Thompson called out in the echoey chamber. 'But obey who?'

'I was just on my way to tell yourself and Mrs Waverley about this when you arrived.'

'Ahh yes, Wink,' Thompson replied. 'We may have a slight problem there.'

*****

The chattering audience of the WI had left the school premises in a euphoric state. Governess Dove and Jennifer Erket had excelled themselves. By far this was the greatest presentation delivered yet and the sheer excitement of requiring the good Institute ladies of Ambledown to help them within the next few days for their first event ensured nervous excitement rippled through their ranks all the way home.

'Last time we spoke, Miss Dove, you alluded to a discovery. What was it?' Erket asked of her ally.

'Not of a discovery as such. More of clarification required,' Dove replied.

'Are you sure, your excitement suggested something greater. Something of note,' Erket probed.

'I was mistaken. There is a new evacuee girl, from London, she demonstrated signs of bruising and I mistook it for the mark.'

'The mark of the moon?' Erket questioned, intently staring at Dove.

'Is what I thought at first,' Dove explained, backtracking. 'But in my excitement to please you I misunderstood and the doctor confirmed it was actually bruising.'

'Perhaps I should see for myself. Which girl is this? What does she look like?' Erket enquired.

'She has a dark bobbed haircut and she lives just up the road, on the Steep. I can find her address if you give me a moment.'

'No need,' Erket replied quickly.

'If I discover any new information, I will be sure to inform Tuchhandler who in turn will inform Dr Mialora.' Dove confirmed.

'You may also inform Tuchhandler that we too are almost ready.'

'Very well.' Dove smiled with anticipation.

'Gute nacht.' Erket smiled as she left the building, sparking up a cigarette.

'Goodnight,' Dove replied cordially, seeing the lady in the zebra-print coat safely outside to where her driver was waiting. Locking the door behind her, she swiftly journeyed to her office. Wheeling what looked like a stationary bookcase around, she unlocked a green vinyl suitcase with a hard shell that was suspended within an inlay cutout behind the books. Sitting it upright, the top half harboured a metal cube, which in turn encascd a circular globe that had a flashing light upon it and a map of the surrounding Ambledown geography. Beneath the top half and lying flat upon the surface was a typewriter, spooling device, microphone and speaker, all of which were protected by the metal casing.

Placing the headset over her ears Dove flipped the switch to initiate contact. 'Tuchhandler this is Taube. Over.'

A few momentary seconds of crackling and a reply came through. 'This is Tuchhandler,' came the wheezing tone of a man's voice. 'What is it, Taube.'

'Erket is onto the girl. I tried to cover up my mistake but she saw straight through it.'

'Are you sure? Are you absolutely sure?' the man replied.

'Nein. Not one hundred per cent. She did, however, inform me they are almost ready to proceed.'

'Then we stick to the plan.'

'If she snatches the girl, we no longer have the advantage,' Dove advised.

'Halt, Taube, Nein! You hear me, we stick to the plan. Until we have the formula, we cannot risk crossing Dr Mialora. Do you hear? I said, do you hear?'

'But, sir, I believe we need to secure her first.'

'Halt, Taube. Nein! That is an order.

*****

Erket slid across the passenger seat and paused for thought.

'Back to the Institute, ma'am?' the driver asked.

'I think we will stay awhile. Drive around back to the top of this road and park out of sight."

Chapter 43
Taube

The chimes of midnight presented Eric Peabody with an ideal opportunity for adventure. He had washed, for the first time in days, and even attempted to comb his unkempt hair. He shimmied down the drainpipe to the rear of his room, above the Poacher, scurried along one of the well-hidden alleyways, and approached 1a The Keep.

Eric wasn't the only one awake. He was being watched from an adjacent passageway by a cloaked figure. Further down the Steep, parked out of sight, he would soon be revealed to the lady in the striped coat.

Aggie was watching from the first-floor window of her bedroom. Nan had locked the front door from the inside and taken the key. She tapped the window as Eric made his way up the stone steps and indicated with his hands that they required the key. Mimicking a silent film star with a cane Eric turned around and walked foolishly down the steps. Purposely overacting every subtle movement, he counted along several cobbles before overturning one and producing a key. Gideon's secret hiding place. Aggie made light work of her descent, unbolted the deadlocks inside, and greeted Eric as he unlocked the door from the outside.

'You smell a lot better,' she said and laughed.

Fortunately, Eric's blushes were hidden in the darkness. 'So where are we off to?' he asked.

'First stop is the war memorial, and then the school,' Aggie informed him.

'School?' Eric frowned. 'What?! I spend most me time tryin' to break out.'

'I know, and I need you to help me break in,' Aggie ordered him.

'That's just stupid.' Eric shook his head in disbelief.

Aggie grabbed his arm and led him down the hill almost skipping. 'Not scared are you, Eric?' Aggie goaded him. Despite her recent fears and an increasing sense of dread when she was on her own, Eric Peabody's presence and knowledge of infinite escape routes throughout Ambledown reassured her.

'Course not!' he said, raising his voice and puffing his chest. 'Sure you don't want to sell that?' he asked, pointing to Aggie's necklace, which was now beginning to glow.

The more the miniature magnifier spent in the moonlight the brighter its beam became. Aggie was quick to hide it beneath her blouse once again as it would expose them when really, she wanted them to be cloaked and hidden in the shadows.

From her car, 'Erket' spotted the brief moment of luminance as it lit up the girl with the black bobbed hair.

'What is that?' she said, directing her driver towards Aggie's neck, while exhaling her cigarette. 'Bring me the girl,' she whispered to her driver as she expelled another subtle wisp of cigarette smoke for his consumption.

*****

'Who can we trust?' Belle asked Thompson.

'As of now, Belle, I'm not sure. My men are treading softly and scrutinising the list. It appears Draper may have infiltrated OSIRIS after all. He wasn't on the list. Nor were Nathaniel or Gideon. As it stands, I trust yourself, and my fellow recruits,' he responded.

'Do you not find it peculiar that Malling and Collingdale fail to remember being given the card but accept it belonged to them?' Belle offered with scepticism.

'It doesn't make sense whichever way you look at it. Something is awry, but that something we need to discover.'

'Have you considered approaching Wink?' Belle asked.

'God no. If she is compromised, I'll be compromising whatever edge we may have.'

'So, where do we go from here?' Belle asked, seeking reassurance.

'Ambledown,' Thompson confirmed.

*****

Night had finally come. Tate stoked the embers of the fully fired steam engine he had spent the last few hours preparing.

'Nathaniel, are you OK?' Gideon asked.

Noone had been staring into the coals of the locomotive for just over a minute. The embers' hypnotic dance was seducing him. By all rights, he should have had the most abrasive fear of any fire but since the evacuation, he had succumbed to its charms. Along with the flames, he saw costumed men dancing, dressed up in masked totems, memories of a distant past, the violet hue burning brightly amongst them as cloaked men hummed softly, and spoke in whispers.

'Nathaniel!' Gideon shook his friend aggressively to wake him out of it.

'Oh, bleeding great. I knew this would happen, just like last time,' Tate chimed in.

'You're paid to get us there, not talk,' Gideon volleyed back, quickly quashing the dissenting smuggler.

''Ere,' Tate replied, taking the shovel from Noone.

'Nate, go up top – on point,' Gideon ordered. 'Nate, do it now and wear a mask, the steam and soot will be unrelenting.'

Noone was handed a rifle from Tate Braggan to accompany his mask and climbed the iron ladder on the side of the engine outside.

'How long?' Gideon asked Tate

'Hour and 'alf or thereabouts,' Tate confirmed

'That's twice as quick as last time. Are you sure?'

'Don't have a couple of cabooses and a small army to chug this time, do we? And the path should still be clear,' Tate confirmed. 'That is, of course, if you can keep up with me, Professor.' He smiled, shovelling coal as quickly as he could.

Gideon took up the task; challenge accepted. He donned a handkerchief across his face, looking more like a bank robber than a stoker as he matched Tate's shovel-load for shovel-load. His dear friend sat sentry just above. The steam-powered machine puffed away slowly as it began to roll into life, soon to be hurtling south, towards the coast and Ambledown.

'Let's try to make it an hour,' Gideon challenged Tate, as sweat poured from both of their brows.

*****

'So, wot are we lookin' for?' Eric piped up.

'Not entirely sure,' Aggie replied as she removed her necklace and began to hover over the stone tomes at the guardian angel's feet that protected the cenotaph.

'Gis a clue at least,' Eric insisted. Always looking around ensuring they were safe.

'C S-M' said Aggie.

Arithmetic was more Eric's forte, particularly if it included gambling on the horses or any kind of haggling. Reading, not so much, but he could just about manage a few letters. Aggie had immediately noticed the names were alphabetically ordered via surname. She moved directly to the end stones looking for S's. Eric began at the opposite end.

'There are a few Smythe's on here, Eric. Any relation to Henrietta?'

'Technically a Huntington-Smythe, as she and her muvva like to remind us constantly. But yeah possibly. She, I mean Henny's muvva Sybil is the daughter of Lord Huntington. '

'Sybil? Seriously? Sybil Smythe? Is that really her mother's name. That's so funny.' Aggie was giggling.

'You've met her, Lady H-S, haven't you? Well, her muvva, Henny's grandma made them two look saintly. Or so the rumour goes. Whatever witchcraft she employed on 'im, it worked.'

'So, she married into Lord Huntington's family and they became Huntington-Smythe.'

'Cunning old cow by all accounts.' Eric nodded. ''Ere we go … Bel-cham-bers … like your name,' he called out phonetically.

'I'm not looking for my name, silly. Anything with C S-M.'

'Belchambers – A – that could be you. Belchambers – G – that could be your uncle.'

'Eric, stop larking about and help me. Someone's bound to spot us if we don't hurry.'

'Belchambers –F … gawd knows who that is.'

'F? No way. Did you say F too? Let me see,' Aggie insisted. True enough, three Belchambers. All of them sharing initials with her family. That's more than a coincidence, she thought, as she took out her necklace to see better.

As it absorbed the moonlight, its glow lit up the shadowy figure over the shoulder of Eric Peabody, emerging from the hidden entranceway of The Crown coaching inn. As Aggie set eyes on the figure staring back at her, the dull tone of an engine came revving down the hill and emerged hastily from behind. The car had been silently stalking them and was now fully revved up to snatch Aggie. The cloaked figure stepped into the road just at the point as the car arrived, forcing it to swerve, sending it screeching down the gipsy road and away from Aggie and Eric.

'Quick, leg it!' Eric shouted, grabbing Aggie by the hand, and directing her into the alleyways just south of the Poacher. It was the one where Lyle had previously confronted her.

'Who was that?' Aggie asked.

'I didn't get a good look. The car was too fast. And put that bleeding thing away.'

Aggie tucked the fully illuminated necklace into her blouse once more.

'Not the car, the man?' Aggie.

'Wot man? I didn't see no man,' Eric replied.

'He was right behind you as if he purposely stepped out. Wearing a long cloak. A Cossack, I think.'

'Oh, dear goodness, not the Priory Friar! You saw the Priory Friar. Ghosts give me the collywobbles, Aggie. I fink we should get you back home. It's too dangerous with ghouls running about the place.'

'Stop lying to me, Eric. Who was it?' Aggie said aggressively.

''Onest, cross me art. Didn't see no fella. Come on, let's get home now.'

'Don't you think they may have followed us from the house?' Aggie asked.

'Well, where then?' Eric asked.

'Let's go to the school, as planned.'

'For pity's sake,' Eric moaned. Taking Aggie's hand, he guided her through the labyrinth of alleyways and shortcuts he knew like nobody else.

'This isn't the right way, Eric,' Aggie whispered.

'It is if you don't want to be seen.'

*****

'So, Professor Malcolm, where does this leave us. Can you deliver on your promise?' asked Mr Louds.

'I am certain the majority of this puzzle has been solved.' Returning to the original scrolls and the negative illustrations he had garnered from them, Professor Malcolm began to run through them one by one. 'The light or at least the god of light, Horus, is responsible for the scarabs' ability to produce such a wonderful display of colour,' he said, stepping through each section very carefully. 'It is this light, and the influence it has, which turns all others into followers. The scarabs themselves metamorphose to mimic their leader, their god.'

'Very good, Professor. Please, keep going.'

'It appears to me that the changelings, the violet Scarabidae and the plants, are then somehow combined together, crushed, by the looks of things.' He pointed to the two women with the pestle and mortar.

'Very good. Very good!' Louds grew excited.

'Then I am unsure. Perhaps smoke or maybe water helps to distribute it somehow.' He demonstrated, pointed to the wavy glyph.

'Or maybe both?' Louds added.

'Then I believe, via your demonstrations, Mr Louds, the rest is self-explanatory.'

Brian Louds laughed to himself. Looking back at him from the puzzle was the all-seeing eye of RA, accompanied by the gods Anubis and Set. He did indeed know how the rest of the cartouche unfolded.

'Bravo, Professor. Bravo. You have succeeded where others have failed. Now, I need you to become those working women and make me the powder.'

'But I have no idea of how much of each to combine.'

'Never fear.' Louds smiled. 'Try to recreate this.'

He held out the small pillbox with a tiny amount of the original dust he had used on the beetles before. Reaching to one of the jars Eric had filled, he removed a writhing example of one of the scarabs. Placing it in a mortar he slowly crushed it underneath until its outer shell splintered and its innards squelched under the pressure.

'There, I have half completed it for you, Professor. You have until morning.'

*****

'Elizabeth, did you hear that screech?' Gemima asked. It was the first thing she had said following her accident.

'Go to sleep, Gem. We've had such a long day.'

Gem looked out of the bedroom window she shared with her sister, and up and down the Steep. She spotted the flash of light as Eric and Aggie disappeared out of sight. He must be coming home. She decided she would go out and greet her brother.

Gemima was not far behind them both and was keen to see both her brother and the girl whose haircut she had copied, following the assault on Henrietta. As she turned the corner there was no one there, just a very dark passageway. She tentatively made her way, following Eric's well-worn route.

'Aggie! Eric!' she called out in a muted tone. She was too scared to step into the smugglers' routes at night and turned to head home.

'Hello,' came Erket's voice as Gem walked straight into her.

She was just about to scream when the sharp sting of a pinprick rendered her unconscious.

The driver pulled up alongside and Gemima was bundled into the boot.

'Where is it? Where is the necklace?' she barked at her driver, who began an unsuccessful search of the surrounding floor in the darkness. In the background, calls diverted their attention

'Gem, where are you?' shouted Elizabeth as she wandered out, bleary-eyed, from the warm safety of the Poacher and peered down the Steep.

'You will have to come back in the daytime,' Erket ordered as they took to their car and sped off once more.

The brake lights of a car were just visible as they sped away

'Gemimaaaaaa?' Elizabeth called in the distance.

Chapter 44
Purrsia

Professor Meticulous Meredith Malcolm rued the senseless crushing of the fascinating scarabs that glowed in front of him. Eric's haul was impressive and the expensive creature cargo would require many hands to convert them from living organisms into ethereal powder when combined with the crushed Sussex Sedge.

Morning was approaching fast and the Professor could well imagine the fate of those before him. He could only hope the pound note had found its way to Professor Gideon Belchambers.

His first attempt to replicate the dust from Mr Louds' pillbox had seen it disperse into the cup of water. It did not quite form the paste he had hoped to dry. The water had also remained transparent without any sight of a violet dilution.

This would be his second attempt and the path he had chosen this time was smoke.

Ensuring the Scarlet Scarab was duly covered in the thick muslin cloth, its remaining light fading now darkness had come, he lit a match and sprinkled his small sample into the glass tank of the Death-stalkers, puffing the tiny level of smoke amongst them. Their hypnotic state now fading from the bright beetle that had commanded their attention, they turned and focused once again on their violet-glowing neighbours.

Professor Malcolm could not be sure if it was the formula or the beetles themselves, so he carefully gathered a small set of tweezers and removed a single Death-stalker from its enclosure. Placing it on the floor, it writhed and lashed out with its pincers as he held the sting securely. Lighting a match once again, he gently blew the formula towards the arachnid before letting it loose. As it scurried off to find cover, he focused the small violet torch beam just ahead of it. As he moved it from left and right, the eight-legged beast pursued the light source as if stalking it like injured prey.

His formula had worked. It was some relief for his own sake but was not what he had been hoping for.

The doors to the laboratory flung open as Mr Louds marched through.

'Eureka! Professor. Isn't that what you like to say?' Louds asked, laughing hysterically. 'Oh, I've been watching you from behind my mirrors. Playing along with your minor discoveries. Well, guess what? Your purpose has been served!'

The orderlies followed their master in and secured Professor Malcolm in a vice-like grip. Removing both the tweezers and torch from the Professor's fingers, Mr Louds coxed the Death-stalker towards his own feet. Carefully picking up the scorpion by the sting, he placed it upon Malcolm's forearm that the orderly was presenting to him with the sleeve now rolled up.

'You see, there were two paths of this particular problem to solve. The first being the Ethereum! The influencing power of smoke as it is inhaled into the body, subtly embracing the ether and invisible in its presence. The second being the Illuminant. The opposing twin, the instructor that directs the ethers path.' Louds stopped for a moment and walked over to the glass of water the Professor had disregarded from his first test. Pointing the torch towards it; the water illuminated in plumes of violet and blue. Invisible to the naked eye but under those certain conditions swirling like brewing summer storm clouds.

'Quite poisonous to drink,' Louds explained. 'But makes the most beautiful paint,' he said, dipping his finger in the glass. Upon the Professor's profusely sweating brow, he drew the eye of RA. He accentuated the pupil with a forceful prod of his index finger.   'You shouldn't have been such a naughty boy, Professor. You may have retained many more of your lives. A bit like my dear friend.'

Louds puckered his lips and called the cat. Its odd, furless body was unlike anything the Professor had seen. The cat hissed and snarled as it saw the motionless scorpion on the Professor's arm. Then Louds picked it up by the scruff and cradled it like a baby over his shoulder. All the while he kept the beam intently focused on the Professor's elbow joint.

'Now, now, Purrsia, what was that?' Louds said as if the cat was talking into his ear. 'I'm sorry, we cannot keep him. I would have liked to but he is as deceitful as any feline.' With that final sentence, he turned the torchlight off, allowing the scorpion to return to his natural predatory state. It motioned forward unfurling its sting and then with lightning precision struck the central vein of the Professor's arm. An excruciating pain coursed immediately through Meredith's body and into his central nervous system. A pain he had felt subtly before. This time it was ten-fold the intensity. He began to shake, foam at the mouth, and within mere seconds his muscles contorted until he was just a crippled wreck slumped on the floor. Professor Malcolm was alive, at least, but frozen in suspended animation, motionless, as he continued to see and hear his captor.

'Don't worry, Professor, you're not dying. I've heard it's actually worse than dying. I may require you in the future.' Louds laughed and walked away with the peculiar-looking cat.   'And as for you, my dear little pussy cat. I think it is time you took your turn on centre stage.'

*****

'I'm telling you, Eric. I saw a man, in a dark cloak. He stepped out as the car came.'

'Alright, alright I believe ya!' Eric replied. 'But shush will you if you want to break into this stupid place.'

'Well, who could it have been?'

'Aggie, a man in a long dark cloak, in Ambledown, please. Haven't you noticed who comes and goes? Could be a brother, or one of those weirdos from the hospital, smugglers and thieves, anyone. I'm more worried about that car. Don't get many cars round 'ere.'

'I couldn't see who was driving,' Aggie replied

'Me neither,' Eric confirmed, agitated. 'It was following us, for sure.'

'Do you think we should go back home now then? Forget about this?' Aggie questioned her own decision.

'You change your mind like the wind. Don't say that. I didn't want to bleedin' do this in the first place, did I?' Eric huffed, annoyed. 'Look, Aggie. I said I'd look after you as did me sisters. Promised Gideon, didn't I? No one else has helped us out more than your uncle. Besides, if that strange car was following us, or that man, *you claim to have seen*, was after you, then I doubt very much they'd actually look for two kids in the school at night time. Your plan may be a touch of genius.'

Aggie managed to smile back at him as he took her hand in reassurance.

'Oh my God, that's freezing,' Aggie said as her ankles became submerged in icy cold water.

'Sorry, shoulda said. We do have to wade through the marshes a bit.'

'We'll freeze to death if this gets much deeper,' she replied.

'Better than being kidnapped by the Priory Friar. Whoooooo!' He laughed and offered a ghoulish impersonation.

'That, Eric Peabody, is not funny,' Agatha scolded him as Goosebumps pimpled her skin.

'You expect me to climb that fence, Eric ?' Aggie asked, frozen from her recent midnight dip in the sub-zero Braggan Marshes.

'It's easy, follow my foot holes. I've done it loads of times.'

'It's so dark, Eric. I'm using my necklace,' she insisted, pulling out and lighting her way.

'Just put it back when we're over. Don't wanna get caught breaking into school. I've me reputation to think about.'

Aggie laughed out loud.

Eric vaulted the top of the fence like a gymnast but as he did so he dropped a small glass jar from his pocket, it shattered on the ground below.

'Oh shit!' he swore.

'No one heard, Eric. Just us,' Aggie reassured him.

'Not the noise I'm worried about. Those little bleeders are worth their weight in gold,' he said bending down quickly, trying to scoop up as many as he could, placing the scrambling scarabs wriggling into and buttoning his pocket.

Aggie joined him in a more gracious descent. As her magnifier lit up, she saw a light from the playground-side windows of the girls' side.

'Look, Eric. Over there, light.'

Eric flashed a glance over but it had already gone. 'Can't see nuffink,' Eric replied. 'Could've been your bleeding light, reflecting on the windows. Told you to hide it.'

Aggie apologised quickly as she hid it once more beneath her blouse.

'Right, where are we going?' Eric asked.

'Sister Harvey's room. She has something from Dove, which I think will help me.'

Eric began a systematic rattling of the boys' side windows. It wasn't long before one succumbed to his touch.

'I unlock 'em all every day.' He smiled at Aggie. 'Stupid Brothers only ever fink to check my classroom. Shan't be a mo,' the adventurous Peabody announced as he disappeared inside.

Aggie waited. She was beginning to shiver in the chill of the night, sodden to the waist. She hadn't waited long before the fire escape door swung open. Eric appeared clutching two cloaks.

'Pssst, Aggie, over here. Might want to slip into these before we freeze.'

*****

'Taube, this is Tuchhandler. Taube, come in. Over,' crackled the voice through the hidden radio.

'This is Taube. Go on,' Dove answered.

'Mialora has the formula. I repeat, Mialora has the formula!'

'And the girl? Over?' Dove asked with bated breath. 'Does he know about the girl?'

'Nein, Taube. Not that he has advised so far.'

The shattering of glass broke the silence as Dove waited for Tuchhandler to respond.

'Taube out,' Dove advised, immediately cutting off communications.

She closed the suitcase and hid it back within its inlaid wooden hideout behind the bookcase. Moving quietly to the wall beside the door, she noticed a small stream of light passing through the corridor.

The light disappeared and shortly after Dove began to follow. She followed the soft footsteps winding through the corridor. She peered through the crack in the doorway and saw the cloaked figure kneeling at the bookcase on the Priory side of the girls' classroom.

'Stand up slowly and turn around or I will shoot,' Dove ordered, producing a Luger from her waist.

The figure did not say a thing, stood up, removed her hood and turned around smiling at the governess.

'You!' Dove exclaimed. 'I knew it was you.'

*****

'Right, Aggie, you make your way to Harvey's. I'll keep an eye out,' Eric suggested.

Covering her head in the hood, she made her way quietly towards the room. Dove's office door was open. Aggie cautiously peered inside, and she saw that she wasn't there. One less thing to worry about, she thought to herself.

Harvey's classroom door was open. Aggie crept to the threshold and peered through the crack in the door. A darkened figure was sitting with their back to them, just in front of the bookcase with the secret vent.

'Miss, Miss Harvey?' Aggie asked as she made her way towards the figure. 'Miss, are you awake?'

Aggie crept up from behind and being careful not to wake her. She rounded the sister to find her gagged and bound.

Eric Peabody rushed into the room. 'What's going on? I 'erd voices?' he said, voice raised.

Sister Harvey was awake, shaking her head and trying to tell them something. Aggie tried to remove the gag but it was too late. The door to the room closed with a subtle click. Eric Peabody turned quickly to be greeted by a cold barrel of a pistol pressed into his forehead.

'Nobody say a single word. Not unless you wish me to prove what little brains this boy has,' came Miss Dove's voice. 'You, Agatha Chatsmore, take the Sister's legs. You, Eric Peabody, take her arms.'

Both Eric and Agatha stared back with incredulity.

'Now! Do it immediately,' Dove demanded aggressively.

Aggie stepped forward feeling the crunch of shattered glass beneath her feet and spying the broken picture frame face down on the floor.

'Hurry Up!' Governess Dove urged them on as they struggled to drag and slide the nun through the corridors under her direction. 'Here. In here,' she ordered them, into the small medical room where Aggie had been examined under the supervision of Dr Beckworth. 'You'll not be found in here,' she confirmed. Passing a ball of coarse twine to Aggie, she ordered her to tie Eric up. Checking the knots thoroughly, Dove ensured they were secured tightly, pinching the skin and making it drain white of the circulating blood, before gagging Eric with a rag, before tying Aggie up herself.

'Should you try to escape, I will kill you. Without hesitation!' Dove confirmed.

Eric was snarling and writhing around on the floor, exhausting himself to escape.

'Such a silly boy. If you do not believe me, allow me to demonstrate.'

Dove removed a small green bottle from her pocket. On the front of it, the small image of the highly toxic Death-stalker. She uncorked it and drew its liquid into a small needle.

'Have you ever been kissed by a scorpion?' Dove asked Eric as her nose drew in to touch his.

He had stopped moving and was now petrified as she danced the small metal sharp in front of him.

'Don't cry, little boy,' she enjoyed saying as tears welled up in his eyes. 'I won't hurt you unless you try to escape. I would never knowingly harm a child. What do you take me for a monster?' She laughed.

Eric relaxed from his flailing and exhaled a huge sigh of relief.

'But adults should know better!' she shouted, thrusting the needle into Sister Harvey's arm.

The nun shook violently. Her body cramped up as saliva poured out from either side of her gag. Her tied hands retracted like claws as she contorted into a foetal position.

The two children's screams were muffled. Agatha shuffled to support the nun's head with her body, much like Florrie's as her aunt had gasped and become overwhelmed by the toxic gas all those days ago.

Dove moved behind her young female captive. Fearing the worst, Aggie flinched expecting a sharp chill to penetrate her neck. Instead, Dove leant her forward and pulled back the hood so she could stare down at her spine.

'That stupid drunk doctor,' she cursed. 'That is definitely not a bruise.'

*****

'Welcome, Tuchhandler.' Mr Louds smiled broadly, welcoming his recent ally into The Silvera Institute.

Accompanied by several men cloaked in long leather coats with pistols at their sides, they followed Mr Louds and his orderlies into the labyrinth tunnels of the huge white building.

'Please, gentlemen, make yourselves comfortable. You are completely safe here,' Louds reassured them.

The barren white walkways with picture-less frames amused them as they followed behind. They were being escorted to the operating theatres where Mr Louds was to present their recent revelations. A crescent of chairs was set out in front of a glass viewing window that was obscured by a set of heavy emerald drapes.

'Excuse me for one moment,' Louds explained. 'Keep watching the curtain in front of you.'

The green drapes parted almost immediately to show Purrsia, the furless cat, sitting in front of a cage of rats that it was eagerly pawing at and trying to attack. Next to the cage of rats sat a large glass aquarium full of water with a small runway leading up to it. A crackling of a public address system announced Brain Louds' voice.

'I give you Dr Mialora,' he said proudly. 'He apologises for the mask but all will become evident.'

A door to the operating theatre opened and a surgeon, dressed in full swabs and sporting a gas mark that obscured his entire face, entered the room. Moving to the cage full of rats, he removed one by its tail and swung it hypnotically in front of the cat. Purrsia pounced immediately and played with the rodent before tearing it limb from limb. The gallery of men sat on observing, unflinching.

Behind the glass, Dr Mialora flicked a switch and plunged the operating theatre into darkness. Holding up the violet torch for all the men to see, he danced its beam around the cage like a cheap vaudeville act. The furless feline, Purrsia, was back at the rat cage trying again to claw at them. Dr Mialora opened the cage, releasing the rats, and sending Purrsia into a frenzy, eagerly pouncing and attacking anything he could catch. The doctor then moved to another switch. On flicking it, an invisible gas descended into the room. Transparent to the naked eye, it was only observed once the violet torch beam was shone and interacted with the plumes to produce swirling clouds of violet and blue. Training the torch beam on the cat, having sufficiently inhaled the gas, it now sat stationary, ignoring its vermin quarry. As the doctor guided the beam around the glass room Purrsia attentively rose and followed its every move. The doctor guided the manipulated moggy right next to the rats that had also stopped moving and were now following the beam alongside the cat in a macabre dance of obedience.

'A clever trick, Doctor,' one of the men hurled towards the operating theatre. 'You trained a cat. You trained some rats. So what?'

The doctor stared back from behind his gas mask. Taking the torch beam, he proceeded to march the animals, single file, around the room as if some bizarre pied piper with a torch, rather than a pipe, was influencing the creatures. Ensuring that the men were watching closely, he marched the creatures slowly up the walkway to the edge of the aquarium before directing the torch beam into the water. Purrsia and the rodent followers immediately dived in desperately swimming down to where the torch beam focused beneath the water. It must have been two, maybe three minutes, during which the thrashing of the animals was furious and until none of them had any more life to give. Then the torchlight went out and the main light was returned to illuminate the room behind the glass.

The top of the tank was overflowing with the corpses of rats and the poor lifeless body of the cat.

The men looked at one another.

Their leader stood up and clapped slowly in recognition. 'Bravo, Doctor. Bravo,' he said in his weasel-like voice.

*****

During Erket's journey through the dark countryside, she had insisted her driver dim the headlights. It was perilous enough on those country lanes at night but she had insisted.

On the outskirts of Ambledown, they sped swiftly past the large iron gates intertwined with HH and down the narrowing road where the cobblestoned bridge arched over the source of the Amble.

Ilya Debrovska had laid his trap here only weeks previously and the fruits of his labour were now coming to fruition.

'Be careful,' Erket warned the driver. 'We will approach another bridge in a few hundred yards.'

The chauffeur slowed on approach as they were engulfed in a foggy mist as the hump of the bridge welcomed them. Out of the subtle clouds, two large green eyes lit up in the centre of the road. The driver swerved and was forced to brake suddenly, skidding the car sideways. Only by luck, not judgement, did he avoid the large female fox and its cubs in the middle of the road and manage not to veer down the nearby ravine. Only yards away, hidden behind bracken and mature trees was the immediate and deathly drop that hid the disused railway line.

'You stupid man!' Erket screamed. 'Run the damn things over next time!'

The driver apologised and readjusted his skewed hat. In the boot, the terrified cries of Gemima Peabody were drowned out by the revs of the engine. The recent swerve of the car had opened up her stitches from her accident that morning. She felt the warm trickle of blood on her forehead again. Her eyes struggled to keep open until there was just darkness, and she slid back into her concussed sleep.

*****

'One hour, six minutes! That's a record,' Tate announced proudly. Holding his pocket watch.

Gideon collapsed backwards, exhausted from the relentless stoking. He patted Tate Braggan on the back before composing himself as he climbed out of the engine room and onto the ladder that led to Nathaniel's sentry point.

'Nathaniel, are you OK?' Gideon asked in a concerned tone.

Covered in soot and dust, Noone had worn his gas mask for most of the journey. Removing it to reveal his clean but terribly scarred faced, he gestured to Gideon to be both quiet and listen towards the steep, wooded banks that aligned and masked the Bracken Line.

'What is it?' Gideon mouthed to his friend.

Nathaniel acted out a circular driving wheel as if he had heard a car.

Gideon grabbed a rifle and joined his friend. He focused through the sight and analysed the dark foliage and trees for any signs of activity. A snap of a twig saw their firearms align straight ahead of them. A moment of silence, and then another snap of a twig from behind them, high in the trees. They rounded to point their guns at the steep banks. Noone cocked the weapon in anticipation.

A whoosh of air through the trees and Gideon's rifle point was weighted downwards as the large black-and-white bird landed, pecking at the sight's reflection of the moon. A bright light ignited from behind them, blinding them both as they turned towards it.

'Evenin, gentlemen,' came the welcome guttural tone of Pop Braggan.

'Was that your car?' Noone asked.

'Don't 'ave no car. Just me pony and trap. Saw it though. Posh like, wiv driver in an 'at, coming from the direction of Huntington Hall. The mutt chased a vixen into the road and almost sent it crashin',' Pop confirmed.

'OK,' Gideon acknowledged 'What news for us, Pop? Is my niece safe?'

'Walked 'er 'ome with Eric meself.' The huge man smiled. 'And plenty to report.'

Chapter 45
Captives

'Ambledown? Are you sure?' Belle questioned, as they made their way back to her father's office.

Closing the door for privacy they planned their next move.

'I'm not sure of anything anymore, Belle. But one thing is certain, Gideon and Nathaniel know more than us,' Thompson replied, staring hard to suggest she too knew more than she was letting on.

'Don't stare at me like that,' Belle bit back. 'I thought he was dead!' she shouted.

Thompson wanted to believe her, yet remained sceptical.

'Look, perhaps we should try and figure this out ourselves. Nate and H–' She paused and started again. 'Nate and Gideon will not desert us. I'm sure.'

'A minute ago, you told me that you thought he was dead. Where's the trust there?' Thompson pointed out.

'I cannot explain it, but everyone I cherished kept that secret far from me. It must have been for good reason. But they are good people. I know they are good people.'

A knock came from the door, interrupting them, and suppressing the tension between the pair. Thompson's subordinates, Smith and Jones, entered.

'We have them, sir,' Smith replied.

'Who? Which ones?' Thompson requested.

'All of them, sir. Everyone on the list,' confirmed Jones.

'Everyone? That was too quick,' Thompson challenged them.

'We agree it was. The most peculiar thing, sir. Nearly all of them were coupled together. Like Noah's Ark, they came in two by two.'

'I don't understand. Why would they be paired up?' Thompson asked, puzzled.

'That's not the only thing. All of them have the same sets of responsibilities. And all of them deny knowing the tiger-lady, but openly accept owning one of the cards.'

The men produced almost a full deck of the OSIRIS calling cards, passing them to their superior.

Thompson looked increasingly perplexed.

Belle returned to the glyphs and the sequence of cartouche they represented. 'What is it that you actually represent?' she spoke theoretically to the 'All-seeing eye' as it stared back at her. 'What is your secret?'

Returning to the original photograph, Belle scrutinised the lady in the cat skin. Tiger-lady was smiling with a cigarette in one hand and using the other to shake Malling's.

'Thompson, fetch me that magnifier will you,' she asked pointing to an old magnifying glass on her father's desk. 'Look, there.' She pointed to Thompson. 'Between her thumb and forefinger.'

'Got him!' Thompson smiled.

'It could be anything, a hankie, even a fleck on the negative,' Belle suggested.

'Oh, come on, who passes a hankie in a handshake? It's one of these cards,' Thompson insisted. 'Come on, Belle, none of us want to say it but they are all lying to us. This goes to the very heart of government. Some way or another.'

'Are you absolutely sure? I'm not convinced. It would be too difficult to manipulate so many. Perhaps there's an alternative explanation?' Belle questioned, as she walked to the tiger-skin coat and reached deep within its pockets.

*****

Gideon and Nathaniel had used the pony ride hidden under hay on Pop's horse and cart for much-needed rest. Noone whimpered in and out of his recurring visions, while Luna, Pop's faithful hound, snuggled up in sympathy next to him.

As the Steep came into view, dawn was breaking and the light crimson of daylight pierced through.

'Red sky in morning, shepherds warning,' Pop announced to wake his two companions.

As they approached the edge of Ambledown and spied the Steep, Pop encouraged his equine transport forward. Two small candlelights flickered and hovered bug-like in the distance where the junction divided the trinity of alehouses.

Wilson Bott, the town's sheriff, who resided above The Hart and kept a watchful eye on the Poacher, had been woken from his comfortable sleep and was being harangued by Elizabeth Peabody on the cobblestones outside.

'You'll be hard-pressed to find anyone willing to look this early for your sister,' Wilson advised her, still yawning.

'Please, you're the sheriff, aren't you? She was here one minute and then gone. Something's happened, I know it. Something has happened to her,' Elizabeth insisted.

'And where's Eric?' Bott yawned again, now conscious he was still in his nightwear.

'He's missing too.'

'Elizabeth,' Bott said calmly. 'They are likely to be together. You know what your brother is like.'

'Please, Mr Bott. Eric went out without her. She went to greet him on his return and then neither of them returned. Please, help. Please,' Elizabeth begged through tearful eyes.

'What's goin' on 'ere?' Pop asked as he halted his large Shire horse.

Gideon, soot ridden and sweaty, unusually dishevelled from his gentlemanly persona, sat adjacent to Pop. His heart sank as he spied Elizabeth's worried disposition. Nathaniel remained hidden beneath the hay.

'Elizabeth, what's happened?' Gideon asked, leaving his seat to comfort her.

'Gem's gone missing and I think she's in danger,' she replied.

'Just Gem?' Gideon immediately questioned.

'Eric's missing too,' Elizabeth added.

Gideon looked at Pop and began to run uphill towards The Keep.

'I walked 'er 'ome meself!' Pop shouted at him. 'Giddy up, girl!' he ordered the horse, clicking his tongue to his palette. The large workhorse followed Professor Belchambers who had launched into a sprint.

Elizabeth was already in hot pursuit just yards behind him.

As Gideon rounded the corner to his black-brick home, he immediately noticed the dislodged cobbles at the foot of his steps. He quickly checked and confirmed the key had gone. Hammering on the metal lion's head knocker, he woke his sleeping housekeeper.

'Alright, alright. Where fire?' Nan hollered back.

'Nan, quickly. It's Gideon. Nan, where is Aggie?' he shouted, peering with fingers pressed through the letterbox.

Nan fumbled with the keys, unlocking the door from the inside. She realised the bolts had been moved since she had last locked them.

'She was here. I tuck her in. But locks, they have moved.'

'Aggie?' Gideon shouted frantically. 'Aggie are you here?'

He vaulted the stairs to the first floor and entered the room. The force of his entrance gusted notepaper off of the bed. The drapes were still drawn shut. He turned the light on. The dolls' house and rocking chair were untouched as was the bedding on top of an un-slept-in bed.

'No!' Gideon cried out, thumping his hand down so hard that it smashed the dolls' house roof.

Hearing Gideon's cries, Nathaniel Noone could not remain camouflaged any longer. He leapt out from Pop's wagon and made light of the steps to Gideon's home. Elizabeth gasped in horror as he sprinted past with pistol drawn. One flight of stairs up and he found his friend hunched over sobbing.

'She's gone. They've taken her, Nate. After all this time, I've lost her. How could they even know? Damn you, Ilya!'

'Well, if they did take her, they were kind enough to let her leave a note,' Noone replied, picking up the folded piece of paper addressed to

Gidcon, which had been placed obviously for him to find upon her bed but had simply blown off upon his entrance.

Gideon read it aloud.

'Dearest Uncle, I am on an adventure with Eric. I shall explain everything on my return. I promise. Just like you promised.

Lots of love

Aggie x

PS – Eric says the pound smells terrible. A hairy man from the Institute gave it to him.'

Gideon was relieved, he wiped his tears from his cheeks then re-read the letter. Noone soon located the banknote from beneath the bed. Examining it, his senses detected the subtle citron zest as it wafted towards his nostrils. Opening the drapes, Nathaniel presented the note to the early morning daylight.

'S.O.S. – PMM,' Noone read out. 'What is PMM?' he asked.

'Who is PMM? is the real question,' Gideon replied.

The grin across his face turning from fear to hope.

*****

Belle had the tiger-skin coat in her hands. With her fingernails, she was scratching at the inside of the pocket and had found the remains of violet-tinted tobacco amongst the lint and fluff.

Placing the tobacco next to the rouged cigarette stub, forming the tiniest pile of microscopic kindling she dimmed the lights.

'Do you have a light?' she asked the man.

Jones produced a neat box of matches.

Sparking a solitary match, she lit the small amount of tobacco while keeping the violet beam fixed on it. It was a minuscule amount but just enough to demonstrate a small experiment to Thompson and his men. The tobacco and saltpetre accelerants duly obliged in igniting the tiny fire while the subtle smoke now took on an ethereal violet hue. Flitting between violets, pinks, and purples, the minuscule clouds revolved and danced until they disappeared into the dust-speckled atmosphere. It was mere seconds in its balletic performance but enough to prove her point. She then switched the light back on.

'The lady in the photo. She has that cigarette in hand. This type of cigarette.' Belle pointed out to the stub. Holding it aloft, the particles of violet shimmered against the darker ginger flakes of tobacco. 'The colouring of these particles, as with the colouring of the smoke it produces, are illuminated by the torch.'

'Go on,' Thompson encouraged her.

'As are the markings on both the OSIRIS cards and the painting in the halls,' Belle confirmed.

Thompson and his men listened intently as Belle explained her theory.

'I am unsure how it specifically works. But all the attendees have the cards. No doubt all of them inadvertently witnessed the markings on the wall, having attended the fundraiser'

'Obey, follow, etcetera,' Thompson added.

'Precisely, but more importantly, the tiger-lady, smoking the unique filters in their company. Who knows? Perhaps she was poisoning them.'

'It's certainly a theory,' Thompson added.

'The thing is,' Belle continued. 'Who else do we know that smokes, literally, all of the time?'

'Wink Waverley,' Thompson replied.

'And she's on the list,' Smith and Jones added.

'Precisely,' Belle reaffirmed. 'But what role does she play?'

Thompson paced the room, scratching his head in deep thought. 'OK, I have an idea, but if we are wrong this may be a treasonable offence so I'll understand if you wish to bow out now.'

'We're in,' Smith and Jones replied in stereo without hesitation.

Belle nodded in agreement.

'Whitehall it is then,' Thompson confirmed. 'Let's go to Whitehall with all our temporary prisoners. I doubt any traitor would keep their cool when presented with such a sight. If Wink or even Malling decides to run, we'll have them. Or we're wrong and we'll likely to face prison. It's a plan of sorts, or the beginning of one anyway.'

*****

'Gideon, where are you going? Who is PMM?' Nathaniel asked.

Gideon had left Aggie's room in a flash and was already mobilising himself to depart for the Institute Silvera.

'We need to go to the Institute. Seek out Professor Meredith Malcolm! Or the hairy fellow as Eric so eloquently put it in the note!' Gideon shouted from his quarters as Nathaniel Noone followed.

'And who is the Professor exactly?' Noone enquired.

'He's already sent me a warning message. Not sure he truly knew what he was dealing with but now he needs our help. Ilya had wanted something in his possession.'

Noone rolled his eye. 'That bloody conniving Russian. He's the key to all of this.'

'Quite possibly,' Gideon confirmed. 'Are you coming?'

'What, all guns blazing? And what do we know about this place?' Noone replied.

'It's forty-fied,' Pop Braggan's deep voice interrupted as he stood dwarfing the threshold to the house. 'That much I do know. But why let us go to the mountain?'

'Pop ... no games now. They may have taken Aggie,' Gideon responded in all seriousness.

'I 'as 'em coming to me, today. And the airy fella Eric describes, I spent the company wiv all day,' Pop advised. 'Man of learning. Big tache.'

'OK. You need to tell me much, much more,' Gideon demanded, slowing down and taking a breath.

'They fink I 'ave perrygrins for 'em. I fink Lyle died trying to get 'em in the first place. Why d'they need 'em up at the hospital.'

'Why do they require birds of prey at all?' Gideon questioned.

'Dunno. Perhaps they want company for the ugly cat or somefink for it to chase.' Pop laughed.

'Purrsia? The bald cat from Cecile's?' Gideon quickly replied. He flashed a worried look towards Nathaniel.

'Do you have a plan?' Noone directed to Pop.

'I does as it goes,' Pop replied. 'And it involves you, Mister Noone.'

Behind the men, staring on desperately was Elizabeth Peabody. 'Aren't you forgetting something?' she shouted angrily. 'Three children are missing. Why is your priority a Professor all of a sudden?'

Gideon exhaled impatiently as if his decision should not be challenged.

Pop stepped in to defuse the situation.

'D'ya know Eric was harvesting the bugs for these men, Lizzy? Just, well you 'ave been nursing Gemima all day. You may not of known they paid 'im. Eric that is, a lot of money. He could've gone after more, roped the girls in or any-fink. Wot we does know is he did it for them. Men from Institute. It's connected,' Pop explained to her.

'Still doesn't explain why all three are missing. Gem went to greet Eric and didn't come back.'

'Eric and Aggie were in it together,' Gideon confirmed, flashing the letter over. 'He used the key from the cobbles to help her escape. No one else knew where they were. They were up to something.'

As the four of them thrashed out ideas, the slight figure of Nelly Parker strolled briskly towards them.

'Oh bleedin' 'ell, that's all we need, Nosey Parker,' Pop moaned.

'Morning, Nelly' Gideon welcomed her. 'How can I help.'

Taking Gideon by the elbow she led him away and whispered in his ear. A few moments later he thanked her with a gentle embrace before she left and he returned to his comrades.

'Nelly saw a large black car with a silver bird parked on the Steep last night. She reckons she saw the driver bundle something into the boot and drive off.'

'Bundle what, a person?' Elizabeth quickly shot back.

'Possibly. Never quite sure with Nelly, her eyes are not the best,' Gideon confirmed. Although Nelly had specifically told him a girl with black bobbed hair but couldn't confirm who, Gideon decided to keep that a secret for now.

'Pop, does that sound like the car from last night?' Noone asked.

'Yeah, could be I s'pose. Heading in the right direction, for sure.'

'Then I think we are right in our assumptions for now. The Institute is our priority. But nevertheless, we should start a search of the village just to be certain Eric isn't up to his elbows in something with the girls,' Gideon confirmed.

'Who, what and where?' came Wilson Bott's voice as he turned the corner now fully dressed. 'Eric caused a revolt at school yesterday. Had all town folk and the Priory tutors rounding up kids for hours. Apparently, they were paid a penny per bug. Lord knows where he got that money from or why.'

Gideon looked towards Pop, whose expression was that of knowing more then he should be letting on right now.

'Wilson?' Gideon asked. 'Is it possible you can help corral the WI into looking for them? The children that is. We have additional, *sensitive*, business to attend to.'

'Sybil Smythe helping the hunt for public "Ericy" number one in her eyes?' Bott replied. 'I doubt it. But I'll see what I can do. They all seem so pre-occupied with their charity work, I really would be surprised.'

'If you would be so kind, Wilson, it would mean a lot.' Gideon smiled.

Wilson Bott agreed and made his way back downhill to begin his thankless task amongst the town folk.

'Elizabeth, I know you are worried. But perhaps you could still go to school. It may be the best place to canvas the other pupils. If Eric owes them money, they'll be quick enough to help find him or even give him up,' Gideon suggested to her.

Reluctantly, she also agreed and followed closely behind Wilson Bott back down the Steep. Once out of sight, Gideon drew his two friends closer.

'Nelly confirmed that car took a girl. It could be Aggie, it could be Gemima, or it could have been all of them. But she was certain she saw a girl with dark bobbed hair. That could be Aggie.'

'She's getting on a bit, old Nosey. You sure she can see that far in the dark? Why should we trust 'er?' Pop challenged back.

'Why wouldn't we? She has nothing to gain,' Gideon explained forthrightly.

'So, Pop, you were saying you have a plan and I'm involved,' Noone said. 'What am I, bait?'

'Not quite bait, Mr Noone, no. But your expertise will certainly come in 'andy.'

*****

The leader of the men, cloaked in long leather, removed his gloves and shook Brain Louds' hand.

'A fine display, sir,' the man wheezed softly.

'Much appreciated, Heir Tuchhandler,' Louds acknowledged. 'Any news on the girl? Rumours serve to advise us of the mark of the moon.'

'Ahh, yes. My informants are closing in on her,' Tuchhandler advised. 'I trust that if we deliver her then the negotiations remain as agreed?'

'As long as you commit to your side of the bargain,' Louds confirmed.

Tuchhandler clicked his fingers and his man produced a patent leather briefcase. They clicked open the double locks and presented two sets of envelopes.

'Perhaps Ms Erket can help you translate.' Tuchhandler grinned.

Louds removed both envelopes. Opening the first was an ordnance map of the Egyptian deserts and beyond the Suez Canal. Lands he knew well. To the bottom right of the ordnance, was a black stamp of an eagle carrying a banner with a Red Swastika at its centre.

'All are guaranteed by the Fuhrer,' Tuchhandler advised pointing to a scribbled signature beneath the eagle. 'If we deliver the girl, we shall retain control of Suez and shipping. You shall only receive entitlement to the secretariat of antiquity and the monuments at Giza. Do you understand, Mr Louds?'

'Perfectly.' Louds smiled back.

Suddenly, two car lights lit all of the men up as they stood there negotiating. All of Tuchhandlers' men drew small long-barrelled pistols and aimed at the vehicle.

'Halt!' Tuchhandler advised as the car screeched across the gravelled drive to within feet of them.

The driver alighted and opened the passenger-side door. The woman in the zebra-skin coat sauntered out. She clip-clopped across the crunching stone underfoot towards the men.

'Guten adend, Sabine. Or is it good evening, Jennifer?' Tuchhandler smiled.

Sabine Erket, Jennifer James or even Jennifer Erket as she was now known, acknowledged him with a confident smile to her former handler. She whispered into Brian Louds' ear to which he chuckled sinisterly.

'It would appear we only require a single envelope after all.' He laughed.

Erket clapped her hands and the driver removed the young girl with the black bobbed hair and carried her past the on-looking men.

'The fact remains we still require a demonstration on a significant number of civilians. Not cats,' Tuchhandler insisted angrily.

'And so, you shall,' Erket confirmed before turning her back on him. She followed the driver into the Institute without so much as a second glance.

'The gods have been kind to us!' Louds shouted, raising his hands to the moon and stars and laughing uncontrollably.

Tuchhandler and his entourage returned to their cars.

'Two days, Louds!' Tuchhandler bellowed. 'You have two days.'

Chapter 46
The search

The route from the British Museum to Whitehall had become increasingly convoluted during the past year as 'Thunder Machines' and their incendiary devices had decimated large swathes of central London in an attempt to quash the government. It was early morning now, the dew glistened against the greenery of the royal parks as daybreak was upon them.

Zigzagging slowly up The Mall, between barbed wire and wooden blockades, Thompson and Belle sat in the lead car as behind them a coach full of twenty-or-so previously reliable men were being escorted under the hidden armed-guard of Smith and Jones. Of course, the men were ultimately civil servants of 'the Executive' and were advised the meeting due to take place in Whitehall was of national importance, which, in all truth, it was, but not as they would understand it and not as Thompson's bait.

Approaching Buckingham Palace and winding left towards Victoria, they would soon find their way to Wink Waverley's hidden office at Number Seven where they hoped to understand the deception at the heart of their leadership. Or at least stop the disease from spreading – any further.

'Are you sure you want to be part of this, Belle?' Thompson asked her for the umpteenth time. 'If you're having second thoughts there is a six a.m. train to the coast where you can connect to Ambledown and track-down Gideon and Nathaniel.' Thompson was obviously trying to persuade Belle to take a different path.

'I'll consider it if all else fails,' Belle curtly replied.

'If all else fails, you won't have that as an option. We may be tried for treason.'

*****

As the German entourage departed, Erket ordered her chauffeur to carry Gemima Peabody into Institute Silvera.

Brian Louds was both agitated and excited. He spoke at speed, jumping from subject to subject.

'Dr Mialora will reward you all well,' he promised them all. 'When do you obtain the birds?' he would suddenly shout at the orderlies. But before they had time to answer he was pestering Erket again. 'It is really her? After all this time?' he followed and prodded Gemima's body. 'I insist you prepare her yourself,' he directed to Erket.

Cautiously entering the hidden rear doorway, the one used to introduce Professor Malcolm just days before, Louds led the way. He paused before entering and berated his orderlies once more. 'I want nothing from you but those birds. Do not return without them,' he ordered.

Instead of directing his remaining cohorts straight on to the tunnel, which led to the hospital where the operating theatres resided and the patients convalesced, or even taking them to the double-mirrored doorway that led to the Professor's laboratory, he led them to a solid stone wall where flanked along the walls equidistant torches were lit and naked flames flickered gently.

Mr Louds walked many paces at speed, he abruptly turned, pressing both palms and forehead on the stone. Slowly using his body weight, he pushed the wall back to reveal the hidden entrance.

Erket was surprised. She had visited the building many times and never been privy to this secret chamber.

Louds took one of the wall torches and encouraged people to follow him. Leading the way, he was followed by the chauffeur and the small girl while Erket took up the rear. A downward set of stone steps led to a room shrouded in darkness. As they waited, Erket sensed Louds move to the centre of the room, where he cranked a chain pulley by hand.

From the ceiling of the room they were in, which linked directly beneath the Professor's laboratory, a hidden panel slid effortlessly to link the rooms together. The early morning light streamed through from the prism situated above. The light blue of night in its final fade, and the crimson red before sunrise lit up the room as its impeccably polished stone reflected each ray.

In the centre of the room, a humongous matt black oblong, honed from a single rock, dominated the room. It was where the sacrifice was to be staged. Where the girl would be offered to the gods.

*****

Wilson Bott had managed to wrangle a few local men. It was daybreak and the hordes of local women destined for the Ambledown Ale factory would soon be making their cautious, slippery, descent of the Steep for a twelve-hour shift. Bott was not confident he could corral enough people to search for Eric Peabody, his younger sister Gemima, and the troublemaking newcomer Agatha Chatsmore, particularly as Lady Huntington-Smythe had made it well-known that the newest evacuee had assaulted her daughter almost immediately upon arrival. Admittedly, that had endeared her to a fair few local residents but the power the lady held in influencing local society, particularly via the Woman's Institute, was more than a match for Bott's laid-back persuasion.

Meanwhile Elizabeth Peabody was trying her hardest to cover as much ground as she could. Her effortless endeavours led her through alleyways and hidden smuggler passages, Eric's usual haunts until she found herself at the bottom of the hill near school.

'Gem! Eric!' she hollered as her throat grew hoarse. 'Please, any of you, Gem, Eric! AGATHA!' she continued. Her shouting was enough to awaken many disgruntled residents.

From within their hidden prison room, deep within the school, Agatha and Eric's ear pricked up at the sound of friend and sister.

'At least someone's looking for us,' Eric mumbled through the cloth gag that made it difficult to both breathe and swallow.

Agatha attempted a smile but her restraints were equally as tight. She looked forlornly upon the contorted Sister Harvey who hadn't moved a muscle since the scorpion venom had overwhelmed her immune system. She was breathing, shallowly, but Aggie was not sure for how long.

As Elizabeth's cries faded, the faint, muffled voice of Governess Dove could be heard. Aggie scoured the room with only her eyes. To the right of Eric's waist, as he laid propped against the wall, hidden beneath the table where Dr Beckworth had previously examined her, she saw the brass cover of another air vent. It was discoloured, rusted over, much like the one hidden in the Sister's classroom.

'Eric, Eric,' Aggie mumbled, catching his attention.

She glared towards the vent, with an unblinking stare, and nodded until Eric realised what she was suggesting. He squirmed and wriggled like a pupa trying to break free from within a cocoon and alight from its mundane shell into a glorious air-bound creature of innumerable colours. Alas, no such manifestation for the young Peabody. Instead his efforts were rewarded with a bump to the head as he lurched beneath the table. At first, he used his cheekbone to try to move the vent, he slipped and it scratched deep into his facial muscle where scarlet red ran down his face and dripped below his chin. Angered by the injury, he thrashed about, expelling most of what little energy he had until he wriggled through one hundred and eighty degrees and presented the soles of his feet to the tiny brass knob. He couldn't move much but his tiny pneumatic hammering of the vent edged it a centimetre to the side so that the air flowed and with it, Dove could be heard with clarity.

'Taube, they have the girl. Repeat, they have the girl,' came the man's voice through the crackling static of the radio.

'Nein, Tuchhandler. Nein. I have the girl,' Dove replied.

'You are certain? Can you be sure? Over. I saw a girl with black bobbed hair being carried into the Institute just hours ago.'

Eric looked back at Aggie, they both realised instantly it was Gem.

'It is the wrong girl. She does not carry the mark of the moon,' Dove replied.

'Then I shall come to retrieve her. Over,' he replied.

'It is far too dangerous Tuchhandler. Not in the daylight. People are already looking for them and strangers will raise suspicions.'

'Then I will send for her tonight. Over and out.'

With that, the crackling stopped, Tuchhandler's voice disappeared once more, and the familiar click and closing of the radio as it was hidden behind the bookcase was heard. A faint knocking was heard and through the corridors came a distant call to the governess.

'Miss Dove? I say, Governess Dove?' came the softly spoken voice of the elderly lady.

Governess Dove composed herself and walked the long corridor to the school entrance. Opening the door, she was greeted by the smiling face of Nelly Parker.

'Mrs Parker, how lovely to see you. Now, what can I do for you at such an early hour?'

'My sister is missing. Sister Harvey. She usually meets me every Monday morning to tend the graves. Have you seen her at all?'

'Oh dear. Unfortunately, not. I've only just arrived myself. I'm terribly sorry. Why don't you come in for a lovely cup of tea and wait for her here?'

'That's ever so kind. Thank you,' Nelly replied cordially.

Elizabeth had been watching Nelly talk to Dove, hidden discreetly in an alleyway out of sight. As soon as Nelly entered, she noticed the door to the schoolhouse left slightly ajar. She crept cautiously towards the entrance and disappeared inside.

*****

'This had better be good,' Wink Waverley demanded as she stubbed out one of her ever-present cigarettes and left the surrounds of her burgundy leather-padded room.

'I assure you, ma'am, it is imperative,' Thompson advised her.

On leaving Number Seven, Wink spotted the coach parked down the road and a steady stream of men being escorted in pairs towards her.

'These are the men on the list, ma'am,' Thompson advised her.

'What the hell are you doing bringing them to meet me?' Wink asked aggressively.

'You would never have met any of these men if protocols had been followed, correct?' he asked.

'Of course. And you are breaking all those rules the closer they get,' she grumbled back.

'Well, let's see if they recognise you, shall we?'

Wink stopped in her tracks. 'Do not forget your station, young man,' she ordered, her good eye staring intently at him. Wink was no amateur spy and had more experience then Malling and Draper combined let alone the upstart Thompson. 'I'll play along with your charade for now. Then I expect a damn good explanation,' she barked.

As Wink and Thompson approached, the men began to salute in acknowledgement – but not at them. Following their gazes, Wink turned and saw Colonel Malling lined up to greet them. He thanked them a pair at a time.

'This is most un-flavoursome,' Wink snarled. 'With me, now!' she snapped.

She entered a hidden door to the side of the street, ordering Thompson to follow, and marched him through a secretive labyrinth of corridors until they were magically re-entering the Burgundy room again.

Belle watched on from the car some distance away. If within an hour Thompson had not returned, she would be on the next train, travelling south. She sat in anticipation as the minutes slowly ticked away.

'What the devil are you playing at, Thompson? You better start explaining yourself before I incarcerate you at His Majesty's pleasure.'

Thompson slid his hand inside his inner coat pocket and produced the list. He placed it on Wink's desk as he took a chair opposite her. In crossing his legs, his hand would be close to the hidden pistol at his ankle. He hoped with all his heart it wouldn't come to that.

'You may wish to turn to the final page, ma'am. It will be of interest to you.'

*****

Elizabeth, after sneaking in, hid behind the large Aspidistra and heard Dove in conversation with Nelly. Seizing her opportunity, she headed for Sister Harvey's classroom. Neither Gem nor Aggie were there, which really was no surprise to her at all. She would have been surprised if Eric was anywhere near the school grounds he detested so much. Nevertheless, she took a moment to quietly scour the room and listen attentively to any creaks from the attic rooms above. She was certain that with the exception of Nelly and Dove, she had the place to herself. As she strolled around the room looking for any clues, though not really knowing what she was looking for, a tiny splintering crack came from the sole of her shoe. Bending her foot outwards, it revealed a slither of glass. It was insignificant in many ways but nevertheless she knelt down carefully to search for more. Combing the floor with her hands in the light of the morning she found a few more slithers of glass and tiny fragments of wood. They appeared to be conjoined and suggested a broken frame or exhibit case of some description. She lay down and scanned the classroom floor. There was no obvious object that matched her thoughts but beneath Sister Harvey's desk, the dark corner of fabric caught her eye. She shuffled over and edging it out carefully she found the charred corner and remaining crest of Priory colours. It was older, different to the badge now and its edges were singed in black and brown.

In the centre of the crest three initials intertwined in perfectly stitched calligraphy.

'C S M,' Elizabeth read to herself before leaving the classroom and taking the crest with her.

*****

'I'm sure there's a perfectly reasonable answer, Mrs Parker, and your sister will turn up soon. She's usually up with the larks so I'd expect her by seven, not long now. Why not wait? Tea?'

Nelly smiled politely towards Governess Dove as she was poured a cup of morning tea.

'Tell me, Mrs Parker. Has the school changed much since your time here?'

'Yes and no,' Nelly replied. 'It looks very similar. And, no doubt, those malevolent Priory girls are still up to their old tricks. This room is almost untouched, from what I recall. I notice the new case though,' she continued, pointing over Dove's shoulder. Dove hardly batted an eyelid to this. 'But I'm surprised the crest has gone,' she finished, pointing to the recently removed framed Priory crest that, which left a clean mark from the dust, where it had been mounted for so many years.

'How so? I'm so new to most of this any enlightenment gratefully received.' Dove smiled back.

'Take no notice of me, dear. Just reminds me of someone very special and the true meaning to be a Priory girl. Not to matter, really.'

The pair smiled cordially at one another waiting for the bells of St Joan's to strike seven.

Aggie and Eric had been listening intently. Aggie more so then ever once word of the crest was mentioned. Eric was just about to start thrashing about hoping Nelly would hear him in return. Aggie stopped him immediately.

'Nelly wouldn't stand a chance,' she mumbled to Eric. Dove had overcome the three of them so easily and had either the pistol or the poison ready to deploy. Nelly was not as strong as her sister and would soon be overcome.

'We need another plan,' he mumbled back, the blood on his cheek beginning to dry.

Aggie nodded as they sat back and began to think.

Seven crystal clear chimes echoed through the spires and broke the awkward silence in the governess's room. Nelly slurped her remaining tea and stood up.

'So grateful for your hospitality, Governess. I shall bake you a cake to accompany that fine tea.' Nelly smiled 'But first I shall go and help with the search party. Perhaps my sister is with the missing children.'

'Missing children?' Dove feigned ignorance.

'That's right, Eric and Gemima Peabody and the new girl, Chatsmore,' Nelly informed her.

'Oh dear, I wasn't aware of that. Perhaps I should help too?'

'That would be very noble of you,' Nelly advised her.

'That's exactly what I will do then.' Dove smiled, not believing her luck. 'I shall close the school today and all teachers and pupils may help with the search.'

'Bravo, Governess. All the children will appreciate that. Though Lady Huntington-Smythe may not,' Nelly said, delighted.

'I am sure she is busy enough organising the WI.' Dove chuckled back.

Aggie and Eric looked at one another. They had no chance of making themselves known now, not if the school was closed. They needed to escape, they needed a plan more than ever, and before nightfall.

*****

Turning to the final page of the list, Wink Waverley smiled, bemused by what she was reading.

Thompson unclipped his ankle holster and trained his gun on her.

'You could hang for that, Thompson. Should you be wrong.' She laughed, unflinching.

'Why would you laugh at such a serious allegation?' he asked angrily.

'Because whatever it is you think you know, it is wrong. I know nothing of this organisation OSIRIS.'

'That's what you are bound to say, just like Malling said it, just like his men said it. All his men! All denying it.'

'I admit it looks more than suspicious. Care to consider what the key denominator is though?' Wink allowed a momentary silence before she then volleyed back. 'OSIRIS! Thompson, OSIRIS!'

Thompson paused with his trigger finger poised. Wink could make any move, any number of hidden switches or alarms, and he would be incarcerated. Though he may take her out before help arrived.

'Cigarettes, pass me your cigarettes,' e demanded.

'I don't buy them pre-made, dear boy, haven't you learnt anything? I prefer to roll my own. Can't stand those damn filters,' Wink replied, throwing a smart leather pouch of tobacco and papers over the desk.

Thompson thumbed the tobacco in the pouch. Strains of brown, orange, amber but definitely no violets or blues shimmering through. It was not like the tigress's preferred vape. No exotic filter, no silk thread, just raw tobacco and liquorice papers. He tossed them back at her.

'Sit,' he ordered.

'Mr Thompson, if I had wished to alert any of any guards, I have innumerable ways to do so. So why don't you lower that weapon? And don't believe for one minute you are in charge.'

'I don't think so,' Thompson replied. 'Not until I speak with Malling too.'

'Very well.' Wink frowned. 'Let's call him in.'

*****

'Good morning, ladies and gentlemen,' Wilson Bott announced as the paltry volume of retirees, drunks and misfits who were willing to search for the children gathered around him at the cenotaph. Not one single member of the WI despite the Sheriff's best efforts. Not even McGregor, much to Elizabeth's disgust as she arrived like a child pied piper up the Steep.

'Mr Bott!' Elizabeth shouted with a steady stream of evacuee children behind her. 'Governess Dove has closed the school today to help with the search for the children.'

'And my sister,' Nelly Parker piped up.

Elizabeth flashed her a look. Sister Harvey was missing too? She wasn't sure what the broken glass and crest meant but she needed to inform Nelly right away.

'OK then, children. Each adult will coordinate the search in a grid like so,' Bott announced, pointing out a marked map of Ambledown. 'You, children, are the eyes and legs of the search. Listen to the adults carefully and hopefully, we will find them sooner rather than later. I'm sure you know Eric and co's preferred hideouts.'

'Eric'll be dead if we don't!' shouted out a few of the disgruntled children owed significant pennies by the Peabody boy.

Wilson Bott didn't have the heart to point out the irony of that statement. If they didn't find the children it was likely they were dead. Instead, he gave a reassuring pat on Elizabeth's shoulder as he blew his whistle for the search to commence.

'Nelly, Mrs Parker?' Elizabeth enquired.

'Yes, dear, how can I help?'

'I'm not sure what it means, but I found this earlier this morning while you were taking tea with the governess.' Elizabeth presented the crest to her. Nelly smiled and a slight tear welled in her eye. 'What does it mean, Mrs Parker?' Elizabeth asked.

'It means many things to many people but in today's context, I believe the children and my sister are in extreme danger. We should inform Gideon right away.'

Chapter 47

The Protocols

'You're treading a very thin line, Wink,' Malling bawled at Waverley as Smith and Jones escorted him into the Burgundy room.

'First, you incarcerate me and then you break all protocols by bringing my men here. None of them knew each other before this day and now you have jeopardised national security,' he continued in a high-pitched yell.

'Please, don't allow me to take all the blame, Thompson. Do bring Colonel Malling up to speed, preferably before your court marshall,' Wink advised.

Thompson was cornered now and the tables turned. However he played his hand, at least one of his superior officers could overwhelm him. Wink had known that all the while and comfortably sparked up a cigarette again. Thompson only had the beginnings of a preposterous theory. Given that Belle Soames was likely to leave for the coast within the next quarter of an hour he had to be fast but at least she could inform Gideon and Nathaniel if all else failed.

'Come on, boy. I don't have all day,' Malling snapped. 'Facts, no fiction, please.'

Pulling the card and photograph from his pocket, he laid them out in front of Malling. Gesturing to Wink, she handed over the list too.

'This list was discovered in Professor Montague Soames' office. Montague Soames is –'

'I bloody well know who he is,' Malling interrupted him. 'Cut to the chase!'

'OK,' Thompson acknowledged, continuing succinctly and at speed. 'The list was found in Monty's office, placed there during the night that this charitable foundation,' he continued, placing the embossed card of OSIRIS in front of him, 'provided a seminar. The list of attendees, if you care to skim it, is almost entirely made up of the men outside, your men. With the exceptions of yourself, Wink, and Major Boyd Collingdale.'

'And Draper, I assume?' Malling replied, pointing to his now-missing colleague in the photograph.

'Therein lies an anomaly. Not Draper, no. He is not on the list,' Thompson confirmed.

'Doesn't make sense. If he is in the photo why not on the list?' Malling replied, surprised by this revelation.

'He may have infiltrated them,' Wink interjected. 'He's missing, remember? Kidnapped, we have presumed.'

'Doesn't enlighten me much, Thompson. More holes than Swiss cheese, my boy. I don't know where to begin to tear this apart,' Malling grumbled.

'If you would be so kind, ma'am.' Thompson gestured to Wink to turn off the light from behind her desk. Plunged into darkness, he lit the ultraviolet beam. 'Do you see it, sir? Do you see it now?'

Malling picked up the photograph and stared intently at the illuminated image of himself. 'What the hell does that mean?' he asked.

'The hawk head is suggestive of a leading Egyptian deity. My expert advises an extremely important presence.'

For a moment Malling issued a self-indulgent laugh before he realised it wasn't praise being heaped upon him. He glanced at Draper's totem too. 'And this? The dog?' Malling asked once more.

'Lord of the Underworld. A guide into the afterlife by all accounts,' Thompson replied

'Doesn't surprise me with that secretive sod.' Malling erupted in laughter.

'Colonel Malling, may I remind you this is of national importance,' Wink interrupted.

'Oh, come on, Wink. A bit of paint, a light show. What next, smoke and mirrors?'

'Funnily enough,' Thompson replied, revealing the flickering luminance within the tobacco at the end of the exotic cigarette stub.

All of them gazed on as Thompson rotated the cards to reveal either a Yes or No, which iridescently illuminated on each revolution.

'Still not convinced it's anything but a sham. A card with words in invisible ink. Christ, we've been using that idea for years.'

'Not like this we haven't,' Thompson was keen to challenge him.

'Someone is doing a very fine job of disrupting the status quo by the looks of things to me.' Malling stood his ground.

'And what about all of these too?' Thompson finished by throwing all the cards from Malling's men on Wink's desk. The illuminated pinks and purples and the multiple instructions shone brightly in front of them. 'So, you think it's still a sham now?' Thompson questioned. 'I have seen bigger and far more significant examples of such writings daubed across the walls of the British Museum, where this all began. I have a witness too. Oh, bugger what's the time?' Thompson changed tone suddenly realising they had been talking for over an hour and Belle may have already departed.

'Five past,' Wink replied, turning the light on.

'Oh no, Belle.' Thompson lowered his weapon and went to leave.

'Oh no, not so fast,' Wink ordered, a pistol now trained on him. She must have had it secured from beneath her desk during those dark moments.

'I am sure Miss Soames is more than capable and trust you put in place a method of communication?' said Wink.

'Bravo, Wink,' Malling replied, snatching Thompson's pistol.

'You refer to me as ma'am, Malling. And for the record, I believe that Thompson at least believes it himself, despite not one of us able to unravel this mystery. Do you trust Miss Soames? Do you believe in this theory?' she said, returning his pistol back to him in front of the protesting Colonel Malling.

'I do, ma'am. But it is yet to unravel, as you say.'

'Then let us stick to what we know. Colonel Malling, I am giving you an express order to explain the Protocols to Thompson.'

'But, Wink–' Malling challenged forthrightly.

'It's ma'am and don't let me repeat myself again. This man risked a court marshall or even a bullet to protect this country. Could've easily popped me if he was a traitor. A little goodwill may just convince him otherwise so the least you can do is explain your day job. Understood?'

*****

Erket examined the hidden chamber. The white polished stone with deep grey and black veins covered the floors and the walls. There was a ceiling of sorts, consisting of a symmetrical framework of wooden joists to support the interconnected laboratory above. The walls sloped inward, joining the room above, and leading towards the pinnacle's glass prism.

Erket had not noticed them at first but as the room lit up around her, two monumental sculptures appeared from the shadows, motionlessly stood guardians at the far end of the large stone altar. The bodies of muscular men with heads of ancient animal deities bore down upon her.

At the foot of the altar, stood a staff of silver and gold. Silver feathers spanned outwards from the centre where a golden talon clasped the crystallised stone at its core. The Scarlet Scarab was awakening. The day was young and the inclement coastal weather saw clouds that denied it its full power from the sun's rays. It sat there patiently, pulsing, as the first chink of light engaged its presence and lit the embers inside. In full daylight, its dazzling display of red would light up like the very flames of an Anubian underworld.

Erket walked around the perimeter of the room. A curved channel, carved in the stone surrounding the sacrificial table. It reflected an invisible liquid.

'I can see you are impressed,' Louds called out across the echoing room.

Erket smiled back as she gazed on in wonder.

'Come, bring the girl.' He beckoned to the driver.

The chauffeur carried Gemima between his forearms and moved to place her at the altar.

'Wait,' Louds ordered. 'Sabine, take the girl. I bestow you the honour of preparing her,' he confirmed as he crept silently to gaze upon Gemima.

Erket took the girl within her own arms. But as she did so, without warning, Louds thrust a dagger into the spine of the chauffeur, killing him. Erket screamed in terror, waking Gemima. Louds meanwhile dragged the corpse on to the large onyx stone as if hauling a haunch of meat to the butchers' block.

Slowly and precisely he positioned the man's dying body star-shaped across the smooth black stone. Shackling him to restraints in each corner he then proceeded to cut into the man's wrists so the blood quickly drained from his body and down through a hidden canal beneath him.

Gemima let out a series of screams before Sabine could subdue her with another scorpion's kiss.

'We could not risk any more witnesses.' Louds laughed maniacally. 'And I had to test my creation.'

At Erket's foot, a small stream of blood began to flow around the carved channel from beneath the altar. Circulating around the large stone table it formed a scarlet perimeter. Louds took the naked flame of a torch and lit it. The blood combined with the ethereal water and lit up around the altar. The glowing eye of RA flickered back for all to see.

'Prepare the girl, Sabine. She must be cleansed of impurities before nightfall comes.'

*****

The large wooden clog remained proudly placed above Tink's shop. The blinds were down and the sign advised it was closed.

The four men huddled around a table to the rear of the shop and far from prying eyes. Pop Braggan took up two spaces as his canine sentry sat attentively at the front, on guard, should they be interrupted.

'Is that it?' Noone replied to Pop's plan

'Got a better one 'ave ya?' Pop challenged him.

Noone shook his head but raised his eyebrow towards Gideon.

'Are you absolutely sure, Pop? It's not without risk to man or beast,' Gideon double-checked with his giant friend.

Pop took a small shiny penny from his waistcoat pocket. It was highly polished and shone brightly under the light within Tink's workshop.

'Eds or tails Mr Noone?' Pop asked Nathaniel as a slight challenge.

'Heads,' Noone replied.

Pop flicked the coin from his large thumb. As it spun through the air, the whoosh and swish of feathers darted past him in black and white. The Lady snatched the coin in mid-air and returned to Pop's shoulder to return the prize and collect her rewarding strand of dried mutton.

'You see, Mr Noone? The Lady will go for anything that shines, anything. And at that moment we seize our opportunity. And the only head that matters is your melted one and the orderlies must see you for it to work.'

'Understood,' Nathaniel acknowledged.

There was a tapping at the window. Luna growled defensively at the door as Tinker pushed passed and opened the blinds to a slight narrowing.

'Good day, Mister Tinker,' came the pleasant voices of two elderly ladies. 'May you oblige us and help with securing the bunting?'

'Bunting?' Tinker replied while his cohorts looked on confused.

'The Women's Institute of Ambledown are proudly raising funds for the war effort you see. All proceeds go to our boys abroad,' came the delicate whispers from outside.

The men concluded their meeting and decided to reconvene at five p.m. at Le Chat Noir. As they left, they noticed many women and many strings of paper bunting being strung across the road leading up the Steep.

'I say,' one of the women said, as Pop's hulking frame squeezed through the doorway. 'Who needs a ladder when we have you.' She smiled pointing upwards.

The three remaining men laughed and made haste as Pop Braggan, the brutal, bare-knuckle giant, succumbed to the ladies charms and helped them secure the bunting above the shop front by tethering it to the iron flame baskets that lined the shops and houses throughout the town.

'Seems more people are interested in decoration then looking for missing children,' Noone said to Gideon.

'It entirely depends on who the children are,' Gideon replied.

He stared towards the very busy Lady Huntington-Smythe. If Henny had gone missing, he was sure her mother would have commanded a battalion to track her down.

'Gideon,' came the call from Nelly Parker striding down the hill with Elizabeth.

'What news, ladies? How goes the search?' he enquired.

'Children and drunks, mainly. None of them,' Elizabeth confirmed, pointing in a disgruntled manner at ladies of the WI.

'OK. We'll join you now. This, by way, is my dearest of friends: Nathaniel Noone.'

Both of the women looked on at Nathaniel's horrific scarring but smiled politely.

'Before you do so, Gideon, may I have a word?' Nelly enquired as she held the charred Priory crest in her palm and presented it to him. 'It is most important.'

*****

Wink Waverley had ordered Smith and Jones to stand watch outside of the Burgundy room. In a gesture of faith, she had provided one of them with the pistol she had recently trained on Thompson and, in turn, Thompson had offered up the ankle gun recently trained on her.

'You have the floor, Colonel,' Wink ordered.

'The Protocols,' Malling began, then took a deep breath before pulling down a map of London that was suspended from the ceiling behind Wink's desk. 'The Protocols are a sequence of communications between multiple parties spread across the city.'

Malling took a large ink pen and drew out the key locations. 'Big Ben, Tower Bridge, Greenwich Observatory,' he began to reel off. 'St Paul's Cathedral –'

'Yes, yes, we get the point, Malling. Cut to the chase,' Wink hurried him.

'The two principles of the Protocols are to protect and to attack. So, during any air-raid, once enemy craft have been spotted, the first protocol that discovers such an event duly informs the second protocol and third protocols, their neighbours.' He drew two arrows pointing either way from any given point. 'There is no set number but a principle of process. Each location is accountable for passing on the locations before informing HQ of completion,' Malling continued, pointing to the flanking locations on the map. And demonstrating a domino effect as each message was passed on.

'And how are messages relayed?' Thompson asked

'By secure wire, each of them within a garrison of anti-aircraft guns, and 1000 watt spotting lamps. You see, what happens is that, in turn, each correspondence continues to inform their next protocol until the circle is complete.' Malling drew a final dotted circular line surrounding the city.

'Why not have HQ inform them all?'

'It's an admirable question and, to be frank, it's actually too time-consuming. We played out many scenarios to realise its inefficiencies and weaknesses. Messages in the current protocols can move quicker than the attacking enemy. Also, if HQ was compromised as a single point of contact, the city's defences would fall. Should one of them, the Protocols that is, be compromised, in this system, the message will be received via the other route until the circle is complete and vice versa. You see once they have informed us each location then branches out and informs their local area network. It's a complex spider's web that spreads like wildfire. Should HQ fail to receive confirmation from any branch we intervene and engage with the next branches to ensure the network of air-raid sirens and anti-aircraft personnel are deployed.'

'The codes between Protocols, are they set in stone?' Thompson continued to investigate.

'Another good question, young man. The answer is no. They change hourly and are symbiotic of one another each being a question and an answer though not actually related. Each Protocol is an answer to a question set out to its neighbours and only provided via ourselves. The answers are not actually the answers, just a word we have decided. So, for instance, if we said the Capital of England is …' Malling encouraged.

'London,' Thompson replied.

'Our answer may be jam. Completely incorrect, of course, but sent out to be expected that way.'

'And who knows about them and sets them?' Thompson asked again.

'Your inquiry is commendable, but I cannot divulge that,' Malling replied.

'Correct,' Wink confirmed. 'Only half-a-dozen or so people, two of which are in this room, the others' way beyond your clearance level,' she concluded.

'So, if these persons are such key components to the security of our nation, what happens when they are not there?' it was Thompson's final question for the day.

*****

'Do you think she knows?' Gideon asked Nelly.

'If not, she is getting close,' Nelly answered.

'Who knows what?' Elizabeth interrupted.

'Agatha,' Gideon answered. 'She was trying to figure out a puzzle that had been set for her.'

'The one about the seven sisters?' Elizabeth asked, innocently.

Gideon was intrigued that had been brought to light but offered no reply.

'I think she's very close,' said Nelly.

'If that is the case, Nelly, then could she have discovered it at school?' Gideon asked.

'How she would've known I don't know. More than likely, Jane was trying to hide it.'

'Who's Jane?' Elizabeth asked

'Sister Harvey to you. Jane Harvey, my sister,' Nelly replied.

Gideon was deep in thought. He couldn't piece all the components together. He racked and racked his brain, playing out scenarios like a chess grandmaster. Upon the Steep, the WI were in full flow, hanging bunting from fire nest to fire nest oblivious to woes beyond their own remit. Gideon had had enough and stormed to the most vocal crowd.

'Don't do anything stupid!' Noone called out as he skulked behind, conscious of hiding his scars beneath his fedora as much as he could.

'What the hell is wrong with you all? Children are missing. It's not a party.'

'The party's tonight,' one of them said and smiled before going on about her business, completely ignoring any mention of the kids.

'And besides, they're only evacuees,' said Henrietta Huntington-Smythe and laughed.

Noone took particular exception and strode forward. He removed his hat and stared nose to nose with her and through his remaining good eye until she burst into tears.

'Monster, you're a monster,' she cried as she ran to seek out her mother. Nathaniel was extremely pleased with himself.

'We'll have no luck here,' Gideon confirmed. 'Elizabeth, Nelly, are you OK to continue the search? Nathaniel and I have preparations to make.'

Chapter 48

The stranger on the train

Colonel Malling, Wink Waverley, and her subordinate Thompson ruminated the position they were in. By some quirk of coincidence, they had found themselves in an environment previously not considered throughout *the Executive's* meticulous efforts to protect London.

They had planned for passwords and the encoding of information. They had men in place and trusted support to those men should they turn or be compromised. Yet somehow, the scenario of all their men and a hidden agenda of deceit widespread across their organisation had not been considered at all. There would have to be more than one leak or several moles to accomplish even half of what Thompson may be suggesting. A chink in the armour only someone close may have considered. Nevertheless, as incomprehensible as it seemed, the three of them considered their immediate options.

'Ma'am, I still maintain this is a ruse. A damn clever one at that, granted. You may just have played right into their hands,' Malling addressed his superior but directed his insults towards Thompson.

'And seeing what I have seen, I disagree,' Thompson argued.

'The fact of the matter is that none of us understands any of this fully,' Wink said, asserting her authority.

'Ma'am, if I may be so bold? We have credible intelligence an air-raid is imminent. The MET advise cloudy weather with the strong possibility of rain for this evening. Perfect for a secret pass by the Luftwaffe,' Malling passionately exclaimed. 'If these men are not returned to their outposts soon, we will have no defence against the attacks at all. We could endanger tens of thousands of citizens.'

'And what if they *are* somehow compromised?' Thompson said, standing his ground.

'Unfortunately, young man, It is a scenario that was never considered. Arrogance on our part maybe but I concur with the Colonel,' Wink responded.

Malling raised a victorious eyebrow and pumped out his chest in what he saw as points scored against the young upstart, as he saw him.

Wink was not as confident as her response suggested but could see no other way, for now.

'Malling, you oversee that the men return to their positions. Under strict observation, you hear me? Two chaperones per man. If any of them look to be straying they are to be removed, all necessary force. Do you hear me?'

'That's dozens of men to find at such short notice. I'm –' Malling grumbled.

'If you are unable to fulfil my request you can always relinquish your command to Thompson,' she interrupted forthrightly.

Malling grumbled despondently then left via a hidden door through the burgundy-padded panelling.

'I hope for our sakes you are wrong, Thompson,' Wink advised. 'Let's forget about that gun you had pointed at me, shall we, for now?' she offered.

'Thank you, ma'am,' Thompson accepted, begrudgingly.

'Don't thank me yet. We could all be buggered. I want you and the couple of men you have outside to continue your investigations. Find me proof; more evidence that leads us to where the answers lie.'

Thompson duly accepted her offer; all the while, hoping Belle was halfway to Ambledown.

*****

Belle Soames was just south of Croydon when the locomotive came to an abrupt halt. Recent bomb damage to the rails had delayed trains entering and leaving London, and she was now stuck in darkness in the middle of a tunnel.

Impatiently, she began to wait for a conductor or announcement saying they were on the move but after half an hour of anxiety, no one came. There was no immediate light in her carriage, just the distant suggestion at the tunnel end, and the empty carriage made her uncomfortable. The only object she had to help her was the peculiar torch with the violet beam. Conscious the battery would not last forever, she flashed it in short bursts and moved ten paces at a time as she navigated the carriages.

'Hello?' she called out. 'Hello? Is anybody there?' she called as she made her way through the darkness to the next carriage with the dimmest of light guiding her.

'Hello,' came a guard's voice as he carried a dimly lit paraffin lamp by his side.

'Thank goodness.' Belle sighed with relief. 'I thought I was all alone.'

'Not many on here today. Lucky for them.' The guard laughed.

'Will we be moving anytime soon?' she enquired.

'Your guess is as good as mine,' Replied the guard, unhelpfully. 'The line's pretty damaged from all the bombing. That's a curious thing though. Don't see that every day,' he said, gesturing towards Belle's hand.

'Oh yes, of course,' Belle replied politely, scrambling for an explanation. 'One of these new blackout torch thingies.'

'Oh right. Is that why it made the tunnel light up with all the pretty colours?' the guard asked.

'I'm sorry, what do you mean?' Belle replied inquisitively.

'I saw it. When you flashed it, as you walked, little flickers of colour cascading outside of the window.'

'Can you show me?' Belle replied.

The guard squeezed past her and stood where she had stood.

'Can you dim your light, just for a moment, please?' Belle asked of him.

Rotating the brass fuel wheel, the light reduced to the tiniest of flickers and they were both surrounded in darkness. Belle flashed her torch beam at the window. Sure enough, tiny sparks of iridescent colour caught the perspiring condensation of the outside window. It was like watching a miniature firework display.

'Beautiful that. Makes a change,' the guard replied.

Belle moved closer to the window and shone the torch intently beyond the droplets of light and water that had accumulated on the pane. Beyond the window, upon the wall of the tunnel, a large curve illuminated in violet-blue and below it the tops of four letters. As far as she could make out the first letter of which suggested an 'O'.

'What's that then?' the guard continued to ask.

Belle switched her torch off. 'May I?' she gestured towards the paraffin lamp.

'Be my guest,' the guard replied.

Turning the lamp to full power, there came a strong reflection of the yellow flame from the window and just themselves staring back beyond it.

'Blimey, that's some trick. Where did it go?' the guard asked in awe. 'I prefer the pretty lights, not his ugly mug. I see that everywhere, every day.'

Belle was speechless. From beyond her reflection, she could see two large piercing eyes and the famous moustache. Something she saw hundreds, if not thousands of times throughout the streets of the capital. The tell-tale pointed finger directed itself towards her.

'Britons, your country needs you!' she read from the giant poster.

*****

Sabine Erket had just witnessed her driver executed in front of her eyes. As she paced anxiously around the altar on which he lay, the carvings and runes subtly carved into it made it much more than a sacrificial stone. It was also a sarcophagus, it had to be. Brian Louds and the secretive Dr Mialora would both execute and bury their intended victim at the same time she immediately thought.

'Sabine, come with me. I need you to wake the Professor,' Louds asked politely as if nothing had just transpired within the room. He ordered one of his orderlies to dispose of the body and at the same time, serving as a reminder of his malevolent intent, he then ordered the other to lift Gem's lucid body and follow them from the chamber.

The slender stairwell allowed Sabine to remove her belt and buckle. Unlocking the Death-stalker clasp her final remaining cigarette served as a reminder that soon the case would be full and replenished to its former glory. But, for now, Mr Louds' orders were clear and the hidden serum was swiftly procured.

*****

'I need to get back to London as soon as possible,' Belle ordered the guard.

'I'm sorry, miss. This train is southbound.'

'I need to get off, now!' she demanded and lurched towards the handle of a slam-door.

'Whoa! You'll end up decapitating yourself or worse,' the guard shouted, grabbing her wrist as right on cue, the flash of light and stream of smoke thundered north on a London bound train.

'Worse?' Belle laughed at the realisation of her stupidity.

'Yeah, worse … then um … losing your head.' The guard laughed at himself. 'And you did almost lose it just then.'

'I need to get back to London, urgently.' Belle begged.

'I gathered that.' The guard said bemused. 'Stay here. I'll see what I can do.'

Belle was tempted to alight the moment he was gone, what were the odds of another train immediately after the previous one? A rush of light and smoke once more heading north soon provided the answer and she sat, exasperated waiting for the guard.

The carriage lurched as a high shrill of a whistle expelled a sound that reverberated and pierced throughout the tunnel. The wheels slowly began to turn as the locomotive's motion moved in the opposite direction. The guard rushed past shouting as he did so.

'East Croydon, ladies and gentlemen. The next stop is a return to East Croydon as we await further instructions.'

'Thank you!' Belle shouted as she sat down for the short journey that would take her to the outskirts of the city.

*****

Professor Meredith Malcolm, the meticulous entomologist and part-time taxidermist, looked nothing like his reputation would suggest. Contorted into the foetal position, his finger-joints crippled a tense white and strained like grasping talons. The bilious drool that now absorbed into his fine facial hair a product of the poison administered hours previously.

It took a lot to surprise Sabine Erket but the state in which the Professor had been left to rot was no reward considering the epiphany presented to his captors. He had solved a riddle that many far more respected experts had not.

'Wake him, Sabine,' Louds ordered.

Removing the small green phial from the cigarette case buckle, she injected a pinhead of serum into his elbow vein. A minute or so later, a huge wheeze of breath exhaled from his chest cavity before violent vomiting began.

'There, there, Professor,' Louds sadistically comforted him. 'You'll be as right as rain in no time.'

The Professor's eyes moved in and out of focus. Sabine Erket helped him to his feet. Where once the laboratory table had been covered with the papyrus and velum cartouche that presented the ancient riddle he had solved; now, in front of him, was the carcass of a recently drowned, furless, cat. Next to it an enamel kidney dish, presumably for its organs, was accompanied by a set of surgical scalpels and a large brown bottle of embalming fluid. Next to that, a set of bandages for the incumbent mummification.

'I believe you know what to do,' Louds expressed, as the Professor returned. 'You may also prepare the girl here,' Louds demanded of Sabine, patting down the same table.

Meredith Malcolm looked on in horror, assuming cat and girl had met with the same fate.

'I will be no party to the butchering of a child,' Professor Malcolm shouted, enraged.

'Oh, she isn't even dead, Professor – yet. Just clean her up. Where would the fun be in a sacrifice if the subject was dead in the first place.' He laughed. 'You'll stay here and supervise until it is finished,' Louds curtly ordered Sabine.

She acknowledged his request with a polite nod.

*****

Thompson, Smith, and Jones had boarded their black saloon and had headed to Shaftesbury. Quite where to start was beyond Thompson but he required additional support and headed for the goods entrance to Fortnum's.

The combination of the advert *The Department* had not authorised, alongside the subterfuge of Miss Jennifer James had meant they were saying a fond farewell to their headquarters which they had only just returned to.

'Sir!' Smith called out from the driver's seat. 'Is she supposed to be anywhere near here, sir?'

Thompson looked through the windscreen. Outside of the entrance and being escorted by two of his plain-clothed officers was Hilary Nevis. Next to her was a very tall woman, with straight black hair, clutching an envelope.

'Mr Thompson? Please, Mr Thompson?' She waved him down and stood in front of his car.

'Shall I deal with this, sir?' piped up Jones.

'It's fine,' Thompson replied, winding down his window. 'Miss Nevis, you are suspended pending further investigations, you know that.'

The nervous Hilary Nevis shook her head in acknowledgement.

'I k-k-know, sir,' she stuttered. 'I know, but something was bugging me about what I said.'

'OK, tell me.'

'Well, first, may I introduce Lady James. Jennifer's mother.'

Thompson looked back confused to his colleagues. Each of them had guns braced in case of any surprises.

'Lady James, a pleasure to meet you, ma'am, but I am afraid I cannot discuss anything with you.'

The good lady, an imposing figure in comparison to timid Hilary, stepped forward and presented the envelope to Thompson. He looked inside and pulled out several photographs.

'Those are the most recent ones of my daughter and my husband,' The lady advised pointing to a smiling Jennifer embraced by her father.

Thompson looked at Jennifer. You could now tell she was definitely the tigress in the photo he held within his pocket. He, in return, produced the image from the OSIRIS fundraiser and shared it with her mother.

'Could this be your daughter?' he asked.

'Of course, it's my daughter,' she replied without hesitation. 'Why on earth she would wear such a garish wig is beyond me? She has such beautiful jet-black hair. But that's her alright. That coat I would recognise anywhere. It was a gift from Donald, her fiancé, well – fiancé to be.'

Thompson was stunned. The Lady didn't even blink or deny anything. Had she been informed of the seriousness of Jennifer's crime? 'Donald?' Thompson questioned.

'Yes, there he is, looking dapper in his tuxedo,' she said pointing out Draper in the shadows. 'Such a sweetie since her father went missing. People talked, about the age gap, you know. But he has been nothing but a rock to our family.'

Thompson took a deep breath. This was certainly unexpected. No one, not even her best friend Hilary had known of their closer acquaintance; and all relationships should have been declared to superiors.

'Your husband, ma'am. You say he disappeared. What did he do?'

'He's Sir Wallace James,' Hilary interjected excitedly.

'*The* Sir Wallace James? The famous surgeon?' Thompson replied.

'Well, I doubt that is such a common name, sir, but yes, he was my husband,' Lady James confirmed.

'Was? I am so sorry. My condolences, did he pass recently.'

'He disappeared; no trace, no note. Very unlike him, who was as conscientious a family man as ever you could meet. We presumed a victim of those dreadful Thunder Machines that plague us,' Lady James continued. 'It was he who first introduced Jennifer to Donald. We did not expect any kind of romance but he offered her a job, without hesitation. Could not divulge much, official secrets and so forth. And rightly so. She has a double first from Cambridge. We were so happy, so proud.'

'And where did your husband meet Draper? I mean Donald?' Thompson asked, correcting himself.

'A charitable dinner. My husband is an expert in the field of rehabilitation for burns victims.'

Thompson's obvious confusion was not lost on Lady James.

'Are you OK, young man? You look like you have seen a ghost.'

'Smith, escort Hilary and the good Lady to the office. I shall return imminently. I need you to corroborate what we just heard; times, places, etc. But, please, all remain here just for now. Jones, Whitehall … immediately. And, Smith, mum's the word. No one knows about this until I contact you via the wire.'

*****

Sabine Erket and Professor Meredith Malcolm did not speak to one another as they independently prepared their subjects for Mr Louds.

The stench of Purrsia's entrails was enough to make Sabine wretch as Professor Malcolm removed them along with the vital organs to create the cavity so as to preserve the cat. Purrsia's final journey would come after embalming.

Softly Sabine dampened Gemima's brow and removed a combination of dried blood and dirt. Still subdued, Gem's body was dead weight and awkward to move.

'Professor, I need your assistance,' she said. 'Help me sit her up.'

Meredith Malcolm did not respond verbally but dutifully placed his scalpel down and moved to assist Sabine Erket. They folded Gemima upwards, her head flopping as she sat 'L-shaped' like a string-less marionette. Sabine moved behind Gemima and continued cleaning the blood from her hair. The injury sustained while skipping, combined with the hustle and bustle of the car journey, had streamed blood through her newly acquired bob and down her spine. As she reached the shoulder blades, she paused and looked at the semi-circular crescent pattern it had formed. She gently ran her index finger over it but as she did so the blood crumbled and smudged away. Her driver had been wrong. It had been dark when he'd checked but it wasn't a scar at all, just a dark mark from the blood. She let out a gasp and turned her back to the door. The Professor momentarily paused, sensing Sabine's concern.

'He's watching,' Sabine whispered, her back to the two-way mirror so she couldn't be seen conversing.

Professor Meredith Malcolm was unmoved and simply ignored her. Requiring another tool, he stood up and stepped across the room. He wasn't aware of the open trap door that lay directly beneath the prism ceiling.

'Watch out!' Sabine cried out as she stretched her slender body to full length and caught the back of his crumpled linen jacket.

It was enough to rotate his body so his step landed on the floor and he didn't fall through to his untimely death on the sarcophagus altar below.

'Thank you,' he replied gratefully. Then continued on with his task.

Sabine carried on bathing Gemima, and she dressed her in a pure white Egyptian cotton robe that had been laid out by Brain Louds. There was a crackling of interference, and tiny speakers, which were buried beneath the vivarium and glass enclosures, made their presence known for the first time since the Professor's arrival.

A deep voice came over against static interference. Repeating itself time and time again as it revolving on a gramophone.

'Work hard, obey. Work hard, obey,' it announced over and over.

Gradually, the voice slowed, becoming deeper and deeper until it was an inaudible deep monotone. Then, in pure contrast, a perky violin concerto began. In the background, drowned out by the string instruments the deep monotone continued to loop.

Sabine and the Professor did not speak, they continued with their tasks.

*****

'My God, Gideon, all this from one man?' Noone enquired.

'Indeed. One very industrious man,' Gideon confirmed.

Both of them stood in Gideon's basement laboratory. The looped strings of developed black-and-white images in abundance in front of them. Papers from Lord Huntington's estate, land registers, images of monuments, ordnance maps, and even a set of documents with nothing on them at all. Each snapped in a hurry, most visible, some blurred and some underdeveloped completely.

'It was everything Tink and Eric could obtain in the time given. He knew damn well we had been sneaking,' Gideon advised his friend. 'We did acquire his torches after all.' He smiled.

'What remains of the originals?' asked Noone.

'That, we are about to find out.' Gideon ran his fingers over the leather satchel he had taken from the dead man at the Museum and painstakingly protected for hours on end. 'I think anything that is no longer here may be of vital importance. Unsure of the rest,' he said as he removed paper upon paper and laid them out uniformly in front of them.

'And you are absolutely sure it was him?' Noone asked for the final time.

'Positive.'

Chapter 49
The Russian Pt.4

On this particularly late afternoon, where summer heat made way for the autumn chill, the residents of Ambledown were still nervous following the flash floods that the storm had brought and the increased presence of the Huntington households' guards seeking out clues to the ransacking and recent break-in at Huntington Hall. Of course, they would focus on the Poacher. It was a den of misfits and thieves, but word on the street was that no one, not even Pop, had any idea who had staged the real robbery. In the aftermath, the servants had been light-fingered enough to suggest more than one man was involved and the black market contraband – particularly, eggs and sides of bacon, which they had illicitly procured – had swiftly been traded amongst the regulars of the Poacher. Pop Braggan was, of course, the prime suspect but the Huntington's did not have the proof or strength to take on the Braggan network.

Several ales had been eagerly consumed as Tink, Pop and Gideon regaled stories and adventures. Their Sunday meetings were often about business but masqueraded as jovial catch-ups and banter. As they left the Poacher, Tink led, Pop followed with The Lady and Luna, while Gideon settled up, as he so often did. Opposite them, stepping out from The Crown was a gentleman dressed in fine fettle, pure white linens, a straw boater and the most marvellous moustache, which he thumbed down eagerly.

      'Oh deary dear, look at 'im.' Pop laughed, pointing at the man. 'The Huntington's are looking for strangers, are they? Look no further.' He chortled loudly.

Gideon stepped out from the Poacher, looked upon the man and momentarily froze.

      'Gideon, are you OK?' Tink asked him. 'You look like you've seen a ghost.' Gideon broke from his stare and returned into the pub.
      'Eric,' he called over. 'I have a job for you.'

The enthusiastic boy jumped off of the barstool and sprung over.

'You see that man, heading up the hill?' Gideon asked. 'I need his room key.'

'I thought our rule was that I am never not to pickpocket anyone ever again?' Eric replied candidly.

'This is an exceptional case,' Gideon replied. And with little encouragement, Eric was gone.

'What is it, Gideon?' Tink enquired, joining him back in the bar.

'Yea, wot's got into ya?' Pop interrupted, re-joining them in the pub for fear he was missing out on a free ale. 'You seen a ghost?' he asked Gideon.

'I believe I actually have,' Gideon confirmed.

'Wot, a real ghost?' Pop replied in amazement.

'Someone I thought was dead already,' Gideon replied as he nervously awaited Eric's return. His friends turned to each other confused.

'Well, that was easy,' came Eric's chipper voice as he re-entered the Poacher in no time at all. 'He was waiting outside yer shop, Giddy.'

Gideon's suspicions were confirmed. This man was masquerading as someone he was not.

'OK, Plan B.' Gideon turned to his cohort. 'Tink, I need to know the name he is using. Here, take the key, return it to The Crown, and find it out. Make sure they write it down.'

Tink left immediately.

'Pop, go to my shop, stall him, and do one favour for me. Make sure you get a good look at his eyes, then report back.'

Gideon didn't have to ask twice. Pop waddled out with Luna and The Lady, whistling a drunken tune.

Gideon waited patiently with Eric, peeping through the shutter gaps of the Poacher. Tink had taken less than five minutes to return having procured the name.

'Professor Meredith Malcolm,' Tink advised, passing Gideon the headed paper from The Crown where he had scrawled the name. 'Professor of insects at the Natural History or something like that.'

'That is very specific, thanks,' Gideon replied with a curious look across his face.

Just moments later, Pop's whistling introduced him back into the Poacher. 'As green as emeralds, his eyes are, Gideon. Green as emeralds,' Pop confirmed to his friend.

Gideon exhaled a sigh of concern, sat down in a corner and began writing on the paper that Tink had just procured for him.

'Pop, I need one last favour from you. I need you to take this letter to London and hand-deliver it to the real Professor Meredith Malcolm.'

'London, but I'm three sheets to the wind already,' Pop argued.

'Plenty of fresh air on those smuggler roads for you to sober up then,' Gideon responded curtly.

'A letter to London, why can't you just post it?' Pop continued.

'Oh, it's not just a letter, Pop.' Gideon smiled. 'You'll have company. Eric!' Gideon ordered the boy over.

'I don't wanna take the boy,' Pop moaned.

'Oh, don't worry, he's not travelling with you. Eric, prepare Geoffrey for travel.'

'A bleedin' giraffe?' Pop frowned.

'A bust of a giraffe, if we're being picky.' Gideon smiled at him. 'Eric will prepare him. Now go, go on, go,' Gideon encouraged his giant gipsy friend.

Pop sauntered out of the pub slowly as Eric rushed before him to help prepare the stuffed animal. Gideon remained behind with Tink.

'Anything you'd like to share with me?' Tink asked of his friend.

'That man we saw, he's no professor. He's a Russian, an imposter, and until many moments ago, I believed he was dead. Pop was right without really knowing. He would be the man that broke into Huntington Hall. That man knows who I am, who we all are, we must warn Florrie.'

Chapter 50
Conundrum

'East Croydon!' came the guard's welcome voice, finally.

Belle was impatient to get back to London. Several hours had been wasted already. All she now required was a Hackney carriage and she would be there within the hour.

'Be careful if you're heading back in town miss,' advised the guard. 'There's a storm coming and you know what follows; thunder and lightning!'

Belle thanked the guard and made her way to find transport. The roads were deserted with the exception of few stranded commuters to the coast that were ambling around. Mostly, however, the streets were empty. She waited patiently to hail a taxicab but with little success. A single street vendor was huddled within their booth trying to shield the daily papers from the wind. The clouds were drawing darker and the gusts beginning to howl through.

'Where is everybody?' Belle enquired.

'Air-raid warning; came through half an hour ago,' the vendor replied.

'In daytime?' Belle questioned.

'Big storm brewing. Reckon Adolf's mob will see it as an opportunity,' the vendor replied. 'Best get indoors, love.'

Belle had nowhere to go. No trains, no cars, just the vendor and a littering of papers and leaves that began to swirl and dance in the air.

'Do you have a street map?' she asked.

The vendor produced an illustrated map of London from behind his booth. Belle reached inside her pockets but she didn't have anything on her but the torch. She had not taken her purse. She didn't even have an umbrella and by the heavy droplets of water now beginning to fall she was going to need one fast.

'I'm sorry,' she said, patting down her body. 'I've misplaced my purse. I'm desperate.'

'No money, no map!' the vendor replied, unrelenting.

'Please? I need to get back to central London. I will send you the money. It's of national importance.'

'Oh, I'm sure it is, Mrs Churchill.' the vendor replied sarcastically. 'In that case … No! No money, no map. Now move along cos I'm buggerin off now before this storm comes in proper.'

Belle was furious. As the vendor turned to button his coat, Belle snatched the map from the counter and kicked the display of daily papers so hard they were sent scattering into the increasing winds. Cascades of Fleet Street's finest danced in black and white forming a barrier between herself and the vendor before she ran for her life back into the station. She ran downstairs, crossed a walkway, and exited the station on the other side. Belle didn't stop running for a full ten minutes, exhausting every breath in her lungs as the heavens opened and lashed down torrents of heavy rain. Certain she was safe, she took refuge in a shop doorway. Opening the ordnance, she then carefully plotted her route to Whitehall. It was quite obvious the map was out-dated and who knew how many roads had changed due to bombing or were blocked on the way. Nevertheless, she calculated if she continued at walking pace, it would take her four hours minimum. That is if she wasn't subject to an incendiary attack, or hypothermia hadn't claimed her first.

*****

'It's time, Gideon,' Noone advised his friend.

Several hours of deciphering maps of Egypt and Mesopotamia, land registers in English and Arabic and much information they had not understood, not really, had taken Gideon and Noone a couple of hours. A picture of what all the moving parts and detail meant was forming in their minds but with many components still missing.

'Did you think Ilya would make it easy for you?' Noone asked him, remembering the dead Russian.

'Not after the robbery. Not ever, considering Cairo, I would have guessed,' Gideon replied.

'Come, they'll be waiting,' Noone urged him.

They finished packing the canvas duffle bag. Predominantly, it held explosives and guns and two large brown cloaks.

'Ready?' Gideon asked his dear friend.

'Ready,' Noone replied with a childlike grin.

Le Chat Noir was a minor amble downhill. On approaching the war memorial, they spied Sheriff Wilson Bott, holding court with a deflated crowd in front of him.

'I'm sorry, ladies and gentlemen. There is a storm fast approaching and we cannot risk being caught out in it. I will not be held accountable for any of your deaths.' Wilson shouted.

Much to the crowd's disapproval they gave up the search and went home, apart from the drunks that made light work stepping into the Poacher.

'Nothing, Gideon. Not a dicky bird,' Elizabeth expressed sorrowfully.

'Lizzy, I think Wilson is right. The clouds look ominous and anyone stumbling into the marshes or caught out could harm themselves. Nathaniel and I have packed to camp out and continue searching into tonight. Heaven forbid an air-raid should come,' he reassured her.

'In this place, please. It's charmed. Not one bomb, not one enemy plane has passed by since we've been here. It would just be Eric's luck to miss it.' She smiled back.

Nelly Parker placed an arm around her and guided her home, towards the Poacher. Nelly looked back at Gideon knowingly and gave him a reassuring nod.

'What are you doing? Eric and Gemima are missing!' Elizabeth shouted at Millicent McGregor who was aloft a ladder painstakingly hanging bunting outside of her public house. Millie failed to respond but carried on cheerily about her business.

'Ahhhhhh!' Elizabeth screamed in frustration and slammed the doorway as she passed into the pub. 'What has got into you?' she screamed at the landlady.

*****

Agatha and Eric were dehydrated and weary. Sister Harvey's motionless body was nothing more than the shadow of its former self. The tiniest inflation of her chest still meant she was breathing but they could not tell how long she would last.

As the clouds outside turned an obstinate grey, the room's tiny letterbox-sized porthole allowed less light in, reducing visibility, as they lay captive in the darkness. They had exhausted themselves intermittently trying to untether themselves but to little avail. Their silence was broken when the door key rattled the lock.

'Any noise, from either one of you, and your fate will follow the Sister's. Understood?' Governess Dove pointed out as she entered with a jug of water, cups, a single sandwich and a needle full of the scorpion venom. First of all, she untied Eric's gag. Held a glass of water to his lips and administered the tiniest of sips. As his mouth opened to receive part of the sandwich, she tightened the gag once more. Eric swelled his tongue and fought the restraint as much as he could as Dove secured it once more. She then moved to Aggie. This time gentler than before, she untied the gag and offered her more than just a few sips. The sandwich was held at her lips for her to consume.

'Please, give Eric some,' Agatha begged but instead, Dove picked up the needle and moved towards the boy's arm. 'No no! I'm sorry!' Aggie begged and begged again.

'This boy is nothing more than a hindrance to me. He is simply alive as a bargaining chip to keep you in control. Any subordination and he receives the scorpion's kiss. Now eat!'

Aggie ate as fast as she could, although it was difficult with such a dry mouth. She was constantly looking with apologetic eyes towards Eric. He simply didn't care. His gaze penetrated through Dove with infinite defiance.

'Why you are so special, I do not know,' Dove directed towards Aggie. 'But we will find out soon enough. The Tuchhandler is coming for you.' She laughed sinisterly.

*****

'Ma'am, we have the men back at their posts and they are fully scrutinised,' Colonel Malling confirmed to Wink Waverley.

'Very good, Colonel. Amazing what you can achieve in certain circumstances,' Wink replied, taking a swipe at his earlier insubordination as she sparked up a customary cigarette.

The phone rang on her desk and she gave it a perplexed look via her good eye before answering.

'Send him in.'

A door opened against the padded Burgundy leather, welcoming Thompson in from his short journey across town.

'Ma'am, Sir,' he said and nodded on entering, sceptical of Malling's presence.

'What conspiracy now?' Malling volleyed at Thompson.

Wink was in no mood for his ego and shot Malling a final warning stare. 'Speak freely, Thompson,' Wink ordered jovially.

Producing the two photographs of the very differing personas of Jennifer James, aka Sabine Erket, he laid them out on Wink's desk. 'You're more than accustomed to this image,' Thompson began, smirking towards the blonde tigress engaging with Malling in the original photograph.

Colonel Malling's blood pressure rose and his crimson appearance would almost certainly increase to camouflage him against the burgundy should Thompson continue in the same manner.

'However, what do we really know about Jennifer James?' he continued, producing a picture of herself and her father, which The Lady James had recently provided.

'Good grief,' piped up Malling. 'Is that Sir Wallace James?' he asked.

'That's correct, sir. It *was* Sir Wallace by all accounts,' Thompson advised.

'I had not realised he had passed. An exceptional man. I met him and his good lady wife on several occasions. My sympathies to the family,' Malling humbly replied.

'That's really just the tip of the iceberg. You see, in the original image, Lady James recognised and confirmed her daughter, beyond a doubt. The "garish coat", as she called it, was a present from her fiancé … or fiancé to be?'

'Wealthy individual is he? I expect so by the looks of that coat and considering the stock she comes from,' Malling blabbed on.

'Donald. That's how Lady James referred to him.'

'Donald? Lucky Donald. Donald who?' Colonel Malling questioned.

'Draper,' Wink answered for Thompson looking at the young spy who duly nodded in affirmation.

'Donald Draper – you secretive old fox.' Malling laughed, once more missing the point.

'That, Colonel, might actually be closer to the truth then you expect,' Thompson advised.

'Wait, wait, hold on. What are you suggesting about Donald Draper? He's a company man through and through. Who's to say who this Lady James is that you're convincing us of –' Malling retracted, his stupidity catching up with him.

'Again, a good question, sir. I have her under my guard at *the Department*. If you have met her, sir, do you think you would be able to recognise her voice?'

Wink Waverley was already on the phone, obtaining a secure line. As she replaced the handset, a large red button lit up at its base. She snatched the handset and turned her back to the men. Several seconds of curt nodding and she revolved back to face them.

'That discussion will have to wait, gentlemen. Credible sightings of a Luftwaffe party heading towards the Channel. We have to bunker down.'

Malling acknowledged the order immediately and opened a door to the right of the room, which Thompson had not seen before. It led directly to a cavernous concrete corridor that was lit with industrial lighting and an abundance of cables suspended below.

'Your chance to see the Protocols first hand,' Wink advised him.

*****

Belle was soaked to the bone. Her teeth were chattering, and her lips turning blue. The incessant rain forced her to take refuge wherever she could find it. Two hours of walking as fast as she could had exhausted her. The streets were deserted. The storm and ominous foreboding of an enemy attack found her isolated with her map as a guide to get to Whitehall. The sky was so dark now it could have been mistaken for nightfall but it was only mid-afternoon. The bright red of a telephone box shone like a beacon in the near distance. It was the first one she had seen since her rapid retreat from the station.

On entering, she sighed a relief for the shelter from the storm. She had memorised the number Thompson had provided her, in case of any emergencies. She steadied her shaking hands, still numb from the cold, and rotated the dial. It took all her efforts now as she just managed to complete the six-digit code. The pips went and her heart sank as she realised she did not have any coins to enter. She slumped into the corner sobbing through exhaustion. Sitting there with the handset loosely held within her hand swaying back and forth as her eyes began to tire, she was almost asleep when the distant sound of a voice awoke her.

'Welcome to Fortnum's. Please, dial the extension of the department you are after. One for Millinery, two for Gentlemen's outfitting, three …' the message continued.

'Hello, is anyone there, hello?' Belle called down the phone.

'Five for Haberdashery … six … ' the message continued.

'No, please, help!' she shouted.

'Nine for home-wares, ten for … .'

Tiredness had become her when Thompson's voice chimed through her thoughts. 'Department Eleven. Dial for Department Eleven.'

She hooked her index finger into the hole for the number one, spun it full circle, and then repeated the process. The line crackled and then cut off to the intermittent beeps of an engaged tone.

'No! You stupid,stupid machine. No!' Belle erupted, hitting the handset against the glass of the booth.

'Hello? Is anybody there? Hello?' came the subtle man's voice.

'Oh yes, yes. Sorry,' Belle replied 'This is Belle Soames. You've been expecting my call.'

'Miss Soames, how can I help?' he replied.

'I desperately need to talk to Thompson. I have found a giant piece of the puzzle. Repeat, Belle Soames for Thompson, most important.'

'Very good, Miss Soames. I will send for you. Thompson is currently sheltering from the imminent air-raid but we will send a car as soon as we can. Are you safe, Miss Soames? You must find shelter. Tell me the number of the booth you are dialling from and stay where you are,' the man replied.

Belle read out the number on the phone dial with huge relief. She slumped into her corner of the booth as the storm outside raged on. It was dark as pitch. She was wet and shivering but she did not care. She would soon be safe. She rubbed the condensation from the glass with the corner of her sleeve, peered out into the darkness, and there he was again, plastered on a brick wall. It was Lord Kitchener intently pointing his forefinger right back at her. Removing her rain-drenched coat she hung it over the telephone to dry as she took a brief moment to step outside and to reconfirm her theory.

Temporarily she left the shelter of the booth and walked towards the poster. She flashed the torch and confirmed that the eyes of RA were staring directly back at her, covering the eyes of the former officer and his dominant recruitment campaign across the city. In the darkness, they only illuminated to reveal their ominous presence.

Beneath Kitchener's predominant digit, the word *'follow'* illuminated in purple-blue alongside his eyes. She moved a few paces to a second poster and that one said 'obey'. Then a few more paces to another. There must be thousands of them across the breadth of London, she thought to herself as she followed them into an underpass and out of the driving rain. At least the underpass was safer than a phone-box she thought to herself and she could still see it from here for when her car arrived. The violet beam was beginning to flicker and falter. She banged hard on its base to encourage the batteries not to die but it did not work. Her sopping wet hands slipped and lost grip sending it skidding across the rain-sodden pavement. As she scrambled to fetch it in the darkness, the lights dimmed from a black car that pulled up slowly alongside the booth. Belle watched from a distance, hidden in the darkness of the tunnel. The car slowed but did not stop, crawling along the kerb. Belle went to cry out as she saw the window wind down but spied the reflective glint of a cylindrical barrel of a gun ominously appear.

Bang! Bang! Bang!

Multiple shots shattered through the glass, sparking against the metalwork and shattering the red phone booth, peppering her suspended coat as it hunched over the phone. As the coat slumped downwards, the car then sped off, without time to witness the lack of a body within it.

Belle crouched into a ball, petrified, hidden in the darkness. As the car sped off in darkness, the wing mirror clipped her elbow, sending her flailing into puddle water and without realising she was there at all. She caught a glint of the man's spectacles as he sat in the back seat winding his window back up. She had definitely seen him before.

Chapter 51
The raiding party

Le Chat Noir was empty with the exception of the four men, Cecile, and a quarry of cats who hid in their lair far from the precipitous storm outside and flashes of lightning that sent them screeching for cover. Tiny candles in jam jars lit the table where the men sat, reflecting their faces ghoulishly as they huddled in secrecy.

'Again, Pop,' Nathaniel asked the giant man to repeat himself.

'Very simple. When the van arrives, the patients embark and 'ed in here. They usually 'elp the wheelchair men in and at that point I make my presence known to them. I will split off with the driver towards Tink's. You two,' Pop continued, nodding towards Gideon and Nathaniel. 'Deal with him inside 'ere. I will then deal with the other outside there.'

'Do you expect any trouble from the patients?' Gideon enquired.

'By all accounts, they're likely to help,' Tink added. 'We need them on-board for part two.' Tinker then pulled out a large box with holes drilled in the side and passed it to Pop.

'They're so she can breathe.' Tink pointed out.

'Just make sure you point your torch in his face,' Pop ordered him.

As the plans were finalised a large deep rumbling penetrated the mossy cobbles of the Steep outside and shook the café's foundations. A jam jar toppled, spilling its tiny waxy candle onto the table. Nathaniel Noone was quick to painlessly quash it with one of his scarred hands.

'That's not thunder. Not as we know it,' Gideon confirmed, stepping out of the Le Chat Noir.

Three doorbell chimes followed him as Nathaniel, Pop, and Tinker alighted from Cecile's and looked towards the heavens. The voluminous black clouds fired silver bullets of rain at them as they struggled to see through the darkness.

'There.' Noone pointed to the skies. 'It's a raiding party.'

Through the cloud break, the rare sight of that evening's crescent moon caught the tail of an aircraft and its ominous squat black cross. Occasionally, a beam would be directed downwards as if the aeroplanes were searching for targets and the storm was hindering progress.

'I ain't never seen them over these parts,' Pop added.

'They must be heading to London.' Tink turned, looking to Gideon.

'Let's just to stick to our plan. We cannot concern ourselves with matters beyond our control,' Gideon advised them all as they took up their positions.

'This is not a drill! Repeat, this is not a drill,' came Wilson Bott's voice through a crackling static public address system. For the first time since war had broken out, the Sheriff was called into action to evacuate the streets of Ambledown. The danger had passed but nevertheless, remnants of the WI continued through gusts, rain, and the threat of bombing to complete their tasks.

*****

'Do you hear that?' Aggie mumbled to Eric. 'They're enemy planes.'

Eric, who had been fighting the gag with his tongue, just managed to release the cloth beneath his chin and took in a huge breath.

'You're joking! Ow's my luck!' he moaned.

'Shhhhhhhh!' Aggie continued to mumble.

With renewed vigour, Eric Peabody slid onto his side and with the energy of a landed conger eel, violently moved himself across the room and behind Aggie. Forcing the weight of his body onto hers, he started gnawing at her gag until finally it loosened and she was able to breathe easily and converse normally.

'If Dove hears us, you're dead,' she whispered to him.

'We're both dead if we don't get outta here,' Eric volleyed back before continuing to gnaw behind her neck.

'Eric, what are you doing? I can breathe now,' Aggie asked.

Eric who now had the chain from her necklace between his teeth was awkwardly trying to manipulate it over her neck.

'If we can hang your necklace outside, the moon will light it up like a beacon. Someone will find us,' he explained.

'During an air-raid? I doubt it. And if Dove sees it first?' Aggie questioned.

'We're bleedin' dead. If she sees it first, I will be for sure. Either way, Aggie, we're gonna die so we gotta try. I'm all ears if you have a better plan.'

Aggie had no response, Eric was right, she couldn't see an easy way out of this either. She bent forward and wriggled in unison as Eric carefully lifted the silver chain and its magnifying glass from around her neck. Placing it between his teeth, he carefully looped it over the brass knob of the tiny rectangle window and allowed it to suspend in the alleyway outside. The storm clouds were unrelenting. Afternoon had moved into evening and the crescent moon could not penetrate through the darkness, let alone cast light into the alleyway, as the overcast shadows blanketed Ambledown, London, and the country beyond.

*****

Through concrete corridors, stairways, and suspended electrical cabling, Thompson followed Wink Waverley and Colonel Malling into a subterranean network buzzing with strategists, analysts, and many of Whitehall's finest. There were many personnel but fewer than usual due to the recent request to guard all the protocol locations.

'We're one hundred feet underground and this concrete is four-foot thick,' Malling boasted slapping a wall. 'We'll be safe down here.'

Moving past rooms with maps and model battleships, to rooms of men in heated strategic debate, they came to a room with frosted glass that Malling entered through. It was cavernous and far larger than Thompson had imagined.

At its centre was a huge magnified map of the City of London stretching into the home counties and beyond. Banks of desks covered in telephony exchanges with operators sporting headsets sat relaying messages inwards and outwards on their secure wire network.

'The Protocols,' Wink announced, moving towards the map.

Thompson observed more detail the closer he got. Tiny diodes surrounded the city in a huge circumference and throbbed patiently in a deep red. It was if the network they represented was the beating heart of the war efforts and the femoral arteries desperately trying to keep things moving. As he canvassed the ordnance's more detailed centre, it was easy to distinguish the key landmarks and defensive outposts his men had recently rounded up Malling's men from. St Paul's, Tower Bridge, etcetera and all with their own individual diode flashing and waiting for advice.

'The first protocol confirmed,' came a voice from a desk.

A runner sprinted to that desk, returned with a small bulb, and pushed it into the map. It was St Paul's, quite often the first, considering its elevated height over Ludgate Hill and impressive observation point across the city. The lamp now replaced the red diode and flashed a brilliant white. Almost immediately, a second voice and then a third came to confirm news from the protocol stations. Runners sprinted everywhere and as if like dominoes falling within an instant, the small red lights were surpassed with white and the map was soon covered in favourable white and not ominous red. Thompson could not believe the speed and fluidity as in a few minutes all Protocols had responded and the halo of white light closed to confirm the security of the city.

'Impressive.' Thompson applauded Colonel Malling. 'Very impressive.'

Malling, who enjoyed praise immensely, shrugged it off as if it was nothing.

'Thompson, that concludes, to us, that all stations across the boroughs of London are exercising their air-raid sirens and posted with anti-aircraft guns and spotters to shoot down enemy craft,' Wink advised him. 'We'll know soon enough how much damage has been inflicted.'

All they could do now was wait.

*****

Terrified, frozen, wet through and at the mercy of the Luftwaffe as well as forces closer to home, Belle made her way through the underpass. Air sirens were now in full symphony warning citizens to stay underground, hidden and safe.

All roads were deserted. All the lights switched off. Only the occasional flash of lightning illuminated the night sky. The rumblings of aircraft thundered through but thankfully not the doodlebugs. Very occasionally, a volley of gunfire blasted from ground to air, deterring the raiding party from exercising their ammunitions and unleashing their non-discriminatory explosives.

Belle had heard and seen enough air-raids to know the Germans were not unleashing hell as expected. With the exception of a scanning light that came from aircraft beyond the clouds, the last remnants of the aircraft were leaving British shores. The storm had proven too difficult to navigate and the Luftwaffe were disappearing into the night.

Struggling to control the pace of her heart and gasping for breath she struggled, broken, and bruised, back towards the red phone-box. Her assailant long gone into the dark belly of the night. The glass now shattered, the ricocheting bullets having torn through her coat and beyond. She slumped inside with the coat covering her like a blanket before exhaustion and the cold became too much, directing her towards unconsciousness.

*****

Professor Malcolm continued with the preparation of Purrsia the cat and its journey into the afterlife. Jennifer James no longer looked like Sabine Erket. The blonde wig had been removed, and her long dark hair replaced the deceit. She had replaced the zebra skin in favour of a long black cloak favoured by the inmates of Institute Silvera. Brain Louds' classical music could be heard repeating over and over in the background as it was piped throughout the hospital.

Leaving Gemima prepared in her long white ceremonial gown for Brian Louds, she left the Professor to complete his task. As she left the Silvera Institute, accompanied by the orderlies, the first of many ambulance trucks were beginning to leave in convoy towards the capital. Their distinct white circles and crosses emblazoned on the sides and on the canvas roofs above. In the distance, the aircraft were disappearing as the thunderstorm appeared to follow them away. The rains were dissipating as they headed towards Ambledown for their final assault.

*****

Colonel Malling turned to the room and congratulated the efforts of yet another successful execution of the Protocols.

'On current information, we are aware of one single bomb deployed near Shaftesbury,' Malling advised them. 'That's the least amount of damage caused by any campaign. You should be proud.'

A round of applause erupted before everybody began resetting their position for future bombing campaigns.

'Sorry, old boy,' Malling directed to Thompson, considering himself victorious in the current debate. 'I will be standing my men down. The Protocols remain intact.'

It was undeniably impressive, Thompson could not deny that, but something did not fit.

'Thompson, shall we?' Wink directed him out of the room and back along to the burgundy room where he expected his immediate court-marshal. Instead, Wink handed him a black-and-white magazine. 'Page ten, society pictures,' she ordered him.

Thumbing quickly as they walked, he came to page ten. A quick scan of the photographs revealed Sir Wallace and Lady James.

'Definitely the lady we have under guard, ma'am,' Thompson confirmed.

'Good, then that means we don't have to include Malling. Let's hope *The Department* remains intact.'

Chapter 52
Jigsaw pieces

Jennifer James alighted via the rear canvas of the ambulance truck and looked upon the shimmering cobbles leading to the market town below. The torrential rain had finally dispersed into a gentle shower as the clouds began to part, revealing the dominant crescent moon.

Raising the hood of the cloak over her head, she slipped into the shadows to exercise her rushed plan. Too much lay at stake for her to fail. The streets were empty but for the tiny band of WI ladies still decorating the far end of the Steep. They were the ones who had inexplicably ignored Wilson Bott's orders and defied the storm.

Much further down the hill, in a tiny bolthole known to less than a handful of historical residents and master smugglers, a tiny silver chain hung in the darkness from a hidden letterbox hole, it's multifaceted magnifying glass swayed in the breeze waiting silently for ignition from its celestial source.

The truck and its two muscle-bound minders continued the slow drive down to the rendezvous with the gipsy brawler and his promise of the birds of prey. Sheathing curved blades, studded with jewels embedded in gold and hidden within their waistbands, they were nervously aware of the size and reputation of their avian procurer and should they fail they were mortally in fear of their employer's dire warning.

Gideon and Noone waited patiently in the café of cats. A canvas bag full of weapons and explosives beneath their table. The scarred man wore a dark cloak with the hood up in anticipation.

Beneath the large cobbler's sign that squeaked as it swung in the wind, stood Pop Braggan, the bare-knuckle brawler, covered in his trademark gold, a single tattooed tear marking his face. The wolfhound Luna yelped at the prevailing moon as its light was a welcome respite from rain and thunder. Inside the shop, Tink was preparing The Lady.

Wilson Bott took a tentative step from his sheriff's office as the rains relented. He was lost for words at the sodden appearance of Ambledown's Women's Institute who had forsaken warmth and safety to hang bunting in preparation for the secretive party they were all so excited about.

The girl with the mark of the moon, prayed for the light from above, and, more importantly, for someone to see the light once it came. Her street-urchin friend was already planning for the endgame, anticipating the worst.

Cloaked opposite from the schoolhouse, just yards away, in her hooded gown, the hidden lady observed from the shadows in her desperate attempt to find the girl.

Inside the schoolhouse, locked within her office, the governess waited patiently with her pistol drawn. She was assured the Germans were coming for her; to help and not hinder. The revelation of the bombers above, thundering and shaking her very foundations, caused her to question her communiqué. She had tried twice to contact Tuchhandler during the storm, via her hidden radio, but with little success. Though a bombing party across counties would send most people underground and clear her path, it still planted the seed of doubt that something was wrong. Nevertheless, her nervousness increased as the clock above her doorway clicked slowly and she waited for that knock from the entrance to come.

*****

'The line is secure,' Wink confirmed to Thompson handing him the handset.

She encouraged him to sit in her chair behind the desk so he could comfortably talk to his subordinate across town.

'Thompson, this is Thompson. Who am I speaking to?' he spoke into the receiver.

'So, pleased to hear from you, sir. We have had a very near-miss here,' Smith replied.

'Good to hear your voice too. How so? What of this near-miss?'

'A bomb landed next to the building, sir. It destroyed an ambulance parked nearby, burst into flames, but failed to explode. No one knows why,' Smith explained. 'By all accounts, there were several similar instances. All bombs failed to detonate.'

'That news had not reached us. That is both lucky and peculiar. Tell me, are evacuations underway? Is everyone accounted for?'

'They are, sir, on both accounts, but we have discovered an anomaly.'

'Explain,' Thompson encouraged him.

'There was an emergency call on line eleven. Just before the bombers came.'

Thompson knew it would have been Belle as he had strictly forbidden any of his operatives to use line eleven.

'What was her message, Smith?' Thompson replied anxiously.

'That's the anomaly, sir. Her call was disconnected or ...' Smith paused

'Or what?'

'I could be paranoid, sir, but it may have been intercepted. I think it may have been intercepted.'

'How on earth could that happen?' Thompson shouted angrily.

'The original call came through to *the* office but when I answered it, it was somehow muted. I just got her name before it changed. I have reached out to telephony but they advised me no one was redirecting calls and the place was empty due to the air-raid.'

'Where was she when she made the call?'

'South of the river, sir. Not one hundred per cent where, but we have a localised search area defined.'

'Send Jones to me. I need a car, and make sure Lady James is escorted, under guard, across town to Whitehall. Deliver her in person to Wink Waverley. We require her full cooperation,' Thompson ordered before slamming down the phone.

'Problems?' Wink asked.

'*The Department* was targeted, near-miss. The bomb destroyed an ambulance nearby but failed to detonate. Apparently, there were several similar instances in and around the area.'

'A saving grace. About time our luck changed. And what of Miss Soames, is she safe?'

'I don't know. I really do not know,' Thompson replied nervously.

'Well, find her and take this to her. We need her permission to use it.' Wink handed over a small black box that contained two phials of green liquid. One a light bilious green, and the other a rich emerald of denser viscosity.

'The light, bilious one, is the remedy. The dark emerald one the poison. They are synthesised from the Death-stalker as Belchambers suggested. One pinprick of either has the desired effect to either resuscitate or render. Our man, the concierge, has been brought around already and he has confirmed Jennifer James stung him with her belt buckle. Seems she is the foe after all. Perhaps she seduced Donald Draper? You cannot blame him, and it's what you originally suspected. I only found out just before the bombers came. The good news is that with his daughter's permission, Professor Soames can be cured and maybe he can complete the picture. Now, go find her. We'll continue the search for Ms James and Draper.'

Thompson appreciated Wink's candour and finally found the correct exit from the room padded with Burgundy leather. He still could not piece the full jigsaw together but would make damn sure he found Belle Soames and save her father. He could be the key to this all.

*****

'Are you finished, Professor?' Brain Louds shouted from the hidden chamber beneath the laboratory. 'As soon as you are finished, join me via the passageway opposite.'

Professor Malcolm tentatively peered into the dark abyss below. Its only source of light was a single wax torch that Louds had removed from its metal girdle on the descending steps leading to the chamber. The prism that sat directly above their heads, reflected tiny shimmers of the moon behind the clouds as the storm patiently left the skies. As Louds paced the room below, muttering to himself, the flare of the flames caught the dark edge of the ceremonial sarcophagus, followed by the stone statues of Horus and Anubis before settling on the Scarlet Scarab suspended in its ceremonial staff and surrounded by bejewelled metallic wings. The classical music could still be heard in the distance, echoing around the hospital wards.

The Professor readied himself, took the mummified cat under his arm and the half-feathered ceremonial mask of Horus, and descended via the opposing passageway to where Louds was residing. Gemima lay unconscious, peacefully positioned in the long white gown soon to be turned red.

'Welcome, Professor,' Louds encouraged as Meredith Malcolm presented him with both the feline and the mask. 'You have endeavoured well. I believe it is time to receive your reward.'

Professor Malcolm stepped back with a sheer look of panic contorting his face.

'Come now, I am not a monster. How many times must I repeat myself,' came his sinister voice and a laugh. Brian Louds took the bandage-wrapped cat and placed it on a plinth at the base of the sarcophagus. Removing the feathered half-mask, he placed it upon Professor Malcolm's head.

'Your fine facial hair almost compliments it,' said Louds and continued to laugh. 'Come, let us retrieve your prize.'

Professor Malcolm was frozen on the spot.

'I will be no part of your game any longer,' he refused.

'So noble, Professor. But the damage is already done,' Louds replied, rounding on him with the small pillbox. Louds removed his surgical mask. The horror below was instantly recognised by the shock on Meredith Malcolm's face. Sinew and muscle exposed where flesh should have been. Visible bone from his jawline exposed alongside molars and canine teeth. A patchwork of scars and squares of grafted skin that were failing him; a product of the failed surgery painstakingly undertaken during the past decade. His mask had been covering his theatrical phantom's appearance all of this time.

A pinch of violet-purple powder and the exhalation into Malcolm's nostrils swiftly took place.

'FOLLOW,' Louds announced in a monotone. 'Follow me.'

*****

The orderlies pulled up just south of Le Chat Noir and blinked their headlights to the waiting figure of Pop Braggan. A nod of recognition confirmed the deal was on. Gideon and Noone observed from a slatted blind waiting for the patients to leave the truck. The orderlies alighted and began moving together towards Pop.

'Oh shit,' Gideon swore. 'There are no patients. They're not coming here first. Pop wouldn't have planned for both at once. Quickly, Nate. You got your gun? '

'Yes,' Noone replied.

'Good. Get ready to fall out of the door.'

Gideon marched Nate to the café's doorway by the scruff, opened it up aggressively, and unceremoniously threw him out.

'And don't come back, ya drunk!' he screamed as Nathaniel skidded across the treacherous cobbles.

The commotion broke the tension surfacing between the marching orderlies who turned back to confront the noise while divulging their weapons in their waistbands.

'They're carrying,' Pop warned Tink who duly noted the whereabouts of the blade hilts.

'Is he one of yours? Eh? One of yours?' Gideon shouted, walking towards the orderlies, holding a candle to Nathaniel's scarred face. 'Must be so proud of your patient's behaviour.'

The confused orderlies broke ranks. The driver ordered the other to approach Gideon and Nathaniel while he continued towards Pop.

'You have them?' he shouted to chief Braggan.

'You got the money?' Pop replied.

The orderly nodded and produced a roll of American dollars. On sighting the green notes, Pop whistled for Tinker to join him. Carefully carrying the wooden box with the holes in, he approached the two of them with a torch in his mouth and passed the box to his friend.

'Open it, slowly,' the orderly demanded, hand fixed in his waistband.

'Sshhhhh!' Pop advised, suggesting calmness so as not to spook the birds as an eerie tension lurked between all parties. The subtle fluttering of wings from inside the box was enough to assure the orderly Pop had delivered on his promise.

Pop slowly opened the box as Tinker held the torch for the orderly to observe the contents. Suddenly, unexpectedly, he flung the lid open, forcing the inhabitant to fly out. Tinker followed his cue, blinding the orderly momentarily with the torch beam that lit up the glint of the gold incisor. The Lady rushed out in a flash of black and white pecking at the orderlies face and tearing his mouth with her talons in the process. The orderly tried defending himself with one hand and reached for his blade with the other. The hulking frame of Pop Braggan grabbed his opponent's wrist and thrust it in the opposing direction. A clear crack and the orderly's wrist snapped. The cry of pain informed his colleague several yards up the hill. It was all so fast, the orderly now examining the candlelit disfiguration of Nathaniel Noone was taken by surprise. As he turned, Nathaniel drew and trained his pistol upon him. Sensing he may still reach for his blade, Gideon thrust his firearm into the man's ribs and unsheathed the weapon's blade as he did so.

'Kill us. We already dead,' the driver announced, spitting at Pop's feet.

'If you insist,' Braggan replied, whistling for Luna to join them.

Passive of nature but terrifying of stature, the wolfhound stood over the cowling man drooling onto his face, her snarling canines on full display.

'Wait, wait!' the other orderly screamed out. 'He will kill us if we return without the birds. He will sacrifice us.'

'Who?' Gideon asked him.

'Dr Mialora!' they both replied.

'Do you wish to live?' Gideon then asked them and was greeted with enthusiastic nods. 'Then you will if you do what we say.'

*****

Thompson was relieved that his two most trusted men, Smith and Jones, had weathered the storm successfully after the immediacy of the air-raid. Jones had been left in the shadows of Whitehall's grounds while his superior had bunkered into the cavernous underground beneath Whitehall.

'I'm glad to see you, Jones,' Thompson confessed.

'Likewise, sir,' Jones politely replied.

'Where did you shelter?'

'I headed towards Shaftesbury, initially, towards the company bunker, but by then it was too late, sir. I spotted lower flying aircraft, much lower than usual but they were spotters, not shooters, sir.'

'Explain,' Thompson encouraged his man.

'Having sped back past the Palace, weaving through the barricades at The Mall, a fighter-plane stalked my path almost like for like. I prepared for the inevitable but it couldn't have seen me or just wasn't interested. It must've seen Buckingham so I fail to understand why it did not attack. I was convinced it would deploy its machine guns at any moment so I took cover outside of the vehicle hiding myself beneath a tree.'

'So, what did it do?' Thompson questioned.

'The thing is, sir. In my experience, those airmen usually deploy rounds upon rounds of ammo once they are that low. But this one didn't. Instead, it had a searchlight and was randomly lighting up targets.'

'Are you sure, Jones?'

'Cross my heart, sir. There was no aerial bombardment, no incendiary devices, and certainly no doodlebugs in that raiding party. It was toothless. Just designed to wreak havoc and remind us the enemy are out there.'

Thompson paused for a moment, trying to understand such an anomaly. Whitehall was celebrating the least effective air-raid of the war. So why hadn't the Nazis struck?

'Seeking something you say? Any ideas what?' Thompson investigated further.

'Well, all I observed was the bomb that headed towards *The Department*. It was no bigger than an infant, sir. Would never have caused the damage we are used to. It rushed from the skies and destroyed an ambulance truck just south of 'Nums.'

'But by all accounts, failed to detonate,' Thompson continued pressing.

'Not strictly true, sir. It ignited alright but almost as if the fuse had been pulled partway through. Instead, a huge plume of smoke rose and then like a proper pea-souper, it was misting away throughout the surrounding streets.'

'Lucky then, would you say?'

'Well, of course, sir. But it happened half-a-dozen times according to different witnesses. Do you think the enemy are running out of explosives? Maybe a faulty batch?'

'It's a nice thought,' Thompson said amused. 'But I doubt they would reveal such a position, do you?'

Jones admittedly did not believe that either and continued driving towards south London. It gave Thompson time to ponder the last twenty-four hours and what they could mean before exhaustion tipped him into a gentle slumber.

*****

'Look, Aggie,' Eric enthusiastically whispered, nodding towards the letterbox-sized hole.

Aggie contorted herself to see the briefest glimmer of moonlight breaking high above them. The celestial beams, though intermittent, were not lost on the suspended magnifier outside. The facets began to reflect and refract the white light through an opaque spectrum and produce a subdued throb of light.

'It's working! it's working, Eric,' she said and laughed.

'Sshhhh!' he reprimanded her. 'Don't want to alert Dove now, do we.' He smiled back. His humour never lost regardless of their peril.

'Let's hope someone spots it first,' Agatha whispered back.

'They will,' Eric reassured her. 'I know they will.'

Still patiently observing the street-scene of the Steep, the cloaked figure had retreated further back into the solitude of a darkened alleyway. Only minutes before, she had seen the two large men overwhelmed by the four locals, their dog and magpie, then bundled into the ambulance truck belonging to the Institute. That was of no concern to her. Her mission was to track the girl. Her patience had now paid off as a chink of light presented itself from the hidden passageway beside the schoolyard. Subtly pulsing in correspondence with the moon, she knew it could only come from one source. The pathway to the hidden bolthole was convoluted but not far. She slipped down the Steep and away from prying eyes.

*****

'How do you expect me to drive with broke wrist,' the orderly contested the orders from Pop

'Cos a broke wrist is nuffink compared to a face without eyes.' He laughed, whistling for his ever-present hound.

Much to his dissatisfaction, the orderly revved the vehicle and pulled away, terrified at the literal prospect of becoming a dog's' dinner. Pop sat next to him with the curved blade pressed to his neck, just in case of any moments of self-doubt.

In the rear of the truck, Gideon and Nathaniel held their orderly captive as they rumbled and jolted through the winding countryside. Whenever the moon flashed its bright light through, the top of the canvas lit up. You could easily distinguish the large white circle and central cross that differentiated an ambulance to the rest of the military vehicles.

'Draw me a map,' Gideon insisted to the orderly, holding out a pen and encouraging him to use the side of the canvas duffle bag.

'And tell us about the girl,' Noone followed up.

'Black hair, down to here,' the Orderly explained. 'He will kill her.'

'We'll see about that,' Gideon fired back, tightening the restraints on his captive.

'He will kill us all! He has an army!' the orderly cried out before Nathaniel Noone gagged him.

*****

Wilson Bott had just finished reordering the public address system within the Sheriff's office when an unexpected knock came at his door. 'Good evening, ladies,' he cordially welcomed them. 'How may I help?'

The gaggle of elderly residents smiled at him and replied in unison. 'We're so glad you asked,' they replied. Before every last one of them forced their way into his tiny workspace.

*****

'Someone's coming,' Eric informed Aggie.

Agatha looked towards the door, fearing Dove had foiled their plan.

'No, not there; outside. Listen.'

Eric was right. The tiniest sound of footsteps trying to make themselves unheard edged nearer. They sat back in anticipation, staring at the hole in the wall and the increasing light emitting from the magnifier.

A ghoulishly skinny hand reached inside and unhooked the pendant from its hanging place.

'Hey!' Aggie shouted, forgetting about Dove momentarily. She was met with the hooded figure's eyes through the hole. One was brown one was blue. It took Aggie by surprise.

'Help us. Please, help us,' Aggie urged, trying to keep her voice down.

The figure stared back at Aggie and then looked towards Eric and the incapacitated Sister Harvey before leaving.

'Hey!' Aggie bellowed before Eric advised her to be quiet.

*****

Governess Dove's silence was broken when she heard 'Hey!' called out for the first time. Reaching for the case containing both the poison and antidote, she was no longer in the mood for games. How much would incapacitate a young child the size of Eric Peabody to the point his lungs stopped moving she thought to herself as she drew the poison into a needle.

As she was leaving her governess's room, a crackling came from the hidden radio, still in its case, and hidden behind the books. A muffled male voice reached out to her.

'Come in, Taube. Over. It is Tuchhandler. Do you read? Over.'

Dove rushed to the bookcase, removed the radio and placed the headset on.

'This is Taube, I have been trying to reach you. Over.'

'Change of plans, I'm afraid. The Fuhrer insists we maintain control over Suez and, therefore, we must accommodate Mialora. We are satisfied with the Ethereum and plans progress at once. Do you copy? Over. At once. You must move the girl to the Institute immediately.'

'You said people are coming. You said the Germans are coming. I did not expect them in the guise of bombing parties.'

'Nor were they. Plans have changed. That was just a reconnaissance on the way to the capital. They are coming, again. So you must move at once. Do you hear me? Secure the girl and get out of there at once.'

'And the boy, the nun?'

'Surplus to requirements. Do whatever you must. Now, I must go. I cannot return from London but will see you in Cairo. Over and out.' The line crackled before dying.

Aggie and Eric heard everything through the brass vent.

'Don't worry, Aggie. There's still time,' Eric insisted as he feverishly rubbed his wrist restraints against the vent. 'Trust me. There's still time.'

*****

Wilson Bott was crushed backwards into what little space he had as the entire Ambledown WI swamped him.

'Mr Bott,' came the suspiciously cheery voice of Lady Huntington-Smythe. 'May I introduce our guest for the day? Ms Erket.'

The tall lady, cloaked in a gown to the rear stepped forward, towering over her fellow females.

'Good evening, Mr Bott,' she said and smiled.' Moving closer to his ear she then whispered into it. 'You can call me Jennifer.'

A sharp needle penetrated his wrist vein as the Death-stalker venom incapacitated him. Contorted, drooling, and foaming from the mouth, Wilson Bott succumbed in a crumpled form on the floor.

'One final task, dear ladies,' Erket announced to her adoring followers. 'We must find the girl.'

Chapter 53

Subterfuge

'Christ, no!' Thompson blasphemed on seeing the shattered glass of the booth. On closer inspection, the bundled torso of Belle Soames lay motionless on the damp phone-box floor. Thompson dashed to the booth, with splintered glass crunching underfoot. He flung the door open and knelt cradling Belle's head.

'Belle, Belle, can you hear me?' he cried.

Belle's pallid complexion, her cheeks grazed and bloodied, lips turning blue from the cold were all that he had feared the most. Rotating her wrist, he detected a faint pulse. A huge sigh exhaled from him. As he gently lifted her head, he noticed her crumpled coat beneath. Charred holes, where the bullets would have executed her had she not been observing from the underpass, appeared to him. He rolled the coat and used it as a pillow as he gently manoeuvred her body.

'Ow,' came the softest of voices. 'My arm,' Belle whimpered.

The limp arm, broken, was now obvious to Thompson. He removed his tie and improvised a sling trying to avoid as much pain as possible. 'Good news, Belle. We have the antidote for your father,' he encouraged her.

The side of her lip curled in satisfactory recognition.

'Picture,' she whispered, her voice fading. 'Picture.'

'What do you mean? The photograph? Belle, what do you mean?'

She mustered the energy to nod and pointed towards Thompson's pocket. He quickly pulled the photograph out.

'What is it?'

Her index finger planted itself on the man's face, before she collapsed, exhausted.

Thompson reached for the telephone that hung off of its hook just above Belle's head. Reconnecting it for the dialling tone he spun the six-digit number swiftly.

'Welcome to Fortnum's. Dial one,' the message began.

Thompson dialled eleven immediately.

'Hello,' came the calm man's voice.

*****

'Thank you. That will be all,' Wink acknowledged Smith as she led Lady James and the ever-nervous Hilary Nevis into the hidden concrete cavern beneath Number Seven, Whitehall.

'Are you OK, girl?' Wink spoke to Hilary.

'I c-could do with a cigarette. T-t-t-to settle my nerves,' Hilary stuttered.

'Me too,' Wink responded.

'Ma'am,' Hilary replied, shaking as she opened her clutch and offered Wink one of her own.

'I don't usually go in for pre-rolled, but needs must,' Wink accepted before ungraciously gnawing the filter off.

'Welcome, Lady James,' Colonel Malling confirmed with a brief look towards Wink as he joined them in the tunnels. 'We have a secure room. Please, follow me.' His outstretched arm directed them towards a door. The room, if it could be described as that, was no more than a cupboard space as the adults squeezed in around a central desk and four chairs.

'Lady James, I need to know all there is to know about your daughter. Start from the beginning. Anything might be important,' Wink asked.

Lady James looked at Hilary who nodded in support. Reaching inside her handbag, she produced a small white card, with brilliant red embossing on it. She passed it to Wink who passed it to Malling.

'Oh yes, OSIRIS. We've seen these before,' Malling confirmed.

*****

Under the cover of torchlight, the men studied the map the orderly had drawn.

'So, explain again. The rear entrance, the hidden one as you call it, that is a single passageway in and out?' Gideon asked.

An affirming nod confirmed the information for the last time.

'It's suicide to enter via that route,' Noone advised his friend. 'We need to find an alternative.'

'Agreed,' Pop added. 'Nafaniel, you, me and the hound. We'll enter by the front, pretend you're a long-lost patient like before.'

'OK. I'll take this route, agreed,' Gideon agreed.

'It's not safe, Gideon. Not on your own,' Noone warned him again.

'We cannot leave an escape route, Nate. We must find her. I'll take my chances.'

The orderlies' nervousness was plastered across both their faces. They were terrified and it was not unnoticed. The driver was clutching his broken wrist.

'You carry the box, like before, and once the exchange takes place, your job is over!' Pop ordered the man who had little choice but to comply.

'Now, what of this army?' Noone directed to the second man.

'The patients are army, all servicemen. Army,' he replied.

'They're ex-army. Is that wot yer sayin'? Not making much sense, are ya?' Pop angered, grabbing the man. 'You can come with us too. We need a guide.'

'Very well, gentlemen,' Gideon finished. 'We'll drop you just south so you can approach via the cliff face. Take this duffle. It has all you need; guns, explosives, masks, binoculars.'

'What about you?' Nathaniel fired back.

'I have these.' Gideon smiled, producing several handguns, a gas mask and one of the orderlies' jewelled blades to which the Lady had taken an instant fascination.

' … not to forget the magpie for company.'

'The Lady, Gideon. You refer to her as The Lady, and you mind you take good care of her,' Pop reprimanded him before they were on their way one last time.

*****

Jennifer James lifted the needle onto the gramophone as static reverberated through the public address system of Ambledown. The residents, returning from their shelter, were greeted with an inaudible screech of feedback before she began to speak.

'Sisters of the Woman's Institute, bring me your children. OBEY! Bring me your children. OBEY!'

Repetitively and monotonously, she repeated the words and maintained the pattern until finally, the gramophone's classical music drowned out her voice and its subdued instruction.

Her cohorts of the WI began to sway in time to her instructions and repeat her words.

'Bring me your children. OBEY! Bring me your children. OBEY!'

Leaving Wilson Bott's office, the WI slowly paced out onto the Steep and spread out in all manner of directions.

Lady Huntington-Smythe headed towards The Crown where Henrietta was entertaining the Priory set at dinner. Millicent McGregor headed back to the Poacher where Elizabeth was behind the bar serving in her absence. In fact, all the women headed towards their family roosts. Those who were without children canvassed the street and alleyways hoping to find some.

Once her plan was in progress, Jennifer James stepped out of Wilson's office and towards the war memorial. The strings of bunting hung in multiple directions from the metal structure of the angel. The bunting, in red, white and blue, suspended ominously down the Steep, zigzagging too, and from the historical iron girdles of the fire society's nests that sat above homes and shops. Jennifer James lit her final cigarette and reached high into the air lighting a dangling remnant of string that led to the first triangular piece of cloth. A spark of ignition and the material burned as brightly as a fuse before moving to ignite the next string and subsequent triangle of cloth. In turn, that burned to the next string and continued onto the next piece until a chain reaction set the street ablaze. Once a full set of bunting had ignited, the fuses of string continued their journey to the iron baskets. The accelerants deposited there exploded, sending plumes of powdered Ethereum into the sky. The more the bunting burned the increasing number of smoke-clouds were ignited, smothering the Steep in an unholy fog of violet purple.

Locals ran to their houses to get buckets of water but were powerless at the speed of the fires. Jennifer James returned to Wilson's office and paused the music momentarily.

> *'People of Ambledown. Bring me your children. OBEY! Bring me your children. OBEY!'*

As the smoke descended upon them, they inhaled the poison that coursed through their veins. The light from the fires lit up the suspended posters of the war campaign – *We need you. Dig for Victory* – all of them now displaying the illuminated and sinister eyes of RA. The large lettering of *OBEY* dominant across them all.

The residents of Ambledown were powerless to resist and began to slowly sway and rock.

> *'Bring me your children. OBEY! Bring me your children. OBEY!'*
they began to repeat.

Jennifer James returned the needle to the concerto. Calming violins sounded throughout the village. She removed the Sheriff's loud hailer and marched down the Steep. The flames burned brilliantly as the war posters were feverishly lit up.

> *'Bring me your children. OBEY! Bring me your children. OBEY!'*

*****

'What the hell is that?' Eric lurched forward trying to peer through the letterbox hole.

'I can hear violins,' Aggie said.

Bang! Bang! echoed the thumping on the schoolhouse door through the brass ventilation system.

Governess Dove was fully alerted. She had heard the music too. She had also heard Jennifer's instructions. People would come for them soon.

Ensuring her pistol was cocked, she crept silently in the darkness. Outside, a hooded figure in a cloak, wearing a gas mask, thumped relentlessly on the door.

'Bring me your children. OBEY! Bring me your children. OBEY!' could be heard through multiple droning voices outside as people moved slowly and relentlessly throughout Ambledown in their pursuit to deliver the children. Cries of children being dragged kicking and screaming, before they too succumbed, by the adults and marched towards Jennifer's voice as she continued her walk towards Ambledown bridge.

'Go away! There are no children here!? Dove shouted through the door.

'Open up Governess. Please, open up!'

Dove had not expected that voice to reply. She unlatched the lock and peered through the gap in the door, her gun ready.

'You? What do you want?' she said to the hooded figure.

Chapter 54

The beginning of the end

Thompson calmly replaced the handset. All colour drained from his face.

'Sir, what is it?' Jones questioned his superior observing the disconcerting expression staring back.

'We have been betrayed, Jones. Duped on an epic scale,' Thompson replied.

'I need you to take us to the Hospital for Tropical Medicine. At least we can treat Professor Soames senior. He may have insight. I'll gather my thoughts on the way.'

The two men lifted Belle Soames and laid her across the rear seat of the black saloon. She semi-consciously wheezed in pain. Unexpected dark rumblings came from above. Thompson looked to the skies. The clouds had parted and the storms were long gone. Several screams began to cry out as above them low-flying planes with spotter lights repeated their plan from the previous hour's trial run.

'It's happening again. Just like before,' Jones informed his boss.

Thompson dashed back to the phone booth. He dialled Number Seven, Whitehall on Wink's secure line and waited patiently until it was answered.

'Ma'am, it's Thompson. We were wrong. Terribly wrong.'

'Of course, you were,' laughed the same man's voice from before. 'Guten abend, Mr Thompson. I really didn't believe we would talk again. Let alone so soon. Good luck following protocol.'

'Jones!' Thompson cried, rushing into the car. 'Shaftesbury, now.'

*****

The small room below Whitehall was a fog of cigarette smoke from both Hilary and Wink's incessant puffing.

'No doubt you have,' Hilary replied, having passed the card around the table. 'If you look very closely you will see its true meaning. OBEY!' she advised, her stutter now completely gone. 'OBEY! OBEY!' she continued until Malling, James, and Waverley were sent into a hypnotic sway and their eyes glazed over with a violet film.

*****

'You look quite the part!' Brain Louds complimented Professor Meticulous Meredith Malcolm.

The blue and gold ceremonial priest robe, the opposite of a pure white line suit, dwarfed the entomologist. It was too large for the Professor's slight frame. It was complemented by the half-feathered mask of Horus that had been placed upon his head. The professor was powerless to resist Louds' plan.

Professor Malcolm's glazed, motionless expression, peered down on the restrained girl in the white gown on the ceremonial sarcophagus in front of him.

Louds placed the gold dagger, encrusted with blood-stained rubies, into the Professor's hand and bandaged it tight so he could not remove it. He then proceeded to gag the Professor, rendering him dumb.

'Soon, at the first light of dawn, when the sun rises and lights your way,' Louds informed him, pointing to the dormant anthropoid encrusted in crystal. 'You will have the honour, Professor. You may sacrifice the girl.'

*****

The cloaked figure removed her mask and began to speak.

'Please, Governess, allow me to enter. I was bringing you the cake I'd promised when, well, all hell has begun to break loose,' said a nervous Nelly Parker holding aloft a lidded cake tin.

'A cake?' Dove replied, completely dumbfounded, and momentarily distracted from her thought pattern. 'What are you talking about?' she replied confused.

Nelly jammed her toe into the gap of the door.

Dove looked over Nelly's shoulder and saw Jennifer James proceeding down the hill. Maintaining her orders, an everyday army of committed resources now searching far and wide for the children.

'Bring me all children. OBEY!' they spoke in unison.

Dove knew it was only a matter of time before the schoolhouse either succumbed to the Ethereum or was ransacked by those consumed by it. She couldn't risk Agatha slipping through her fingers, she needed an escape route and Nelly Parker knew this town better than most.

'Do you know a secret way out of here, Mrs Parker,' Dove asked. 'I am fearful for my life.'

'Likewise, and yes, I do,' Nelly replied. 'Let me in, dear. I can help.'

'Quickly then,' Dove encouraged Nelly through the doorway before bolting it and peering through the blinds to the chaos ensuing outside.

Nelly passed her the tin as she entered. 'Thank you, dear,' Nelly replied, fully removing her gas mask.

'I don't want your cake,' Dove replied motioning the tin back to Nelly.

'Nor I,' Nelly replied, raising her hand upwards and pointing a gun at the governess.

Dove dropped the tin and went for her own firearm but Nelly deployed a round that ricocheted off of the tin lid, rendering the futile attempt useless.

'Now about this secret escape,' Nelly spoke softly. 'Were you considering my sister and Eric too or just the young girl, Agatha?' She smiled.

'What can you see?' Pop asked of Nathaniel Noone as he peered through binoculars towards the Institute.

'Not much with one eye,' Noone admitted.

'Give 'em 'ere,' Pop said and snatched them off him.

The modernist structure had a clear benefit for them. The steel and monolithic glass gave a perfect perspective on what was occurring inside.

'That's odd,' Pop advised. 'It appears all the men are just sitting there, staring into space. Looks like supper time with food bowls.'

'Just sitting there?' Noone questioned.

''Old on. Ere we go. There's a man walking around. Wait a minute, he's feeling their faces. Moving from one to another. I know him. He drinks at Cecile's. Definitely that man Goodfeller!'

'I don't understand what they're doing,' Noone replied again, confused.

'He's blind. He probably doesn't know 'imself. I can't see nuffink else. No guards, nuffink.'

'You,' Noone spoke pointing to the orderly. 'You, go ahead.'

The orderly was terrified to do so but Luna's guttural growl convinced him to comply.

*****

Jones floored the car as fast as he could. The bombers were coming and they had not heard the air-raid warnings. People were still lining the streets making their way home from the previous attack. Chaos ensued.

'There, sir. Look.' Jones pointed through the windscreen.

A Messerschmitt dived through the darkness, peppering an ambulance with ammunition. The vehicle burst into flames. No show of dramatic pyrotechnics. More an autumn bonfire, and before his eyes, Thompson saw exactly what they were doing. The purple plume of flames turned to smoke and wafted through the air and across the city.

'They're targeting those ambulances!' Thompson called out.

'Evil, they're animals, sir. Targeting the infirm,' Jones responded.

'No, it's for another reason,' Thompson assured him.

People were too focused on running for cover from the planes. Their gas masks were scattered and left as they did so.

'Posters!' Belle cried from behind them.

'Belle?' Thompson turned to see her presenting the broken torch towards him.

He snatched it quickly, it did not work despite his attempts to influence it. He fumbled through the glove compartment for his own torch. Removing and replacing the batteries from one to another and with subtle cajoling, it flickered to reveal the violet beam.

He shone the torchlight revealing dancing plumes surrounding the outside of the car and being inhaled unexpectedly by unsuspecting passers-by.

'Shall I stop?' Jones inquired.

'No, don't you bloody-well stop. Drive as fast as you can.'

Thompson trained the beam out of the window on to the recruitment posters and Kitchener's dramatic stare. The eyes of RA lit up as poster upon poster that lined London's street, expressed its image and were accompanied by orders.

OBEY, FOLLOW, KILL

The iridescent clouds of purple were sprouting up and filtering throughout the city. They were filling the lungs and entering the bloodstreams of its inhabitants.

'Gas masks, now!' Thompson ordered.

*****

The driver tentatively stepped towards the rear entrance of the Silvera Institute carrying The Lady in her box. His brow dripping in anxious perspiration, he slammed the solid brass knocker.

Gideon Belchambers was well-hidden behind the wheel arch of the ambulance truck. His pistol was trained on the doorway, should the orderly have a sudden change of heart or his enemy be revealed.

'Did you hear that, Professor?' Brian Louds excitedly laughed at the catatonic Meredith Malcolm. 'You will soon have your mask in all its feathered finery.' Skipping excitedly up the stone staircase and through the stone-walled corridors of dim torchlight, Louds opened the doorway to greet his guard.

'You have them?' he asked enthusiastically, eyes trained on the box.

The guard stalled and did not respond immediately. A drip of sweat fell from his brow and dispersed onto the box.

Louds immediately opened the lid, releasing the black-and-white bird inside.

'What is this, a mockingbird? Traitor!' Louds screamed, slashing the man across the face with the poisonous spike on his ceremonial ring.

The guard shook violently, slumped to his knees and fell into the doorway. Brain Louds moved to slam the door but the hulking figure of the orderly blocked the path. He let out an ear-piercing scream as he stepped over the body to pull it from the door.

Gideon readied his shot and then caught the eyes of Brian Louds. His heart raced and he became breathless. His fears had come true. The rumours were real. Fourteen years ago, he had stared into those very same eyes. The man looked very different back then but his eyes were as evil as he had remembered. Gideon squeezed his trigger and sent the small metal bullet hurtling towards him.

'Ahhhhhhh!' came the deafening scream as the bullet hit its target and sent him tumbling back over the orderly and into the passageway.

*****

'Did you hear that?' Pop turned to Noone.

'Was it Gideon?'

'Dunno.'

'Come on,' Noone replied, arming himself. He followed the safe passage to the Institute the orderly had carefully trod in front of them. He rushed to the glass window of the Institute and with short sharp thuds alerted Archie Goodfellow.

'Who's there? who's that?' Archie Goodfellow called out.

'Your name Goodfeller?' Pop asked muffled through the glass. He trained a gun at him, although the poor man could not see.

'Archie *Goodfellow*. Wait, I know your voice. Braggan, right? You are Pop Braggan.'

'Archie, my name is Nathaniel,' Noone interrupted them. 'A good friend of Professor Belchambers. Do you know of a young girl being brought here?'

Archie directed them to a door along the external balcony. The steel and glass balustrades reflected the crashing seas from the cliffs as the moon shone down behind them.

'I'm sorry, I have not seen, so to speak, or heard any child here,' Archie confirmed.

'What's wrong wiv this lot?' Pop questioned Archie, moving into the building. He examined more closely the hundred or so men who sat in silence staring aimlessly into space.

'They change when the music comes,' Archie explained. 'I've never known them like this.'

'Archie, how well do you know this place? Can you guide us?' Noone asked.

Pop flashed him a look and gestured towards Archie's eyes.

'I know this place better than most. I see beyond the walls,' Archie confirmed.

'Eh?' spoke Pop, confused.

'I smell things others do not sense. I feel draughts and breezes others do not feel. There are hidden doorways and corridors for sure. All is not as it seems.'

'We'll follow you then,' Noone confirmed.

'This place is giving me the creeps,' Pop said, staring at the servicemen with their many scars and disabilities who remained motionless where they sat. 'What d'ya suppose this stuff is?' Pop asked, reaching over one of the stationary men, and holding up the pestle and mortar bowls with the remains of ground-down purple powder.

'I don't know, Pop. But this place is beginning to creep me out too,' Noone replied.

Following Archie's lead, the men descended past the white-washed walls with the picture-less frames and the abundance of mirrors. Noone couldn't understand them. The last thing he wanted was a constant reminder of how he looked.

'The operating rooms, or so he calls them,' Archie announced with an outstretched hand.

'Who?' Noone questioned

'Dr Mialora.'

*****

'If you please.' Nelly gestured to Dove to drop her weapon. 'After you.'

The governess duly complied and walked slowly towards the room where Aggie, Eric, and Sister Harvey were captive.

'Slowly, very slowly. An old lady like me has very shaky hands,' Nelly advised, threatening her with consequences.

Dove unlocked the door. Nelly shoved her in with the point of the barrel.

'It's you.' Aggie smiled, relieved.

'Of course, it's 'er.' Eric laughed.

'You knew?' Aggie turned to him.

'Course I knew,' Eric smirked.

'Nelly Parker, I am so pleased to see you.' Agatha welled up as she spoke.

Nelly removed her darkened glasses to reveal her dual coloured iris. 'Nosey Parker, some might say.' Nelly smiled.

'Or the Priory Friar,' Eric added, referencing her disguise.

Aggie looked at him in disbelief. It had been her. Aggie had not imagined it to be Nelly, however, wrong her recollection was.

'Such happy families now,' Dove criticised spitefully. 'They're coming soon and no one will survive.'

'Is that so?' Nelly answered in a far more serious tone. 'Well, talking of happy families, what have you done to my sister?' She finished by cocking the arm of her gun and pressing it into Dove's temple.

*****

Gideon approached the entranceway with caution. The contorted figure of the orderly lay half in and out of the building, foaming at the mouth. There was a pool of blood nearby where Gideon's shot had maimed its target. The dimly lit passageway of candlewax torches provided just enough light for him to follow the bloody trail deeper into the inner sanctum of Silvera.

The shattering of glass broke the eerie silence and Gideon's heart rate increased. He edged down the corridor, deeper into the Institute. The carved blocks of stone that supported the walls, the shadowy use of old wax and torches, transported him back to the hidden tunnels of so many years ago. Wiping the stinging sweat out of his eyes, he hoped his contemporaries were faring better. A second shattering of glass alerted his senses and he composed himself as he crept nearer to their sound.

He glimpsed through the open glass doorway towards a room completely at odds with its surroundings. Walnut and mahogany cases, full of books. Strange collections of insects that writhed in their enclosures of glass. An extended laboratory bench full of the most complete set of scientific instruments he had seen. A third crash of glass just feet away turned him to turn quickly and fire his gun into the darkness. A flap of black-and-white wings tore through the lab and hid amongst the inverted ceiling joists that pointed to the glass prims at its pinnacle.

'Stupid bird, I could have shot you,' Gideon whispered to himself as he stepped forward, looking up to the moonlit sky above.

He couldn't have seen the exposed trapdoor as his footing gave way. He slipped, falling through it. Dropping his gun at the realisation of his plight, he made a last chance attempt to grab the floor of the lab as he fell. The gun landed feet below firing off another round on impact and sparking up the marble room below.

*****

'Did you hear that one too?' Archie called out to the confused onlookers. 'Two gunshots I have counted so far,' he confirmed.

'Are you sure?' Noone asked. Neither Pop or he had the sensitivity of Archie's hearing. 'Can you guide us towards them?'

Archie agreed and began to walk them through the operating corridors. Passing glazed room upon room they moved swiftly, one having the rotting corpses of rats, spilling out of a large glass tank.

'This place gets worse,' Pop added to the conversation.

'There. From over there,' Archie pointed unknowingly at his own reflection at a dead end with a floor to ceiling mirror

'That's just a mirror, Archie,' Pop told him.

Brian Louds gazed on through the two-way mirror as his only blind resident pointed a finger directly towards him. The face of the melted man unwittingly stared back as did the gold-laden giant with the teardrop tattoo. The blood streaming from the bullet wound that had cleanly entered and exited his left bicep was flowing quickly. Louds applied a gauze, makeshift tourniquet, and cleansed the wound with iodine as he stared upon yet more quarry with murderous intent.

'Nathaniel, no! Seven years of bad luck!' Pop shouted.

'My luck was expended years ago,' Noone replied before hurling a chair in the direction of Archie's pointed finger.

An ear-piercing shatter sent a thousand shards of reflective glass crashing to the floor and revealing Louds' hidden network of stone-built tunnel-ways. The orderly seized his chance and ran back into the Institute to escape.

'Luna,' Pop readied his dog.

'Forget him. He served his purpose,' Noone ordered Pop, as he took in the sight before him. 'Wow!' Noone expressed stepping inside. The sand-coloured blocks were reminiscent of the labyrinths of Giza. 'You were right, Archie. You were right.'

'God 'elp us. Wot 'ave we got mixed up in now?' Pop offered.

Noone pointed towards the fresh bloodied footsteps leading away from it.

'Here it comes. Can you hear it?' spoke Archie moments before the sound was audible to the rest.

A crackling of static started overhead, and through hidden speakers the voice came. 'Where on earth have my manners been?' Louds' voice penetrated. 'Welcome to the Institute Silvera, gentlemen. Seeing as you have already made yourselves at home, allow me to introduce to you my guinea pigs,' he finished abruptly.

Pop and Nathaniel stared uncomfortably at one another. Pop rolled up his sleeves while Noone cocked his pistol.

'OBEY. OBEY,' Louds repeated over and over again before introducing soothing classical music.

Upstairs, there came the sounds of chairs shuffled out as their occupants rose, copied the call to OBEY, and began to march on the spot. The deafening sound of over 100 men preparing themselves for battle. A blood-curdling scream rebounded downwards as the terrified orderly cried out in the distance.

'What the hell is happening?' Noone asked of Archie.

'Wait, it's coming again,' Archie nervously replied as the static played out.

'Kill them. Kill them all.'

Chapter 55
Captives

Thompson and Jones's saloon arrived quickly at the rear of Fortnum's. A stationary car greeted them as they rushed through the open security gates. Slumped outside of his driver's seat, was the lone body of a man.

'Is that Smith?' Thompson asked of Jones.

'It's definitely him,' Jones confirmed, slamming the brakes on, and rushing to his friend.

'Wait, carefully now,' Thompson informed his man 'Do not remove your mask at any cost.'

Screams of civilians echoed through the streets as foreign planes would skim across the rooftops flashing light as they went. Occasionally gunfire and explosions followed.

Both men were armed as they cautiously approached the lifeless body next to the abandoned car. Belle reclined in the back of the car, nursing her arm, regaining what little strength she had left. Her heavy breathing was clouding the mask's visor.

'Smith? Smith, can you hear me?' Thompson whispered into his colleague's ear, cradling his limp head.

There was no response. His pulse was still active but his pupils dilated as he stared into oblivion.

'Check for blood; a gunshot wound,' Thompson ordered Jones.

Between them, they turned the man and checked all over but no bullets had passed through him.

'Sir, here sir,' Jones directed his superior.

A tiny crimson trickle on the palm of his hands led to a recent hole from a sharp needle that had punctured the skin, forced the poison through, and rendered the man incapacitated.

'The treacherous swine,' Thompson angered, fumbling quickly into his pockets.

The two phials, one of light green and the other a thick viscose emerald, were well-protected within their black casing. Thompson uncorked the lightest fluid, took the accompanying needle and injected a tiny pinhead of anti-venom into the already tiny hole created via the assailant. All they could do now was wait.

*****

'She poisoned 'er!' Eric shouted out as Nelly untied Agatha.

'Did she now,' Nelly replied, forcing Dove onto her knees.

Aggie, in turn, untied Eric. Using their best efforts, they sat Sister Harvey upright, her drooling mouth lent against Dove's shoulder. Eric frisked the governess, searching for the poison in her pockets but it wasn't there.

'Where is it?' he demanded. If he had Nelly's gun, he would surely have ended any more malevolence from Dove.

'You silly child. You have all lost. They are coming for you all.' She laughed.

'I only asked to see how co-op-ri-tiv you'd be.' Eric smirked back, turning Dove's belt buckle to reveal the two phials of liquid. 'I'm guessing the poison one is the one with less liquid, doubt she's ever used the other for anything good.' Eric suggested to Nelly, examining them towards the light of the letterbox window.

'If that's right how much to administer the cure?' Nelly directed towards Dove, who remained defiantly silent.

'Very well. Poison it is,' Nelly confirmed, drawing the remaining dark green fluid and moving to Dove's neck vein.

'No, no, that will kill me!' Dove cried out. 'Please, no, just a drop. A pinprick is sufficient to bring her around.' She screamed as Nelly pierced her skin and administered a pinprick of the darker poison.

Dove shook while her muscles contorted. Her hands retracted like claws before she fell down slobbering on the floor.

'Nelly!' Aggie screamed in shock.

'I don't trust her. Do you? She's a rat. Why not make her a lab rat?' Nelly replied un-wielding. 'I need to be certain. My sister's life is at stake.' She then reached for the second liquid and began to tease a tiny droplet out.

Static interference broke the tense atmosphere in the room. It reverberated through the brass vent they had listened into so carefully.

'Come on, Eric,' Aggie encouraged her friend. 'Let's find what she was hiding.'

Nelly nodded her permission and Aggie led her friend along the winding school corridors. They stopped temporarily at the large Aspidistra as the violins continued through the public address outside and throughout the village. Purple light shone through the cracks between blinds. Creeping quietly towards the slatted window, Eric peeked outside. The town folk were moving slowly and swaying. One or two firmly clasped children in their hands and were marching them down the Steep towards Amble Bridge. Above them, the bunting burned brightly and the smoke engulfed them all.

'Bring me your children, OBEY. Bring me your children OBEY.'

Eric Peabody, who was rarely lost for words, turned to Aggie with a stunned silence.

'What, Eric? What is it?' Aggie asked worriedly.

'They're rounding up all the kids. I don't know what's going on.'

'Let's find that radio first. Then we can decide what to do. Nelly will know.'

The two of them continued into the governess's room. Apart from a square of pristine wall, where the Priory crest had recently hung, nothing looked out of place at all.

'Think, Eric. What did we hear? Think,' Aggie said out loud, searching for items in the room.

'It was like opening a case. Two clicks, always two clicks. We need to look for a case. Two clicks and then the crackling.'

'Yes, that's good,' Aggie encouraged him.

The two of them looked high and wide for a case. Nothing under the table, not much furniture at all, the room was reasonably bare. Eric opened the drawers to Dove's desk and tossed everything out with great exuberance. Ransacking a head teacher's room was a long time coming for him.

'It's not here. Perhaps it's in another room?' Aggie suggested.

'There are too many rooms to search, Aggie. It's gotta be 'ere. She'd never risk letting it out of her sight,' Eric shouted, kicking the desk in anger.

'Think, Aggie, think,' she said to herself once more, tapping a finger on her forehead as if Florrie was encouraging her in a lesson. 'Think!' she shouted at herself.

'I got it,' Eric answered. 'Nelly said the room hadn't changed much, didn't she?'

'Apart from the case,' Aggie quickly responded.

'Bookcase, not suitcase,' Eric answered, pointing to the neat piece of furniture propped against the wall.

Eric took one end and Aggie the other. The hidden wheel bearings allowed it to turn smoothly and there it was, a suitcase, hidden within the bookcase. Static crackled louder on the revelation. Right there beneath, where the case had been hidden against the wall, was an elaborate brass vent. Dove could not have known how it was revealing her secrets.

Two clicks, from the locks at each end, and they had opened the suitcase between them. A radio transmitter, recording spools, microphone, and headset all perfectly placed for clandestine communications.

'It's still on. Still working,' Eric whispered to Aggie, the crackling of interference feeding back to them. 'Say something,' Eric encouraged. 'pretend you're Dove.'

Aggie shook her head in defiance. 'Absolutely not.'

'Just say something. What does it matter? You 'erd 'er. They're already coming for us. If you don't, I will, and then the game will definitely be up,' he insisted. Eric thrust his hand down on a large black button in front of the microphone preparing himself to speak.

'*Guten abend*,' Aggie improvised, impersonating Dove. She was hoping the static and interference would mask their vocal differences. 'This is Taube, over, Tuchhandler are you there?'

Gideon held on with both hands. The drop below could be any number of feet down. The moonlight beamed through the prism above and reflected onto the staff below where the Scarlet Scarab was set against silver and gold razor-sharp wing casings. He began to pull himself upwards when the distant sound of violins began in the background.

'What on earth?' he said to himself before the smashing of a glass pane penetrated through the corridors.

The echo of footsteps paced closer to where he hung. They disappeared momentarily while descending the stone steps in the adjacent chamber, before falling silent.

With a final surge of energy, Gideon hauled himself up and clung onto the trapdoor from below his elbow joints. His chin resting on the wooden surround using every notion of leverage he could.

'Dear friend, leaving so soon?' came the sinister voice from the darkness beneath him. A voice he had not heard in a long, long time, but recognised instantly.

'Ahhhhhhh!' Gideon screamed aloud as the ceremonial staff, with its gold and silver wings, was unceremoniously thrust into his leg.

Brain Louds slowly tore the ornate, razor-sharp wings of the scarab through Gideon's calf muscle. The excruciating pain was too much to bear. Gideon lessened his grip and crashed into the chamber below.

'Nice to see me after all this time?' Louds laughed, removing his facemask and smiling through sinew and bone.

*****

It wasn't instant and therefore Thompson doubted his actions immediately. Turning to Jones in despair he shook his head.

'Wait,' Jones replied as Smith's diaphragm retracted and a volley of breath shot from him.

Coughing and spluttering, Smith vomited bile and blood as his body reacted to the poison leaving his body. Thompson quickly removed his gas mask and placed it on his colleague, clutching his own airways to stop the smoke penetrating. Jones sought one from the boot and replaced in onto this friend.

Smith struggled to get his words out. 'In there,' he advised, pointing towards the previously hidden entrance to the department.

The bin that covered the hidden cellar way was displaced several yards from its position of stewardship. The oak doors hidden beneath were now upright, leaving the entrance exposed.

'Get them to a hospital, now,' Thompson ordered Jones.

'I'm coming with you,' came Belle's voice from behind.

'You're too weak, Belle,' Thompson told her.

'And you are too few. I can help. I can,' she insisted.

'Come on then,' Thompson said, having no time to argue. 'Stay behind me.'

Descending into the underground cavern, they were greeted with pitch black.

'Torch?' Belle asked.

Thompson passed it over as he kept his gun raised. She lit it up. Its now-familiar violet guiding their way under sets of illuminating eyes.

'They're everywhere!' Belle cried. 'Everywhere.'

The overwhelming sense of defeat crippled Thompson's confidence. What were they fighting?

'Sshhh … listen a minute,' Thompson said, stalling. 'It's coming from outside.'

The welcome sound of the air-raid sirens arrived at last. A moment of relief as the Protocols remained intact.

'*People of London, OBEY. People of London, OBEY!*' came the surprise voice following the first siren before being overtaken and drowned out by violins.

Belle looked towards Thompson. They acknowledged to each other their theory had come to fruition.

'Listen,' Belle directed Thompson tugging on his shirtsleeve.

'I know. I heard it too,' he acknowledged.

'No, really listen,' she replied, tapping her ears. Her voice was still muffled under her mask.

'*People of London. OBEY! People of London OBEY!*' they heard against a screech of feedback, this time echoing and near, not just from the public address speakers across the city.

Thompson suddenly realised where the sound was coming from. An index finger raised to his gas mask was sufficient enough for Belle to remain silent as they crept through the daunting corridors.

*****

'You need to do something quick, Archie,' Pop fervently suggested as the army of veterans began their slow march down the winding ramp.

'I don't know this part of the building. It was hidden to me,' Archie replied.

'Just listen for any sounds or feel those breezes, Archie, or we are all dead,' Noone hurried him.

'It's difficult to concentrate with that damn distraction,' Archie replied, pointing towards the hidden speakers.

Pop walked towards their direction. He felt the wall. It was lathe and plaster, not stone. He thrust his fist through it and tore out whatever wires he could find. The speakers in their immediate vicinity rang silent.

'Thank you. That's better,' Archie informed them

Noone and Pop could still hear the many hidden speakers playing out the concerto, and informing the imminent army to *Kill* them.

'I can't find them all. There's too many,' Pop advised.

'Perhaps there's a master relay,' said Noone.

They started looking for any cables or piping, which would carry such wiring.

'Pop, up there, the thick black pipe.' Noone pointed out.

'Here goes nuffink,' the giant gipsy said, clasping his ham fists around the pipework.

As the pipe yielded to his great strength the lights of the Institute began to flicker. The more he pulled, the more the intermittent they became.

'Wait, Pop, wait!' Noone cried out – too late!

Bang! The sparks of electricity flew above their heads. A live cable hissed and thrashed serpent-like, just missing the huge man. Immediately, they were plunged into darkness. The music stopped too.

'Yes!' Pop applauded. 'It worked, kinda.'

'What's happened?' Archie asked.

'We've lost the music but also the lights. Everything has gone dark,' Noone

'Welcome to my world.' Archie smiled. 'Wait, what's that?'

The whirring of static as a gramophone, slowly coming to life, came across the speakers once more.

'Kill, kill, kill,' it repeated in its deep monotone.

'Oh great,' said Pop, as if things couldn't get any worse.

Then, in the distance, tiny flickers of lights began illuminating the Institute once more.

'The back-up generators, I think,' Archie piped up.

The purple lights that replaced the fluorescent hospital tubing in times of emergency, stuttered and came to life, illuminating the walls to reveal the secrets of Silvera. The hidden eyes of RA staring back from the picture-less frames.

Kill, Obey, Follow, daubed across every surface, walls, floors and ceilings.

'You were saying?' Noone said to Pop. 'Run!'

Luna barked rapidly, snarling and snapping as the army had moved to within feet of them, following them through the hidden chamber. Unrelenting, they drew closer and closer.

*****

Thompson gestured to Belle to enter the room cautiously as he carefully opened the door. The banks of desks, headsets and telephone relays hastily rearranged so that cables ran in an incomparable interconnecting web.

Removing his mask very slowly, Thompson encouraged Belle to follow, helping her as her broken arm hung in its makeshift sling. Whispering into her ear, he brought her up to speed.

'This room is wired. He can eavesdrop. That we definitely know.'

'What is all this?' she mouthed back softly.

Thompson shrugged as he perused the room. The complexity of the telephone exchanges was as new to him as it was to her. 'He's orchestrating communications somehow,' Thompson suggested.

Belle looked back confused. Static reconvened as an incoming message announced itself.

'This is Taube. Over. Tuchhandler, are you there?'

A momentary pause elapsed as Thompson and Belle digested the message.

'I told you to leave,' the man's voice replied.

Belle pointed to a small microphone where the voice had come from and which fed the larger relay.

'He's still here,' Thompson mouthed to Belle. Ghosting past her with his gun drawn, he slid up to the side of the corridor. The unmistakable letter D, faded in gold leaf on the door, greeted Thompson as he stared at the suicidal passageway ahead. The blinds were drawn and only the faintest of shadows flitted from within the room. Gesturing to Belle to find a suitably long object, Thompson crouched down and removed his fedora. Belle returned with a wooden metre ruler that Thompson used to suspend his hat upon. Belle squatted towards the floor, grabbed the ruler with her good arm and held it up to mimic Thompson's head height.

'Are you sure, Belle?' Thompson asked. 'You're in the line of fire.'

'Of course,' she replied.

Thompson slid down onto his stomach. Gun loaded and aiming at the door.

'On three,' he mouthed. 'One, two … '

BANG! BANG!

Two quick shots smashed the frosted glass, the golden D shattering into a million pieces. The bullets fizzed through the corridor towards them both. The first penetrated the hat and sent it spinning on the ruler. The second splintered the stick itself.

Thompson volleyed several rounds back through the hole in the glass.

'Oww!' Belle cried out.

'Are you hit?'

'No, it's just my arm,' she replied, clutching the arm in the sling. 'Go, go,' she ordered him.

Thompson burst into a sprint.

With the exception of the chrome balls shining from Newton's cradle, discarded on the floor, the office was empty. The book-cases behind the desk, with their many hidden exits, had all doors left wide open. It was a fool's errand to even try to follow him down the dark passageways. Even if you chose correctly. Thompson returned to Belle.

'We need to make sense of this all,' he said, scratching his hatless head. There was a renewed enthusiasm now they knew the enemy was close.

Returning to the communication room, they took a step back to observe the mass of cables and telephony exchanges in front of them. The banks of desks surrounded a central desk. These were not the uniformed line of organisation that Draper had stringently set up when in charge. This was not the logical systematic approach Thompson expected of him. Lines, wires, and cables led in and out in a tangled bird's nest of information exchange, culminating towards a central hub with a predominant desk in the middle of the room. A web of deceit and misdirection they had to try and fathom out.

Belle approached it stepping carefully over wire after wire. 'I am sure the message came through to this one,' she said as she approached the central exchange. 'Do you speak German, Thompson?' she asked.

'Not nearly well enough,' he replied, now canvassing the communications room.

'Tuchhandler – well, now I understand. It's German for Draper. You were right. And Taube … well, that means Dove,' she advised him.

'Very good, but who the hell is Dove?'

'Why don't we find out?' she said, pointing to the exchange where the message had been received.

*****

'I told you to leave,' Tuchhandler had replied.

Aggie and Eric jumped back from the microphone startled. They hadn't expected a response.

'What do I do now?' Aggie turned to Eric.

'Dunno, didn't fink that far,' was his unhelpful response.

'He was adamant to get out of this place, at all costs. Something bad is coming, Eric.'

'Somefink bad is already 'appening,' he said, gesturing to the outside.

They waited patiently, nervously.

'What on earth do you think you are doing?' Nelly Parker said, making them jump as she entered the office.

'Who's guarding the gov'ness?' was Eric's first response.

'I am,' came the welcome voice of Sister Harvey pushing Dove from behind with the point of a barrel.

Dove shuffled forward, gagged and bound, looking the worse for wear. The antidote was working on her too.

'It worked then.' Eric smiled looking towards the poison.

'It did, clever boy,' Nelly acknowledged.

Static began to flow back through to the radio device once more.

'This is *not* Tuchhandler. Repeat this is *not* Tuchhandler,' came the cut-glass accent down the line.

Aggie and Eric turned to each other, confused. The three adults all equally confused in the room. A silence fell amongst them as no one was willing to speak.

'Cat got your tongue, Taube, or should I say Dove?' the man spoke confidently. 'Your game is over. We have captured Tuchhandler. It's over.'

A disbelieving shrug of shoulders as his eyes lit up and jaw dropped painted a victorious picture across Eric's face. Aggie was too late to stop her friend as he lurched and pressed the microphone into action, rolled his shoulders over, and stopped anyone from trying to snatch the microphone.

'We've got her too. We caught 'er. We caught Dove. We want the reward. Just kids but we stopped 'er!' Eric enthusiastically announced.

'Well done, son. I am sure the reward will be yours. What's your name, son?' came the reply. 'Can you give me your name? I am Thompson of The Department.'

'Peabody, sir, Eric Peabody of Ambledown. And me mate here is, is A –'

Aggie snatched the microphone from him.

'Hold on,' came a female voice back. 'Ambledown, did you say?'

Aggie was berating Eric. He shouldn't have said their names or location. She took the microphone from him and refused him to use it.

'You could have given us away,' she told him.

'But we already are. They're coming. You 'erd the other fella? Right?' Eric angrily replied.

'Hello, are you still there?' the lady spoke again over the speaker. 'OK, I understand. It's about trust and trust me we do not know who to trust. If that makes any sense. But if you just said Ambledown I wish to ask you one question. OK?'

Aggie nor Eric could decide what to do next. Nelly and Sister Jane Harvey held back.

'My name is Belle Soames. My father, who is poisoned and lies dying in hospital, was … wait … is good friends with a Professor from Ambledown. Would any of you know him? We desperately need his help. His name is Professor Gideon Belchambers.'

*****

'Quick, Archie! Quick! Find us a secret exit or we're mincemeat!' Pop shouted

Luna continued lurching at the oncoming army. Despite drawing blood and tearing clothes, the men did not flinch as they proceeded towards their targets.

'Kill, Kill, Kill.'

'Here, Nathaniel, here!' Archie stopped. Feeling a breeze from the stone surface in front of him.

'It's just a wall,' Noone replied looking on at the stone complimented by two large torches.

'I can feel something. I assure you,' Archie confirmed.

'Pop, start pushing,' Noone ordered.

The giant, Braggan, placed his hands between the torches as Noone and Luna desperately held off the advancing men.

'It's moving,' Pop cried out through gritted teeth. 'Archie, help me.'

Goodfellow positioned himself under Pop's frame and shoved with all his might.

'Quickly … then!' Pop called out as enough space was created for Nathaniel and Archie to squeeze through. 'It's closing … Nafaniel, 'urry up!' Pop hollered.

Noone and Goodfellow squeezed through.

'Take care of me dog,' Pop told them, shoving Luna by the collar through the closing gap.

'Pop, no! Pop!' Noone cried out unsuccessfully as the stone wall reset itself.

Pop Braggan swung and didn't stop swinging his bear-sized fists as he fought off the advancing army. As brave and strong as he was, the weight of so many men finally overpowered him. The first few men had fallen quickly, but as the advancing hoard became more and more, they sent him tumbling to the ground. Gold chains were breaking and crushed underfoot, they were suffocating the huge man.

Chapter 56
The exchanges

'I am so glad you are here to witness this.' Louds laughed loudly into Gideon's face. 'The "old gang" back together again. Stand up!' he ordered.

The bleeding tear of his calf muscle was excruciating but bloody and bruised as he was, Professor Gideon Belchambers was relatively unscathed. He hobbled under the encouragement of Louds' gun towards the black ceremonial sarcophagus that was almost hidden in the darkness.

At the head of the sacrificial stone, both altar and coffin, stood a man with arms outstretched as if preaching to a crowd. His hand was joined to the ceremonial knife of gold and bloodied rubies. The long robe shimmered and caught what little light was available and on top of his head the half-feathered mask of Horus.

'Look closer, Professor. I believe you know each other,' Louds urged him, squeezing Gideon's cheekbones from below and forcing him to stare at Meticulous Mcredith Malcolm's opaque eyes.

'Professor Malcolm?' Gideon spoke softly as Malcolm remained unresponsive.

'Indeed. So worthy of the honour of killing your niece!' he said and laughed loudly.

'No!' Gideon rounded to grab the gun but before he could do so, Louds shot him in the opposing calf. Gideon cried out in pain as he collapsed to the floor.

'Tut, tut. Now, look what you made me do. You'll just have to crawl around on all fours, Professor, just like my feline brother used to.' Louds laughed again, pointing at the mummified body of Purrsia at the foot of the altar. 'You don't think the irony was lost on me?' Louds continued. 'The furless animal, all skin and bone. Purrsia or should that be Persia, the Prince of Persia as you referred to me?' He laughed. 'Genius.'

'Grotesque, Salazar, that's the word you are struggling for – a grotesque.' Gideon winced.

'So, you do remember me. How kind. And I too remember you, Professor Gideon Belchambers or should I say – Halcombe?'

'I do not follow. You're talking in riddles,' Gideon replied through gritted teeth, trying to confuse his adversary.

'Such a unique name. I thought it would have taken us mere months to find you. Months, not fourteen years. I was losing hope and then imagine my luck after all that time. The Russian finally pays the debt he owes.'

Gideon defiantly refused to acknowledge him and remained silent.

'Ignore me all you like. Perhaps you'd care to take a look on the sacrificial altar instead?' Louds continued.

Gideon closed his eyes, refusing to acknowledge him.

'Look!' he screamed, forcing Gideon up by the scruff. 'Look!'

Gideon's head was planted against the black onyx at eye level. He tried as he might to ignore the inevitable until Louds forced his eyes open. Gideon's tears were streaming before his lids parted. Staring directly into the young girl's eyes he bowed his head down and let out an eruption of laughter.

'The girl with the mark of the moon. Your niece, the usurper's heir. Do you know how strict the secretariat are? Do you know that without her body I can never fulfil my rite?'

'It's not her.' Gideon looked up at him. 'It's not her!' Gideon laughed uncontrollably.

'You're lying. You are lying!' Louds aggressively replied. Forcing Gem's body upwards and revealing her back. 'You see the mark!'

'I see a mark.' Gideon laughed hysterically. He leant forward, licked his finger and rubbed the crescent mark of congealed blood from Gem's back. 'Betrayed once more.' Gideon laughed.

In a fit of rage, Louds lashed the gun hilt across Gideon's face, knocking him unconscious. 'If I cannot kill her, I'll take the next best thing!' he screamed upwards towards the statues of the gods.

*****

'Are you still there?' Belle continued down the microphone. An extended pause greeted her back. 'If you decide you can trust us. Just call back. My name is Belle Soames. Not sure how you could ever check that what I have said is true but … well, anyway, that's all I have. I must go now.'

'Look,' Thompson pointed to a flashing light at the central desk. 'What do you think that is?'

'I'm not sure,' Belle replied.

'Wait, can you hear that again?' Thompson added.

It was distant but the violins had started over once more.

'*People of London, OBEY, People of London, OBEY. Come onto the streets,do not be afraid. Do not be afraid,*' came the recognisable voice of Draper.

Thompson left Belle waiting for a response from the children and ran back down to the cellar entrance. Donning his gas mask once more, he peeked out into the chaotic city of London. The skies were turning mauve. A combination of purple and violet the likes he had not seen. Lord Kitchener's eyes were lighting up from the posters that plastered every street. Overhead, the final aircraft was lighting up targets before plumes of smoke dispersed their poison into the ether.

'What in God's name is happening?' he said to himself.

A blast of light, a powerful beam, shot across the rooftops. Followed swiftly by another. They were anti-aircraft spotters. The type deployed by the Protocols to help shell enemy craft. But they were not tracking the Messerschmitts, which swooped and dived. Instead, they were directed towards the metal zeppelins that flew above the city to deter the bombing raids. In turn, the angular metallic surfaces sent the light onwards cascading the city in a blanket of colour.

'It's not the Protocols,' Thompson confirmed to himself. 'He's using them against us.' Sprinting as fast as he could he returned to Belle. 'Any news? '

'Not yet,' Belle confirmed. 'But look, all the desks are lighting up now.'

Thompson stepped back. Looking at the central hub and the surrounding desks feeding into it. Like a circle of dominoes, the lights came on one after the other. Just like the white light rush as Protocol after Protocol was completed.

'It's the Protocols, Belle. But not for any good.'

'What are the Protocols? What do you mean?' she replied confused.

'If I am right, Draper has initiated them. It's a system for communicating across the city at rapid speed and to protect us from attack. Draper is using them against us. You need to stay here in case I need you, or the children need you. I am off to Ludgate Hill.'

*****

Luna scratched so ferociously at the closed stone doorway her pads began to bleed.

'Come, girl, come,' Archie encouraged.

The hidden room was small and echoed.

'Who's that?' Noone asked, training his gun towards movement in the corner. 'Speak. Who are you?'

'My name is Dr Mialora. My name is Dr Mialora. My name is …' came the repetitive tone.

'You!' Noone walked cautiously forward, gun drawn, and barely enough light to see in front of him. 'Put down your weapon.'

'Wait, Nathaniel, wait,' Archie stepped in front of him. 'I know his voice.' Archie walked forward and passed his palms over the gentleman's face. 'It is the Doctor. But not as we suspect,' Archie confirmed. 'This room. It's not as I expected. Not as they should have been keeping him. Start searching, Nathaniel. Start feeling for anything but brick or stone.'

In the darkness, Archie ran his hands along the wall. Noone joined him. They had finished three sides when Noone felt the stone shift to a much colder surface.

'Here, what is it?'

'Glass, I think,' Archie replied.

'Glass? I cannot see a thing through it,' Noone replied in the pitch black.

'Perhaps it's for seeing in, not out.'

'If that's so, then, excuse me.' Noone stepped them both back and fired a shot straight at it.

The glass shattered and tore through the hung drape beyond, instantly flooding the room with light. Noone, Luna and Dr Mialora shrouded their eyes from the brightness.

'Told you,' Archie said and smiled.

Noone looked through. Yet another room but well-lit, separate from the purple lighting of the rest of the Institute. In front of him, amidst a bank of communication wires and a telephony exchange, a spooling recorder played *Kill, Kill, Kill* over and over again. Next to it, not a gramophone as they thought but a second recording device playing the symphonic sounds of the gramophone.

'I don't suppose you two are our problem?' Noone said sarcastically as he ripped the spools apart.

The music stopped immediately. The repetitive orders to kill them desisted. The footsteps of the soldiers had stopped. Brian Louds' army had frozen where they stood. Noone turned to see Dr Mialora in the light.

'I know you,' Noone said to him. 'You are a doctor, but not this one. You must remember me, Sir Wallace. It's Nathaniel Noone. Sir Wallace, Sir Wallace?' Noone repeated clicking his fingers in front of the man's unresponsive stare.

'I am Dr Mialora,' Sir Wallace James repeated.

'No,' Noone insisted to him. 'You are not!'

*****

Thompson drove the saloon to its fastest limit. His sight was impaired by the misting gas mask as he breathed erratically and deeply, swerving constantly to avoid the people peppering the streets. The skies were a deep purple now as night time crept in. The fog of ethereal smoke engulfed the citizens, who were powerless to resist the continued commands. Thousands upon thousands took to the streets in swaying unison and aimlessly walked around. Should a Thunder Machine strike now, they would all be exterminated.

St Paul's Cathedral, perched high on the hill at Ludgate, was always the first protocol and looked down upon the city above all others. Thompson pressed forward towards St Paul's.

Belle Soames sat patiently for the children to respond. The full bank of desks was now flashing back at her. If Thompson was right, Draper had total control over London.

'Miss Soames?' came the young girl's voice through distant interference. 'I have a question for you.'

'This is Belle Soames. Please, go ahead.'

'How well do you know my uncle?' Aggie asked.

Belle Soames was just about to answer when she paused.

'I'm sorry, could you repeat that?' Belle began to well up.

'How well do you know Professor Gideon Belchambers?' Agatha replied.

'That's not what you actually said,' Belle replied, beginning to sniffle.

'Agatha, that's quite enough now,' Sister Harvey suggested.

'You said uncle. Did you say uncle?' Belle questioned.

Agatha was looking at Harvey and Parker, who she knew knew so much more than they were letting on. Both of them were discouraging her from saying anything else.

'That's right,' Aggie continued defiantly.

Belle erupted into a flood of tears. Her sobbing could be heard back through the exchange.

'Miss Soames, are you ok, why are you crying?' Aggie asked.

'Because if you are telling me the truth, I attended your memorial when I was no older than I suspect you are now.' She continued to cry.

Aggie turned in disbelief. 'What is she talking about?' she demanded of the Sister and her sister.

They refused to divulge any more.

'Miss Soames, I do not understand what is going on and people here are refusing to tell me. So, I ask this last question of you, did you ever know my uncle by the name of Gideon Belchambers?'

The lengthy pause was almost too much to bear. Belle gathered herself and replied.

'No, I did not. Not back then. His name is … well, was … as I knew him, Halcombe Stubbs-Moffatt.'

This was not quite how she had intended being informed of the answer she was seeking. Aggie stared at Sister Jane Harvey who, in turn, looked to her sister, Nelly Parker, as they both bowed their heads knowingly.

'Why didn't you just tell me?' Aggie angrily asked them. 'And my mother, did you know her too?' Aggie questioned via the receiver.

'I did. Your mother was named Charlotte,' Belle confirmed.

*****

Louds unceremoniously dumped Gem's body to the side of the sarcophagus and hauled Gideon's concussed body onto it.

'Damn you, Jennifer! Damn you, Sabine!' he screamed out. 'I will execute your father for this!' Louds shouted out. Restraining Gideon upon the altar, Louds walked behind Professor Malcolm.

'You may kill him now. Kill, Kill,' Louds repeated over and over again

Meredith Malcolm raised his arm, with the blade secured in his hand, above his head and pointed it towards Gideon's heart.

'Now!' Louds screamed, sending the Professor's arm downward. In the darkness, Louds felt a gust of wings flash by him, hurtling towards the Professor. The large magpie landed on his arm, trying to pull the ceremonial blade and its shiny rewards from his clasp. The knife was bound so tightly that rather than release it, the Professor spun off-balance, crashing towards the sarcophagus, and knocking himself unconscious as he did so.

Louds shot Gideon's weapon at The Lady who scrambled back through the trapdoor and into the room above. 'Why have you stopped?' Louds cried out. 'Why?' he called out as the silence of the Institute suddenly overwhelmed him.

*****

The screams of children, far greater than they had been, broke the tension in the room and across the exchange. Eric dashed out to peep through the blinds. Children were now being marched, accompanied by two adults either side, with a willing army of adults to help with the task if they struggled.

'Heellppp!' screamed Elizabeth who had been forced from the Poacher by Millicent McGregor and the barfly Doctor Beckworth, then dragged kicking and reeling down the Steep. 'Eric, Aggie, Gemima!' she hollered. 'Ruunn … if you can hear me! Run!' It was only a minute of struggling before she too succumbed to the Ethereum and the power of the Illuminant as she wilfully paced down the street with the two adults.

'Aggie, they've got Lizzy,' Eric shouted. 'But where's Gem?'

'What's happening?' Belle spoke down the exchange.

'Our town has been taken over. Adults are rounding up the children. It's some sort of magic. It's as if they're possessed!' Eric shouted.

'The same is happening in London,' Belle confirmed.

'Haha!' Dove laughed beneath her gag.

Nelly reintroduced her to the poison again and left her to convulse on the floor.

'Ignore that. Please, continue,' Aggie said.

'Can you see illuminations? Do you have any army recruitment posters in your streets? Are there images of eyes, and are they violet or purple-blue?' Belle quizzed them.

'The 'ole town is purple. Even the buntin'. it's burning throughout the streets. It's alight. The ole place is alight. There's smoke everywhere and that's purple too,' Eric confirmed.

'Anything else? Can you hear anything for example?' Belle continued.

'Violins,' Aggie and Eric replied together.

'Good, good, and with them, orders, over and over giving repetitive instructions.'

'How did you know that?' Eric replied.

'Now, listen to me. We are experiencing exactly the same thing. It could be all over the country, heaven knows. But put out the light. That seems to influence everyone. That's my best guess,' Belle offered.

'No chance. The whole of our street is ablaze. It would take everyone in Ambledown, and all the adults are rounding up the children,' Eric explained.

'Then, stop the music. Stop the orders. Can you get to them?'

'I think they're in two separate places,' Eric said.

'Wilson controls the public address,' Nelly confirmed. 'We can get to him, I'm sure.'

'Eric, you go with Sister Harvey and Nelly. They can use you as a decoy. I'll mind Dove,' Aggie insisted. 'It's all I can think of. Go, now.'

*****

Passing Trafalgar Square, the enormity of his task played out in front of him. Thompson did not stop but slowed to avoid the thousands of people who now lined the streets. Buses were deserted and strewn across roads, as too was the occasional automobile. People wandered aimlessly. The sheer volume of those who would otherwise have sought refuge underground lined the streets.

Those who had succumbed were quickly followed by loved ones trying to help. The removal of the gas masks proved their undoing. As he stared upon Nelson's Column, a dazzling beam shone down from upon it as violet light illuminated the streets. The citizens were mere fodder should the Luftwaffe initiate a strike.

St Paul's, he thought. All he could do was continue onwards to St Paul's.

*****

'Follow that gunshot, Archie,' Noone insisted as they guided Sir Wallace James out the way they'd come.

The swaying army stood motionless and subdued. Luna barked and dashed off ahead as they passed hordes of men in momentary suspension.

443

'Pop?' Noone called out as he saw the hulking man trampled on the floor.

His hound bent at his face and licked his wounds. If she'd had the strength, the wolfhound would have dragged him to safety.

Archie knelt down. 'I can still feel some breath. I think he's still alive,' he confirmed.

The Braggan leader was battered and broken on the floor. His lifetime of jewellery had been crushed and broken like many of his bones.

'We can't lift him. We'll need help. Archie, continue towards that gunshot.'

'Most people run from gunfire, Nathaniel. Has anyone told you that?'

Noone cocked his weapon as Archie moved onwards. Luna the wolfhound barked once more and led the charge in front of them.

'The dog's right. There's a very strong breeze coming this way.'

'Carefully does it now, Archie,' Noone advised him as they accompanied Sir Wallace between them.

*****

Sister Harvey and Nelly Parker restrained Eric by the wrists.

'Alright, alright, I'm not the enemy,' Eric moaned. 'Loosen your grip.'

'Need to be convincing, young man,' Harvey replied, in slight enjoyment.

'The moment we leave, we're heading for the Sheriff's. Do you know where it is?' Nelly asked Eric.

Eric's face was a picture of amusement. He had spent plenty of time under the watchful eye of Wilson Bott.

'Eric, to be convincing, we really shouldn't be wearing masks. We'll retain ours but you must take a deep breath until we replace yours when we arrive. Got it?'

''Course I 'ave,' he replied

The three of them burst out of the schoolhouse. Eric took a gigantic breath from inside just before passing over the threshold. Pausing to observe the men and women they knew so well being subdued in front of them, they then continued with their plan. Eric had dashed that route hundreds of times but now, on one breath, it seemed like a mountain to climb. Quicker and quicker, he encouraged his makeshift, elderly, captors.

Standing guard outside of the Sheriff's were Messrs Closet and Cleave. They looked both imposing and macabre, though nothing more than puppet sentries. Sister Harvey did not break stride. As the men swayed in front of them she belted Mr Closet, the funeral director, as hard as she could around the face, sending him tumbling down the incline of the Steep. Closet, stout of frame and rotund, was unceremoniously tripped and rolled like the barrel he was, even further.

Eric beckoned them inward as his cheeks turned purple and his chest struggled with its final oxygen.

Once inside they secured the door behind them and watched on as poor old Wilson was subdued on the floor.

'There, next to the microphone!' Eric shouted, ripping the tape machine spool from its continuous revolution.

Outside, the violins stopped. The residents of Ambledown also stopped swaying and all that could be heard now were Jennifer James' orders.

'Bring me your children. OBEY!'

As it dawned on her the music was no longer playing, Jennifer James knew she had one last ace up her sleeve.

'You, step forward,' she directed to the girl. 'Tell me your name,' she ordered.

'Elizabeth Peabody!' she called out, emphasised through Jennifer's loud hailer.

'And how would you like to die?'

*****

'Ow, bloody hell!' Archie called out as he tripped over the torso beneath him. 'Didn't see that lying there.' He chuckled.

Nathaniel looked down at the contorted body of the orderly below them. 'Archie, are you able to get Sir Wallace out of here? I need to find Gideon and then figure out how we move Pop.'

The continued barking of Luna grabbed Nathaniel's attention as he moved cautiously back into the passageways.

'What is it, girl?' Noone asked, entering the impressive laboratory.

Luna was standing astride the open trapdoor, barking down into the darkness below, the dark hole, almost unrecognisable to a human eye, reflected back the ceremonial staff of the Scarlet Scarab.

A flap of wings from the corner and Nathaniel spied The Lady surreptitiously moving in the darkness.

'What can you see?' Noone asked them, staring into the darkness of the chamber.

'Curse the gods,' came the voice Nathaniel had dreaded hearing. 'And some people call me grotesque,' it echoed and laughed.

'Salazar!' Noone replied.

Chapter 57
The three P's

Sir Christopher Wren's most impressive architectural triumph drew before him. The baroque monolithic dome that was well-positioned upon Ludgate Hill and imposed itself over London, now shrouded in brilliant violet as light emitted from the ginormous lantern beneath the famous ball and crucifix that protected the city for centuries.

It was amazing at how the three Ps: Parliament, Palace and Paul's had remained unscathed. But now the master plan of Draper's deception played out in front of them. It had been a long time coming and born many years earlier in a much hotter country many miles away.

Ensuring his gas mask was secure, Thompson armed himself with two pistols then took to the steps outside. He recognised the two men standing guard at the entrance. Rifles loosely carried to their sides. They were the protectors of the Protocols. Only a day before had Smith and Jones rounded them up and ensured their scrutiny before Colonel Malling had insisted he was wrong.

The two men swayed as the violins played louder. Thompson couldn't see how they could harm him, how they would know how to target him but he approached them with caution.

'Fire!' came a man's voice from within the cathedral. The two men raised their rifles and shot through the air. Their bullets fizzed far from Thompson, clipping stone pillars and indiscriminately wounded a subdued civilian.

'No!' Thompson cried out before the words came again.

'Fire!'

The men reloaded and took aim again. It was obvious they were not in control of their minds or bodies as the bullets were far from hitting him but laden with murderous intent nevertheless.

Sprinting towards them he disarmed the men swiftly. Taking the rifle from one, he peered through its sight to the upper floors.

'Fire!' came the shout once more. Thompson caught a glimpse of shadow from above and fired in return. It sparked against a railing as footsteps echoed into the darkness.

On entering the cathedral, he felt its eerie calmness, so at odds with the outside world surrounding it. You could almost hear a pin drop. Keeping aim through the rifle sight, he sought an opportunity to bring down his prey as he studied the upper galleries for sight or sound of his former superior.

'This is Tuchhandler. Over. Commence the attack. Commence the attack,' echoed the familiar voice.

*****

'Lizzy!' Eric cried out, dashing to leave via the Sheriff's door.

'Think, Eric! Think!' Sister Harvey cried out as the two elderly ladies tried to restrain him.

'She's gonna kill her. She's gonna kill her.' He burst into tears while his flailing arms resisted them.

'She's not. She needs her to bargain with. If you go out there, she'll have two of you and one of you will be disposable,' Nelly tried to reason with him.

'Put on your mask. We need to come up with another plan, and quickly,' Sister Harvey ordered him.

Just down the Steep, hidden in the governess's office, Aggie waited anxiously for her friend to return.

'What's happening?' Belle Soames spoke softly down her microphone, the flashing lights reflecting from her pale skin.

'They've stopped the music. I think they've stopped the music,' Aggie enthused.

'That's great. Has it worked?' Belle continued to question.

'I'll be right back.' Aggie crept to the school doorway.

The music had indeed stopped. The inhabitants of Ambledown were motionless. An opaque film covered their eyes.

'Elizabeth Peabody,' Aggie heard announced from outside.

'How would you like her to die?' Jennifer James repeated.

Elizabeth swayed motionless and silent in her grasp.

'Very clever, children,' said Jennifer James and laughed, acknowledging the death of the symphony and its suggestive monologue. 'But if you do not come to me now, I will begin executing the children one by one.'

Aggie desperately looked up the Steep towards the Sheriff's office. Sister Harvey, Nelly, and Eric were yet to reappear.

'Five ... Four ... Three ... Two ... One!' Jennifer counted out. 'So be it.'

She cocked her pistol and held it to Elizabeth Peabody's temple. The crisp click sounded out clearly.

'Five ... Four ... Three ... Two ... One ...'

'No! STOP!' came the child's voice from the middle of the Steep.

*****

'Seems we are at an impasse,' Louds called up to Noone. 'What can you offer me for your friend's life?' He laughed.

'I can't see that you have my friend,' Noone replied.

'Where are my manners?' Louds replied. 'I'll switch the lights on.'

A spark from two flints being scuffed together chinked in the darkened chamber. Then, slowly around the circumference of the black stone sarcophagus, flames began to bob and weave. Slowly, they rallied to form the perfect eye of RA around the ceremonial altar. The orange and amber danced, momentarily hypnotising Nathaniel Noone who collapsed backwards sweating and breathless. Visions of whirling mean and ceremonial beast masks danced through his mind.

'Oh, I forgot. Do the flames still haunt you, Nathaniel? Remind you of when you once had a face?' Louds giggled aloud.

'I could ask you the same thing,' Noone replied, shielding his eyes from the direct flame-light.

The Scarlet Scarab gently throbbed as flame-light influenced her revival.

'Do you see her,' Louds directed towards the ceremonial staff and increasing presence from the crystallised stone. 'The prophecies are true.'

Noone scoured the room as Louds continued talking. As far as he could ascertain, there was no other way out apart from the stairwell. Not that he trusted the man he once knew.

'If I recall, your sacrifice should be the girl. And not that girl.' Noone laughed back.

Louds flew into a rage. 'Her uncle will suffice, for now. The gods will understand. Besides, she will come for him. She will come.'

'I'll kill her first,' Noone replied. 'If I have to. I will ensure your rites are never fulfilled.' Noone spat as he spoke.

'The melted man, he who almost burned himself alive to save her all those years ago. I do not think so,' Louds rebuked him.

Noone angled himself to find a shot. Louds lurked in the shadows but as the flames grew orange, light began to illuminate the marble white room and showed the veins of the stone as dark amber. The carved deities cast solid shadows onto the walls, and between them, the forearm of Louds was exposed.

Bang! Bang!

Two deft shots flew from Nathaniel's gun. A thud echoed across the room as the body slumped to the floor.

*****

'Where are you?' Thompson whispered to himself, trying to locate his adversary.

'Where are you? Where are you? Where are you?' echoed back at him, though it was his own voice. He paused. He heard the locks of a suitcase click and their sounds also bounced around the walls and sounded back, just behind him. He turned quickly but there was no one there. There was a sign on the wall:

The Whispering Gallery.

Each sound echoed and reverberated but announced itself far from where it had been created. It was a vocal hall of mirrors.

'I'm getting closer,' Thompson announced, momentarily raising his gas mask, as the sounds bounced and repeated themselves throughout.

'It's already over. Join me?' Draper said and laughed before his footsteps echoed and disappeared once more.

Thompson followed the route he could determine would lead him onwards. Yet more steps; steps that led to St Paul's pinnacle.

*****

'Hello? Are you still there?' Belle Soames called through the radio. 'Hello?'

No response came from the children as Belle waited desperately to hear from anyone. Unbeknownst to her, the governess's room was now empty.

*****

'STOP!' came the young girl's voice from outside the schoolhouse.

Jennifer James looked up, un-cocked her gun and pushed Elizabeth aside. It was too far to confirm her identity but, nevertheless, the girl with the black bobbed hair was walking straight towards her. Her hands were held high and there was a brilliant glow emitting from one of them.

'Let her go. Let them all go!' Agatha called out. The magnifier in her hand increasingly grew brighter as the crescent moon smiled down upon them and the facets beamed out brilliant white light.

'It's you. It really is you,' Jennifer replied. 'Turn around. Walk backwards to me.'

Accompanied by the two subdued American guardsmen, whose eyes were covered with an opaque film, and who held rifles to their fronts, Jennifer James approached Aggie's cloaked figure. Quickly forcing Aggie's head forward, Jennifer peered upon her spine. Between her shoulder blades, the raised birthmark of the moon revealed itself to her.

The light of the magnifier was beginning to heat the ebony handle and burn Aggie's fingers but as she held it aloft, its shining brilliance subdued the purple hues and they began to pale into insignificance. The nearer the town folk were to Aggie's light the sooner they snapped out of their induced service and confusingly looked towards one another.

'What's happening?' people asked as they began to wake up and recover. 'Who's she?' they said pointing towards Jennifer James.

Jennifer snatched the magnifier, scolding her hand in the process. She thrust it back into Aggie's cloaked pocket.

'Fire,' she said to the Americans who duly obliged and volleyed shots across the crowd, allowing her time to escape. Snatching Aggie by the scruff and forcing a gun to her back, she passed the hump of Amble Bridge towards the munitions factory where the Americans' jeep was parked.

Aggie turned for a second to see Eric in his gas mask desperately sprinting down the Steep as fast as his legs could carry him. The boy's sister was safely slumped on the bridge.

'In, now,' Jennifer ordered her. She shoved Aggie into the passenger's seat.

'Where are we going?' Aggie asked.

Jennifer's response was a sharp spike into her arm.

Aggie began to shake violently as her muscles were overwhelmed with the poison.

'Aggie! Aggie!' she heard Eric's voice disappear into the distance.

*****

Thompson's gas mask was covered in a hazardous mist, condensation, and sweat. It was impeding his vision and making him breathless. His instinct was to remove it and indulge in a huge gulp of the air outside, but he resisted. He stumbled out and supported his back against the doorframe. The glare of brilliant violet forced his arm upwards to protect his eyes.

'Beautiful, isn't it?' came Draper's voice as his pistol hilt cracked into Thompson's ribs, winding him and doubling him over. 'Remove your mask. Take it all in.'

Thompson gazed outward from the top of St Paul's, took a deep, clean breath and gazed upon purple skies. The smoke had not penetrated to such lofty heights just yet but was being consumed by the tens of thousands of people, insect-like, on the streets below who it overwhelmed and left senseless.

From his elevated perspective, he looked down upon the white circle and illuminated purple cross of an ambulance truck's canvas roof, the perfect target from a pilot's perspective. A final fighter peppered it with ammunition, sending a burning plume of ethereal spores into the smoke below.

'The Thunder Machines are coming and with them the real smoke and fire,' Draper advised him. 'Pity you won't be here to see it. Shame, I had such high hopes for you, Thompson,' Draper encouraged him with another crack to his ribs.

Thompson exhaled, winded, and fell exhausted to his knees. 'Not sticking around to enjoy the view with me?' Thompson mustered up enough energy to say.

'I have a plane to catch. The Fuhrer has grand plans for me.'

'Traitor!' Thompson screamed reaching inside his left-hand pocket towards his final firearm.

'No, no, no.' Draper eased his gun downwards, placing pressure from the gun in his right hand on Thompson's temple. Disarming Thompson's weapon with his left, Draper continued. 'Why would you want to do that? Why did you reveal your hand? I trained you better than that,' Draper replied, annoyed.

'You're right, you did,' Thompson confirmed. 'Because as you were disarming me with your left, I was readying myself with my right.'

Thompson snatched the broken phial from his right-hand pocket. The second blow from Draper had ensured the glass had cracked.

'What?' Draper replied confused.

Thompson stabbed the glass phial downward, piercing Draper's skin at the ankle, and ensuring the dark-emerald poison flowed freely. The immediacy of such a potent poison caused Draper's nervous system to capitulate. He shook violently at the extreme dosage and collapsed towards his subordinate.

Thompson bent forward, allowing Draper's motion to carry him over. Unable to grasp or clamber in a last-ditch attempt to save himself, Draper's catatonic stare did not blink as his frozen body rolled, tumbling towards the edge of the dome until St Paul's ball and lantern disappeared into the distance His spectacles scattered to the wind as he fell several hundred feet to his death without so much as a scream, fully conscious, until shattering onto the pavement below. An unidentifiable blood-splattered torso broke into a thousand pieces as he left this world in unbearable pain.

Thompson steadied himself, retrieved his guns, and emptied the barrels into the huge lantern. The light faltered and faded as the beam stopped signalling across the city and beyond. The outlying Protocols soon followed as the domino effect toppled the enemy's illuminations.

'Tuchhandler? Tuchhandler,' came the nervous static voice, echoing up the stairwell from the radio inside.

*****

As ordered, Eric had kept his gas mask on as he sprinted between the static adults down the Steep.

'Lizzy! Lizzy!' he cried out on approaching his sister.

Elizabeth Peabody lay motionless but was still alive. With no music or orders to follow, people began to revive.

'I'll be back shortly,' Eric reassured her. Dashing back to the shop where the large shoe hung outside, he banged the glass window as rapidly as machine-gunfire. 'Tink, Tink!' he shouted from his muffled mask.

The blinds were down, and the shop was locked and closed. Eric Peabody stepped back, removed a cobblestone, and launched it through the window. It smashed into a thousand pieces that he kicked through the doorway and went through to Tink's workshop. A tiny light surrounded the secured vault door. Eric thumped again and again. Tink who was concentrating on the radio in front of him with both earpieces on was oblivious to the world around him.

Eric encouraged remaining purple smoke through the doorway, wafting it through the tiny holes of the door edges. A sharp cough and shuffle of feet and Tink's attention had been gained. Grabbing a gas mask, he opened the secured vault to find Eric Peabody furiously staring back at him through his own.

'Get another mask. Now!' Eric screamed at him, snatching one before Tink could react.

They both left the shop, and Eric went and placed the mask on his sister's head.

454

Tink revolved and observed the sight in front of him. Gobsmacked, he wandered about the motionless human statues through their fog of purple smoke. The Steep continued to burn from above.

'She's taken her. She's taken Aggie,' Eric informed him.

*****

Thompson heard the radio but was confused as to where the sound was coming from. Wandering back to the whispering gallery, the same voice was desperately trying to contact Tuchhandler. Thompson's plan was to search in the opposite direction from where he thought the sound was coming from. Arches of stone, covered in red velvet drapes, led to priest holes, and, beyond them, hidden chambers. He searched two or three before finding the large metal machinery staring back at him.

In front of him were three sets of hidden telephone exchanges. To the right, one flashed with a red light. The one to the left crackled and buzzed as if communications were still on-going. The central one was connected to a wire and a recently deposited suitcase discarded beneath it. He grabbed the wire and followed its elastic curl beneath the machines. There, a tape was spooling, playing classical music. He immediately ripped the spool, leaving silence to fall upon the city. Outside, people stopped swaying and just stared motionless into space.

'Tuchhandler, Tuchhandler,' came the increasingly aggressive German voice.

Thompson pressed the accompanying microphone that cut the incoming message and prepared to return an exchange. The flashing red light to the right caught his attention and delayed any communication.

'Why are there three of you?' he thought to himself. The red light was throbbing curiously.

He swapped his left hand for his right and pressed the opposite microphone's button, but once again refrained from speaking.

*****

'So glad you remember my name, Nathaniel,' Brian Louds replied.

'How could I forget it?' Noone responded, desperately seeking another angle.

'I'm not surprised your best friend changed his. Halcombe Stubbs-Moffatt, I mean, really, what sort of a name is that? His sister on the other hand –'

'You don't get to talk about her,' Noone snapped.

'Still burn a candle do you? Forgive the pun.' Louds laughed.

Noone fired two more shots in anger.

'Would you sacrifice yourself again, Nathaniel? I might consider a swap for your good friend if you let me finish the job.'

'If that's your final offer, I may consider it,' Noone continued.

'Your friend is dying down here. Tick, tock.' Louds laughed.

Gideon lay upon the altar, and blood from his wounds flowed through the hidden channel, feeding a dark crimson into the flames. The deeper red was encouraging the Scarlet Scarab to throb and find strength as the light burned brighter.

'The thing is, all he required from me was to protect his niece and ensure you did not escape. He didn't factor his safety into the equation,' said Noone.

'Selfless. How kind of him, Nathaniel. Quite a literal statement, wouldn't you say? It'd be careless to lose two great friends, wouldn't it?'

'You wouldn't understand,' Noone said. 'By my reckoning, if you could have escaped already you would have, the coward that you are. Perhaps, I'll go now. You've nowhere to go. I've people to save.' Nathaniel Noone moved back from the trapdoor and waited. Luna barked aggressively as The Lady flapped about the laboratory.

'Noone!' Louds shouted. 'Nathaniel Noone!'

Noone did not reply.

*****

'Hello?' Belle replied to the voiceless static she was presented with.

'Belle? Is that you?' Thompson replied, surprised.

'Thompson? Thompson? I'm confused. I was expecting the children.'

'Draper is dead. I managed to bring the lights down, and stop the music, but I fear we are under imminent attack regardless. I am sat at several exchanges in the cathedral of St Paul's with German voices furiously trying to contact Tuchhandler – who must be Draper!'

'And he's dead?' Belle confirmed. 'But they don't know that?'

'No. They couldn't possibly.'

'OK. Patch them through to me. Just press down on my microphone so I can hear.'

'What are you going to do?'

'Tuchhandler is dead, but not Taube. I have an idea. Just patch them through.'

Thompson and Belle didn't have to wait for long.

'Tuchhandler!' came the furious German voice.

Thompson pressed the buttons simultaneously and Belle took over.

'*Nein, das ist Taube.* (No, this is Dove.)' Belle announced '*Tuchhandler is tot.* (Draper is dead). *Tuchhandler is tot.*'

There was a sustained silence. Both Thompson and Belle waited nervously for a response.

'*Taube, das ist Geschwader Führer eins.* (Dove, this is Squadron Leader One). *Wir haben unser licht verloren.* (We have lost our leading light.)'

'*Abbrechen, abbrechen.* (Abort, abort.)' Belle improvised.

'*Verstanden.* (Understood). *Weiter zum zweiten ziel.* (Moving on to Target Two.)'

Thompson waited for the conversation to conclude.

'Belle, what did they say?'

'They're aborting their first mission,' she replied.

'Yes!' Thompson shouted punching the air.

'But they're moving on to Target Two.'

'Target Two

Chapter 58
The second coming

Luna's occasional growl towards the room below was all that Brian Louds, better known to Nathaniel and Gideon as Salazar, could hear from the laboratory above. Occasionally, The Lady would inadvertently extend her wings, causing a flask to fall and smash as the moonlight reflected upon them and she was helpless to resist their shimmering charms.

'You see, Nathaniel Noone? I can still hear you, fumbling in the dark. You would never abandon your friend,' Salazar called out.

Salazar was greeted with yet more silence as Nathaniel did not respond. He was already exiting the Institute. He was using what little time he could create to initiate his plan.

Stepping over the body of the unconscious orderly, Archie Goodfellow was tentatively guiding Sir Wallace James as he stumbled through the dark. Noone grabbed an elbow of each of them to help them on the way. His firearm clutched in his hand.

'Archie, I will need your help soon. I'm sorry to ask this of you. First, we must ensure Sir Wallace is safe. Then we must try to rescue all of the veterans, your friends.'

'You have it, sir. You have it,' Archie replied.

Beams of light flashed over the hill and Noone was caught like a rabbit in the headlights. The vehicle skidded on the stone-gravel driveway and halted in front of them, blinding Noone and Sir Wallace. Caught with nowhere to hide, Nathaniel thrust Archie and Sir Wallace in front of himself to shield him from the light. The tall dark woman stepped out of the car, fired a shot at their feet, and issued her first warning.

Staring into the graphic horror of Noone's melted face, she began to speak. 'I have her. Now, you let him go. You tell Tuchhandler, you tell Louds, my bidding is over. I have fulfilled my part of the deal. Now let my father go.'

'Tuchhandler?' Noone questioned back. 'Your father?' 'Archie,' Noone whispered in his ear. 'Do you have a daughter?'

A slow shake from his head and the truth dawned on him.

'Jennifer?' Noone called out.

*****

'What is the second target?' Thompson fired back.

'I have no idea,' Belle replied.

'Well, find out,' Thompson panicked. 'I'll pass you through after three. Ready, one, two, three.'

The crackle of static ran for several seconds. Calmly and with authority Belle continued.

'*Geschwader Führer eins, bestätigen sie ihr ziel uber.* (Confirm your target.)'

Minutes went by with no response.

'Belle, try again. We must know. Patching you through now,' Thompson interrupted.

'*Das ist Taube. Vorbei,* (this is Dove. Over,)' she shouted in a demanding voice. '*Bestatigen Sie ihren Standort.* (Confirm your location.)'

'*Taube, das ist Geschwader Führer eins.* (Dove, this is Squadron Leader One.). *Wir haben den Kanal betreten,* (We have entered the Channel,)' came the reply from the German pilot.

Thompson removed his hand and spoke directly to Belle. 'Where are they?'

'Flying across the Channel. Put me back through, now,' she demanded.

'*Geschwader Führer eins* (Squadron Leader One). *Ihr endgültiges ziel?*' Belle fished for an answer and waited.

459

'*Die Munitionsfabrik bei Ambledown.*'

Belle immediately cut off the communiqué. 'Thompson! Thompson, did you hear that? Did you understand?'

'I understood enough,' he replied.

'Children! Children!' Belle screamed down her exchange, directing her calls back to the village. 'Please, somebody, you must evacuate! Repeat, evacuate, now!'

Silence.

*****

'I don't know you. Whatever Tuchhandler's plans might be, I am finished. I have delivered on the promise. Hand over my father.'

'Jennifer.' Noone stepped forward, tossing his gun towards her and relinquishing his supportive arm of Sir Wallace. 'Somehow, I believe we may be on the same side. However perverse that seems to us both right now. I am not your father's keeper. I am escorting him from the Institute. The girl you speak of, is she still alive?'

'I doubt we are on the same side. And, of course, she is still alive,' she replied, firing a shot past his ear.

'My name is Nathaniel Noone. I am not Tuchhandler's servant. Think back, hard. Your father saved my life. We have met before; many years ago now. You were only a girl. Think, Jennifer. Think, Jennifer.'

'It's a trick. You don't know me.'

'Take your father. Here,' Noone offered, gently encouraging Sir Wallace forward. 'I'll step back. I need you to trust me.' Noone placed his hands on his head and stood there unprotected.

'Young lady, he is telling the truth,' Archie interrupted.

Jennifer knew of Archie, the single man who could not be influenced by the Ethereum due to his lack of sight. Louds had tried many times.

'Shut up, both of you. Shut up!' Jennifer James called back.

Muttering to himself over and over again, Sir Wallace James shuffled towards his daughter.

'I am Dr Mialora. I am Dr Mialora..'

Still training her pistol on the men, Jennifer cautiously approached her father.

'Dad, it's Jennifer. Dad, can you hear me?' she said through trembling lips. Her eyes were welling up. 'It will be alright. We need you away from this place. It will subside, I know. Trust me, I know.'

'Jennifer, you do know, don't you?' Noone began to speak. 'I have seen you since. In a different guise. I couldn't recall it at all, and most likely you would not have remembered me like I did not remember you at first. Dressed in animal skins, standing out from the crowd, and influencing those who Tuchhandler defined. Though we both knew him as Draper.'

'You know Donald?' she shot back.

'Your father saved my life and Donald Draper took me under his wing. He was my mentor, it pains me to say. He stopped me from going insane, despite my obsessions. He saved me from my numerous attempts to end my own life.'

'We were to be married, Donald and I. Father insisted on it. I wanted to make him so happy.'

'Do you really believe that? Do you really believe that is what Sir Wallace would have wanted for you? Think, Jennifer. Think. All of us just pawns in a far greater game. Draper the grandmaster.'

'I don't understand. Nothing makes sense to me.' Jennifer continued to weep, with her father cradled against her.

'No one has all the answers, I assure you. The only truth we know is that little girl, in the back of your car, connects everything. The man you know as Brian Louds, the man your future husband seduced you for, he is known to me as Salazar and all he wants in the world is to sacrifice that little girl.'

Jennifer James stepped back to the car, buckling her father in the passenger side and looking down on the comatose teen.

Barking echoed down the passageway as Luna announced herself into the big wide world outside.

Noone turned to see the hound bounding their way as bullets had encouraged her to leave.

'Nathaniel. Nathaniel,' came the sinister voice of Salazar. 'A peace offering,' he announced.

From the shadow of the doorway walked Professor Meredith Malcolm. The ceremonial knife had now been removed and held beneath his throat as he carried Gemima in his arms.

'Sabine Erket or do you prefer Jennifer James now?' Louds called out. 'Bring the girl to me. Bring her to me now. I will release your father from my service as promised.'

Jennifer dipped her head before rising up obediently. She scooped Aggie from the rear seat and began to march towards Louds. Noone stepped in her way, his back blocking Louds' sightline.

'Don't do this,' Noone begged.

'Kill him!' Louds cried out.

Jennifer looked Noone directly in the eyes and then fired.

*****

'Children, please! One of you, please! You are in immediate danger,' Belle's voice continued in desperation.

'Miss Soames,' came the welcome reply. 'We have lost the girl. They have her,' Nelly confirmed.

'Listen to me, the bombers are coming. They are targeting the munitions in your village. You must evacuate immediately.'

'Nosey – I mean, Nelly, sorry,' came Eric Peabody's breathless voice. 'Tinker's on his way to Bott's. He has an idea. He wants this radio too.'

'Miss Soames, we'll be back to you as soon as we can be,' Nelly said disconnecting the cables. 'Where's your sister?' Nelly asked.

'Fishing someone out of the Amble. Then she'll be helping us proper.'

A swift jaunt through the purple smoke to the Sheriff's office and they joined Sister Harvey, Wilson Bott, and Tinker the tailor as they reorganised the room.

'Here,Nelly. Place it here,' Tinker encouraged her, grabbing the flailing cables and connecting them through his own suitcase device. Pressing the microphone into action Tink began.

'Miss Soames, they call me Tinker. Tell me what you understand.'

'A German bombing party are on their way. They are targeting your munitions factory.'

'If they are successful the South Downs may fall,' he replied.

'You must suppress the light source you must suppress the lights. It guides their path.'

Eric shook his head. He had been trying to douse the flames and bunting but the water just encouraged them.

'We're lit up like a beacon. They'll find us easily,' Tinker replied.

'Then you must leave. Save as many of you as you can. Leave now.'

'Wilson, connect that public address system and wait on our orders. Eric, Sister, you know what to do. Go now,' Tinker ordered.

Eric Peabody leapt from the room and raced down the Steep, an armful of gas masks dragging behind him. Rushing as fast as he could, he placed a mask on every child he approached. As the Ethereum filtered out, he encouraged them to follow him and do the same. Soon, child after child came round. Sister Harvey followed in the same vein, approaching the adults. Stunned and bewildered, they gradually came round.

'People of Ambledown,' Wilson Bott's voice reverberated around. 'We are under attack. Move calmly and quietly to your shelters.'

*****

Nathaniel fell to the floor. Aggie stared back at the scarred man whose voice she had recognised all those days ago. Motionless as she was, she had still heard every word. How wrong she had been. He was far from the monster she recalled that infamous night just weeks ago when he'd kidnapped her at Florrie's. Remembering her Uncle Gideon's note, all made sense now.

Trust *no-one,* as she had understood it, actually meant, Trust *Noone. Nathaniel Noone.*

Nate smiled upward at Aggie while he lay there on the ground as Jennifer James carried her away. A single tear fell from her eye as his face slumped down upon the floor.

'Come, child,' Salazar encouraged them. 'Soon, it will all be over.'

Aggie felt a sharp prick of pain as Jennifer James administered the final shot into her arm and led her into the passageway and through to the sacrificial chamber.

*****

'What's going on, Belle?' Thompson asked nervously.

'They're evacuating. They're not sure how long they have.'

'And the children? Are they safe?'

'The girl was taken. Belchambers' niece,' Belle confirmed with a tear. 'Lord knows the whereabouts of Belchambers and Noone.'

Thompson left his station and returned to the dome to look down on London. The smoke was dissipating, and people were beginning to move once more; frightened, confused, but alive. He could only hope Ambledown would survive.

*****

'That's the lot, Tink. They're moving on out,' Eric announced, returning to the Sheriff's. 'Any news?'

Tink's disappointed shake of his head saw Eric's shoulders slump.

'Come on, Eric. Let's find your sister and seek shelter,' Nelly encouraged him.

'I'm not going back to the Poacher, not never.'

'Come. I know just the place.' Nelly guided him.

*****

'I take it she is still alive?' Louds asked.

'Of course, she is,' Jennifer James replied. 'Shall I wake her?'

464

'Now, wouldn't that be sadistic?' Louds laughed.

The descending stone steps challenged her as she gripped Aggie tightly.

Louds eased the stone wall entrance back into place and closed it behind them. 'Place her here,' he said excitedly. 'Such a pity you couldn't stick around to see the finale,' Louds whispered into Gideon's ear.

Raising the ceremonial blade by the hilt. He flashed it downwards towards Gideon. Jennifer flinched as the knife made contact with the restraints and not the man himself.

'I will not waste the ceremonial blade on him any longer or tarnish it with his blood. He is dying, slowly and painfully. He has bled and soiled the chamber enough' Louds announced. After hauling Gideon's shoulders forward, and dispersing him off of the black stone, Jennifer James was directed to step forward with Agatha's motionless body.

What little light remained of the flames sent sinister shadows up from below. Louds draped the ceremonial robe upon himself, finally confirming his true historical identity, Salazar. The half-mask of Horus sat upon his head. Its feathers and beak reflected back upon the namesake of the statue that overlooked the altar. The statue of Anubis in his darkest stare looked down upon him with envious eyes.

'The girl. You may lower the girl,' Louds ordered. 'Wait, turn her around.'

Jennifer cradled Aggie as his blade tore through the back of her cloak.

'The true mark of the moon,' he confirmed, running his cold hands over the girl's back. 'Do you think I would have forgotten?' he stared at her, expressionless.

Jennifer James began to retreat from the altar, and out of reach of the blade.

'Come, come. You have given me more than I could have wished for. Do not be afraid. There is still a place for you by my side,' Salazar reassured her.

A smash of glass from the laboratory above sent shudders down her spine. Salazar pulled the blade out and moved towards her.

'What was that?' he screamed.

Nervously, Jennifer went to offer a response just as The Lady flapped through the trapdoor, once more attracted to the shimmer of the blade as it caught the crescent moon.

'Kill it! Kill it!' he ordered Jennifer James. 'Its feathers can finish my mask.'

Jennifer reached deep within her cloaked pocket.

'What are you waiting for?' Salazar hurled at her. 'Shoot it.'

Clutching the instrument between forefinger and thumb she looked at the prism above. A short cloud-burst darkened the room.

'I need a clear shot. I need the moon,' Jennifer explained.

'Just start firing. That room is insignificant now.'

'Three, two, one,' she counted down.

'Fire!' Salazar ordered.

She opened her hand and the magnifying glass revealed itself as the moonbeams penetrated its multifaceted face. Instant, brilliant light blinded him and forced him backwards.

'Now, Aggie! Now!' Jennifer screamed.

Agatha transformed from motionless victim to immediately sitting upright. She put her hand in her pocket and reached the gun that Jennifer had set there just moments before. She instantly squeezed the trigger, sparking the gunpowder, igniting the bullet, and hurtling it down the barrel. Salazar flew to attack her with the blade, allowing the gunshot a clear path to his ribcage. As the single bullet tore straight through him, it sparked on the stonework behind. The sheer force sent him backwards.

It could have been the gods or sheer adrenaline but he did not stop. He stumbled forward once more, blood now gurgling from his mouth, and made one last dramatic lunge to murder Aggie.

Bang!

A single shot from above the trapdoor sent Salazar crashing to the floor. His own blood now filled the all-seeing-eye that surrounded them.

The light from the magnifier illuminated the room. The moonlight had supercharged its powers. The Scarlet Scarab ignited. Its brilliant red responded to the light burning through the room. The heat became too much to bear in the laboratory as the books began to catch fire.

'Jennifer, enough! Enough!' Noone cried from above the trapdoor as the heat began to rage.

Jennifer James dropped the magnifier. Her hand was blistered and burned. Aggie fell from the large black stone. Gideon unconscious was by her side.

'Uncle Gideon! Uncle Gideon!' Aggie clutched at him. She still felt the lightness of breath flow from his chest. 'He's alive! He's alive!'

Fire leapt from book to book. Noone's scarring was more resilient than most to the heat but nevertheless, he was beginning to choke from the smoke.

'We have little time. Come on!' he screamed to them.

Forcing the hidden doorway backwards he descended the stairs.

'Come on! Go, go!' he yelled at Aggie.

'I'm not leaving him,' she cried back.

'None of us are,' Jennifer comforted her. She took Gideon's legs as Nathaniel secured him under the arms. 'Quickly, now move.'

The acrid black smoke descended quickly as they forced their way onwards.

Finally, fresh air as they stumbled over the orderly and to safety.

'Nathaniel, is that you?' Archie cried out. 'I smell smoke.'

'The institute is on fire. We must move quickly.'

'But what about the men? They're just ordinary men like you and me?' Archie replied. 'What about Pop Braggan? Is he safe too?'

Noone stared back quizzically. The army of men had been employed to kill them just moments before and Archie wanted him to save them?

'He's right,' Jennifer agreed. 'They would not have been in control. It isn't their fault.'

'What?' Noone replied in disbelief.

'I know this place as well as anyone,' Jennifer advised. 'I can help them. Look after my dad.'

Sprinting back into the passageway, Jennifer James was soon engulfed in the suffocating smoke as the laboratory burned.

'Jennifer, wait! Jennifer!' Noone screamed. He cried out and chased after her.

*****

'Eric, you know the hidden-tunnel-ways out of Gideon's, don't you?' Nelly asked.

'Of course,' he replied.

'Get yourself and your sister there. It's the safest place in the village.'

'Come with us, Nelly.'

'I'll join you shortly. Jane is still rounding up the last of the children.'

Eric led Elizabeth to the cobblestone home of the keys at the foot of la The Keep before entering Gideon's house.

'Halt!' came the accent from within the cellar. A shotgun pointed at them both, a gas mask covering Nan's face.

'You stupid old bag!' Eric screamed back at her.

'I have my orders, Eric. To defend this house for Gideon.'

'Well, Gideon and Agatha are gone. You hear me? And if you're stupid enough to sit here when the bombers come, so will you be.'

The housekeeper looked out of the doorway. The purple smoke was now subsiding as Nelly and Sister Jane Harvey wrangled several children towards them.

'Gideon won't like this,' she announced.

'Well, that proves how little you know him,' Elizabeth replied, snatching the gun away from her. 'What's so damn important in that cellar?'

Nan tightened her lips as the children flowed in.

'Wait,' Elizabeth halted them. Henrietta Huntington-Smythe and her friends were trembling pitifully. 'Nan, find them all blankets. Grab supplies.'

'Follow me,' Eric shouted as they traipsed upstairs and into Aggie's room. 'Through the wardrobe. All of you, follow Lizzy through the wardrobe.'

Elizabeth held a solitary candle as they crouched down in the long stone alley.

'Stop at that torch,' Eric advised them. 'No further.'

The torch splintered the hidden junction. Should they have to take flight, Eric knew where to go. Gideon had drilled him plenty of times. The tower of The Keep certainly wouldn't be the safest place this time.

*****

'Jennifer, Jennifer?' Noone called out in the darkness. Soon the light from the Scarab offered up a route through the stone.

'Nathaniel, this way. Follow my voice.'

Noone entered the room they had sought to destroy. The exchanges and spools were cast out in front of him. The stark difference between the smoke-filled tunnel and fluorescent bulb light caused Nathaniel to squint.

'I take it this was your handy-work?' Jennifer replied pointing out the spoilt reels of tape. 'Never mind,' she replied before continuing. 'Men of Silvera. OBEY! Men of Silvera OBEY!' she began to repeat.

Throughout the Institute the men began to sway in unison. Her voice was reinvigorating them.

'Awake. Awake. Awake.'

The men's senses began to regain control. They were beginning to resist the influence that the smoke and light had seduced them with. Startled and confused, they were greeted by real smoke and fire.

'OK, that's just the start,' Jennifer advised Noone. 'We now need to help them out of here.'

'Wait, what's that? A radio exchange?' Noone asked. Jennifer duly nodded 'Do you know how to work it?' he questioned.

'Of course.'

'Contact Ambledown 71273.'

'Why?'

'They'll send ambulances, supplies, and anything we will need. Please, Jennifer. Do it now, quickly. We have to go straight after.'

*****

469

'Belle, this is Tink. I'm leaving now. To the best of our abilities, we have evacuated. Wish us luck.'

'Any news of the children?'

'Those we are aware of are as safe as they can be.'

'Good luck,' Belle finished, sickened to think of where Agatha may be.

'Come on, Wilson. We've done all that we can,' Tink advised him.

Tink replaced his headset and headed to the door with Sheriff Bott.

'Ambledown, Ambledown, are you receiving? Over,' came the crackling voice of a female over the exchange.

The two men stared at each other.

Tink scrambled back to his head-piece. 'Belle, we are leaving, as advised.'

'Going where?' came the rasping male voice as it took over.

'Nathaniel, is that you? Nathaniel?' Tink replied.

'We're in a bit of fix, old friend,' Noone replied. 'Send supplies to the Silvera Institute as soon as you can. We need transport, ambulances, food, drink, for at least 100 men. Gideon is in bad shape. Be quick, this place will be burned down within no time at all.'

'Nate, I hear you loud and clear, but the bombers are coming. We've had to evacuate or hide. Ambledown is compromised. It too is burning and lit up like a beacon. I'm so sorry. We cannot assist.'

'I don't understand, Tink. How do you know? About the bombers, I mean. If they hit that factory much more than the village will be lost.'

Tink patched through to Miss Soames. 'Belle, I have Nathaniel Noone on the other line.'

'Belle? How the hell are you involved with this?' Noone spoke through, his voice distant.

'Long story short, Nate. Thompson has killed Draper and foiled his plan, but that inadvertently redirected the bombers from London. Unfortunately, they are heading for Ambledown as we speak.'

'That was bloody kind of him. Christ' Noone blasphemed, punching the desk. 'How do you know, anyway?'

'I am talking to them. They think I am Dove?'

'Dove? Who is Dove ? Oh God, I am so confused. Belle, what are they looking for? How are they coming?' Noone asked once more.

'They're coming along the coast. They will head towards anything that is lit up.'

'Anything?' Noone asked back.

'I believe so,' Belle replied for the last time.

'Belle, you tell them to search for the brightest of red lights. That's the brightest of red lights. Over and out.

'What the hell, Nathaniel?' Jennifer looked at him.

'Just get the men out of here. Come on, hurry. Get them out of here. We've little time.'

Chapter 59
Well red

'*Geschwader Führer eins, das ist Taube. Kopf fur rot.* (Head for rcd.) *Wiederholen.* (Repeat.) *Kopf fur rot,* (Head for red,)' Belle said calmly into her microphone

'*Das ist Geschwader Führer zwei.* (This is Squadron leader two).*Wir sehen das violette licht.* (We see the violet light) *Sollen wir vorrucken?* (Shall we advance?)' came the second pilot's voice.

'Ja,' came the first squadron's commander.

'Nein.' Belle reinforced. 'Nein, nein, nein.'

*****

Tink and Bott sprinted up the Steep towards The Keep. A lead Messerschmitt flew between the buildings directly towards them. Its first rounds peppered the cenotaph before moving onwards to the brewery.

The enemy pilot scanned below as the purple bunting still burned brightly, but the deserted streets offered no real targets.

'They've come!' Wilson callcd out, dashing upstairs to join Eric and the children.

'Eric, we just heard from Nathaniel. He's safe.'

'Aggie, Gideon, Pop ?' Eric replied quickly.

'He didn't really say. Just mentioned lots of them needing help.'

'Hurry up, you bloody bastards! Do your worst!' Eric screamed towards the ceiling.

*****

'What were you thinking?' Jennifer turned to Noone. 'We'll all be killed.'

'No, we won't. Now get going!' he yelled at her. 'Save as many of these men as you can.'

'Nathaniel, you can't. It's a one-way ticket. The heat from that thing will burn straight through you.'

'We'll see. Now give it to me,' Noone ordered her. 'Now! Then go.'

Jennifer passed the magnifier over.

'Follow me. Follow me,' she repeated. 'Help those who cannot help themselves and follow me. An air-raid is coming and we are not safe!' Jennifer James called out as she disappeared back into the Institute and up the steep incline to the front of the glass and steel structure. She was redirecting the men to the safety afforded via the cliffs.

Moving through thick smoke, and back to the hidden sacrificial chamber, Nathaniel clasped the magnifier and hid it well, should the moonlight unexpectedly present itself. Descending the stairwell into the dimly lit stone chamber, he retrieved the ceremonial staff. The Scarlet Scarab was still intact. Its emission was subdued temporarily without its elemental source. He approached the body of Salazar motionless on the floor and kicked him for good measure before finally retrieving the ceremonial staff.

He placed the magnifier around the staff's neck, making it spin and refracting above the scarab's head. The prism directly above allowed the moonlight to pour through. The magnifier fed life into the crystallised rock and the beating heart of the anthropoid pulsated as it stirred once again. Noone sprinted from the chamber as the deep-red illuminations grew hotter and hotter, turning the chamber a superior shade of scarlet and the beginning of an unfathomable furnace. The laboratory above burst into flames. The secrets of the scrolls disappeared in mere moments. From out of the fire, phoenix-like, the brilliant beam flew out brightly into the atmosphere above, lighting up the night sky with pyrotechnic exuberance.

The flames burned down the corridors, chasing Noone with ferocious intent. With the orderly's body now having been removed from the entrance, Noone exploded out of the building as the gulf of energy erupted like a volcano, sending him through the air crashing across the gravel driveway.

*****

'*Das ist Geschwader Führer zwei.* (This is Squadron leader two). *Das Ziel war falsch.* (The target was fake.)'

'*Ja, ja. Das ist Geschwader Führer eins.* (Yes, yes, This is Squadron Leader One). *Schau zu deinem horizont.* (Look to your horizon.)'

The fighter pilot raised his aircraft and peered out towards the sea. There on the coast, mere miles away, the scarlet beam of light tore through the clouds with atomic power, lighting up the night sky.

'*Attacke, attacke, attacke,*' came the German pilot's voice.

*****

Eric quivered with the rest of the huddled children as the first shots were fired. But little came after that. He waited and waited, even though patience was not his strongest virtue. Instead of rounding and a revisionary attempt to attack the deserted village once more, however, the fighters' engines roared off into the distance.

'Sod this!' Eric exclaimed and ran further into the tunnel. He made light work of the tight stairs that led to the hidden room within The Keep. He peered through the archers' windows of The Keep. Lead and glass caught the purple hues from below, but they were at too acute an angle to see much more than just that. He turned and peered at himself in the mirrored doorway, ran towards it and pulled it open from a gap at its base. The tunnel beyond, of soft torchlight, led to the roofs of Ambledown. He snuck through a window and climbed between chimney pots until he perched himself to find the perfect vista. Over the cliffs and into the distance, a stark red light burned brightly into the sky. Rumbles of thunder came from its surrounding clouds. A full arsenal of enemy aircraft tore towards it.

*****

'Get as far away as you can. Find cover, shelter, anything,' Jennifer encouraged the men as they ran, hobbled and wheeled their way from the burning mass of the Silvera Institute.

The wooden panelling of the laboratory and its exquisite collection of books were mere firelighters to the spreading furnace that now took on the concrete and glass. Lit up in brilliant red, it was an obvious target from the air, as it burned brightly across the English Channel.

'Nathaniel, can you walk to the jeep?' Jennifer asked, helping him by his elbow.

'Luckily for me, you missed.' He smiled back, pointing towards the bullet hole in the flank of his coat. Looking up from his gravel-worn face, the melted man saw Aggie sobbing over the slumped body of Gideon in the back of the jeep.

'No, no!' Nathaniel cried out, running over.

'He's alive, just,' Sir Wallace called back. The influence of poison had left his bloodstream with the new intake of fresh air.

The barks of Luna and intermittent caws of The Lady directed his gaze past the vehicle. Archie Goodfellow, assisted by three other men, pushed the hulking if somewhat broken frame of Pop Braggan in a wheelchair.

The rumbles then began. In the distance, and along the cliff-tops, the Luftwaffe was coming. The scouting Messerschmitt indiscriminately took fire at the men desperately trying to leave the hospital. Its furious machine gun cast clouds of gravel dust as it passed the driveway to the burning Institute.

'Hide! Seek cover!' Noone called out.

The pilot looped his plane high in the air readying for a return run. The Scarlet Scarab continued burning brightly as the magnifier increasingly provided celestial power from above. It was a power source that no one could understand or explain. Positioning the beam directly at its centre and between himself and the fleeing hordes of terrorised servicemen below, the pilot smiled and thrust the engines forward, faster and faster towards his prey. His thumb upon the trigger as he steadied his aim through the crisscrossed sight.

As he hit the scarlet beam of light that so kindly guided his way, the plane immediately ignited into a ball of flame, tearing the hull in half, and exploding the fuel tanks as it did so. The plane disintegrated into the night sky and fell into the furnace below. The oncoming entourage of support fighters had no time to move. Meteorites of molten Messerschmitt peppered their planes and ignited them into flames, setting the sky alight. The larger bombers, lethargic and slow to turn, narrowly missed the crashing shells but inevitably were too late to evade the ferocious scarlet beam. A crescendo of destructive violence exploded and engulfed the night sky as the passing fleet exploded within their very own munitions. The Luftwaffe party was spread to the winds in glorious Technicolour.

*****

'Take that, Adolf!' Eric whooped and cheered from the rooftops miles away. The destruction and flames spread far across the south coast.

'*Das ist Taube. Jemand?*' (This is Dove, anyone?) Belle asked as the screams of enemy airman disappeared into the static.

'Is he going to be alright?' Aggie turned to Sir Wallace James who was nursing Uncle Gideon.

'I will ensure he is,' he replied.

'He'll be fine, Agatha,' Nathaniel Noone replied. He stepped forward as the red skylight lit up the true horror of his melted face. He winked at her through his remaining good eye. 'I'm Nathaniel, by the way.'

'I know. Nathaniel Noone. My uncle always advised me to trust Noone.' She leaned over and placed a peck on his cheek.

Chapter 60

The Seven Sisters

'Belle, are you still receiving me? Over,' Thompson asked nervously. 'Any news from Ambledown?'

'I'm still here. Nothing but silence, I'm afraid,' Belle confirmed.

'Bear with me,' Thompson advised, leaving the exchange and once more journeying to the top of St Paul's.

Far away, from the coast, a red light shone brightly into the sky. Billowing clouds were casting dark destruction along the vista. He had heard of such bombs and their devastating ability but did not understand the enemy's ability to deploy them. He sprinted back to the microphone and receiver.

'Belle! Belle!' he shouted urgently.

'I'm still here,' Belle confirmed.

'I'm sorry but I think Ambledown was hit. I'm so sorry.'

Belle sat there in silence. Agatha's voice repeated itself in her head. She had been trying to fathom the secrets and lies that had kept her hidden all these years, but now it was all lost.

A static crackle from her radio broke the depressing silence.

'Ello, ello ... Isbelle?' came the young cockney voice.

'Eric?' Belle responded immediately.

'Present and correct, Miss.' Eric laughed back. 'We're all safe. Ambledown is on fire, but most people are accounted for. Gotta go.'

'Eric, Eric? Agatha? Is she there with you?' Belle asked.

There was a momentary pause before the relay spoke to her again.

'Belle, this is Tink. Eric has just left for the Institute, which, on last account, people were being rescued from. We haven't heard from Nathaniel since the bombs and they were one hell of an explosion. I'm heading there now too.'

'Thompson, can you hear me? Over,' Belle said, switching the relay.

'Go ahead, Belle.'

'Ambledown is safe. A different, second target, however, was hit.'

'Understood. I must leave for Whitehall. Stay where you are. I will come for you, I promise,' Thompson assured her.

On leaving St Paul's, the sheer volume of dispossessed and disoriented people dawned on Thompson. Had that attack been successful in the capital, thousands of citizens would have been lost, if not the war.

*****

he Silvera Institute burned brightly. The red beam that tore through the sky had been quashed as the crashing fuselage of the Luftwaffe's bombers collapsed into the steel and glass structure. The Scarlet Scarab was crushed and buried beneath monumental carved stone. The magnifying glass had been discarded into the embers.

The Institute continued to burn as the many servicemen began to make their journey by foot into the countryside and towards the market town of Ambledown.

Jennifer James was accompanied by Nathaniel Noone at the front of the Americans' service vehicle. Gemima was huddled across him. Aggie cradled Gideon's head in the rear while Sir Wallace maintained his pulse and dressed his injuries as best he could. As the full beams sped down the country road, a large ambulance truck blocked their path. Its lights blinded Jennifer into an emergency stop.

A shadow approached them. The bun on top of her head was reminiscent of a governess.

'Holster your weapons!' she ordered, pointing a weapon directly towards them.

Aggie looked on in disbelief.

*****

Whitehall was as dazed and confused as the rest of London. A disoriented army of people were aimlessly wandering around. Thompson spied the nervous Miss Nevis crouched idly against a wall outside. Clutching a cigarette and shaking nervously.

'Hilary, are you OK? Hilary?' Thompson asked, but was met with a blank stare as she pointed towards the entrance.

Thompson entered Number Seven, which was the now unprotected realm of Wink Waverley and Colonel Malling. Alighting the vast subterranean corridor, he was greeted with dozens of civil servants still in subdued paralysis, non-functioning. The Protocols were a shambles; complete disarray. He searched room after room until finally he happened upon the tiny broom cupboard that held Wink, Malling and Lady James. All of them had succumbed to the Ethereum. Immediately realising his mistake, he sprinted out of Number Seven, but Hilary had disappeared, forever.

*****

'Please, put down any weapons you may have,' the woman continued with the shadow of her weapon pointing directly at them. 'Raise your arms, slowly.'

Nathaniel tossed his guns and placed his hands in the air.

'Hahaha. Fancy being disarmed by an old lady with a broom handle, Nathaniel Noone,' she cackled.

'Florrie?' Aggie yelled with excitement. 'Florrie, is that really you?'

'Hello, dearest girl,' Florrie replied, putting the broom handle on the floor.

Floods of tears erupted from Aggie and streamed down her face. Small droplets dripped onto Gideon's brow and encouraging the tiniest curl of a smiling lip.

Florrie whistled loudly and from the rear of the truck, five other women presented themselves. They were Aggie's teachers, Fairfax, Grace, Woes, Fargo, and Lovegood.

'Governesses? What are all of you doing here?' Aggie asked, confused.

'I really should explain,' Florrie replied. 'We all should,' she said and smiled, encouraging her sisters.

'We are the forty-two,' they all replied together. The women all smiled towards Aggie and helped her out of the jeep. This, in turn, enabled them to lift Gideon onto a stretcher and to the rear of the ambulance.

'Are you joining us, Nathaniel?' Florrie asked.

'I'll go back to the village. No doubt Eric is already on his way and will require an explanation.'

'And them?' Florrie asked pointedly, towards Jennifer and Sir Wallace James.

'I'll take them with me,' Noone replied. 'They have their own loved ones to inform.' He smiled towards them both.

A bark from behind them hailed the entrance of Luna. The Lady landed on the windscreen frame and cawed.

'I say, is that Nathaniel Noone I can hear?' came the welcome sound of Archie's voice. 'Any room for quite a big one?'

Noone turned to Archie who had Pop Braggan propped upright in a wheelchair. He was semi-conscious and most definitely alive.

'I 'erd that, Goodfeller,' Pop wheezed at Archie before clutching his ribs in agony.

'Until next time then, Nathaniel,' Florrie bid him goodbye. 'Don't make it a decade, for pity's sake. I may not be around.'

'Next time, soon. I promise.' Noone smiled.

As Aggie's great aunt revved the truck and pulled away, the teenage girl he had unceremoniously kidnapped weeks before waved Nathaniel Noone goodbye with a longing smile as he disappeared into the distance.

'Where are we going?' Aggie asked of the chaperoning women.

'Home, dear,' they replied together.

'London?'

'No, not London.' They all laughed, as they began humming the skipping rope song.

The truck made its way along the coast until, not far by, they reached the sign to the Seven Sisters.

'You've lots of explaining to do, you know that?' Aggie directed towards them all.

'We'll leave that to Gideon,' they advised.

'Oh, Gideon, is it?' she replied back. 'Not Halcombe then?' she questioned.

'It's complicated, Aggie,' came Gideon's soft voice as he struggled for breath. 'It's really complicated.'

'I'm just glad it's all over,' Aggie said and sighed with relief at the sound of his voice.

'Oh, it's far from over,' Florrie whispered under her breath. 'Far, far, from over. If anything, it's only just begun.'

The end ... for now.

Printed by Amazon Italia Logistica S.r.l.
Torrazza Piemonte (TO), Italy

10428565R00276